THE UNSEEN HOUR

SILAS REAMES

Cover Design: David Gardias
Chapter Header & Scene Break Art: An-Nhien Nguyen
Ebook ISBN: 978-1-961057-28-9
Paperback ISBN-13: 978-1-961057-27-2

Mom,
I know you love a good romance story.

Your copy might be missing a good portion of 43, and part of 47, and maybe even part of 52. Oops!

CHAPTER I

NEW YEAR'S EVE
THE 98th HOUR

There were tales in my homeland that said the end of the year was once cause for celebration. People would set off fireworks in the sky—beautiful flashing shades of greens, reds, and blues—to mark the occasion. Many threw lavish parties, toasting one another at the moment one year ended and another began. I had no idea if that was true, or merely legend, but it wasn't how things were now.

I hurried through a near-empty alleyway, my only company the rubbish abandoned outside of local shops. I tried to keep my steps quiet, but my boots echoed on the cobblestones underfoot. It would have been easier if Temple's shoes fit better, but my brother's feet were considerably larger than my own. Then again, it would have been easier still if I were a man and didn't have to wear someone else's clothes. Then I could have gone wandering the streets without anyone questioning it, instead of having to resort to thievery and deceit. Although, was it thievery if I fully intended to return his trousers and overcoat before he'd noticed their absence?

It was late enough that I needn't have worried about being spotted. I didn't see another soul as I made my way out of the town of Fox Haven and back towards Scops Hall. I placed one hand atop my hat, where it threatened to bounce loose from my head and send my hair tumbling. My thick, lustrous, deep brown locks were a source of pride for the family, alongside my other features, at every gala or soiree we attended. In my family, looks mattered. In this instance, though, they were a nuisance.

An echoing bong sounded from behind me. I knew well enough what it was. The clock tower. The immense stone structure loomed like a monolith. All major town squares throughout the country of Emrys had one. What they did in the other kingdoms that made up Rayus, I did not know. I could only assume each country had its own warning system.

The bells within our clock tower sounded all year through, but on this night, their toll changed from melodious chiming to a solid, heavy sound. A deliberate alteration so that no one could mistake its meaning.

I counted to eleven silently.

"Bollocks."

It was a good half hour's hard ride back to Scops, and that was after I retrieved my horse. Perhaps leaving the grullo stallion feeding just on the outskirts of town had been a poor idea. I hadn't worried about his being stolen. After all, I was the only one the animal would tolerate riding him, much to my brothers' chagrin. The stallion was finer than any of their horses. Pellix and I had an understanding—I didn't try to break his free spirit, and he helped me to retain mine.

There was also the fact that I was the only soul foolish

enough to still be out at this time, on this night. Undoubtedly another deterrent for horse thieves.

"Pellix!" I hissed into the darkness as I ran past where the cobblestones ended and onto the gravel trail outside the town walls. I was lucky the watch hadn't barred the gates yet. The thought hadn't even fully formed when they both slammed shut behind me. I'd have worried about town sentries, but I knew they pulled the gate closed from within the towers on this night, unseen by the world and unable to see anything in turn.

Pellix strode toward the road from the trees, reins dragging the ground as he continued pulling grass up by the roots. I ran to the horse and gave him a pat across his grey neck before swinging myself over him. I knew that if I were found out, I'd be chastised several times over. Out late, with no chaperone, in men's clothes, riding not only astride but with no saddle to speak of—the scandal of it would send Mother into a fainting spell.

And even if none of that fazed her, there was the problem of my timing. If I was caught at the wrong time on *this* particular night, my mother's reaction would be the least of my concerns. But I'd had to do it. I'd been tracing my father's steps for months, and now my suspicions were all but confirmed. Thanks to one very unapproved visit to the most restricted shelves of the town's library, I had found the book my father had left.

All I had to do now was read it, once I was safely away from Fox Haven and back home.

Pellix moved into a canter and I leaned into him, welcoming the wind that whipped my hair. My brother's hat flew off and was left in the fields. I relished the sensation of flight as Pellix ran full speed through the night. We made it back to the stables on my family's estate without anyone stopping me at the entrance of the grounds. No one stood guard on this night. I coaxed Pellix into his stall with the promise of barley and a carrot I'd snuck into my brother's coat pocket.

Success and exhilaration thrummed through my veins. I was one step closer to uncovering the details of the tragedy that had hung over my family for years, and no one was the wiser.

After giving Pellix a final pat, I double-checked that his stall was latched shut. Animals had never been victims of the hour, but a lost horse was bad any time of the year. After reassuring myself that the stall was secure, I began to make my way out of the barn.

"Have you *any* idea how much trouble you are in?"

Wincing, I turned what I hoped were repentant pink eyes toward my eldest brother as he stepped out from one of the empty stalls.

Of all the rotten luck. Of my three brothers, Ambrose was the one most likely to turn me over to Mother. As the eldest, he took his role of faux-parent all too seriously. He took his title as Marquess of Scops even more seriously.

"I was merely—"

I clamped my mouth shut as Ambrose held his palm in my face. After several seconds of silence he withdrew the hand and placed two fingers on his forehead, squeezing.

"Merely. Merely? As if whatever excuse you have is some half-measure. Some small deviance or miscalculation. Sister, you have *no* reason. None. To be out at this hour, tonight of all nights! Don't you appreciate the severity of this day? Have you any understanding of what could have happened if you were still out at midnight?"

The question rankled me, and if it *had* been any other night, I'd have shot off a retort to my eldest brother. Given the circumstances, however—he surely missed Father as much as I did. I couldn't hold it against him that he wanted reassurance that I understood the risk I had taken. Of course I did. Everyone in the country knew. This night was an unavoidable terror that all citizens were forced to live with each year, its mere existence haunting them.

If the legends were meant to be believed, the changing of years had once moved smoothly. Midnight of December thirty-first rolled straight into January first of the following year. But that was not how things worked in my world. For my lifetime, and generations before me, we'd lived with one additional span of time buffering the years.

The Unseen Hour.

This night was its ninety-eighth anniversary. In the grand scheme of things, it wasn't such a long time, but the curse hung over all of Emrys.

No one could speak to its cause, but all knew its cost. Anyone not in their homes, with doors and windows latched tight when the clock struck midnight at the end of the year, fell victim to its evils. As the year ended, the world stilled. It was said that no breeze stirred the grass. Fog filled the streets; even the stars stopped twinkling in the sky. Any lamps not dimmed by that point were snuffed out, never to light again. They'd had to replace a whole row of lanterns on Bailey Street once, when the dimmers had run into a delay and failed to get them all extinguished in time.

It was as if the Unseen Hour took not only lives but also the light within anything it saw.

The clocks themselves refused to move so much as a second until the fog dissipated. At that point, lights flickered on and time began to move forward again into the next year.

While we had no way of knowing how long it actually lasted, the name Unseen Hour had stuck. That cursed span of time was the one of the Taking. Any who were outside succumbed to it, cursed with a terrible fate, their lives snatched away.

Every year, the watchmen emerged from their homes before the rest of the town on January first so they could collect the bodies of any unfortunate individuals taken by the hour's curse. Each was frozen as solid as ice, no matter the weather.

We cleared away the hour's damage and began counting down for the next year. However long it really lasted, the Unseen Hour felt as if it stretched for eternity.

There were many theories as to the hour's origins, but none proven.

One legend said Death had gotten greedy and had chosen to take more than his due in that one hour. Another said it was a way for both gods, Day and Death, to keep mortals humble, aware always of their powerlessness against forces unseen. Still others held the citizens of Emrys and the other countries of the world responsible, viewing the hour as punishment for their actions.

It didn't matter to me what caused it. I was determined to best it—and had been ever since the Taking struck my family three years before. Which is why I'd sneaked out into the night. If my theory was right, then we might need to endure only one more year of the Unseen Hour without Father by our side. Not that I was about to tell Ambrose such a thing.

He waved a finger under my nose.

"Celia! The next time you—"

Ambrose went still, finger mid-wag, voice cutting off mid-lecture as the town clock began to sound. The clock towers of each town were carefully configured so that their tolling at the end of the year could be heard even in the most remote country manor. On this night, there was an extra warning.

It was a quarter of an hour until midnight. We were running out of time.

"Bed. Now," Ambrose instructed, hurrying me out of the barn and into the manor house.

Once we were inside, he instructed one of the staff to secure the front doors, and then followed up the stairs after me. I didn't bother to argue; I didn't even remind him, as I often did, that at twenty-four I could certainly look after myself. No one, no matter how brave, wanted to be anywhere near the outdoors during the Unseen Hour. I all but sprinted toward my rooms and only resented Ambrose a little bit when I heard the click signifying he'd locked me inside. It was for my protection more than anything else.

The curtains on my windows had already been pulled shut, no doubt by a harried maid eager to finish the chore and lock herself in as well. It didn't matter to me. I knew what was coming, even if I couldn't see it.

Outside in the dark of night, the twelfth gong sounded.

CHAPTER 2

JANUARY
THE 99th YEAR

Icy slush threatened to seep into my brown leather boots, though they were laced up just past my ankle. I lifted my skirts as I crossed over the puddle. The outer layer of the dress was an unrelenting shade of vibrant pink, a perfect match for my eyes.

When I am managing a household of my own, I shall outlaw this wretched fabric color, I swore to myself as I continued to trudge through cobblestone streets full of mud and melting ice.

Pellix snorted, and I cast a forlorn glance back to where I'd left him tethered. It was criminal, truly, that horses weren't allowed more places. As far as I was concerned, Pellix behaved with more chivalry than many of the noblemen in Emrys. Not that anyone was asking my opinion on equine etiquette. I supposed I should consider myself lucky that I'd been allowed to ride side-saddle into town with a formal chaperone. The way my mother described it, only a generation ago, anything but a carriage would have been out of the question, particularly with the weather as cold and dismal as it was currently.

My destination loomed over me, an imposing row of brick buildings. The one I needed was second from the left and took up several businesses' worth of space. It also, I thought with more than a little bitterness, was unlikely to provide what I needed.

Back where Pellix was tethered, Finneas gave me a small wave as he tied off the white horse he'd ridden for the morning. He'd been one of our footmen for years, and while it meant another lecture from Mother on how just a generation ago simply a footman to accompany me would have been a scandal in and of itself, I was glad he was who she'd chosen to ride with me into town.

He followed me up the lane.

"Do you think Pellix's shoes are looking a bit worn?" I asked him.

I knew that Finneas had taken a liking to the blacksmith's daughter and spoke to her whenever he got new shoes for the horses. Our horses' hooves were better looked after than anyone else's in Emrys, primarily because Finneas visited the blacksmith and skilled farrier so frequently.

He grinned.

"You're sure you don't need me to go with you to the library?"

"Thank you, but no. Charlotte will be meeting me there." I *was* meeting one of my closest friends later, but I'd intentionally set things up so I would arrive earlier by at least a couple of hours. "Her brother will have escorted her, so I will be fine."

"I'll be waiting by the horses when you're ready, freshly shod!" he promised before disappearing down an adjoining street, a bounce in his step.

I strode toward the library, with Mother's voice echoing in my head.

"In my time, ladies would not have been caught alone for all the money shipped across the Talwin Sea! Ruination for certain!"

If Mother was to be believed, then ladies in generations past must have sat on their duffs doing nothing but needlework most of the time. The idea made me itchy all over again with the need for action. As I reached the library doors, I lifted a hand and used the black metal handle to pull the left one open.

Treading across the tiled floor of the library's entrance, I was thankful my boots didn't echo too dreadfully. I could see the towering shelves of books beyond, but before I could go through the stacks I had to make my way past the librarian. The man behind the desk was balding, spectacled, and cleared his throat a good three times before I reached him. His ruddy cheeks and reddened nose had me wondering whether he was ill or just old and blustery.

He wasn't the usual man at the front, and the scowl on his face as he examined several pieces of old parchment did not instill hope for a friendly welcome and easy interaction.

I planted myself, in all my hot pink glory, in front of him. When he didn't acknowledge me after a few moments, I leaned forward and tapped my finger on the top of the desk. When that didn't work, I took a note from his book and cleared my throat.

He glanced up, eyes huge and watery behind his spectacles.

"Excuse me," I started when he said nothing, "but I need a pass for the Estates section, please."

He looked me up and down, smacking his lips and chomping on nothing but air before giving another scratchy throat-clear.

"Which aisles?"

"Wherever 'H' would be." It was becoming a struggle to

hold on to my friendly demeanor. When I'd come in the past with my brothers, no one ever cared which sections of shelves they wandered about in. Maybe we hadn't advanced past Mother's time very far after all.

He leaned to the side, looking pointedly over my left shoulder, then repeated the movement to the right.

"Companion?"

I let out a small sigh.

"Just me," I replied with a forced smile plastered on my face.

"I'm not certain Miss ..." His eyes flicked down to his book, and then back up to my face.

"Celia Hipnosi," I supplied.

The man's eyes went wider behind his spectacles, and his gaze zeroed in on my eyes. The moment of recognition. Honestly, if he'd been more attentive we could have avoided the entire interaction. Vibrant pink eyes were a renowned Hipnosi trait, and we were the only family in any country known to possess them.

Even so, the man continued to frown, tilting his head side to side like I was a strange and unfamiliar creature he couldn't quite decide whether to pet or hunt.

"My attendant is just outside, securing the horses. He should be around before long," I lied. With any luck, if I made it to the stacks the librarian would go back to his reading and forget all about me.

He huffed.

"Very well, proceed to the left. You'll go through the archway to the second room, and then eight rows back on the left."

I nodded along with the instructions, thanked him and then scurried past before he could change his mind. I knew very well where the books I sought were, but I had no intention of telling him that. Admitting to the librarian that you'd spent the evening just before the past year's Unseen Hour breaking into the library wasn't likely to get one invited back in as a patron.

"At least all this pink is good for something," I muttered to myself as I made my way to the familiar shelf of books.

The librarian had probably only let me near it because he'd been face to face with a Hipnosi. Rubbish. Not that his reaction had been earned by me. Our family had been powerful and respected for generations.

I did have a hunch, though, that the bespectacled book guardian would have thrown me out if it hadn't been for the pink. Very few dared to refuse a Hipnosi.

I couldn't help a furtive glance as I passed the Royals shelving area. Unlike my current destination, the shelves there had intricate carvings on the side, inlaid with shimmering gold, and more impressively a second desk with not a librarian, but a guard. Very few people were allowed in there, since it contained important papers pertaining to the royal family and their dealings. Only nobles with letters bearing the seal of Her Majesty or the prince were allowed.

It was the area I'd sneaked into just before the Unseen Hour, with a hunch that my father's writings had ended up there. I had been right. Our family sometimes worked closely with the royals, and he'd been pursuing something for the queen when everything had gone wrong in the first place.

I had found the book I was seeking, but it was missing a couple of pages.

I needed to go back to the beginning and try to piece what I had together.

CHAPTER 3

I found my way to the Estates section in no time at all. After a glance around to make sure no one else was lurking in the stacks, I bent down and peered at the next-to-bottom shelf. Gently, I pulled out a set of four books; then I reached into the gap behind them.

Relief and a sense of triumph coursed through me when my hand closed around the well-worn journal I'd hidden in the space behind the other books. Each time I visited, it was the same—untouched except by me.

I had no idea why anyone else would bother with this section of the library, but I couldn't be too careful.

Had I been less worried about potential prying eyes and probing questions, I'd have checked out the book. And if I were just a bit less scrupulous, I'd have stolen it ages ago. I'd have to, soon enough. My family was set to leave our estate at Fox Haven and return to the capital of Karith in a couple of months.

I had chosen not to take the journal before the last Unseen Hour for a silly, sentimental reason. I'd found it in the stacks, and this area felt like my spot. Once I removed the journal, that went away. But I would have to take it before we left for the capital.

We went there every spring, and for the past several years that trip had meant enduring 'the season'—multiple months of hot weather, endless promenades, needlessly intricate balls, and other such events, all designed to throw the young people of Emrys together.

Romance wasn't the goal, but a proposal was. The queen of Emrys herself hosted at least two events for the nobility each season, one at the onset and one at the season's end, to celebrate all newly married and engaged couples.

I hated courting season, and it was a point of pride for me that I had so far escaped it without a betrothal since my entrance into society. This year in particular, it would serve as nothing but an unwelcome distraction from my research.

The diary would have to come along with me to Karith; there was no way around it.

"As if I could leave you behind, R. Holmes," I whispered to the small book with the blue cover.

I put a hand to my cheek, certain I was blushing.

After my father's disappearance a few Unseen Hours ago, I had taken refuge amidst the books. Admittedly, the first time I'd come, it had been because I couldn't bear the morose mood at the estate a moment longer. Finneas had accompanied me into Fox Haven, and I had followed instinct to enter the library. Books had always been an escape, and that time proved no exception, although not in the way I'd anticipated.

I had headed toward the emptiest section I could find, since tears had already started running down my cheeks. One simply did not sob in public, at least not if one didn't want to become the focus of gossip.

Emrys had plenty of that, and partaking in it while avoiding becoming the one spoken about with derision was a popular pastime for the country's population.

The Estates stacks beckoned on the day of that fateful visit, empty of a single soul aside from myself. I'd chosen an aisle at random, turned to make it appear I was examining the books, and started to cry.

After that, it had become something of a ritual. I held myself together for my family, and at public events, and I let myself grieve in the forgotten stacks of the library, Estates section, row 'H'.

Those who say time lessens grief are wrong. Time creates space. It gives you more moments around the grief, to cushion you a bit. But the grief is always there, and anything can trigger it. For years, section 'H' had been my refuge when I needed somewhere to be alone.

Only the past fall, before the ninety-eighth hour, I had been in town and seen a man that looked just like Father. Only a trick of the light, coupled with his distance down the road. No one else had those pink eyes. But grief does funny things to the senses. Less than a second of mistaken identity, and I sank into fresh grief.

I'd run into the library, desperate for my familiar stack. Most blessedly, thank both gods, that day a kindlier librarian had manned the desk.

October. My birthday. A day when everything changed for me, and probably why I'd been missing my father enough to see him in a stranger's face.

Once I hit the stacks, I sank to my knees and began to cry. An act both absolutely unbecoming if someone had found me, and an impressive feat of maneuvering. Corsets and dresses aren't made for sitting on the floor.

Even so, I managed. While trying to use the shelves to hoist myself back up to a standing position, I grabbed hold of some books.

A few tumbled out, including the blue diary I held in my hands at present.

The Estates section housed exactly what the name suggested: publicly available information pertaining to various estates. It wasn't often visited, because you could just as easily obtain the information, if you were a man, through business transactions, meetings, and your own familial records. In my case, though, the library was my only means. But the diary was not some boring set of ledgers on some nobleman's finances.

Last October, I'd put the other books neatly back on the shelf, but the blue-bound journal caught my attention. I leafed through it on a whim.

Per the first page, it had belonged to an R. Holmes. It must have ended up in the library along with other estate papers upon his death.

And it was the death that intrigued me.

Everyone in my region of Emrys had heard of the Holmes family. They had been the most powerful dukes of Emrys, going back as far as anyone could remember. They were still one of the most prominent families in the realm, although a shadow had fallen over them nearly a hundred years prior.

During the first of the Unseen Hours, the heir of the dukedom had been Taken—a special name for a special death. Emrys recognized two gods: Day and Death. Day was depicted often in sunny repose, warm and welcoming; Death as the opposite.

Our clergy interpreted the frozen bodies as a sign of rejection, determining that victims of the hour would find no rest in the next life. Instead, an endless and horrible fate awaited them, taken not only from this world, but also from peace in the next.

All three Holmes brothers had died during the hour of that first year, some of the earliest victims of the horror.

At least that was the theory.

I had my doubts.

I'd sat in the library on that October day a few months prior utterly enthralled. I'd read the diary through many times since, and I'd come to the conclusion that perhaps the hour itself wasn't what had been the downfall of R. and his siblings.

The diary made mention of what I found to be rather suspicious happenings surrounding the Holmes brothers in the months before their supposed deaths: Items disappearing from their manor with no explanation. Sightings of dark figures outside the windows, but when staff were sent to look no one could be found. And an illness that plagued all three brothers simultaneously, all the way up until their bitter ends.

What was even more compelling evidence was that all was not as it seemed pertaining to the matter of bodies, as odious as such a topic was. All Unseen Hour victims were found in the streets the following morning. That's how it had been since that first night. Souls were Taken, bodies remained. Only two Holmes brothers had been found. For a while, some had thrown around the rumor that one brother had murdered the others and absconded, but no one had ever found motive or proof.

Why give up an estate you had every right to and go on the run as a murderer? It made no sense.

All that had piqued my interest, but the most compelling thing about the diary had nothing to do with Holmes. In the margins was a second set of handwritten notations. Holmes's own entries were swirling, stately, and easy to read. The notes in the margin were stilted and rushed but familiar to me. They were written in my father's hand.

When and how he'd come into contact with the diary I couldn't be certain, but he'd written all sorts of things in the open spaces. Theories on Emrys, and the Unseen Hour, and how a live person might get Taken. By the end of the diary, my father's notes had even suggested the hour itself was just a problem that needed to be solved and not an unavoidable punishment by the gods.

He made mention of looking into his ideas, for himself and the crown. But three years ago he'd vanished during the Unseen Hour.

In the past few months, since discovering the diary and Father's writing, I had become a woman possessed. I would pick up where he'd left off, and I would finish his mission. With any luck, I thought, and some help from both blessed gods, I could still save him.

Everyone else believed him dead, but after what I'd read I was no longer sure, because my father's situation mirrored another to a curious degree.

With my father, there had been no frozen remains.

Just as with the elder Holmes, there had been no body, and no trace of him since.

CHAPTER 4

MAY

THE 99th YEAR

The drawing room felt stifling, but I was reasonably certain the cause was my outfit and not the temperature. I gave a quick glance around the room, ensuring no one was looking at me, before I tugged at my too-tight bodice in a futile bid to loosen it. I knew I should have been thankful Mother had given in to my requests for a sapphire blue dress instead of the parade of pinks that otherwise lined my wardrobe. The endless sea of fabric in varying shades of the color was meant to remind everyone of the Hipnosi legacy. As if anyone could forget, least of all me, when I was covered in a color only otherwise seen on cakes and sweets, or fields of flowers.

The unique Hipnosi eyes had become synonymous with money, influence, and success. For generations we'd been close to the crown, and my father had taken an already impressive estate and made it even more profitable.

The blue dress was a coup, but if I couldn't breathe in it then it hardly mattered. When I had complained about the restrictive garment, Mother had just brushed me off.

"Just be thankful the fashions have evolved since I was a girl. Our waistlines sat just below the bust, and I can assure you that wasn't any more comfortable," she'd insisted, falling into her favorite pastime of comparing my experiences with her own.

Perhaps my *bust,* as Mother insisted was the only polite way to refer to the area, was able to breathe easier, but my lungs certainly weren't. The whole idea that, in the years between my mother's social seasons and my own, men had decided to be attracted only to women whose top halves looked like an upturned triangle was absurd. I tugged again at the offensive clothing.

"Keep doing that, and you're bound to scare off even the most determined of suitors," a familiar voice teased in my ear. I turned to see Bram, the youngest of my three brothers and the only sibling younger than me. Ambrose, Temple, Celia, and Bram—the prodigies of the famed Hipnosi household.

Bram circled me like a shark in the Talwin Sea.

"The color is nice," he conceded, "but the fidgeting is bound to leave you devoid of a single dance request."

"Then it will have been an evening well-spent," I retorted.

Bram winked at me, taking the sting out of his earlier statement, and I had to hide my giggle behind a gloved hand. At twenty-one, he was expected to start at least considering marriage this season, but he was the least of our mother's concerns. After all, she had three other children to settle first.

Bram ran a hand through his dark brown hair, messing up the careful style that fell just below his ears. He grinned at me.

"You do realize you might receive less chiding from Mother and Ambrose if you took to the floor a bit more often during these events," Bram informed me before offering his arm.

We made our way out of the manor and to a waiting carriage.

"I'm afraid my dance card is full-up for the evening," I responded before flashing it at him from where it hung around my wrist. I'd written incomprehensible squiggles into most of the lines.

Most, not all.

I knew I had to occasionally venture out onto the floor if I wanted to escape the worst of my mother's ire.

Bram sighed as Shrewsbury shut the door to our carriage, no doubt ready to report back to my mother and eldest brother whether I was behaving. Mother rode in a second carriage with Ambrose and our middle brother Temple.

I stuck my tongue out at the carriage door once it was safely closed and there was no chance of Shrewsbury spotting me. Not mature, I had to admit, but the only rebellion I could muster in the moment.

Bram chuckled, then reached across for my hand.

"Humor Mother. It's not as if she'd actually hand you over to most of those fools," he reminded me as the carriage began to move.

In that, I knew he was right. Since our father's disappearance, Mother had become a shadow hovering over us all. That was actually an improvement, as she'd practically shut herself into her rooms for the first few months. If I had to choose, I'd settle for the hovering. While it meant she was maddeningly involved in all our affairs, it was also likely why, in spite of her threats, she hadn't pushed any particular suitor on me—or my brothers, for that matter. Deep down, she didn't want to let go.

It was well enough for the boys; they'd all stay at one of

several family properties if they were married. I, on the other hand, would be expected to move into my betrothed's household.

Truthfully I had considered it, but in spite of our bickering I cared deeply for my family. That, and the suitors available to me in Emrys left something to be desired. We spent most of the year in Fox Haven, the largest city aside from the capital. For the season, we had to be in Karith, because the queen did not deign to travel outside the capital without good reason.

Unfortunately, neither location had presented me with appealing options for a husband. Occasionally, nobles would travel from Mejje, across the Talwin Sea. I'd once seen an emissary from Sez and its jungle-filled islands southwest of Emrys. I'd never met anyone from Tang or its icy tundra to the northeast. And, of course, no one had ever met anyone from the lost country.

Not that I anticipated their men being any more appealing than ours, if they were the sort of individuals who attended fêtes and art exhibitions, where it was the people on display rather than the paintings.

No, I had yet to meet a man that made me want to leave my family, as bothersome as they sometimes were. And certainly not in the past few months, now that I had a much more important mission.

Saving my father, in my mind, was certainly a worthier use of my time than simpering and flirting just enough to look interested but not enough to appear forward. It was more enjoyable spending my hours absorbed in the writings of Father and the intriguing R. Holmes than pretending to show interest in the men of Emrys, or for that matter men from any country in Rayus.

After all, was it my fault that my options were almost all either dull, self-absorbed, womanizing or some combination of the three? I didn't think my standards were too farfetched, but the available bachelors in Emrys begged to differ.

Still, I at least had to make a show of it; make it look like I was trying to win over the hearts of all the eligible men of the season. I hardly had the stomach for it, or the inclination.

Especially this year. I'd set myself a deadline of December. My father had been interested in Holmes and his diary, and after scrutinizing his notes I had a theory on why. I suspected he had tried to imitate Holmes in some way. They'd met the same fate, and he'd read the same information in the diary I had. I hadn't yet figured out how he'd managed to get Taken, but I suspected the missing pages might have something to do with it.

And it stood to reason that the Unseen Hour was my window of opportunity. I did not intend to wait an additional year. The pages were my mission, and now that we'd arrived back in Karith, I was about to get my chance.

I just had to suffer through the season's opening ball first, because Mother's eyes had been on me since our arrival and would remain so until she was assured I was safely ensconced in the season's activities.

With any luck at all, I'd make it through this season as I had the previous ones, without an engagement. Truth be told, I wasn't against marriage, but I wanted someone adventurous. Someone open-minded, bold, and intelligent, like the author of the Holmes journals. He wrote of travel and a longing for more of it. His words convinced me that he'd loved his family, and held them dear, but balanced it with a desire to explore. It sometimes felt like reading a mirror of my own soul.

Someone like that could set my mind and my body on fire.

Completely scandalous. Utterly inappropriate.

I could imagine Mother's face if she knew.

"Sorry, Mother, but I've fallen for the intelligent, well-spoken man who wrote about a life of ambition and adventure. Oh, who is he? A long-dead nobleman of Emrys. That shouldn't complicate things too much, should it?"

The carriage came to a stop, and when I stepped out I was staring at the well-lit entrance hall of Swiltshire, where my best friend, Charlotte, resided.

At least the evening wouldn't be a total loss.

CHAPTER 5

"Ambrose, Temple, Celia, Bram," our mother called. I joined my brothers as the carriages moved behind us. They would be waiting when we were ready to return home. There would be no windswept rides on Pellix this evening.

I huffed, and my mother shot me a glare. Fixing my face into a smile, I followed her as we made our way into the manor and an extravagant ballroom. Mother didn't need to know that I'd managed to loosen my corset on the carriage ride over.

Bram had pointed out that I looked like a duck trying to do a somersault, but he'd kept his laughter to a minimum and had sworn not to mention a thing.

Chandeliers, twinkling lights, and too many bodies made the room more stifling than the drawing room back home, loosened corset or no. Another reason to hate layered dresses. I knew, because my mother never failed to remind us all, that I was lucky to have such opportunities. It didn't stop me from stewing; it just meant I did so with guilt.

"May as well put that blue dress to use. Perhaps a turn around the dance floor would even put a smile on your face,"

Bram prodded me. His hair was a shade darker than mine, and his eyes just a shade lighter. Among the four of us siblings, only Temple took after our mother, with blue eyes. Bram's pink practically sparkled as he teased me, which was one of his favorite pastimes.

As if his words had the ability to summon potential suitors, Bellamy Bonds, the Marquess of Umpert, came striding across the room toward me. He bowed at the waist when he got close.

"Lady Hipnosi, you look positively radiant this evening. Would it be too much to hope that you still have an opening on your dance card?"

"I'm certain she has a few, actually." Bram smirked and made himself scarce before I could think of a retort.

I plastered on a forced smile, knowing Mother would be watching from somewhere in the crowd.

"Lord Bonds, it would be a pleasure." I held out my wrist and tried not to cringe as Bellamy plucked the card and wrote his name on a line for a waltz later in the evening.

Because things were not quite as archaic as in generations past, it was fine for those in our generation to call each other by their first names once someone gave their permission to do so, but in this case I was just fine allowing Lord Bonds his formalities.

Bellamy bowed again as he dropped my wrist, and a strand of lanky red hair fell in his face before he hastily smoothed it back. His eyes were a leafy green that might have been handsome on another face, but Bellamy's resting expression was a sneer, and no features really suited his lack of personality.

When the waltz came up, I allowed myself to be led onto

the floor.

Bellamy was a perfect example of the *bore* portion of my options. He was neither toe-crunchingly dreadful nor gracefully adept at the waltz. Then again, neither was I. My ladylike talents included a passable singing voice, an admittedly more than passable level of skill on the piano, and a keen interest in novels. Although reading was only a valuable quality when husbands wanted a wife who wouldn't meddle too much in their affairs, being otherwise distracted.

Throughout the dance, Bellamy maintained polite and completely acceptable conversation, about such thrilling topics as the weather and the *hors d'oeuvres*. For my part, I responded and smiled in equal measure, as was expected of me. After all, it wasn't entirely Bellamy's fault he was so mind-numbingly dull. The parameters of society didn't lend themselves to dashing, daring, or delinquent behaviors. Which was a shame, given that nearly all of my interests fell into just those categories.

There were, of course, trysts every season, but the subjects were pounced upon with merciless gossip when found out. I wanted adventure, not public censure and ridicule.

As I extricated myself from Bellamy's company, I saw Ambrose take to the floor with Penny Montgomery. He was likely to take a wife this season. He'd expressed multiple times throughout the previous winter that, with Father's businesses finally in order, this was the next sensible step.

I had no complaints. Penny and I weren't particularly close, but she was always polite to me at these functions. The two of them spun in a circle as the musicians played one of the livelier tunes of the evening.

"Pardon me, Miss Hipnosi, might I trouble you for a spot on your dance card?"

I swallowed a beleaguered sigh and turned, then felt a genuine smile spread across my face.

"Thomas Huberts! I didn't realize you were here for the season!"

"I am indeed, and Charlotte insisted I be here with our parents, hosting this evening's soiree." He leaned in conspiratorially. "I think she wanted another set of eyes on everyone so she could have twice as much gossip tomorrow. I'm sure she'll tell you herself, though."

I glanced behind him and spotted my best friend headed our way. Charlotte and Thomas shared similar honey blond hair and hazel eyes.

"I'm sorry I didn't say hello sooner. It took me a while to go around and greet everyone in attendance. Did you see the queen brought one of the princes with her?" Charlotte asked as she smoothed out her dress.

It had been impossible to miss. Eligible ladies and status-climbing men had been crowding him all evening, or crowding the queen herself.

"I've heard the prince has shown an interest in Lady Kellers." Charlotte gave a side-eyed glance at the woman, who was sipping champagne and watching the dancing with interest.

Thomas rolled his eyes.

"Ah yes, the most exciting thing happening in Emrys. Lady Kellers dancing with a prince. How did I ever survive while I was away, with such succulent gossip occurring right here under your very nose, Charlotte?"

I smirked at Thomas.

"If Charlotte and I were permitted to travel, I have no doubt we would have stories just as interesting as yours," I countered. Thomas had spent the better portion of the past year in Mejje and had most recently been traveling on the islands of Sez. "We are prepared for you to astonish us with what you have learned."

Jealousy twisted my gut, but I kept the smile on my face.

Thomas began regaling us with tales of the golden-sand deserts of Mejje and the buildings constructed in such a way that people stayed cool even on the hottest of days.

One thing that was once better, not in my mother's time but a couple of generations prior, was travel. Families would cross the seas and couples might take trips together. After the Unseen Hour began, however, people feared travel delays and being caught unaware.

A few years after the Unseen Hour began in Emrys, it spread. First Mejje, then Tang, and finally the islands of Sez had been hit. The lost country, farther even than Tang, no doubt felt the sting of the hour too, if any individual in fact still lived in the wilderness of its abandoned lands. The other nations saw the hour as a curse Emrys had inflicted upon them, and relations had been strained since, which only added to the difficulty of travel.

Charlotte nudged me, and I realized I'd been scowling with my arms crossed. I fixed my posture and face before anyone in my family could see me—and hopefully any others who might twist even the smallest look into gossip about a romance gone bad or some equally ridiculous nonsense. I viewed Thomas and Charlotte in the same way I viewed my three siblings, and I had no desire to fuel suspicions that Thomas and I were embroiled in some sort of affair. As much as I enjoyed his company, I felt nothing toward him in that way. If I was to marry, I wanted to long for someone. Ache for them with the same desire I felt for real adventure, or at least the way Holmes described such travels.

When I lay eyes on the waves, it's as if they carry my heart along with them, pulling me out to sea and whatever awaits beyond.

I'd memorized an embarrassing portion of the entries, and I

wanted my heart pulled by a man the way Holmes's had been by the sea.

Charlotte snapped open her fan, blocking our faces from the crowd and bringing me back to the moment.

"It may interest you to know, brother, that I actually do have news that is more pressing than yours. It pertains to you, Celia. Your mother and mine were speaking. She says this is the year she's determined to find you a suitable husband. You and at least one of 'those mischievous sons of mine,' in her words. You'd best be watchful."

I froze. The music in the ballroom became an annoying buzz in the background, and I reached up and tugged on my bodice. The dress was still too tight after all.

"I didn't want to distress you"—Charlotte chewed at her lip —"I just wanted you to be aware."

I flashed her a small smile.

"Yes. I appreciate it Charlotte, truly. I just need some time to ... oh, Bellamy is making his way over again. I can't handle another dance with him. Not now."

Thomas held out his hand and bowed.

"Allow me to help."

It would lead to gossip, because the three of us were already so often in each other's company, but at the moment I didn't care.

I was in no state to make inane conversation with potential suitors. Thomas wouldn't require conversation at all.

While we spun around the dance floor, I plotted.

I'd ask to ride in the carriage home with my mother and find out just how serious she was about this marriage plan.

Then, either way, I would ignore her and double down on my efforts to go after my father. If I brought him back, marrying me off would be the last thing on anyone's mind.

CHAPTER 6

Normally at these sorts of events, I looked forward to the end of the evening. While I enjoyed seeing Charlotte, Thomas, and a select other few individuals, I enjoyed getting away from the pack of marriage-obsessed mothers and suitors even more.

I was also firmly of the belief that being able to get rid of a corset and constrictive dress was perhaps the best part of any evening.

In this instance, however, I'd put myself in the lion's den. My mother, Vinia, smiled at me from across the carriage, and I awaited her commentary on the evening. She'd looked so pleasantly surprised when I requested we ride home together that I felt a tad guilty, until I saw her eyeing every gentleman I danced with before we left the ball.

"Lord Huberts was admiring you this evening," she started.

I sighed.

"Mother, Thomas and I are friends. Just as Charlotte and I are friends."

With a frown, my mother sat back in the carriage; but she rallied within seconds, leaning forward again.

"What about the Marquess of Umpert? I saw that he danced with you this evening. His properties are small but lovely. His estate to the northeast has that charming lake."

I made a noncommittal noise in the back of my throat. The estate my mother referenced was far outside the capital and near the coldest region of Emrys. Worse, Bellamy Bonds was the Marquess, and I could only imagine being stuck on a dreary estate with nothing to do and no one but him and his staff for company.

Plus, his lands were just about as far from my family as I could be. As annoying as Mother's prodding sometimes was, I had fond memories of growing up at Scops. Family walks through the woods. Riding together. Lawn games, even though I rarely won, with laughter and joking. Back before my mother had disappeared into her grief and then re-emerged with nothing to occupy her but high society.

My father's disappearance had taken the spark from my mother, and if she got him back, the spark would return as well. I was sure of it.

"I have no interest in Bellamy Bonds either, Mother. He has all the personality of a wet blanket."

Across the carriage, Mother frowned again, deeper this time. Her whole face managed to turn downward. For a moment it looked as if the pile of orange curls pinned atop her head might fall off like ice cream from a cone. I had to bite back a laugh at the thought. Her eyes seared into me. They were a saturated shade of blue that complemented her other features. She had faint freckles across her cheeks—terribly out of fashion in her time, and still not the standard for beauty in mine, but one of her singular holdouts against the norm. My father had always found them charming.

While the shades of our hair and eyes might be different, I did share the shape of my mother's eyes, although I rather thought mine never bore the same severe look. We also had the same cheekbones, and the same straight nose. It was like watching an older, more serious version of myself.

My mother sighed, falling back against the seat again.

"You know, you could at least *try* to involve yourself a bit more, dear. It was one thing your first season or two out, but now people are beginning to talk."

I just bet they were. Whispered barbs behind gloved hands. Gossips feigning civility and concern. All young women and ladies made their society debuts during their twentieth year. I'd be twenty-five in the fall, marking it as my fifth season. Most women were married by their third. Tongues were wagging.

In the face of such scrutiny, it was foolish to think my mother's desire to hold her children close would win out. I had been distracted while it had slowly been chipped away, carved and shaped into conformity.

"And what should we care for the gossip of a bunch of sodden-headed bores?" I grumped in my seat.

I suspected I'd gone more than a hair too far when Mother gasped, but instead of chastising me she sighed, reaching out to take my hands in hers.

"Do you know, when I was your age it was even worse. We didn't refer to other nobility by even their last names, as we do now. We had to refer to them by the title of their estates. You would have been dancing all night with Marquess Umpert, not Bellamy or Lord Bonds, as you refer to him. When your father and I were betrothed, I had to go around addressing him as Marquess, or Your Grace, if you can imagine."

I had heard this information from her dozens of times before, but accepted the gesture for the peacekeeping attempt it was. I smiled, letting myself be drawn into the story.

"And what changed everyone's minds?" I asked, already aware of the answer.

Vinia looked around the carriage as though someone might overhear a secret before turning back to me, whispering conspiratorially.

"The queen. She loved the missing king, may Day and Death save him, and insisted that she would not spend her entire life referring to him by a title when she ought to have the right to call him *Frederick*." The missing king's name was whispered quieter than the rest. It might have been all right for the queen, but no one else was foolish enough to refer to the royal family by anything but their titles. That had *not* changed.

King Frederick had chosen to travel to the other continents, determined to repair relationships and attempt to work together with foreign emissaries on better defenses against the Unseen Hour. Instead, his ship had disappeared during a fierce storm in the Talwin Sea, somewhere between Emrys and Mejje, during the hour. Everyone agreed the king had either drowned, along with the rest of the crew, or been Taken and his body lost to the waves. But no one dared argue with the queen.

What I *did* have of Father's writings included notes that appeared to relate his interest in the Unseen Hour to the missing royal. Whatever the queen suspected, or whatever she hoped to find by enlisting my father's help as a trusted noble, I wondered if she had a similar suspicion to my own: that being Taken was not necessarily the end—at least not when there was no body left behind.

At the moment, the queen ruled in place of her eldest son. There was some law stating that if a monarch was indisposed due to health for more than twelve years, then the next ruler would be crowned. The queen had a few years left in power before the officials of Emrys could legally declare the king deceased and place one of her sons on the throne instead.

While I was as far in power from her as she was from the gods themselves, our positions were oddly similar.

Both firmly stuck in our circumstances. Both of us running out of time to delay.

Father had disappeared during the Unseen Hour months after my first season. I hadn't been able to move on from it. It was as if going through each year in a repetitive pattern somehow preserved our lives, in case he came back. Not that anyone else expected him to. Even before finding Holmes's diary, such action had felt to me like a betrayal. Moving on and settling for a mediocre and shallow life.

While the missing king might indeed be at the bottom of the sea, I had always felt I would know if my father were dead, and now I had every reason to suspect I'd been right from the get-go.

After all, the individuals who were Taken had to go somewhere. All of Emrys believed in Day and Death. It stood to reason, in my mind, that if Death was responsible for our plight, he had the souls safe.

And since my father's body was gone as well, it made all the sense in the world that, wherever the souls were, there he was, still alive and waiting for rescue. The diary and his theories had only solidified my belief.

He'd only been out on the night in question to fetch the Fox Haven physician for one of my mother's debilitating migraines.

When two weeks had passed with no news, we held a funeral for him and that was that. I was expected to go back to my life and the role I was meant to play.

But I couldn't. I remained stuck between my life before, and whatever awaited after.

Then, I found R. Holmes and his diary, alongside my father's writing.

Every night since October had been consumed with new purpose, the fire inside me finally stoked again.

And this night was no exception.

I just had to handle my mother first.

"Really, Celia, I bear some of the responsibility for this. I let you drag your feet these past few seasons. I wanted to give you time to grieve, and I needed the time as well. But your brothers are moving on, and so must we. Ambrose has already expressed interest in a proposal this season. You need a suitable match of your own. I'd feel better knowing you were cared for. After all, with your ... habit of running off ... I need to make sure you have someone to ensure your safety."

I huffed, working hard to keep a glare off my face. Mother would never tolerate both at once. I could hardly explain to her that my habit of sneaking off was to follow my father's bread-crumbs, and those of R. Holmes's diary, to try to find a way to follow them both wherever the Taken went.

I tackled the issue of suitors instead.

"How am I supposed to make a match when there is no one I would consider marrying? I have no interest in Thomas in a romantic way, and none to speak of for Bellamy whatsoever. That will not change."

"Really, Celia! It does not matter if you feel that way. Your father and I married for love, but that isn't the case for many young ladies. If I had possessed a firmer hand the last few years, you'd already be settled and running a household of your own. I admit that I should have pressed harder, sooner."

I shook my head, dazzled at how my hair stayed in place even as my neck whipped about. My attendants were truly skilled, and I inwardly groaned at how long it would take to remove all the pins after our arrival home, when all I wanted to do was sleep and forget this conversation.

Not that I'd be sleeping even if my hair were loose. I turned my attention back toward Mother.

"You didn't do anything wrong. I preferred it that way. In fact, we could wait another few years if—"

"You have delayed long enough! Arguably too long! Within another year or two, people will be saying you're an old maid, and what of your options then?"

Then I'd be free to live in peace and get into whatever mischief I wanted. At least that was what I was tempted to retort with. The problem was, my mother was right. In one small detail only. I didn't want to be alone. I *did* want marriage and a relationship, but I wanted it on my terms. I wanted romance and passion, *and* I still wanted freedom.

"And what about a loveless marriage? What about being forced to become nothing more than a woman who has babies and exists on her husband's arm?"

Mother flinched, and I regretted my words. After all, Mother had done just that, dedicating herself to her children, and prior to my father's death she had been vivacious and charming.

"Mother, I'm happy your choices brought you joy, and that's what I'm asking for myself. I want to be my own person, and have my own adventures. You used to encourage that. When Father was here—"

"When he was here we had more safety and security! It was his own reckless choices that took him out that night and cost us all. I will not have you following in those footsteps. I could not bear to see something happen to you, Celia."

Tears glistened in the corners of my mother's eyes, and I bit down on a retort. I knew the fear and pressure was coming from a place of grief, but that would mean nothing if I ended up married to someone like Bellamy for the rest of my days, doomed to talk of nothing more interesting than the unusual amount of rain or whether the bread was particularly dry at dinner.

My mother sighed, putting a hand to her forehead and giving it a sharp squeeze before dropping her hands in her lap and looking at me again.

"I'm thinking only of your future, Celia. At some point I won't be around, either. I know your brothers will look after you, but I want you to have your own home. I want you to have your own security, and that means a good marriage."

I almost pointed out that the queen ruled just fine in the king's prolonged and mysterious absence, but I held my tongue, knowing the argument would make no difference. The queen was the queen, and she didn't have a mother pushing suitors on her. She had the officials of Emrys, constantly trying to push her out.

My mother reached back out, taking my hands.

"If the other choices are really all so unpalatable, why not marry Thomas? The Huberts are a good family. You have a friendship with Charlotte as well. Your life would be comfortable."

True, I'd rather spend my days at the Huberts' estate than anywhere near many of the other men who had been interested in me, but it seemed fair to neither Thomas nor myself. In spite of any rumors, we had no desire to wed each other. I knew, having seen it in past seasons, that friendships could blossom into something more, but that hadn't been the case with us. I truly viewed him as platonically as I did my own siblings. Just the thought of being intimate with and having children with Thomas made me uncomfortable.

Even if I was willing to set that aside and marry him to prevent a worse fate, I couldn't ask it of him. Thomas, like myself, had his own dreams. He wasn't interested in marriage at all, from what he had shared with Charlotte and me. I couldn't ask him to sacrifice that to save me from a lifetime of living with a boorish man.

Besides, I reminded myself, *if I can hold Mother off for just the remainder of the season, it won't matter. I'll rescue Father, and she'll have other things to focus on.*

My future would hinge on my success during the Unseen Hour, just like my father's fate. This whole conversation was meaningless, and I could afford to give in for appearances.

"I will seriously consider potential suitors. Lord Whipples did look handsome this evening, did he not?" It was a safe choice, because I knew the earl in question had eyes for Charlotte, but my mother beamed nonetheless and spent the remainder of the ride discussing the various advantages of his family.

When the carriage arrived at Scopshaven, I breathed a sigh of relief and returned to my rooms.

The conversation had driven home the need for me to maintain my focus.

Everyone else would be as exhausted from the evening as I was, but that meant I had to take advantage while I could.

This was the perfect opportunity to follow the next step on my father's trail.

CHAPTER 7

I bit back a yawn. Merely having a clear goal didn't mean I relished a night without sleep.

If I can figure out Father's part in all this, it will be worth it.

I'd spent months reviewing the same writings over and over, but I wanted those missing pages. They hadn't been anywhere at Scops that I could find, and our property in Karith was my next guess. The capital was where Father conducted a lot of business, and it made every bit of sense in the world to me that the pages might be in his office. Particularly since his research was being done at the behest of the queen.

I'd briefly considered approaching the monarch at the ball, but there was no simple way to explain how I knew my father had been looking into the hour at her request. And no good way to ensure the conversation was private.

In the end, I'd decided to find the pages before doing anything else.

This was our first time back to our Karith property since I'd discovered the diary, and while we'd been here for days, I'd had someone watching me near constantly. Now, when everyone was tired from the preparations for the ball and the event itself, was the best time to look.

The house was dark and quiet as I made my way down the imperial staircase. As I came upon the landing where the two sides converged, I was careful to step over the portion of wood I knew would emit a squeak liable to wake someone.

I was driven by determination and desperation in equal measure. I placed a fist over my heart, then brought it up to my lips and kissed it. A plea to both gods, Day and Death, to help me. Whether the theory of Death being responsible for the hour was true or not, no one dared defy a god. Most people had only grown more pious in the years following the hour's appearance, in the hopes one god or the other might show mercy to us all.

It had yet to work, but at least the services held in the gods' honor were full of song, in addition to endless recitations of prayer. The music was something I had always enjoyed. All respectable families attended services. Fox Haven had a gorgeous church with stained-glass windows depicting the gods themselves and various scenes within Emrys.

There was another church, though, of which I was even fonder. No more than a stone ruin, now, surrounded by a crumbling cemetery, it sat on a brush-covered portion of the Hipnosi property. We'd purchased the land generations ago from the Holmeses, and that connection had only strengthened my love of the crumbling old structure in recent months. A small area where I could escape with Pellix, away from our fields where workers harvesting crops might spot me.

Our gardener had told me once that the ruin may well have been dedicated to one of the other gods—a blasphemous statement in Emrys, which was probably why he refused to say more when I pestered him on the subject.

Other countries had their own ideas as to which gods existed, and how many, but Emrys was a country of Day and Death. The two gods brought balance, and to shun one would surely bring even worse devastation down on us all. So we continued to worship the deities until the day one of them might take pity on their worshippers. I tried not to be completely sacrilegious about it, but I believed strongly that we'd do better taking action for ourselves rather than awaiting intervention by deities of whose existence I had certainly never seen any true sign.

Not that such thoughts kept me from offering my prayers and songs when the occasion arose.

Perhaps the gods appreciated my acknowledgment, because I made it to the bottom of the staircase without incident. My candle illuminated only a small circle of the blue carpet that lined the stairs beneath my slippered feet. Blue. The color was a tribute to my mother, and Father had insisted blue accents be added to his properties after their marriage. I found it a welcome break from all the pink that filled our wardrobes.

I reached the study doors.

Now, here was the real trick. Mother ensured the house-keeper stayed on top of all household maintenance, with this room being the one exception. She hadn't been able to bear entering it after Father disappeared, and so it had remained shut and untouched, aside from Ambrose going in to clear out any paperwork necessary for running the estate. Even then, Ambrose had gone to the trouble of renovating one of the other rooms on the ground floor to serve as his own office, rather than disturbing Father's legacy.

If the hinges creaked, I might bring someone running. I had several excuses at the ready—needing a glass of milk, sleep-walking, simply missing my father. But if I was seen trying to get into the office, it might put Ambrose and Mother on alert against a second attempt. It would be far better if I got this done in one try.

I held my breath, then tugged on the door.

My luck held out, and the left door to the office swung open silently. Scurrying inside, I hastily shut it behind me.

"It's like having you home again," I whispered to the room.

The scent of dust and books hung heavy in the air, but beneath that I could smell oranges and bourbon, a favorite drink of my father's. I was on the taller side of average, but my height was nothing compared to my father's. I had to pull the chair back from my father's desk and climb onto it to reach the candelabra hanging over his desk.

I'd thought ahead enough to bring along a few handker-chiefs, stuffed into a pocket. It wouldn't do to leave prints on everything. I pulled one out and used it to swat cobwebs off the candelabra before lighting it with the tip of my candle.

Soft, warm light spread over the desk.

I searched the items on the top first, but they yielded noth-ing. An atlas, a pair of reading spectacles, an empty candle holder, and a few loose pieces of parchment next to an open bottle of ink with a quill still sitting in it.

The desk had three drawers on each side. I started on the left, not wholly surprised to find the first two were empty. When Ambrose went through, he'd probably taken anything he thought was important, and it only made sense those items would be in the higher drawers.

When I'd finished on the left, I started on the right and identified nothing of value in the first drawer there, either. Just a few pages of blank parchment and an unused quill. If I were stupendously lucky, there would be a document with the words Unseen Hour printed across it.

I hit upon just such an item in the second drawer. My heart leapt into my throat momentarily, beating fast as I reached a shaking hand in the drawer to retrieve what I'd seen. My hopes sank just as quickly as they'd risen when I realized it was just an old copy of a warning. They plastered them throughout the country every December, reminding citizens to prepare themselves and to barricade themselves inside before midnight on the thirty-first of December. As if anyone needed reminding.

In the early years, people discovered the key to safety through trial and error, along with observation. Once it was clear the hour was a continuing pattern, it didn't take long to discern that it was only those outdoors who were in danger. And it took only a little more discussion to realize that hiding places like barns with open doors or ruins like the church I enjoyed didn't keep one safe. Whether closed shutters and bolted doors were necessary along with simply staying shut up indoors, I couldn't say. But I supposed everyone had decided it was better to be overly cautious than a frigid corpse on January first.

I was tempted to crumple the warning up and burn it but couldn't bring myself to destroy anything of my father's, no matter how minuscule its importance. Doubt began to creep in. I knew what I was doing was possibly a fool's errand, but it was also the first time in years I'd felt a real sense of hope.

And I couldn't deny that focusing on this instead of the season made me feel more adventurous than I ever had. Except perhaps when I was with Pellix.

I couldn't give that up, and I wouldn't give up on my father.

It was that thought that had me leaning down, wiping the dust from the drawer's interior, when my handkerchief caught on something. I tugged, then cursed when the thing came back frayed. I detested needlework, and it would be my responsibility to mend it.

"Blasted fabric!" I scowled at the offending handkerchief.

Grabbing a candle off the desktop, and determined to find and remove the offending splinter from the wood lest I prick myself on it, I leaned back toward the open drawer. Cut into the wood was a tiny notch, so small it would be missed if someone wasn't looking specifically for it. I reached down and placed a finger in the groove, then pulled.

The bottom of the drawer came away, revealing a hidden compartment beneath. Inside were a couple of folded pieces of paper, tied up in a blue ribbon. I reached in and retrieved them. I recognized the ribbon as one my mother had worn in her hair in the past. Careful not to drip wax on my discovery, I pulled the ribbon loose and unfolded the pages. They were torn along one edge, and I greedily devoured the last words my father had for me.

The key is the Thipp's.

That single sentence was scrawled across the top. Below it was a list.

– Retrieve Thipp's
– Test on next hour (away from family – physician's?)
– Results to Her Majesty
– Replicate
**Only at the brink of death can I greet Death*

My heart was a hammer inside my chest as I read over the list several times. He had left us on purpose; at least, that's what the writing indicated.

Thipp's root was something I'd seen referenced in Holmes's

diary as well. The brothers had been taking it prior to their own disappearance, to help with the insomnia brought on by whatever ailed them. It struck me because Thipp's was now known to be dangerous sedative. It was still used, but only by medical professionals during surgery. It was never given out as a mere sleep aid. Which meant, if my father had gone looking for it ... was this what I needed if I wanted to follow him?

The first portion of the writing looked more like a plan, but the final section read like a diary entry, my father spilling his thoughts onto the pages.

> *I don't need the money, or a reward, that awaits if I achieve this. I've sworn secrecy, but there can be no harm if I'm only telling myself.*
>
> *Her Majesty is determined to retrieve her husband and to fight the hour. She thinks, as I have come to as well, that there is a way past this side to whatever waits beyond. If she wants to retrieve the king and send an army to fight gods, that is her business.*
>
> *Monarchs think everything can be solved with the strength of an army. Even death.*
>
> *I seek a solution to protect my family. Each year, this wretched hour takes even those who think they are prepared.*
>
> *My children are almost all of marriageable age. What of Celia? How can I protect them when they aren't under my roof?*
>
> *Something must be done, and for them I will sacrifice anything.*

The paper wrinkled in my hands, and I jumped, unclenching my fist. He'd disappeared for *us*. If he had succeeded, he was wherever or in whatever lay beyond the hour. If he had failed? It had been because he wanted to protect us.

The Unseen Hour and its lost souls were a terror for everyone, but to the most unlucky in Emrys and all of Rayus, it was personal. My father had lost his only brother to the hour, delayed on his way home during a winter storm. He'd never have risked the same happening to us, not if he thought he could prevent it.

The extent of the queen's involvement was interesting, but I was most intrigued by the Thipp's. That was the key. Holmes had mentioned it, and now Father had indicated that's how he'd done it. I would do the same.

I just had to come up with a way to get my hands on the stuff, and then wait for the hour.

From out in the hall, a telltale squeak sounded. It had to be one of the housemaids, awake early and preparing the manor for the day. I tucked the paper into my pocket.

Taking care to remain quiet, I stood on tiptoe on Father's office chair and blew out each candle, then slid all the drawers shut before peeking out the door. Seeing the coast was clear, I slid out and shut the door behind me. I made my way to the foyer and then sprinted across to the kitchens.

Tilly, one of the housemaids, was straightening a vase of flowers on an entrance table when I emerged back into the foyer.

"Good morning, Tilly."

She jumped, jostling the vase and only just managing to grab it.

"Miss Celia! I didn't realize anyone else was about."

"I'm sorry if I frightened you. I wasn't able to sleep much

last night. I thought I'd get a bit of breakfast and then lie down again. Would you like to join me for some juice?"

Tilly beamed.

"Of course, Miss."

I patted my pocket, reassuring myself the papers were still there before following her.

CHAPTER 8

OCTOBER
THE 99th YEAR

We were well into fall, and by some miracle of both gods I had managed to make it through another courting season, and another birthday, without an unwanted proposal of marriage.

When we arrived back in Fox Haven in mid-September, I finally felt safe to breathe. We'd stayed in the capital longer than normal, for Ambrose's wedding and associated festivities. While I was happy for my brother and glad that Penny was an agreeable person, having a marriage so close felt almost contagious.

To my horror, Charlotte and Thomas had informed me that Bellamy had been very close to speaking to Mother about a request for my hand once he'd heard of Ambrose's engagement —a sign that the Hipnosis were ready to wed.

It was Thomas who had come to my rescue. He'd gone to one of the gentlemen's clubs in the evening and sought Bellamy out, plying the dull Marquess with drinks and then pretending to let slip that he'd always admired me. Thomas had gone so far as to lie and say he'd been in communication with my family regarding my hand.

It was a bold and total falsehood, but it bought me time. Bellamy had, no doubt, figured out by now that Thomas and I were very much un-engaged. As he'd pursued no other women, there was every likelihood the Marquess would renew his attempts the following season, but each time I thought of that and my breathing went shallow and quick, I reminded myself that it wouldn't matter. By that point, I'd have Father back and it would be a non-issue. At least, that's what I repeated to myself at night when my confidence in my plan threatened to crack.

Father would never let me be married to someone against my will, I was sure of it. And with him back home, Ambrose could relax and Mother could go back to her more vivacious self, rather than the nitpicking and traditional creature she'd morphed into in recent years.

I was thankful that her anxiety seemed to have been eased somewhat by Ambrose's wedding. It was beautiful and took place at the Huberts' estate, which they had kindly lent on the day.

While everyone else was focused on planning for the festivities, I'd used the months to solidify my plan. I read my father's notes and Holmes's diary until I could quote both by heart.

I had to admit that while it was all informative, R.'s writing proved distracting for an entirely different reason.

If we could see beyond the edge of the known realms, beyond even the lost country, what would we find? What horizons lie past our experience, ready for exploration?

A question that I myself had asked. I'd awoken more than once from dreams involving an entirely different sort of exploration. They always involved the mysterious Holmes, his features shaded, his words turning from poetry to seduction.

In a few instances I'd roused from sleep to find my own hand trailing over my sleeping gown between my legs, though I'd been imagining his touch just before waking.

A part of me longed to linger on the fantasy, but it was one I couldn't afford. Holmes had been gone for nearly a hundred years, and no amount of infatuation was going to change that. I had one person I could rescue, and I needed to put all my focus toward that goal.

The diary also helped me tailor my plan. The Holmes brothers had taken Thipp's in regular and increasing dosages leading up to their disappearance, with no way of knowing in their time how dangerous such a practice might be.

While I was far from a medical expert, I suspected that the amount he indicated could have brought him to the brink of death—which was exactly my father's goal, during the hour. There was only one place where I could both retrieve the Thipp's and find notes as to how much to take. It was also the most likely place to find the antidote, which I fully intended to bring along with me.

I was not an unintelligent woman. I knew the risks were high, the chance of success low.

It didn't matter to me. The alternative was unacceptable, and if there was even a small chance of reuniting my family, I would take it. Nothing had been right in my life since Father left. Mother had lost her spark, and Ambrose had become even more severe. Temple was rarely home and seemed to deal with his grief by engaging in near-constant travel. Only Bram and Pellix had kept their sweet natures.

Pellix had been my companion more and more frequently as

the need to expend my nervous energy increased. Waiting for the hour proved tedious, and I felt jumpy and confined when I had to stay away from him for more than a couple of days. Once we returned to Fox Haven, I took him back near the ruins more and more often. I even began practicing some tricks. My family would have had a fit if they found out, but it kept my mind off everything else.

I could ride astride, and sidesaddle, and with no saddle. Pellix would even let me ride without reins. I'd taught myself to mount while he was moving and even how to jump from some of the stone ruins onto his back. He was an excellent sport about all my attempts, in exchange for a supply of his favorite snacks.

And the worst I had done with all these tricks was to bruise my legs and arms.

There was a time, years before, when Pellix and I had run into a wolf on one of our rides. In a panic, I steered us into the trees, and a branch slashed into my leg. I tumbled off, and when the lone and probably desperately hungry wolf charged me, Pellix ran forward. He stamped his hooves, nostrils flaring as he chased the predator away. Then, he stood patiently while I got myself mounted once again.

I almost lost my riding privileges that day. I still bore a scar on my leg, and it was to my benefit that no suitors could see it. Scars were frowned upon. My parents had only relented on the riding when they heard how Pellix had protected me, but it was months before I was allowed to venture any farther than the gardens.

What a suitor might think of my legs had been far down my list of concerns at that time, but now the possibility of an engagement crept into my mind. My plan was both a distraction and my best chance to change things.

I pulled the journal, my father's notes tucked inside, out of my pocket.

"I will follow you, and find you, and bring you home," I swore, making my way through the garden and to a favorite bench.

Now that we were in Fox Haven, I could check one item off my list.

I'd find a ruse to go to the physician's and cause a distraction. Then, I'd take the Thipp's, as well as the ingredients for an antidote. Once the hour was here, I'd find Father and give us both the antidote. I lacked my father's investigative prowess, but it was the best solution I could come up with. If the Thipp's had kept him in a state unable to return, perhaps the antidote would remedy that.

I sat outside on the bench, leaning back and spinning a pink flower between my fingers. There was no Thipp's root here. I propped Holmes's diary on my knee, holding it open with my other hand.

R. had grown suspicious of those around him, wondering if his sleeplessness, and the cure that was causing him horrid side effects, were intentional. He thought he was being poisoned by someone. On the night of his disappearance, in his last entry, his jumbled writing described his symptoms. He'd grown worried for his life, and not without reason. He'd mentioned going after the culprit. Had he found the individual? Was that why he and his brothers had been out in the middle of the night?

Whether Holmes had made it to his destination or not before being Taken, I wasn't sure. My father's theory in his writings, however, was that he'd been just close enough to death to be Taken body and soul.

My father had intended to use the Thipp's to get Taken, but surely he'd intended to return. That part still troubled me. Had someone trapped him wherever he'd ended up? Was he merely lost? Had he not considered bringing a Thipp's antidote along with him? Had he miscalculated the dose, or the timing? Herbs and cures were tricky things, and I had no more experience than he had.

Information on exact dosage and measurements would be kept under lock and key at the physician's apothecary in town. Not that sneaking bothered me, but the physician's office didn't have hours where I could trust it to be empty. There were a few physicians in Fox Haven, and at least one of them stayed at the apothecary at all hours, so they could be available to sick individuals around the clock.

My brothers had told me, after going to fetch medicine for one of my mother's headaches, about the sleeping quarters in the back to ensure someone could always be on the premises.

The key to the antidote might be within our own garden, if I could find it.

To give my mind a break, I turned from my plans to the other portions of R.'s diary. He was beginning to feel like a treasured companion, just as close to me as Charlotte or Thomas.

The way he wrote, up until his last frenzied entries, was lyrical. I pictured R. as a poetic soul but adventurous as well. He'd written in earlier entries of his travels, and I lived vicariously through the descriptions of the rugged and icy terrain of Tang, the lush jungles of Sez's islands.

In some of my daydreams, I thought of going with him. It was ridiculous, but I couldn't always stop my mind from picturing a life next to someone both bold and eloquent.

"My Lady, your mother has requested you meet her inside."

I jumped, looking up from the journal to see Tilly.

Flustered, I hastily tucked the diary between two other books I'd brought out with me.

"Thank you, Tilly. I'll be up momentarily."

Tilly was fidgeting, twisting her hands.

"You'll want to be prepared, Miss."

She rushed off before I could ask anything further.

"By both gods, what could that have meant?"

I raked my fingers through my brown waves and followed her.

CHAPTER 9

When I entered and saw Mother standing in the great hall with Bellamy, I froze. I told myself the shot of anxiety that went through me was merely instinctual. I'd done so much snooping and sneaking lately that I was bound to feel on edge even when walking through a doorway in broad daylight, wearing a pink dress of which my mother could do nothing but approve.

Bellamy probably had business with my brothers and was stopping in to be polite, nothing more.

Telling myself that did little to stop the steady increase of my heartbeat.

Bellamy shot me a victorious smile that made me want to turn around and bolt to the stables, his perfectly white teeth managing to look predatory instead of handsome. I wanted to sprint for Pellix's stall, then ride all the way to the capital so I could disappear. There was no way my mother could know about my plans, but I clutched the books closer.

Mother had a strained smile plastered on her face, and it didn't quite reach her eyes.

I'd seen her wear the same expression at society functions a number of times. It always meant she wasn't pleased with the situation but was determined to endure it, because that's what decorum called for at the time.

"Bellamy has made a formal request for your hand in marriage. Isn't that ... interesting, Celia?"

Bellamy swept into a bow at his waist.

"My lady. I do hope you will forgive me the unusual timing, but as I'm sure you know, engagements do occasionally take place outside the season. One of the queen's children had just such an engagement a few winters ago. While I would never dream of attempting to outshine Her Majesty, I thought perhaps a Wintertide wedding would be perfection. I would have expressed my interest in your hand sooner, but I was under the mistaken impression that it had already been spoken for. Thankfully, that misunderstanding has been cleared up, and I am here to rectify my error before the opportunity eludes me. As it stands, I look forward to a winter celebration of our nuptials."

My mother made some inane comment about the beauty of the ground covered in snow during that time of year, and how lovely it would be to have the ceremony on a holiday. Bellamy reciprocated, and I had to remind myself to breathe. I could hear the blood rushing behind my eardrums.

Bellamy didn't even wait for an answer; he just continued prattling on with Mother about his idea of all the arrangements and the timeline.

I'd been wrong. Thomas's delay tactics had failed, and any hope that my mother would have shut Bellamy down flat were clearly not going to happen. My dress felt too tight; my heart pounded against my chest like Pellix's hooves across the frozen ground.

I cast my gaze around for my brothers. As if summoned by my thoughts, I saw Ambrose tucked back into a corner, looking grim. He made his way over to me, standing so he momentarily blocked me from Bellamy's view as I unleashed my rage on him.

"How could Mother agree to this? She knows that I do not—"

"She didn't agree. I am the head of the household, and I agreed on her behalf. Really, Celia, you had to know you could not continue on riding around in stolen breeches forever. I proposed to Penny, and it's time for you to find a suitable match as well."

I clenched my fists, scrunching my eyes to try to hold back tears. My face felt hot.

"Is that what this is about? You have a new bride, and it's time to clear your sister out and make room? Too crowded here now, is it?"

It wasn't a fair accusation, and I knew it, but to believe this of Ambrose was the last thing I wanted. My eldest brother was dropping lower in my esteem by the moment.

"I won't marry him. I will not, and you can't force me," I spit out.

Ambrose's frown deepened so much that his forehead creased with the worry lines of a much older man.

"Do not do this here, Celia. You cannot make a scene. We will discuss this later, and you can scold and shout at me then, if you must. But know this: the wedding will go forward. Mother expressed a concern for your safety, and I must say I agree. I am starting a family of my own with Penny. I will always support you, but I cannot have my eyes on you at all times. I kept your secret last year when you showed up just before the Unseen Hour, but I cannot follow you around like a child who continues to throw herself into danger. This way, you'll have a husband of your own to make sure you stay safe. I am doing this for you."

"Do you think me nothing more than the cattle in the fields, or numbers in this estate's ledger, that you can so easily sell me off?"

Ambrose's cheeks reddened.

"I would never send you to a dishonorable man. Bellamy is a gentleman. There are no complaints with how he runs his house, no unseemly chatter from his staff, and no rumors circulating anywhere that he is anything but an honorable man. You will wed him. And do not look at me like that. You're staring as if I've just disowned you and thrown you into the streets. You can bring a maid with you; I know you've always been close to Tilly, and she's agreed to go. And of course you'll have all your things."

"And Pellix?"

I grappled for any ounce of control I could get.

Ambrose sighed, running a hand over his face.

"If the horse is that important to you, I'm sure it could be arranged. The gods know none of us can ride him. Bellamy's estate has a large stable area, but you must know you won't be able to continue riding as you do now. He's already assured me that he has a room with a piano, so you'll be able to keep up with your music."

Small recompense. My future stretched out before me in my mind. Pellix stuck in a stable and without my companionship. I'd be trapped decorating Bellamy's estate, standing on his arm at formal functions, and, horror of horrors, sleeping in his bed and …

It did not bear thinking about.

There was only one way out of this, and I'd been working toward it all year. Now the stakes were even higher. I just had to delay a little longer.

I strode past Ambrose and over to my mother and Bellamy.

"Not Wintertide," I interrupted. Bellamy frowned, and my mother for once did not point out my rudeness. "I mean to say,

I've always thought a spring wedding would be perfection. The flowers just in bloom and all those beautiful colors serving as a backdrop. An ethereal outdoor ceremony."

As I spoke, I realized that it did sound beautiful. But I was just stalling.

Bellamy ran a hand over his chin, scowling as he appraised me.

Swallowing down my hesitation, I reached out and placed a hand on his arm, an acceptable gesture for two newly engaged individuals.

"Having the pink flowers we keep around the estate incorporated into the ceremony would be a touching tribute to my father, and a wonderful gift from my new husband. A fitting backdrop for the joining of two noble houses."

Bellamy smirked, and I tensed, forcing myself to keep my hand on his arm.

"It would eliminate any potential issues caused by an unexpected snow," he mused. "And some people are wary of traveling at Wintertide, so close to the Unseen Hour. All right, if that is what my bride desires, so it shall be. Springtime."

"Shall we discuss the details over tea?" Mother offered. Ambrose and Bellamy readily agreed.

My mother rushed off to speak to the staff about preparing tea, and my brother moved across the hall as Penny entered.

Bellamy leaned down, and his hands squeezed my own. They were sticky with sweat.

"I'm thrilled you've accepted my proposal, *Celia*." The way his voice lingered on the syllables in my name made my skin crawl. "I'm sure you'll be very happy with me. And I am sure you'll please me as well." His eyes dipped downward, and I felt a sudden desire to tug the neckline of my dress higher.

My mother announced the tea was nearly ready and beckoned us all to the sitting room. I tried to yank my hands away from Bellamy, but he held on for a few more seconds before letting go.

He followed me through the halls, and Mother didn't meet my eyes when we swept past.

The rest of the details for the wedding were hashed out by Ambrose and Bellamy, along with Mother's occasional input. I hardly said another word.

Instead, I sipped my tea, taking another drink any time I felt tears threatening to form.

I'd done the only thing I could—bought myself time.

There was one solution to all my problems, and a fool like Bellamy was not going to stand in the way of my happiness.

After the Unseen Hour, I'd be gone and Bellamy Bonds could find a new bride.

CHAPTER 10

DECEMBER
THE 99th YEAR

With the 99th Unseen Hour looming closer, along with my wedding if I didn't succeed, securing the Thipp's and the antidote was paramount.

I had feigned a stomach illness not long after the engagement, which my mother had chalked up to nerves. She'd summoned one of the physicians to visit us at Scopshaven, rather than giving in to my insistence that I could make it into town. That first attempt at snooping around the apothecary was thwarted before it began. It was a reaction I should have anticipated, but I didn't let myself dwell on disappointment.

My guess was that our manor wouldn't be a successful location from which to launch a plan, and I'd need to be in Fox Haven already before trying again.

I'd come up with the perfect ruse: a migraine. Mother suffered from them, and it stood to reason that I might have them as well.

The only issue was the timing and the location. If I feigned the headache at home, my brothers would simply send for a physician to be brought to me again, and I'd get no information at all, stuck in my rooms and under the watchful eye of Mother, Ambrose, and all the staff. Bram might have participated in my mischief, but it would have meant telling him my plan. I didn't want to risk being stopped, or even worse, having him insist on joining me.

I knew what could happen if this whole scheme went wrong, and while I was determined to risk myself, I wouldn't put the lives of anyone else I loved on the line.

I'd have to be in town, and preferably late enough in the day that only the overnight physician would be in the apothecary. Someone was always available for the ill, but if I tried my ruse in the afternoon, there would be multiple doctors or assistants running about. I stood my best chance if I only had one person to get past.

In the end I had to resort to a few tactics I wasn't entirely proud of. I'd been skirting the rules all year, and honestly before that, but I didn't like to draw anyone else into my troubles. I simply hadn't figured out a way around it. I couldn't go into town alone, and I couldn't risk going with our own staff or my family. They wouldn't let me out of their sight. I needed someone close enough to act as my chaperone, and lenient enough that I could manipulate the circumstances a bit.

A carriage pulled up in front of Scopshaven, and when the footman opened the door Charlotte gave a merry wave. Thomas sat across from her and lifted his hand as well.

"My sister tells me I am to take you both to the library," he called.

The footman offered me a hand. I accepted and put my other one around my skirts, lifting them as I climbed into the carriage. Today's ensemble was just another wave of hot pink. This one matched my eyes almost exactly.

"You look lovely," Charlotte gushed, wearing another green gown that brought out her eyes. She'd made it through the season without any proposals, although she'd actually been hoping for one. Lord Elmond Whipples had spent half the season promenading with Charlotte and danced with her a gossip-inducing number of times, but then his father had taken ill and he'd had to return to his larger estate in the northwest.

"Elmond wrote to me," Charlotte confided. "He has been in contact with our parents as well and has expressed his intention to formally propose as soon as matters at his estate are settled."

I gave her a genuine smile, reaching for her hands. If she was happy, then I was happy for her.

"That's wonderful news, Charlotte! You'll be moving, then, in the new year?"

Charlotte stared at her feet, fidgeting.

"Yes, but don't think this means you'll be rid of me." She looked back up. "I'll write you weekly letters, and it's not so difficult for us to make some trips to the capital. Please say you'll visit more yourself. I'm sure you could convince Temple or Bram to accompany you! Especially now that Ambrose will be getting Penny settled in. You will promise, won't you?"

Thomas was smirking at me across the carriage, his head

quirked to the side. He knew I didn't care much for the capital and its smoggy streets and crowded buildings. Even so, that wasn't the reason I hesitated. Thinking of how my family and friends would react to my disappearance was something I'd tried over and over to ignore, but it was difficult to do with Charlotte's hopeful expression panging my soul.

I chewed on the inside of my cheek, grasping for any answer that didn't stack one lie on top of another. I could tell the two of them my plans, but they'd probably have me committed. At the very least they'd feel they had no choice but to report my intentions to Mother and Ambrose.

After all, a plan to poison oneself and wander around during the hour could hardly be coming from a sound mind. Even if they didn't panic, I ran the same risk that had kept me from telling Bram. I couldn't ask Charlotte and Thomas to put themselves in danger.

"If you are there, it will be well worth the visit," I managed, not quite a promise to go.

When we got to town, Thomas bid us farewell and headed toward a law office to complete some estate filings on behalf of his father. One of the Huberts' maids, who had been out shopping, met us near the town gates.

"Marie will accompany us to the library," Charlotte explained.

Thank both gods I hadn't based my plan on limited company. It would work just as well with Marie present. Perhaps better.

The three of us made our way into the library and spent a pleasant few hours perusing the shelves, reading poetry, and then having tea at a small cafe across the street. Thomas had yet to return, which further helped my plans.

After Marie twice suggested that we head back on our own,

and I twice insisted we should wait just a bit longer, she started to look truly nervous.

"We'd really better be leaving. It's getting dark," Marie fretted, glancing up and down the street and watching for Thomas.

There was nothing to fear about a normal December night, but as the hour drew closer, some people grew more superstitious.

Charlotte gave Marie a comforting smile.

"If we need, we could take the carriage back and leave a note for Thomas at the town gates. He'll borrow a horse from the watch or remain in Fox Haven for another day. I know he was planning to return later this week regardless," she offered.

Most of the time I was thankful for her compassionate and generous nature. This was not one of those times.

The city watch at the gates of towns often kept a stable of horses for when a fast response time was needed. Nobility technically had the right to request them in cases like this and were trusted to return the horses. As members of the nobility helped fund the watch, it had never presented an issue.

Marie relaxed, and since more insistence on my part to wait would look odd, we made our way back to the carriage. If I wanted to ensure the apothecary held only a single physician when we arrived, I needed them to stay at least until the sun had fully set. This time of year, that just about coincided with the close of many shops, including the apothecary. Then it would only be approached in emergencies.

The footman helped Charlotte and Marie inside the carriage, then turned to me.

My moment had come.

"Oh no! I've dropped one of my gloves. My hands are like ice." I shivered for good measure, the glove in question having been stuffed down my bodice.

"Do we need to go back and look?" Marie asked. Her face

was tight, and I knew she wanted to get home before we were on the road in pitch darkness.

"I'm sure I had it when we left the cafe. It can't be far," I insisted.

Charlotte turned to her footman.

"Harold, would you mind just retracing our steps up the street? We can spare a few moments."

Charlotte's footman nodded, striding quickly back up the road, which was fast clearing of people.

"I'll check out here by the carriage. No need to get out," I called. I made my way around the carriage and loosened the horses' hitch.

"Hyah!" I waved my arms at the horses.

The two of them whinnied and began running toward the open town gates. I grabbed up my skirts and ran several steps away, far enough not to look suspect.

"I found it, and ... oh my!" I shrieked, bringing Charlotte and Marie's heads popping out of the carriage. "What was all tha—oh no!" Marie's mouth gaped open, eyes wide as she watched the horses run through the gate.

Harold was already hurrying back, no doubt having heard my shrieks.

"I'll round them up, Misses, don't worry! I'll get someone from the watch to help me."

I only hoped the horses were the flighty type.

"We may be waiting for some time. Perhaps we should go somewhere warmer, and well-lit?" I suggested, glancing at Marie. "It's getting awfully dark to be out here alone, and the sun will be fully set soon. Surely there's somewhere we could get dinner? Aren't you growing hungry, Charlotte?"

"Oh yes, very." I knew my best friend would agree with me if it meant a fresh meal and getting out of the cold.

The plan was working perfectly. Harold had rushed off after

the horses. Charlotte's chaperone had been somewhat reluctant about staying out in the dark with two young ladies she was responsible for, and it was only too simple to persuade her that obtaining some food at a local inn, regardless of what types of "ruffians," as Marie put it, we might see there, would be much more respectable than freezing in the quickly darkening streets.

My plan was further helped when Thomas finally made an appearance at the inn where we had taken refuge, having heard of our troubles when one of the horses proved tricky to catch. Harold had found him and led him to us.

"We managed to get the horses rounded up, but it's too late to go home at this hour. I'll secure you ladies some rooms at another inn in town. There's one that caters specifically to women, and it's quiet and clean. We'll keep the horses in the watch stables and return home tomorrow. Hopefully your family won't be too worried, Celia."

My stomach clenched. Everyone would be worried, and Thomas and Charlotte were kinder than I deserved.

"Thank you, Thomas," I managed.

"I'll walk down the road to secure your rooms, then come accompany you when they're ready."

The lamps outside were being lit, and it was well and truly dark. Perfect timing.

"That sounds wonderful. I don't think I could have made the ride back home. I'm beginning to feel rather ill. My head is splitting." I threw the back of my hand against my forehead and slid back in my seat. The posture no doubt was undignified, but it would absolutely make me look even more unwell.

I'd been wheeling my feet under the table as well, trying to work my cheeks into a flush. Judging by the concerned look on Charlotte and Thomas's faces, it had worked.

"It's been a long day. A good rest should help. I'll check on the rooms and return quickly." Thomas grabbed his overcoat and threw it over his shoulders, rushing out the front door of the establishment. I bit the inside of my cheek.

It's necessary. If I told Thomas and Charlotte, they'd only worry for me.

They might be my friends, but they were naturally curious. If I'd told them the headache was fake, I'd have had to explain why I was trying to conjure a way to get into the physician's office at night.

For all the sneaking about I did, I wasn't a natural liar. I considered the two things separate. It was one thing to try to gain more freedoms, another to deceive my friends.

But my hands were tied.

I waited maybe five minutes after Thomas had left, and then flung my upper half down on the table with a moan.

"Oh, I don't know that I'll make it through the night without assistance. This must be what my mother talks of with her own headaches. Oh, it's awful, Charlotte, truly it is."

Charlotte's maid stood hovering over me and worrying her hands.

"Could it have been the food? Perhaps we shouldn't have stopped here," Marie fretted.

"No, her mother gets this same affliction," Charlotte said, putting a reassuring hand on my back and patting me.

"And only the physician works for Mother. Oh, I wish we'd brought some of her medicine with us and ... Ah!" I clutched my head. By this point, several patrons were looking over at us.

Marie's eyes went wide, seeing the amount of attention we were now drawing.

"Perhaps we should take her to the physician's, then. People are staring here, and we don't want to make a scene."

Charlotte turned toward me.

"Celia, do you think you can walk that far?"

I made a great show of trembling as I pushed myself up, and

when I nodded to Charlotte, I winced and put a hand to my temple.

"I really must, I think. That's the only thing that ever helps my mother."

I was so close, and after tonight, I'd be ready.

CHAPTER II

The three of us made our way through the darkened streets and toward the apothecary, where two lanterns lit the sign in front.

"I'll get the physician," Charlotte promised, dashing ahead.

Marie walked slowly next to me, fretting.

"Surely the physician can fix this. He must."

I heard the familiar *clop* of hooves on cobblestone as Marie stepped into the street ahead of me, still talking to herself.

"Marie no!" I lunged forward, grabbing the maid around her wrist and hauling her back onto the side of the street as a carriage sped by. All four horses were running, the driver whipping them on. He didn't even turn to look at us.

Marie stared, wide-eyed, at the spot where she'd been standing, directly in the path of the carraige.

She started to shake.

"I almost. If I had. You saved me."

"You would have done the same," I said, blushing.

After all, it was my fault we were out late to begin with. I'd never intended to get anyone hurt. I was the only one who was supposed to be in pain, and that was fictional.

I gave a moan and reached for my head again as I remembered my supposed crushing migraine.

Marie helped me across the street. Charlotte was rapidly knocking on the physician's door. It creaked open, and we were met by Dr. Stephans. He had impeccably styled brown hair, and silver-rimmed spectacles gleaned in front of hazel eyes. My mother had seen him a number of times for her debilitating headaches. He hadn't been the most sympathetic of all the physicians in town, but he'd been just as willing to accept payment for treatment as any of them.

He stared at the three of us, one eyebrow raising almost to his hairline. Marie strode to the front of our trio.

"I've brought Celia Hipnosi. She's suffering a dreadful headache and said you'd know what to do. She says her mother has the same affliction."

"Bring her in," he instructed.

While the apothecary was a place that reminded me of ailments and illness, I couldn't deny being intrigued. There were wooden shelves lining each wall. Small cutouts and large, housing tiny vials, oddly shaped jars, wooden boxes, and all manner of containers. Some of the glass ones glinted in shades of teal, turquoise, and red from a lantern that the physician had lit. A library of medicines instead of books.

Charlotte and Marie assisted me to a chair within the shop. I knew, from previous visits, that the physicians disappeared into the back when they needed to look for additional inventory or check instructions for a specific medication. That was where I'd need to go, and I knew just how to do it.

"The light is too blinding in here. I can't possibly stay in this room. It's an onslaught to the senses, truly it is." I threw a hand over my eyes, cringing away from the relatively dim lantern light within the shop. I knew it wasn't overdone; my mother was sensitive to light for days when she had her migraines. She remained in her room with the curtains drawn, and a second set of curtains behind the first to block as much light as possible.

Dr. Stephans frowned, his forehead creasing, then gave Marie a hard stare.

"You really should have brought her as soon as she displayed symptoms. I can put something together, but it will take some time to have an effect. She'll need to remain here for a little while."

Marie's face reddened as she bristled.

"Of course I brought her as soon as she expressed a need for medical care! I am not irresponsible, Doctor. We have had quite an evening. Loose horses and waiting in the cold and runaway carriages. She's no doubt overwrought. And she expressed full confidence in your ability to assist in this matter."

Now it was Dr. Stephans's turn to bristle. He sputtered as he tried to recover from the maid's tirade. No doubt it wasn't the usual level of respect he was shown. I had no idea whether Marie was acting out of thanks toward me, or whether her nerves had caught up to her, but I liked the more assertive attitude she was displaying.

"Of course I shall assist the young lady. I'll begin putting together a remedy for the pain immediately and—"

"And I am feeling rather off. My stomach is rolling. I fear I may be ill." I clutched a hand over my mouth.

Dr. Stephans sighed, looking past me and at the darkened street, no doubt thinking of all the sleep he wouldn't be getting.

"Yes, and I'll give her something for the nausea as well."

He spent a few minutes shuffling around the front of the apothecary, pulling things off of shelves.

"This is most unfortunate. I'm out of one of the herbs needed. We sold it all just a few days ago, and I haven't had the opportunity to collect more. Is the medication for nausea truly necessary?"

I lurched forward, and made an incredibly unseemly retching noise.

"Truly I think it is," Charlotte insisted. "Is there none in the gardens?"

The apothecary kept its own gardens for some of its ingredients, in a space just outside the town walls of Fox Haven. They had an enclosed greenhouse and made use of the fields closest to the town gates.

Dr. Stephans sighed again.

"I'll go retrieve what I need. If this had happened during the day, I'd have an apprentice available." He grumbled the last bit to himself.

Dr. Stephans retrieved his coat.

"Oh Marie, Charlotte, I don't know that I can handle these lights. Surely we can find somewhere darker?"

"Is there nowhere else she could wait without the lanterns?" Charlotte asked.

"It's quite irregular, but she could utilize the sleeping quarters in back, with her chaperone of course." Dr. Stephans sounded uncomfortable, but I felt a thrill zip through me. One step closer.

He left for the gardens, and Marie accompanied me to the back room.

"My, it is gloomy in here," Marie commented in the darkened room as she felt around for the cot and lowered me onto it.

"Truly, Marie, you don't have to wait in here. There's no other way in but through the shop. You shouldn't have to sit in the dark."

"Well, I—"

"And even the slightest noise is hurting my head. With no one else in here it will be quieter," I insisted.

Marie didn't need too much convincing and soon swept out the door.

"I will be just out front," the maid promised.

I counted a full minute in my head and then swung off the cot. I felt my way along the wall and out of the room. The apothecary was small in the back. There was a doorway leading to the front of the shop, and one on the opposite side of the hall. I pushed it open and was just able, as my eyes adjusted, to make out a desk and several sets of shelves and drawers pressed against the walls.

"Day and Death be praised," I whispered.

I'd need more light to find what I was after, though. Thankfully a lantern hung off a hook inside the door, and it lit when I twisted a small mechanism on the side that felt like a key. I'd gotten lucky. Not all homes and shops had lamps like this that could be lit without a ready source of flame. It made sense for the apothecary to have one, with the need for light at all hours and the urgency of their work, but I was thankful all the same. Otherwise I'd have been toting papers to and from the hall where a bit of the shop's light lingered, and that would have been riskier by far.

After a few false starts, I discerned the organizational system. Various cures and ingredients were listed based on malady. The most dangerous substances were on shelves back here, along with warning labels. I found the shelf with Thipp's quickly and shoved a stoppered glass container of the stuff into my dress pocket. Then I searched for the paperwork that would tell me how much I needed to take.

I rifled through a drawer until I found a file for Thipp's root.

There was a shuffling outside, and I froze.

"—should check on her," Marie's voice sounded. I dropped the file, prepared to hurry into the hall and state that I'd gotten up to be sick.

"Marie, we should let her rest. She'll call for us if she needs us," Charlotte's voice answered.

Day and Death preserve you, Charlotte, you absolute gem.

I didn't catch Marie's response, but their voices moved away from the doorway to the back rooms, and I breathed a sigh of relief.

I picked the file up and brought it close to the lantern, where I could see better.

"Here we are. Precautions due to dosage complications. Suggested dosages based on height and weight. Only referenced for men, of course. Come on, come on … yes!" I threw a hand over my mouth; I'd been louder than intended. After a few moments, when Charlotte and Marie didn't come running back in, I continued reading.

The antidote was listed as well. Both gods be praised, all the ingredients I could either buy in town, without the need for all this sneaking, or find them in our garden at Scops.

A chime rang at the front door, signaling the physician's return. I stuffed the paper listing the antidote ingredients into my bodice, next to my glove. I was going to have things falling out of every nook and cranny in the fabric of these layers when I returned home.

After shoving the rest of the files back into a drawer, I doused the lantern and scurried back to the physician's quarters.

I'd barely made it inside when he came to the back rooms. I leaned against the doorway, feigning as though I'd been on my way to the front of the shop.

"I heard a noise."

"Yes, I have everything I need now. Come back to the front and have a seat, Lady Hipnosi. We'll have you sorted in no time."

He was much cheerier now, and Thomas trailed on his heels.

"My brother promised him double his usual fee," Charlotte leaned down to whisper in my ear as we passed.

Guilt gnawed at me. Retrieving my father helped my family, but it did nothing to make up for the hurt I would bring to those closest to me. If I could, I'd gather information on the hour itself while rescuing Father. Surely I could learn something useful when I was wherever it was that the souls were Taken. Maybe there really was a way to rescue even more souls, or take royal troops to the mysterious destination of the Taken and wage war on a god.

Either way, I owed my friends a great debt.

One remedy for headache pain and an ironically stomach-churning treatment for nausea later and I was seen safely to the inn, accompanied by Charlotte, Marie, and Thomas. Thomas took a room down the hall from the three of us, an exception to the 'ladies only' boarding policy, since he was technically responsible for the lot of us.

I didn't have to feign exhaustion. The headache medicine caused extreme drowsiness. The horrid aftertaste of the nausea medication lingered on my tongue, but it had been worth it.

I had a few weeks left to gather the antidote ingredients, and now I knew my plan was possible.

In less than a month, gods willing, I'd see my father again.

For the first time, I was looking forward to midnight.

CHAPTER 12

NEW YEAR'S EVE
THE 99th HOUR

"Stay safe, Tilly. May both gods see you and save you," I said to the housemaid as she began to close the double doors of my room.

"And you, Miss," Tilly responded, voice shaky as she pulled the doors closed.

It was the customary exchange for anyone you saw on December thirty-first, no matter how familiar you were or weren't. Everyone clung to the same phrases, as if the words alone might keep them safe, instead of their windows and doors firmly shut and locked.

There were two hours remaining until midnight.

I was antsy, my muscles tight and jumpy with the desire to spring from my bed, lest I miss my opportunity, but I willed myself to wait. I focused on my breathing. One, two, three, in. One, two, three, out. Over and over.

I checked my small shoulder satchel for a third, and then a fourth, and then a fifth time. I had four vials of the antidote nestled within, along with the journal and Father's notes. It was probably far too late to glean any helpful information if I wasn't on the right path with my plan, but I felt some comfort at having the two men with me in some way. I'd also tucked in a bit of food from the kitchens, and a few pieces of jewelry—a last-minute decision when I was restless. For all I knew, I'd have to bribe our way out of wherever Father was.

After what felt like the longest wait I'd ever endured, I heard blessed silence. No more squeaks in the floorboards, no more slams or bangs as windows and doors were shut. No more soft footsteps as Mrs. Fig and Shrewsbury checked each one for the fifteenth time, ensuring not even a mouse would be able to sneak into the manor unannounced. Even then, I made myself count my breaths for several more minutes, creeping to my wardrobe to change. I flung the doors wide. At the base, under a pile of folded shifts, sat my disguise. Temple wouldn't be thrilled that I'd stolen his favorite riding outfit, but it couldn't be helped.

I'd always been closest to my middle brother in height; not surprising, given we were only a year apart in age. He was hardly my senior, whereas Ambrose had five years on me, and Bram was younger by three. Growing up, I'd been allowed to be tutored alongside Temple. Over the years I'd been forced to dedicate more of my time to acceptable pursuits such as music and sewing, but I'd spent plenty of time with him. He'd been a competitive classmate, each of us challenging the other to improve.

Once we'd reached adulthood, the distance between us had grown of its own accord. After all, what was the point in competition when his gender alone granted him freedoms I was doomed to be forever denied? He'd spent a fair portion of this past year traveling throughout Emrys as an official of the crown.

I scowled down at the clothing, torn between compassion for my brother and ugly, twisted jealousy as I pulled on Temple's riding breeches. The tailcoat was a striking blue. Since his eyes matched our mother's, he hadn't been forced into nearly the number of shocking pink outfits that I had. Ambrose and Bram had garishly pink neck scarves and even socks, but Temple had the most muted wardrobe of us all.

I did up the silver buttons of his riding coat before pulling my own brown boots on over the breeches. I wasn't risking ill-fitting shoes this year, and Temple's feet were several sizes larger than my own. I needed to be able to move quickly.

I pinned my curls up carefully and shoved them under a felt top hat, borrowed from Bram. If I did happen to be spotted, better someone think I was a local lord rushing back home than a lone woman out in the dark.

If they were real, then both gods must have approved of my plan, because I managed to make it out of the house without anyone stopping me. I imagine I had paranoia to thank for that. On this night of all nights, no one wanted to stir from their beds, regardless of what creaks or moans they might hear. Too terrified of being Taken, of chancing a meeting with Death.

I shivered, then shook myself. It wouldn't do to get nerves now. What was done, was done.

Once I'd made my way out the doors and down towards the stables, I met Pellix, who was brushed and waiting.

I'd insisted on an afternoon ride, claiming it calmed my nerves. Ambrose had relented, knowing as well as the rest of us the shadow that fell over the household on the days leading up to the anniversary of Father's disappearance. Mother haunted the halls like a ghost for a good week prior, eyes red-rimmed and constantly dabbing at her face with a handkerchief, refusing to manage anything as she did the rest of the year. Mrs. Fig took over all household duties for that week.

Now all I had to do was put a bridle on Pellix, and I'd be off. No saddle for this; I was keeping things quick and simple.

Pellix whinnied, nudging me as though urging me to hurry up. Once I was astride I leaned down and patted his side.

"Don't worry, friend, I would never risk you."

I would remove the bridle from my equine friend before I enacted my plan. He'd be free to wander the grounds. The only worry I had was causing him distress, but I couldn't avoid it, any more than I could avoid worrying my family with my absence.

I could only hope my plan worked and that I could retrieve Father and return quickly.

Pellix and I reached the old ruins near the edge of our property without incident. I guided him around the cemetery and stopped at what had once been the front of the structure. I'd chosen the spot partly for practical reasons; it was close enough to the house to reach before the hour, and far enough that I wasn't worried I'd bring danger to my family's door.

I couldn't deny, though, that some of my reasoning was sentimental. The ruins were still on our land, which made it feel tied to Father, but it had once been Holmes property. I reached into my satchel, clutching the journal in one hand.

"For my father and everyone, like you, who was taken by surprise when this wretched hour began."

If there was a way to get Taken at will and then bring missing people back, that could be revolutionary. And if my father was still waiting, as I hoped, he surely knew even more about the hour.

I left Pellix grazing outside the ruins, making my way into what might have been a sanctuary, years and years ago. At the very least it was the largest portion of the partially collapsed structure. Open to the sky, so I had no worry of missing my chance.

The clock tower sounded. Eleven-thirty. I'd made it with time to spare. Last year I'd needed more of a buffer. I'd broken into the library using a lock-pick set I'd given to Bram to mark a previous birthday. He was always in motion, and it kept his hands busy while doing tedious things like conversing with Ambrose about the manor's affairs. He'd readily offered to teach me once he'd figured it out for himself.

This night I had no locks, and no Fox Haven watch at the gates. I just had Pellix's snuffling, and the occasional *rip* as grass was torn from the ground. I could see his withers if I craned my neck over some of the crumbling stones.

I wasn't worried about anyone finding me here. No one else was fool enough to risk being out after eleven on this night. Now I was simply waiting on the clock.

When I read the file on Thipp's at the apothecary, I learned it rendered you not only unconscious but unreactive to painful stimuli during a surgical procedure. Breathing and heart rate slowed down so much that they could become undetectable. Take too much, and your heart and lungs simply shut down. Like so many parts of my plan, my dosing required hope and faith that I'd read the physician's notes correctly, and Father's, and Holmes's.

R. had grown suspicious of the substance he was being given nearly a hundred years ago and had tracked his symptoms and amounts. For a moment I wished he were with me. He would have understood the significance of the root and the nervous chill that ran through me at the idea of ingesting such a dangerous substance.

But that was ridiculous.

I didn't know him, no matter how much I felt that I did.

The clock rendered its next warning. Fifteen minutes until midnight. It was nearly time.

I checked my satchel a final time for the antidote and decided to tuck two of the vials in my pocket.

Somewhere in the dark, a wolf howled and I nearly jumped out of my skin.

"Bloody ghosts!"

Pellix's head appeared, looking over the stones at me.

"It's all right. I'm just nervous. I'll be fine," I reassured the stallion. With a snort, he went back to grazing. I took a few deep breaths, then reached into the satchel and took out the container with the Thipp's. As the first gong of the Unseen Hour sounded, I said a small prayer to the gods I wasn't even certain existed.

"Please let this work. Please let me find my father."

I tipped the container back, sending the minced Thipp's to the back of my throat. It tasted a bit like bitter ginger as I swallowed it down.

My racing heart began to slow, and the edges of my vision went hazy within moments. I couldn't run from my decision now, but I still took a few steps forward, my body responding to what it perceived as a threat.

I stumbled against a wall, sliding down to a resting position.

"At least it's warm for a winter night," I mumbled, staring at the sky and the fog beginning to descend.

I started to send a final prayer up to the gods, that my family wouldn't find me frozen in the morning. Maybe they were finally answering, or maybe I was dying and my mind was playing tricks on me.

I could hear singing—the most beautiful voices calling me home.

My thoughts went black as the twelfth gong sounded.

CHAPTER 13

Acophony of noises woke me—wailing, urgent whispers, even a few screams. Above all the rest of the noise rose a singular voice. Smooth, male, and authoritative.

"Everyone form up over here. Quickly now!"

Though his tone was harsh, the words had an almost melodic quality, soothing and welcoming.

I shook my head, moving to push myself off the ground.

"Bloody ghosts!"

I was already on my feet. Had I been sleepwalking?

The last thing I remembered was the Thipp's root, the clock's warning, and music. I felt along my arms, chest, and neck. There was a steady pulse. Not dead, then.

And most certainly not in Emrys.

The ground underneath me was grass, but tinted blue instead of green or the dried-out beige of winter. Staring overhead, I saw that the moon might be partially responsible for the shade. Instead of a stark white, it had a bluish tint as well.

An orb of light floated by me with no discernible means of

staying aloft. I jumped backward, throwing a hand out to catch myself. My nail beds had a bluish tint similar to the grass. Was I dead after all, then? Had I miscalculated?

I glanced left and right, my hair loose and slapping at my shoulders. Where had my brother's top hat gone?

Were hats disallowed in the afterlife?

A hysterical giggle worked its way up my throat, and I slapped a hand over my mouth to suppress the sound. I needed to calm down. To think. I'd swallowed the Thipp's just as the Unseen Hour had begun. That meant that, unless I was in some sort of medicine-induced stupor, I'd been Taken as intended. As for the hat, it had probably tumbled off my head when I'd stumbled in the ruins. My gait had been wildly unsteady.

I jumped again when I heard the sound of a woman wailing and the authoritative voice repeating his instructions.

I was not in Emrys, and I was in who knew what level of danger.

Around me, other men and women were throwing confused looks at one another. Several had tears running down their faces. If my own heartbeat hadn't been enough, a good look at those around me would have convinced me that I was in a much different state than the other people here.

All the vibrancy had leached from the hair, skin, and eyes of those around me. When I looked closer I saw that they were all swaying to and fro as they moved. Their feet trailed the ground, but just the toes.

They weren't walking; they were floating.

I choked down a scream.

"Not too much farther. Come along, then!" The man up front continued to coax us all away from wherever we'd arrived.

Everyone—the crying, the calm, and those who looked lost —followed the soothing voice.

"Don't worry, the memories will fade soon. You won't be scared in a moment. You just need to follow me this way."

The others moved toward the voice, drifting like the very ghosts they were.

I checked my own feet, but they were still firmly planted on the ground.

"Hurry now!" the voice called, more urgent but no less musical.

With no better plan, and not wanting to draw any undue attention to myself, I fell in line with the others. My legs shook as I walked, probably helping me blend in. I tottered, partially out of terror and partially because of a leaden feeling in my limbs. Could the Thipp's still be having an effect?

Another glowing orb floated by, and I managed not to jump this time. Aside from the moon, these orbs were the only thing lighting the way. Spherical lanterns. The next time one passed, I reached out to tap it and discovered the casing wasn't hard like glass, but soft like a flower petal. I was too shocked to try to see what the light source was inside.

As we continued forward, the bluish grass was broken up by clusters of flowers, in shades of violet, ivory, and soft champagne.

It was the middle of winter in Emrys. Even though all the clues pointed to us no longer being anywhere near my home country, let alone any country in all of Rayus ... the whole setting was a bit too comfortable for how I'd always envisioned death.

"No time to waste! Line up!" the voice from before barked again. Even when he sounded impatient, I felt an urge to listen instead of run.

One of the floating souls, if that is what they were, moved past me. I reached out and grabbed the arm of his coat, which had more color than his sallow skin.

"Excuse me, but do you know where we are?" I questioned, reaching out to place a hand on his shoulder to get his attention.

As he turned toward me, I took a step back. His eyes were void of any emotion or recognition. Though he was staring straight at me, I felt as if he were looking right through me.

After a moment, without answering, he turned and moved toward the voice that instructed us all.

With nothing to do then but follow the orders being yelled at us, I fell into a row forming as hazy men and women took their places. The initial wailing had stopped, and all of the others seemed almost eerily calm. Their faces expressionless, they formed precise rows, everyone's spacing even. I took a place in one of the lines. Clutching at my riding jacket— *Temple's* riding jacket—I realized as my shock wore off that I was dreadfully cold, in spite of the springtime surroundings. In Emrys it had been a mild night, but here it was frigid even with the flowers and lush grass. I shivered.

"All right then, I believe we've got everyone."

I craned my neck, finally getting a look at the cloaked leader of this horrible parade. His hood prevented me from seeing him clearly, and it was a stony gray.

The souls around me continued to sway like leaves in a breeze. I did my best to imitate them, smoothly swaying to and fro as if the slightest breeze might shift me.

The number of people around me had swelled.

Some wore fashions popular in Emrys, but I also spotted the loose and baggy clothing worn in Mejje, said to keep people cool in the heat. Having never been, I had to make do with what I'd learned from books, but I recognized the fashion just the same. Another man wore thick furs I recognized as being from Tang. They were known to hunt the wolves and elk in their lands and used the hides to keep themselves warm on the icy tundra. There were a few people holding weapons, small daggers and knives, and I was shocked to see even the women in pants. They had to be from Sez.

For a single moment, curiosity overrode my concern and I snapped my head around, trying to discern whether anyone from the lost country was here.

The cloaked man at the front yelled again, and I turned my attention forward.

Goosebumps rose on my arms and I willed them to stand down lest even that small detail come to the attention of the figure that stalked in front of our rows. It wasn't like he could see them under my sleeves, I mused, but maybe I was wrong. Maybe he could.

What if he was Death?

If the god was real—and the fact that I was standing in an entirely different realm was quickly making a true believer of me—there was no telling how he would react to my intrusion. He might be impressed at my ingenuity, or he might be offended by my trickery.

Whether because of the goosebumps, or my breath that clouded the air in front of me, I caught his attention somehow. Of all the rotten luck.

The cloaked figure froze, his stillness even more disconcerting against the background of shifting souls. He, too, kept his feet firmly on the ground.

He lifted his head, and I saw the gleam of his eyes under the hood. Eyes more vibrant than that of any of the souls before me. They were grey, but even from a distance I saw small flecks of blue. They locked onto me, and he began moving toward me, shoving the other souls aside.

My fear ordered me to run, and my traitorous, hammering heart set the speed at which I ought to escape, but I held my feet firm. After all, I had nowhere to go. I didn't even know where I was. Perhaps I might still fool him.

I held my breath so it wouldn't fog in front of me, swaying awkwardly even as the figure drew closer.

He reached up, grabbed onto his hood and pulled it back.

Brown hair with just a hint of a wave framed his face, a loose piece falling over his forehead.

My arm jerked as I fought an instinctive reaction to reach out and fix it.

He had a defined jaw with the shadow of stubble, and sharp cheekbones that would have made him look severe if not for the warmth in his eyes.

He was handsome. Undeniably so.

I hadn't expected handsome.

Then again, wouldn't the gods have given themselves a face that could tempt people?

His eyes were wide as he pointedly gazed at me, his eyes moving from the top of my head down to my boots. Then he looked back to my face.

Maybe it was the Thipp's and its lingering effects, but I was short of breath. During the season I had done what I could to avoid drawing too much attention, but now I couldn't help but look boldly back at him. If anything, I wanted to get closer, to trace my finger along his jaw and see if he was as solid as I was.

The space around us was quiet enough that I heard the soft whoosh of his breath as he gasped and then uttered one word.

"Starlight."

I looked around me, trying to figure out what he meant. I craned my neck upward, only then noticing there were no stars to be seen.

"I'm sorry, I don't know what you mean."

One of his hands reached for me, but he stopped before he touched my skin, pulling back.

My breath caught, and a part of me wished he'd kept reaching.

If I'd already been found out, I should at least try to make a good impression.

I dipped into a curtsey.

"Hello. I'm Celia Hipnosi, and—"

He threw out an arm, cutting me off.

The other individuals surrounding us still wore blank expressions, but a handful of them had turned to look.

Without a response, he turned away from me, and my heart sank.

I'd already upset him. If he was indeed Death—and who else could he be?—then I needed to fix this. More than that, I wanted to fix it. The very air felt more frigid as he walked away.

I scrambled for something else to say. Something to do.

Before I could manage anything, he glanced around at the individuals getting out of line and snapped his head in their direction.

"Back as you were!" he yelled, turning on his heel and marching back to the front of the formation.

I let out several quick, shallow breaths as I regained my composure.

Starlight, he had said.

What did he mean? Had it been a test? Had I failed?

At the front of the group, his voice boomed over the crowd once more.

"Welcome, new Shades, to the Ether. You are here under the hospitality of Charon, god and ruler of this plane. I am his Head Shade. For now, I'll be taking you to where the others linger. You may rest there until it is time to realize your purpose."

So he wasn't Death, and apparently neither was the leader of this place. *Charon*, he had said. Then who was this man?

Another living being like me? Trapped here, or was he here on purpose? And who was Charon?

Emrys worshiped only two gods: Day and Death. There was no one else.

The questions swirled in my head as I followed the other Shades farther into the Ether.

The crowd began surging forward again. I stood on my tiptoes, craning over the floating souls to try to catch a glimpse of the Head Shade once more.

Everything he'd said about Charon and the Ether and Shades had left me reeling, but he was the one leading this crowd. In my mind, that also made him the person most likely to have the answers I needed, and since I'd already been spotted I might as well approach him. I ducked and wove through the crowd, feeling only a little guilty when I bumped a few swaying and floating individuals.

"Sorry," I murmured to a woman who didn't even spare me a glance.

The ground had shifted from fairly flat to rolling hills, with even more wildflowers.

"Please excuse me." I slid between two men who looked like they were from Mejje, their already billowing pants swaying as they floated along.

I'm surrounded by victims of the hour. Dead people. Likely good people who lost their lives just for being in the wrong place at the worst time. I should be screaming, or sobbing.

But I couldn't quite manage it. The rest of the Thipp's must have worn off. I was still uncomfortably cold, but my limbs felt lighter. A nervous energy ran through me, fighting against an undeniable buoyancy brought on by my success. I'd made it! Whether this place was even real, and if I could get here, had been a massive hurdle in my plan.

The difference between death and victory.

The difference between never seeing my father again and having the means to find him.

No doubt I would eventually have to grapple with more obstacles. I'd been unconscious on arrival, so I really didn't know how to get back. Was time still frozen in Emrys? Was it already January first? Would the antidote get us home, or would it even help if the Thipp's no longer had an effect here?

All problems for future Celia. I'd spent over a year working toward this destination, and I needed to focus and continue with what I'd set out to do. This journey couldn't be for nothing.

The Head Shade, as he'd called himself, was only a handful of rows in front of me.

Another one of the illuminated orbs floated past. This time I reached out and placed my palm under it. It was warm, but not burning hot like fire in a lantern.

"We're here," the Head Shade's voice rang out.

I released the orb, and my fingers curled, already lacking the small amount of warmth it had provided.

There were more and more people surrounding us now, and I guessed this was the resting place of Shades. I could see people in clothing that I knew was from the fashions of generations past.

The chill in my fingers had spread, and my extremities were growing numb.

If I couldn't find my father quickly, I'd need somewhere warm to rest until I could look for him.

My body was getting stiff, this time with chill instead of the effects of Thipp's, but my mind raced. I spun in place, looking at the new faces for my father. I didn't see him anywhere, but my hand flew to my mouth when I spotted a familiar face: a man whose name I couldn't recall, but whom I recognized from Fox Haven. He'd been a woodworker. I had gone along with my father once to have a table made for our entrance hall. The man had been kind and welcoming, asking my opinions and thoughts on the craftsmanship, and smiling at my answers.

He'd disappeared years before my father. The woodworker's shop had been closed for months after his death, and for the past ten years it had been run by another man in town.

But he hadn't aged a day. Aside from the pallor of his face, and his floating form, he looked the same.

It made sense that the dead, or the Shades, as the man had called them, didn't age. But it was disconcerting, seeing familiar faces after so long, when only I had changed.

The Head Shade called for attention.

"This"—he gestured at the rolling hills, littered with trees —"is the Meadow. You are free to remain here. In this form you will have no need to sleep, or eat."

A few of the faces had slightly widened eyes that might have registered surprise, but for the most part no one showed an outward reaction. It was as if the farther they went into the Ether, the less engaged they became. The Shades were aptly named: mere shadows of whoever they had been before.

I, however, was no Shade, and I did not intend to fail due to starvation or succumbing to the elements before I located my father. Not after coming this far.

· "Excuse me," I said, quietly at first and then louder when the Head Shade didn't respond. "Excuse me! What do you mean 'new Shades'? And where is the Ether? And what are the options if we *do* need shelter and food? Or sleep?" I'd intended to ask only one question, but once the first had spilled out, so had the others.

I clamped my mouth shut as the Head Shade turned toward me, a frown on his face and his grey eyes flashing. The ridiculous thought that he was even more handsome when he was incensed entered my mind, but I dismissed it when he started moving in my direction.

He shoved back through the crowd until he was face to face with me again.

"Keep your voice down," he urged me. "Now that we're here, you will be in the presence of Charon at any moment. You don't want to draw his attention, trust me."

He'd said it with a glance to each side, and a worried look that told me it was a bad thing. But from what he'd told us earlier, didn't he work for Charon? Besides, the deity of this whole place was even more likely to have answers than the Head Shade. I'd spent my whole life praying to Day and Death, even if I hadn't been convinced of either's interest in my world. I was already in the Ether, and if addressing a god was the next step in finding my father, I'd gladly take it.

The Head Shade turned away from me, but I couldn't afford to let him dismiss me.

I followed him.

We walked in silence for a few moments before he turned again.

"What do you think you're doing? Go back into the crowd and try to blend in!"

"I'm not trying to frustrate you, but you're the only one who will talk to me and I need your help. You see, I came here to—"

"*Came* here? On purpose? Are you completely mad?"

I took a step back, his words hitting me like a slap. Not that he was wrong; it's what many people would have thought if I'd told them my plans back in Emrys.

"I had to. But now that I'm here, I can finish what I came to do and then I'll be on my way. If you don't want Charon to know about me, that's fine. If *you* could tell me what I should be doing in this place as a not dead, dead person?" I faltered then, still questioning the status of my own mortality.

Being dead would ruin all my plans.

The Head Shade sighed.

"You're not dead. Not technically. But unless you'd like to be, I advise you to keep your head down and stay near the back of the group."

"Why? What's going to happen if I stay at the front?" Was there something dangerous here? Something aside from the god?

While I wasn't a soldier by any means, I was strong. I rode Pellix and hiked through the hills around the estate. I lifted heavy things in the garden. I wasn't skilled, but I wouldn't be going down without a fight.

"Maybe I can help," I offered.

"While I appreciate the offer, the only person in danger here is you, and you're in way over your head."

I gave him a good look then, waiting to see if he was the threat. But he just kept watching me, blue flecks in his eyes glinting. When I lowered my arms, he spoke again.

"Please. Hide now, and I'll promise some answers later. It would be better if we had something to conceal you."

I debated whether I should listen to him or take my chances when Charon arrived. I was drawn to the Head Shade, but that could merely be because he was the first and only person here to speak to me.

I was in an unfamiliar place, and he was someone who

looked refreshingly alive. A reminder of everything I was trying to return to as soon as I found my father.

But if the Head Shade *was* to be trusted, then Charon was a god. Likely the god responsible for this hour, or the damage it wrought. And if that was the case, then he really could be trying to protect me from an angry deity who wouldn't like finding a living soul in his realm.

The Head Shade came upon a gentleman I judged to be several years Ambrose's senior.

He reached out and pulled at the cloak the man wore. It came loose with no sign of protest from its former owner.

"Just going to borrow this, if you don't mind," he told the man.

The Head Shade passed it to me, and I hesitated before taking it.

"Won't he be cold?" I gestured at the floating man.

"They don't feel cold. Make sure to tuck in your hair, and look down so your eyes don't show. The color is too saturated for a Shade."

After another moment's hesitation, I tugged on the deep grey cloak, yanking the hood over my hair. The strands were a mess, some in the front determined to stick out, but I pulled the remaining pins out from my ruined hairstyle and used them to pin the hair framing my face down. I'm sure I looked laughable, but the Head Shade still wore a somber expression.

"Better," he acknowledged, "but remember what I said about keeping your head down. Your eyes would reveal you right off."

When he said it, another strange look played across his features. It was gone before I could question it, and he returned to the front of the crowd, walking until he stood under one of the trees that topped the nearest hill.

Head down, hair hidden, wrapped in a cloak taken from a

dead man, I watched the Head Shade until he came to a stop, then turned on my heel and worked my way to the back of the crowd.

As I reached the last few rows, the already wintery temperature dropped starkly. I clutched the cloak tight and looked up to see a figure descending from the sky.

CHAPTER 15

A few of the people surrounding me cried out. It was the first sign of emotion since our arrival. Several of my fellow Taken cringed, and I even saw the Head Shade ducking back as the figure descended.

Large feathered wings sprouted from the being's back. When he landed, he tucked them in toward himself, and then they vanished entirely. I heard my breathing as it sped up, aware that I was on the verge of hyperventilating and powerless to prevent it.

With the Head Shade I had wondered, but now I was certain to my bones. This was a god.

When the figure lifted his head the sensation got worse. If this was Charon, as the Head Shade had indicated, I couldn't see much of him. He wore a hood, and its opening gave way to a black void. Not a darkness caused by a lack of light, but an intense and heavy emptiness, purposeful and yawning. I wanted to look away, yet my eyes were riveted on the void that reigned in the place where a face should have been.

How had I ever assumed the Head Shade was a god? This being was terrifying and awe-inspiring.

I squeaked as I swallowed down the scream that threatened to erupt. Even so, the figure turned toward me. I looked at the ground and started swaying like my neighbors.

"This year's Taken, Charon," the Head Shade announced, and the figure snapped its hooded head back towards him.

"A large number this year. Good. I had worried people were growing too wary of my hour. But it seems we have many this year who were foolhardy. Perhaps doubting the power I exert between the years? Of course, this will be nothing compared to the centennial celebration I have planned."

The voice from within the hood was booming and deep. It rang out and seemed to linger in the air, grating on my nerves. It sounded less like the echo of a voice and more like the sound of metal sliding against metal. A ringing you felt in your bones. Jarring and disconcerting. When the Head Shade spoke, I'd felt as if his very words were music, drawing me closer. When Charon spoke, I wanted nothing so much as to turn and run without ever looking back.

As the god continued to look over his Shades, he removed his hood, and I had to wonder if my mind was playing tricks on me. Not surprising, given the night I'd had.

Charon had human features after all. Dazzling and simply too much, in a way I couldn't quite describe, but human nonetheless. He had black hair and grey eyes, similar to the Head Shade. The god's eyes, however, held none of the spark that the Head Shade possessed. No flashes of blue. Just a steel wall, cold and unyielding.

"You now belong to the Ether. I am Charon, your ruler and host. You have died, but you are not in the realm of Death. You should be thanking me for that. Her domain is far less pleasant. Think of my kingdom as a state not so much as between life and death, but more as an aside. You have been removed from the cycle of life and death. Omitted from its plan. Death's domain is vast, but mine grows at a rapid pace. You're all here at the most exciting time, because soon we'll be able to implement the plan I've so carefully nurtured all these years. In return for my hospitality, you will have a job to do during the Unseen Hour, under the guidance of my Head Shade."

Charon floated over the ground as he spoke. His Shades were swaying, pale imitations of their former selves, toes trailing the ground, while the god moved with purpose. He walked on air, seeming to command the very elements in his realm.

The extreme cold, and my close brush with death, were catching up to me. Only adrenaline and fear were keeping me upright and awake.

Even when exhausted, my curiosity remained intact. Charon had confirmed Death was real, and *she* had a realm of her own. Emrys had been wrong about the gods, in more ways than one. Charon's name sounded familiar, and my tired mind just barely grasped a memory of seeing it in a book about Tang.

The gods, it appeared, were above trivial things like national borders.

"Acclimate to your new forms. By the time the next Unseen Hour rolls around, you will all be ready with your songs."

Charon floated down the lines, and I swayed and turned my head away from him as he passed several people down the line from me.

I didn't dare turn to look at him, praying instinctively to both gods that he would pass me by without noticing my feet planted firmly on the ground. Not that I expected praying to work. I was in the presence of a different god, and this place belonged to him.

He gave off a chill exceeding that of the surroundings, and I felt him growing closer. He had to be only a few individuals away when I heard the Head Shade call out.

"Charon, I have a final count for you, and the information you asked me to gather. Would you prefer to review it now?"

The wall of cold froze several feet from me, then receded. My muscles relaxed as he moved farther away.

"Yes."

"Then I'll settle the Shades and convene with you."

The two of them murmured some more words I couldn't hear, and then Charon retreated beyond the Meadow and out of sight.

The Head Shade didn't immediately follow, instead approaching me.

He leaned closer than was decent and whispered in my ear, his breath pleasantly warm.

"Remain here. Do not make a scene. I will be back soon, but if Charon finds you, it will not be good. Nod if you understand."

I leaned even closer to him as he spoke, desperate for any source of heat.

I nodded, too tired to fight him on the request.

"Good. I'll return shortly."

He whisked away, taking his warmth with him.

I was stuck with the Shades, with nothing but my questions for company.

CHAPTER 16

The other Shades had broken from their ordered lines and were floating and wandering through the flowers but not leaving the Meadow.

Was this to be my life until I escaped? Pacing and roaming listlessly until I managed to find my father? If I had to wait for the Head Shade's return, I might as well get started.

The crowd was vast, and I wandered well past the group I'd arrived with. Father disappeared years ago, so I might need to check everyone. But the veritable sea of wispy Shades in the Meadow made it clear that would be a longer task than I'd hoped.

Nearly a hundred years of souls.

My limbs grew heavy again as the realization sank in. Charon had indicated this hour was over; he had his souls for this year. Time was probably moving forward in Emrys, and I was only just beginning my search.

My family and friends would know soon enough that I was missing, if they didn't already. The moon was still high overhead here, but who knew if that reflected time in Emrys? My original idea of trying to make it here and back within the confines of the hour was laughable. I could only hope Father was here in the Meadow and that finding him would be simpler than the presence of thousands upon thousands of souls led me to believe.

The Head Shade had warned me not to make a scene, and I had no desire for Charon to come back, with his frigid demeanor, but I wouldn't find my father by standing around.

"Father! Calden Hipnosi!" I called out, making my way through the crowd.

Yelling hadn't worked. The Shades only looked up occasionally, and no one responded to me. I'd had to revert to checking everyone individually after all.

I'd barely made a dent, spinning yet another person around only to be disappointed when I didn't recognize him, when someone shouted.

"What do you think you're doing?"

Turning, I saw the Head Shade had returned. He raised a hand, beckoning me toward him.

"No," I muttered to myself, trying to resist the pull the Head Shade's voice created. I had come here for my father, and I had no intention of leaving without him.

Across the crowd, the Head Shade's eyes widened, and he marched over to me.

"I've left him with some figures to look over, but Charon could still choose to come back at any moment. His whims at this time of year are difficult to predict, and you do not want to be here looking *alive* when he returns. You need to be gone before that happens."

Was he going to try to send me back to Emrys? For a

moment I felt relief, followed immediately by a strong surge of shame. I'd come all this way, and I couldn't be deterred just because of one individual. Even if they were a god. Even if they sent a chill deep into my bones that made me want to curl up and cry.

"You can't send me back yet. I'm looking for someone," I told the Head Shade.

Upsetting the only other living being here was perhaps not a great strategy, but I couldn't let him stop me.

"Send you back? I can't send you back."

I blinked.

Couldn't send ... but he didn't know I had the Thipp's antidote. Didn't know how I'd gotten here in the first place. He was used to Shades. I was different.

I had to be, because if I wasn't, then I was trapped.

"Are you all right?" He reached for me, placing a hand on Temple's jacket sleeve. My breathing calmed.

There was still something I could do, even if I didn't know how to escape the Ether.

"I still need to find him. If you could help, he—"

"I hate to be the bearer of bad news, but if anyone was with you during the Unseen Hour, they're dead. In fact, it'd be much better for you if they aren't down here, because then they got away alive. If they're a Shade, you don't want to see them like that."

He really did look apologetic.

I shook my head.

"The person I'm looking for disappeared during the Unseen Hour years ago, but I'm convinced he's not dead at all."

The Head Shade leaned forward, looking more closely at me and tilting his head to the side.

"Who did you say you we—"

The other Shades froze around us, and a cold wind hit me. I shivered inside my borrowed coat.

"That'll be Charon coming back. You can't be here."

My heart began pounding again, which could give me away as much as anything else. With a last, panicked glance at the other Shades, I admitted to myself that it could take days, if not far longer, to find my father. I couldn't do that if I was discovered by an angry god.

"Where can I hide?"

I had no choice but to trust the Head Shade, for now.

"Come on! This way!" He grabbed my hand, yanking so hard I nearly went tumbling. I would have if he hadn't caught me underneath my arms. He was so warm that I leaned against him until another gentle shove pushed me back on my feet.

"Steady, and move quickly."

I stumbled after the Shade, my limbs moving sluggishly with the cold that ate at me. I might have arrived alive, but surely the temperature would finish me off.

The farther we went from the field, the more the scenery changed. At first it was one or two clusters of short and twisted trees. Dead and lifeless. Then, some with sparse leaves. Soon enough we were surrounded by trees that towered above us, as tall as several buildings each. He'd led me from the more open Meadow into a forest. Not a bad idea. There were plenty of places here to hide.

The bark of some of the trees was cedar brown, and others black as pitch. The limbs were largely bare near the base of the trees, but there was what appeared to be blackened foliage farther up in the branches. Bushes similar in shade to the grass of the Meadow dotted the area between the trees.

After a lengthier trek, we were surrounded by the towering things, their trunks looming, as thick as some of the smaller shops in Emrys. The farther into the trees we went, the warmer it got, and I sighed in relief when the feeling returned to my fingers and toes.

The leaves on the massive trees were illuminated by streaks of green and blue light that had appeared in the sky, ribbons that created a dazzling glow.

"How—" I began, before feeling a tug once again.

"In here!"

I was practically shoved through a door I hadn't even seen moments before.

The Head Shade stepped in behind me and closed the door. He had brought me to a cottage built between the trees. The whole dwelling was one open space. A cot and disheveled blankets were tucked against one wall. A roaring fire in the hearth in one corner, venting smoke into the dark sky. There was a singular chair, constructed of the same cedar that made up the forest. Against one wall was a set of wooden shelves built directly into the side of the structure, and a small water basin and some wooden bowls sat atop the makeshift counter. The walls themselves appeared to be made of wood, with mud and dirt packed between the spaces. It must have been built between several of the larger trees I'd seen outside, which kept it propped up at the corners while concealing it from the outside.

I edged toward the fire, craving warmth.

"Get under the blankets," the Shade urged me, steering me toward the cot.

I'd gone a few steps when my survival instincts kicked in, along with the realization that I was very much alone and unchaperoned, with a man I didn't know in the slightest, being led to a bed.

"I can't do that! I don't know who you are, or even what you are. I don't know where I am, but I am *not* putting myself in a compromising position." Technically, I was already in a compromising position, but this was a chance to gain back some level of control.

I stamped a foot, crossing my arms over my chest and doing my best imitation of Mother when she was giving an order she expected to have followed. Inside, though, I was trembling.

I was standing in front of a man, and the Shade was certainly a man, while wearing my brother's riding clothes, of all things. My reputation would have been irreparable if anyone in Emrys had seen us.

Blasted ghosts, what must the Head Shade think of me? What would anyone else think?

I might not like the constraints of Emrys, but I'd done my best to abide by them enough that I didn't risk my family's reputation. It could be toppled along with my own if I wasn't careful.

The Shade ran one hand through the back of his brown hair, tousling it.

"I'm not used to guests. I didn't consider how it might come across. I just wanted to keep you away from Charon and prevent you from freezing to death."

His body language was comforting as he created more distance between us, giving me an open path to the door if I wanted to run.

"This was just supposed to be a rescue mission," I whispered, staring between the Head Shade and the door. "I didn't mean to create a mess for anyone else."

If Charon really would be upset to find me here, it was likely that I had put my host in a poor position as well.

"We'll get to all that, but for now, why don't you warm up?"

The Head Shade didn't move, and I plopped down onto the cot. Only then did he step forward, reaching over me to pull a thick blanket around my shoulders.

After a few moments, the warmth began returning to my limbs. I was so cold that the process felt painful.

Soon enough though, the tingling passed, and comfort took its place.

"Thank you."

He nodded in response, moving to the single wooden chair in the small cottage and sitting down.

Maybe he felt more secure since I no longer looked like I might run. He was in just as uncertain waters as I, alone with a stranger.

It was time to rectify that particular issue.

"I am Celia Hipnosi, daughter of Marquess Calden Hipnosi and Marchioness Vinia Hipnosi. My eldest brother, Ambrose, currently holds the title of Marquess. I traveled here from Fox Haven." If he was from Emrys he'd probably recognize the name.

"Fox Haven," he murmured.

"You know it?"

The Shade dipped his chin toward me. His brown hair had glints of bronze, and I wondered if it was as soft as it looked. It was also longer than what was currently fashionable.

I stared at him for a moment, my cheeks growing warm when he met my gaze, and I noted how long I'd been looking. I cleared my throat, trying to force my features into an expression of nonchalance.

"Now then, who are you? Are you a god, like Charon?"

He took a deep breath and let out a prolonged sigh.

"I've been Head Shade for so long, I can't even remember the last time someone asked me about myself. I'm no god, just another person from Emrys who made it down here alive. I was Taken during the very first hour, and I've been Head Shade for nearly a century. Before that, I was Orion Holmes."

CHAPTER 17

"You're one of the doomed Holmes brothers?" I shouted, then clapped a hand over my mouth, aware how rude the reaction had been.

I still had my small bag slung over my shoulder, and I took it off, nesting it in the blanket in front of me.

Shock rolled through me, and I swallowed down the other emotion that threatened to push through: disappointment. For over a year, I'd been falling for the words of R. Holmes. Against all odds, one of the brothers was alive, but he was O.

I longed to ask about the other two, but if they weren't here, that didn't bode well.

Orion blinked.

"People know about us?"

I dropped my hands, nodding.

"Everyone knows of the three Holmes brothers. You all … well, you … during the first Unseen Hour, you …"

His face was impassive.

"We died. You can say it."

If he was giving me leave to discuss it openly, I might as well ask after his siblings.

"Yes, that is the assumption, but only two bodies were ever found. And the last place people had seen you was in your home. At first, people thought you were murdered, but then, when the hour continued, people realized you'd been victims of it. Since it was the first year of the Unseen Hour, you had no way of knowing the danger you were in, being out at midnight."

Orion scoffed.

"It was foolish for us to leave at that time of night, even if we didn't know the hour was coming. My brothers and I only left our home because of extenuating circumstances. Even then, only one of us made it far enough to go past the boundaries of the Holmes family estate. Me."

"And your brothers?"

I held my breath.

Orion frowned, staring into the fire as he answered.

"Reginald and Remington are deceased. I'm the only one who made it here"—he gestured to himself—"like this."

That settled it, then. The mysterious gentleman I'd found myself drawn to, more than any of the men I'd met at balls or while promenading or attending any number of mind-numbingly dull affairs in Emrys, was dead.

I hadn't known R. Not really. I'd just been drawn to his words. But to Orion, he had been a brother, and judging by the way he scowled into the fire, the memory was still painful.

"I'm sorry. I've got a few brothers myself, and I can't imagine being without them. I'm sure you all had your reasons for going out that night. After all, there were mysterious happenings going on at your estate—and had been for weeks before you disappeared."

His eyes widened.

"People know about that as well?"

"Not everyone." Truthfully, I wasn't certain how much attention had been paid once it was decided the brothers were victims of the hour, or how much investigation had been done before that determination was made. The only reason I knew more was because of R. and his writing. Otherwise, I'd have heard of the three brothers who died during the first hour, when the Holmes family lost an entire generation of its house, and nothing more.

I wasn't about to admit that I'd been snooping around his brother's journal. It was highly possible that learning their personal possessions had ended up on a dusty library shelf would be just salt in the wound. A bolt of longing tore through me as I thought of the journal's author, but this wasn't the time to linger on fantasy.

"Most people just know you all died during the hour, and that your estate passed to a cousin whose side of the family still holds the estate to this day. There were some questions initially, about whether the missing brother—you—was involved in the demise of the other two. But that theory was quickly abandoned," I assured him. "Everyone assumes you were all three victims of the hour."

"They're not wrong to say that."

"Our estate abuts yours," I said, as a way of explaining my additional knowledge.

Here without his family for so long. My heart went out to him, but so did my curiosity.

I stood, leaving the satchel on the cot but keeping the blanket draped over my shoulders as I took a few steps across the small cottage to observe him closer. I walked in a circle around Orion, tilting my head as I took him in.

"Yes?"

"Well, if it's not too impertinent to say ... how are you still alive? It's been nearly a hundred years. Shouldn't you be dead?"

Orion winced and I bit my lip, regretting the harsh words. I wanted to know, but that didn't excuse cruelty.

After all, I was in some mystical realm called the Ether. Who was I to tell people whether they were dead or not? Tact had never been my strong suit. I'd worked hard to fake it when necessary—during balls, for instance—but this entire episode had shaken me. I was having a harder time feigning decorum than usual.

Orion laughed, but the sound fell flat.

"You don't have to be worried about niceties with me. This is my first social interaction in quite some time, so I'm just pleased to have someone to talk to. I *would* be dead, if I aged like I did in Emrys, but the Ether doesn't work like that. There is no true passage of time here. You can track the days and feel time slipping by, but you remain the same. Frozen bodies are left behind after the hour, and frozen is what I am here as well. Stuck at twenty-seven for years. At least, that's how it's happened for me. I assume you'll be similar."

Orion stood, removing his cloak and hanging it on a wooden peg on the wall.

His outfit wouldn't have given away his age. In his generation, materials for men were more embellished. Golden thread, bright colors. In my time the trend had reversed, with women tending to wear the vibrant colors and men's outfits being more subdued.

Orion's clothes were simple. Tan trousers, black boots, and a flowing cream shirt with the tie at the neck left open, revealing the very top of his chest.

Once again, I found myself staring without meaning to, this time at his broad chest. I cleared my throat as he moved back to his chair.

"And is that how it is for everyone else like you, everyone still alive in the Ether?"

"I'm the only one like me. Aside from you, that is. Everyone else down here is a Shade, except for Charon himself."

"Oh." I slumped back down onto the cot. My exhaustion caught up with me as I deflated.

Could I have been wrong?

Maybe my father *was* a victim of the hour. But he'd been following the Holmes journal, and he'd used Thipp's. The Ether seemed like a big place.

"You could be wrong, though, right? There could be someone else? Maybe they're hiding from Charon, like you're helping me to do. Maybe they're camouflaged in these woods, just like you, and you simply haven't come across them."

Orion flashed me what I took to be a sympathetic smile, one that didn't reach his eyes.

"Perhaps," he allowed, although his voice didn't sound certain at all. "The Ether is vast. It's possible someone slipped my notice. They could be in hiding. When I arrived here, I was a novelty. Charon never intended for beings like us to exist. His Shades serve a purpose, and he only wanted the dead. He's since realized he can use me to his advantage, but my initial months here were ... unpleasant."

His eyes darkened as he spoke, reminding me of a storm building over the seas.

I was torn between wanting to know more about what had happened to him and the thought that maybe I didn't want to hear it, if it was the fate that might await me.

I waited for the expression to fade before interjecting with an idea.

"If he has a use for us, should I have hidden? He rules this place, so it stands to reason he's the one with the power to keep us here or return us. He'd also know all the Shades, right? Maybe he could help me find my—"

"Charon helps only himself. Whether you realize it or not, you've stumbled into something much bigger than the lives of all of Emrys, or the other countries. This is a battle between gods. Trust me, you don't want to be stuck in the middle."

"We were always taught that there were only two gods, Day and Death."

Orion sighed.

"Emrys was wrong. Now, you're bound to be weary after the night you've had. You should get some rest." He raised a hand before I could protest. "I will sleep on the floor, and I can assure you that you're much safer here with me than you would be wandering about the Ether. Shades aren't the only thing Charon has around here. You don't want to meet some of his other creatures unprepared."

As if on cue, a cry rang through the night. It sounded like a cross between a wolf's howl and a blood-curdling scream. I jumped and snapped my arms around myself.

"See what I mean? Now then, why don't you get some rest. I have some more comfortable attire you could change into. Are ladies really wearing their own riding outfits with trousers now?"

He gestured to my borrowed outfit.

I gave a nervous smile, along with my admission.

"No, women are still relegated to uncomfortable dresses in an array of unfortunate colors and patterns. These are my brother's clothes. He doesn't know I have them. Well, I guess he might by now."

"I'll get you something else to—"

"No, these are fine. I'll be perfectly comfortable sleeping in these."

It was a horrible idea, really. I was dingy and dirty from my journey through the fields and woods, but I couldn't exactly ask the man to leave his own house, and no matter how terrible I was at behaving as a proper lady, I wasn't willing to take my clothes off in front of a man I'd just met, no matter how helpful and handsome he might be.

Orion shrugged.

"Whatever you think, then."

Even as I settled under the blankets on his cot, which was more comfortable than it first appeared, I would have guessed it would be impossible to sleep.

But I was wrong.

The exhaustion of being taken from Emrys to the Ether caught up to me, and I fell into a deep sleep without even dreams to disturb me.

CHAPTER 18

The events of the previous evening had shaken me, but when I woke the following morning, I was refreshed and determined to get answers. Before getting up, I patted the Thipp's antidote in my pocket, reassuring myself that it was still there. I left my satchel tucked underneath the blanket.

This morning, I was going to do whatever it took to convince Orion to help me. I'd made it this far, against all odds. There had to be a way to find my father, and a way out. If the Shades entered the Ether in that open field that led to the Meadow, it made sense that one could exit from there as well.

Resolute, I threw the cover off, wishing for a fresh change of clothes. A quick glance told me Orion wasn't anywhere in the small cottage. Surely he wouldn't leave me alone? When I opened the door, though, he was nowhere to be seen. I was hesitant to call out for him, not knowing what else might show up. As I scanned the trees, I noticed something that had me stumbling back.

It's still dark.

Bluish moonlight filtered through the trees. Brighter now

than before, but there was no sunny sky that I could see. There was a colorful flash between several of the trees. Those same dancing lights that I'd seen in the forest when we'd arrived at his home.

"Orion?" I called.

He didn't answer. He'd told me to stay inside, but I couldn't accomplish anything alone in front of his fireplace.

"I'll be right back anyway," I reasoned aloud to myself.

Decision made, I wandered away from the path we'd come in on the night before, and farther into the woods. Not far from Orion's home, I walked into a clearing, and the vibrant colors had me throwing a hand over my brow. The sky was filled with those same ribbons of lights, but these were purple and orange, and even brighter now.

I missed the blue and greens of the previous night.

They're the same blue as the specks dancing in Orion's eyes.

I was mentally chastising myself for that frivolous thought when something tapped me on the shoulder.

"Bloody ghosts!" I jumped a good foot in the air, and when I whipped my head around I saw Orion, laughing behind his hand.

The sound of his laughter set my heart fluttering, or maybe it was just nerves.

"Is this how ladies have been talking since I went away? Well, well."

He was smirking. It was the closest to happy that I'd seen him.

I winked, hoping to keep his smile in place. I much preferred it to the somber Head Shade I'd first met.

"We talk how we like. At least I do. You should know, though, I'm no model of the ideal lady. Not by the queen's standards and not by my mother's, either. In fact, I'm afraid that I'm somewhat of a societal disappointment compared to many ladies," I admitted.

"And I'd wager neither your mother nor the queen got themselves in a mess like getting Taken to the Ether," he teased, still grinning.

I took a step closer to him, remembering how much warmer it had been when he'd held my hand. It was still cold out, though not nearly so bad as it had been with Charon in the Meadow.

If he was in a positive mood, then this was as good a time as any.

I took a deep breath, willing myself to hold my nerve.

"It's clear that you've got a whole life constructed down here, and I don't mean to disrupt that, but I have no intention of staying. I'm here with a purpose. I have someone I need to find, and if I'm right he's been down here for four years now. Once I've found him, I intend to go home. And I think I have the beginnings of a plan. If it works, you're welcome to come with us." I tacked the last bit on as a bargaining chip, although I had no way of knowing whether Orion even wanted to leave.

He must, though, with an entire world waiting for us back home. Either way, I'd made plenty of antidote, assuming that method was at all helpful. Fully prepared, that was me. Ambrose and my mother would have been so proud, and then equally disappointed that I didn't put my efforts towards more acceptable pursuits.

"You'd be back in Emrys again," I prompted when he didn't respond.

Orion ran one hand over the stubble on his chin.

"Finding another Shade like us would be the easiest part of what you're suggesting, and even that could take quite some time. Are you actually saying you have a way to get back to Emrys, and stay there?"

I'd mastered the art of inane conversation and providing just enough information to keep the conversation moving when it was necessary. I couldn't do the same here. What I was asking of him was enormous, and I had to give more if I wanted something that important in return.

"I was Taken because I poisoned myself with Thipp's root; not enough to die, but nearly that amount. It was a close call, if I'm being honest."

His face darkened into a scowl. I was well aware of how it sounded. I'd put myself at great risk on purpose.

"I had no intention of *really* dying, only getting down here to enact the rest of my plan," I assured him, "and I brought along the antidote. That's how I hope to leave. There's plenty for all of us. If you can guide us to the Ether's entrance, it could work. I still have my body, and you still have yours. We just need to get home. If we can enter, there must be a way to exit, right? Well, anyway, that's my plan. What do you think, Lord Holmes?"

I straightened my shoulders.

He blinked at me.

"There's no need for that. Orion is just fine."

Even without him holding my hand, I felt warmer. My use of the title might indeed be ridiculous, because I addressed Charlotte and Thomas by their first names. It was done fairly often in my time, but it hadn't been in his.

A hundred years ago, using his given name would have been a serious expression of intimacy.

Then again, I was his only company. That could easily explain it. It probably didn't mean anything special.

"All right. *Orion.* Will you help me?"

"The Thipp's antidote is clever, there's no denying that, but I'm not sure it will work. You can't just waltz out of the Ether, you know. It's not a door that you can open at your leisure."

My shoulders slumped, but I rallied. I was here, and I had a potential ally.

"I managed to come down here just fine. I already know the location where I came in, even if I don't know how it works. There must be a way, though."

Because if there wasn't, I'd be in the Ether for an eternity, and I was nowhere near prepared to accept that fate.

"Logic doesn't come into play much in the Ether," Orion muttered.

I was undeterred. He might be somewhat surly, but the conversation could have gone much worse.

My whole plan could have gone much worse. I could have died, or Charon could have caught me, or I could have been alone in my endeavors. This was still, relatively speaking, the best-case scenario.

"You've been down here for quite some time. I'd wager you've gleaned at least some information that could be useful to our aims."

Orion sighed.

"You've got your location correct but your assumptions wrong. You think you'll be able to exit the Ether because you're still alive. And I'm here to tell you it wouldn't matter. The Shades all leave the Ether once a year, and only once a year. At the onset of the hour they return to Rayus, and then come back to the Ether again when the hour is over. It's how Charon lures souls down here. Shade song."

I put a hand to my head. The forest spun around me.

"The Shades return to Emrys and the other kingdoms? All of them? Song. Is that ... I thought I heard music, but—"

"Do you need to sit down? Maybe try a few deep breaths."

I hauled air into my lungs, staying on my feet but leaning against a nearby tree trunk.

Orion was right. I'd relied on my living status to be part of my exit strategy. Being able to leave regardless was excellent. I could blend in with the Shades, and Charon would be none the wiser. But *only* being able to leave during the hour? My family would be without me for a year. My friends. Pellix.

By the time I returned, they would have held a funeral, mourned me.

I'd tried to be a good daughter, and instead I'd ended up hurting everyone else I loved.

This was always a possibility. You'll still return home, and they'll just be happy to have you both back. Come on Celia, rally!

What was done, was done. This gave me a year to find my father, and a year to process what my decision was putting the rest of my family through back in Emrys. Now, though, I had to handle what was in front of me.

I stared up at Orion. Even if I hadn't been slouched against a tree, he would have been taller than me by several inches.

"You admit there's a way back. You know the way the Ether works, and I have the antidote we could try once we're actually in Emrys. If we truly have to wait for the next hour, that leaves us a year. We could work as a team. Please? Wouldn't you do anything to rescue someone you loved?"

He stared at me for several seconds, the flecks in his eyes, as I'd thought, a perfect match for the lights from the previous evening.

"All right. I'll try and help you, but don't get your hopes up. As I told you, there's no one else down here like us. I don't want to raise your expectations only for you to end up disappointed."

"But he could have hidden from you. Maybe he's got his own spot in the woods, staying safe from you and Charon. You're Head Shade, so maybe he didn't trust you?"

It's possible I shouldn't, either.

But he'd been nothing but kind so far, and it's not as if I had other options. I'd much rather work with Orion than face an unknown realm alone.

Orion was staring at me again, studying me.

He cleared his throat.

"Fine. We'll look. That's all I can promise."

I nodded, trying to appear as though I'd anticipated the answer all along. In truth I was ready to fall back against the tree again with relief, but I didn't want him to think he'd paired himself with a weak ally.

"Then let's get going." I turned on my heel, fully prepared to march straight back to the Meadow.

"Right now?"

"Yes, of course. No time better. Although"—I glanced down at myself—"I think I would like that change of clothes after all, and at some point I'll need to wash these."

"They'll be loose on you, but you can wear some of my other clothes."

It didn't take long for him to lead us back to his small home in the woods. The clothes he'd offered me the previous evening were sitting folded on the chair that sat near the fire.

"They'll be too big, but we can belt the pants and roll the sleeves."

Before I could even ask, he stepped out and closed the door behind himself. I changed quickly. As soon as I'd removed Temple's riding breeches, I realized how good it felt to be out of the dirty garments. I longed for a bath, but that would have to wait. It wasn't as if there was a tub inside the cottage. I'd have seen it immediately.

After tugging on the new trousers and a soft, long-sleeved linen shirt, I felt much better. The trousers were a light tan, the shirt a muted blue. Both were too large, as expected. I found some rope on a shelf that could be used as a belt. The shirt sleeves took several attempts to fix, but eventually I rolled them tightly enough that they stayed at my wrists. I threw the Shade's cloak Orion had given me yesterday over the attire, already anticipating the chill of the Meadow.

"Ready!" I announced, throwing the door open.

Orion raised an eyebrow at my outfit, but if he had any negative opinions, he was smart enough to keep them to himself.

"In that case, Celia Hipnosi, let's show you the Ether. I didn't have time to tell you much about your new surroundings yesterday, but this walk will be a good opportunity. After all, if we're partners, I should try to make sure you don't get yourself killed before you can return home."

His tone had left open to interpretation whether or not he was kidding.

He'd spoken of death in such a nonchalant manner. Before explaining himself, he turned and walked into the forest.

"You did warn me not to wander. Aside from Charon, what dangers does the Ether hold?" I demanded as I ran after him.

He turned with a smirk.

"Unfortunately, many things, but if you stay with me you should be safe enough."

"Is that confidence speaking, or cockiness?"

Orion pulled the neckline of his shirt to the side, revealing his shoulder and the top of his chest. A raised scar bisected his collarbone.

"Experience."

I reached a hand up, but he slid the shirt back in place before I could be so foolish as to touch the scar.

"That looks like it was deep. Something here caused that?"

"I've been in the Ether for a hundred years. I've had more than one thing go wrong and leave me with a scar. Not that I didn't have a few before I arrived here. You said you weren't the 'ideal' lady, and I guess I'm not much of an ideal nobleman. I was more interested in collecting experiences than tailored suits. And those experiences occasionally resulted in some mishaps."

I snorted with laughter.

"Be grateful you were up against suits and not corsets."

"Ah, yes, fearsome and constricting devices, so I've heard. They're still using those, then?"

"To my undying resentment, they are indeed. If you'd met me on any day other than New Year's Eve, I'd have been wearing both a corset and a vibrantly pink dress."

He looked into my eyes.

"You don't like pink, then?"

I started to shake my head, then stopped, chewing my lip.

"It's complicated. My father has pink eyes. Many Hipnosis do. But sometimes it would be nice to just be myself and not a well-behaved Hipnosi."

It felt a little bit like a betrayal of my family, but it was how I'd felt. Searching for my father, sneaking into the library and reading Holmes's journal. All for a purpose, but also the greatest adventure I was ever likely to have. A substitute for the traveling and exploring I wanted to do, but couldn't, unless I wanted to devastate my relatives and their reputation.

"I understand 'complicated,'" Orion said.

His expression fell back into a frown. He scanned the trees around us. The lights that danced in the sky were still vibrantly orange and purple.

We made our way in silence for a while. When the trees grew sparser in the distance, I guessed we had to be nearing the Meadow.

Orion turned to me.

"Who are we looking for? Your husband? He's fortunate, having someone dedicated enough to follow him here."

I shook my head, and for some reason felt my cheeks heating at his assumption. I realized that while I'd mentioned my family, I'd never said who I was searching for.

"Not a husband. My father. He disappeared during the Unseen Hour when I was twenty-one. There was no body, but I knew he'd been Taken. He never would have left us otherwise. Then I started snooping. I found out he wasn't the first to disappear without leaving a body behind. One of the Holmes brothers ..."

"Go on," he urged as I gave a sheepish smile.

"And some others over the years had gone missing during the hour. The king was lost at sea during an Unseen Hour, and the queen believes he might still be out here. At least I think so, given some things my father was working on for her. Either way, I thought it was possible. I just had to find a way to follow my father, and I did it using y— ... some writings."

I felt it best not to mention that I'd dug through his dead brother's private possessions. There was no way that would endear me to him. It made me sound like a silly, lovesick girl at best, and a ghoul at worst.

We'd hit the treeline, but Orion wasn't looking out at the Meadow. He was watching me.

"Your father is lucky to have a daughter this dedicated to him. My brothers and I were that close as well."

"I'm sure they were wonderful. Did you have a lot in common? Did they also get involved in a lot of experiences and *mishaps*, as you put it?"

He laughed.

"Not the same as me. I was the heir, and later the duke. I had to be a little more composed, earlier than my younger brothers. They had more opportunities to travel just for the joy of it, but somehow they managed to do a better job avoiding trouble. Or at least avoiding the consequences. I stepped in to help with that."

"You were protective of them," I observed.

"Very. When I ended up here and realized they weren't also … that they'd died …"

"They were very lucky to have a brother who cared about them so much."

Definitely the right call not to ruin things by blathering that I had fallen half in love with his dead brother's words on a page, while reminding him of the fact that a bunch of papers stuffed in a rarely used section of a library were all that remained of the people he loved.

Orion cleared his throat, adjusting the neckline of his shirt.

"So, the Shades."

"Right. With any luck, I'll find my father today, and then we can discuss the trip home."

For a moment Orion froze, then he tilted his head at me.

"Today? We're not finding anyone today. Oh no, Starlight, we are merely observing, so I can show you what goes on in this realm."

I wanted an answer regarding the nickname, but not more than I wanted answers about my father and the Shades.

"Why not today? Why drag me back to the Meadow if we couldn't look?"

He sobered.

"I wanted you to see this realm, and the part housing the Shades is one of the most important. I doubted you had much of a chance to observe yesterday, still acclimating to the realm. The only area with more meaning than the Meadow is Charon's home, and we aren't even going to get close to that. I'll tell you which areas of the Ether are safe, and which to avoid. For now, though, let's focus on the Shades."

In the distance, I could see the crowd of Shades, swaying in the still air.

"Can we get closer?" I asked.

Orion shook his head, and for a brief moment I wondered whether Pellix might have been a better partner for this endeavor. Unlike humans, the stallion never argued. He'd have gone cantering into the field of Shades without a second thought.

Orion sighed.

"I'm not trying to frustrate you."

"You're very good at reading people, aren't you?" Or I was very easy to read.

He shrugged.

"The Shades are my only neighbors, and they're not exactly expressive. In comparison, you're positively theatrical."

His blue-flecked gaze lingered on me again; then he cleared his throat.

"This is the first day after the Unseen Hour. At some point, Charon will be patrolling, checking the count I provided of his newest recruits. He's likely to summon me as well."

"To ask you about the Shades?"

"And rant and rave about his issues with the other gods and his ultimate plan for his centennial hour."

"What *is* his plan?"

Orion took a breath and started to speak, but nothing came out. He cleared his throat and tried a few more times before giving up.

"The thing about gods, or at least Charon, is they're powerful. I'd wager he's as lonely here as I've been, but he doesn't want to risk me spilling his secrets. Even to the unresponsive Shades. If he orders me not to discuss something, then I have no choice but to remain silent."

I drew back, eyes wide.

"That's awful!"

A hundred years, and no one but the wilderness and a god for company, one who was sounding worse by the minute.

I gulped when something else occurred to me. I hated to ask, but ...

"He noticed something wrong yesterday. If he asks about me, will you have to tell him?"

Orion shook his head vehemently.

"No. We may not know each other, but I promise I wouldn't have whisked you into the forest if I wasn't trying to help. I'd have just handed you over first thing. Charon does not appreciate secrets or delays. He wouldn't be pleased to find out I lied to him. It's a risk, but I wouldn't have done it if I didn't think I could pull it off."

Orion shuddered, and my anger for the god whose existence I'd only just learned of grew even more.

"Now then"—Orion pointed, and I looked back at the Shades—"let's start with Shade basics. They're exactly what they sound like—shadows of their former selves."

"That's exactly what I thought yesterday!" I blurted, shocked that he'd captured my own thoughts.

"The Ether holds their souls, but make no mistake, they are dead."

The entire concept was still overwhelming. The churches always preached that when our lives ended, we went to a realm of Death or Day, but what happened there was only discussed in vague terms.

"If they still are, or have, or whatever the wording would be ... if they still possess their souls, does that mean they remember themselves? Could I speak with one?"

They hadn't been helpful yesterday, but they'd been new to the Ether, just as I had been. Maybe they were different once they were settled.

Orion shook his head, then paused.

"Well, yes, and no. Their emotions and thoughts are dampened in the Ether. Something about this realm suppresses it. You'll have noticed when you arrived that emotional reactions were quickly squashed. They just float around the Meadow."

"But?" I pressed, sensing there was more.

"You *can* talk to them. It can be frustrating, and it's difficult to rouse them enough that one stays engaged long enough to respond, but it's possible. I've attempted it quite a few times over the years. It never turned out as I'd hoped."

His shoulders slumped, and I reached a hand out, placing it on one of his arms.

I had been on the verge of another question but bit my tongue. He'd been down here, virtually alone, for nearly a hundred years. What did that kind of isolation do to someone? I sometimes felt alone and trapped in a house full of family.

Orion, though, had none of that.

He was right. The Shades, for all they looked like people, did not behave like them. Even as blurs in the distance, I noticed how they didn't appear to engage with one another beyond clustering together.

"What *does* make the Shades interact?"

Orion ran a hand over his neck.

"During the Unseen Hour, they come alive, so to speak. It's as if ... as if all the longing and grief and fear that they must have felt when they arrived are bottled up all year. When the Unseen Hour arrives, Charon sends them to the world, and it's all unleashed. The closer we get to the hour, the easier it will be to get a response from them. After they call the new souls down, that's when they're most deflated. It would be hard to talk to any of them right now."

My eyes widened, and I threw a hand over my mouth.

"The Shades? Are they the ones who ..."

"Yes. Using Shade song, as I mentioned earlier. Charon's fog covers the Shades during the hour, so they move around Rayus virtually unnoticed, unless you hear one. All Shades sing. I don't think they can help it. My theory is they're drawn to the ones they once loved. Shades from Emrys go to Emrys, those from Mejje to Mejje, and so forth. There are even Shades that haunt any ships unfortunate enough to be caught on the seas."

Ships like the one the king was on when he disappeared.

The need to scream was growing. I'd stuffed down the terror of my arrival the previous day, but now it was being brought viciously to the forefront of my mind. Using the souls of our loved ones to attack us.

As for the Shades—if the hour was when they were most aware, did they know? Did they have to watch, helpless to intervene, as they lured their neighbors and friends to their deaths?

Orion took my hands in his, the resulting warmth distracting me from my terror.

"The Shades lure the souls, thanks to the magic they derive from Charon and this realm. I used to love music," Orion reflected. "I attended every concert. I followed the news of every new cellist, or singer—anyone with talent. After hearing the Shade song, though, I could go without ever hearing music again."

Something in my heart broke. I loved music as well. I remembered when I'd first met Orion, how even his terse voice had sounded like a melody.

"Do you sing, too?"

Orion looked at the ground, purposefully away from me.

"I command the Shades and sing the new souls back here once they're already deceased. I can resist singing in Emrys, but I have to call the Shades."

"Why? Why not resist? Surely you could—"

Orion put a finger to his lips.

"Charon," he whispered. Not seconds after he spoke, a chill ran through me.

Orion pulled on my hands.

"We need to go. Now."

He led us back into the woods, where the trees grew thicker again.

The chill of Charon's arrival had sent goosebumps running up my arms, and the fear in Orion's voice had me moving all the faster.

We were well away from the cold when it registered that my hand was still in his.

It wasn't like this was the first time I'd held hands with a man. I'd had men escort me, and I'd of course danced with them, but running through the woods together was somehow more intimate.

I wondered if his hands would feel just as warm caressing my face, holding me around the waist as we danced, sliding underneath my borrowed shirt.

Cursed ghosts.

It had to be the Ether. I was otherwise alone, in an unfamiliar place. I was away from Emrys and all its constraints. That had to be what had my mind thinking such ludicrous and scandalous things. And mere months ago I'd thought myself nearly in love with the mere memory of a different man.

Then again, Orion wasn't a memory. He was very real.

"Why are we running?" I asked, pulling my hand away, and immediately regretting the empty chill that spread through my fingers.

"I intended for us to be gone before Charon arrived. Normally I have a warning before I see him. Getting this close to the centennial hour, he must be growing excited, changing up his routine."

"Where does he stay the rest of the time? Could another not-Shade like you be hiding there?"

"I'm not showing you Charon's residence. I'm not even sure I could, and if I did, could you promise you wouldn't run straight in looking for your father?"

I scowled at him, but had to admit the truth.

"I would if I thought there was a good chance of finding him. I didn't go through all this, and come all this way, only to be denied."

"And I'll help you as much as I can. But I won't risk you to Charon unnecessarily. I don't want you to get hurt."

He glanced over his shoulder as if he expected Charon to materialize behind us.

For all I knew, he could.

"You barely know me," I countered once I saw that we weren't being followed.

The blue in his eyes blazed.

"I know enough. I just mean ... I haven't had anyone *real* in my life for quite some time. I don't want the first person I get close to put in any more danger than absolutely necessary."

For a fleeting moment I thought the look on his face was one of longing. It certainly mirrored the expression that men wore at balls when they were gazing at women I knew they wished to be with. The sky was transiting from orange and purple back to green and blue. I put it up to a trick of the light.

"Why look out for me? You're close to Charon; you've admitted as much. Why work against him for the sake of some woman you've just met?"

"I might be close to him, but I have just as much reason to despise him as any victim of the hour."

It made sense, and yet ...

"You could still work against him without me, though. You

don't owe me anything. Wouldn't this just be dangerous for you?"

With every word I uttered, Orion looked tenser. His jaw twitched, and he began to pace.

"I have to help you. You're the only one I can save. All the others who made it here like us are dead." Orion clenched his fists. His voice was anguished, and the wild look in his deep grey eyes told me he was haunted by whatever he remembered.

The problem was, he'd previously told me that, as far as he knew, we were the living Shades.

I was trapped in the Ether with a liar.

CHAPTER 20

Orion had sworn I was the only other being in the Ether who wasn't a real Shade, but he'd just admitted there had been others. I planted my feet, praying to both gods that I'd misunderstood.

"What do you mean *dead*? I'm the only other one like you who's appeared, right?"

"That's not exactly what I said."

"Bloody ghosts," I muttered, squeezing my hands into fists, "It might not have been what you *said*, but now I'd like to know what you *meant*."

It was too important a distinction to leave to chance or miscommunication.

If he actually was helping Charon to somehow harm others like me ... I'd run. I'd hide and find a way to fend for myself. But I sincerely hoped it didn't come to that. I was quickly becoming accustomed to company, and to the freedom that came along with the Ether and the absence of Emrys's rules. Spending all my time merely trying to survive against a god *and* a man with a hundred years' experience in this realm was not something I wanted to attempt.

And, I had to admit, being around Orion was nice.

"You're right, Celia." His use of my actual name made me look back up at him. "I was ... dishonest. Not intentionally. I shouldn't have said you're the only one. I mean, you are currently. I've never spoken to another, because I was always too late before meeting you. But I've seen a few others like us. Not dead, but Taken and in the Ether regardless. I would have helped them, too, but Charon got to them all first."

He shuddered, and I hung on his words.

"And what did he do when he discovered them?"

"Obliterated them. Smote them into nothing but ash that floated away into the air. I don't even know if *dead* is the right term for them. Charon despises Death, and he is loath to relinquish anyone to her clutches. I imagine he simply erased the souls off the face of Rayus, or the Ether. Simply gone."

My breath came in shallow bursts. It was enough to shatter even the most devout believer's view of the gods, and I was far from exemplary when it came to religious devotion. If Death was real, shouldn't she be doing something? Shouldn't Day? Because if she existed, and Charon existed, surely he did as well?

It didn't matter, though. At least not as much as the very real scenario staring me in the face and breaking my heart. Tears pricked at my eyes.

"Then he could already be gone. It could be that my father was here and eliminated as well. Did you get a good look at any of them?"

I clutched at his shirt, tugging on him and then leaning into him for support when my knees threatened to give out. He wrapped one arm behind me, and it was the only thing keeping me upright.

I'd come all this way. I'd been so convinced ...

I tilted my chin, looking up at him and the pity on his face.

"My father was tall, broad-shouldered. He would have been not far past fifty when he made it down here. He has hair just a shade or so lighter than mine, and striking pink eyes. He—"

Gently, Orion pulled my hands off his shirt, steadying me as I tilted. He squeezed both my hands between his own, the warmth centering me.

"None of them were men that age. There was a lone woman. She looked like a housemaid. There was a younger man once, and he appeared to be a blacksmith's apprentice. Another man had black hair and a short black beard. He looked like a sailor, based on his clothes. The only other man I've seen was old, grey-haired and bent. He was dressed in furs like those from Tang. None had pink eyes."

Orion slowly sank to his knees, lowering us both, until we were seated on the ground. He leaned me up against a tree trunk for support, then moved so he was crouched in front of me.

"I didn't mean to worry you about your father. I just wanted to be open with you. Are you all right?"

I was still trembling, but I managed to nod.

"It wasn't him, then. He could still be here," I reassured myself. "How embarrassing."

Reaching up with one hand, I wiped the tears that were running down my cheeks. I wasn't afraid to show my feelings, but showing them outside my own home would have started all sorts of rumors in Emrys. You never knew who was watching. You never knew what they would say.

That the house was in trouble, that I was involved in some tryst gone wrong, that I was a hysterical woman prone to fits. The possibilities were endless.

It was simpler to pretend. But I was so incredibly tired of pretending.

Orion reached up, tucking a piece of loose hair behind my ear. My breath hitched.

"I'm sorry. I should have clarified right away, but I was most concerned with getting you away from the Meadow, and then making sure you trusted me enough to stay away from Charon. I haven't had anyone else I could really talk to in so long … I guess I'm not very good at conversation anymore. Not very good at being human at all, really."

"I wouldn't say that. I'm still breathing, right? I'd say that's a success." I smiled at him and received the smallest shadow of a smile in return.

I sniffled.

"I warned you I'm not much of a lady, and so if you're not much of a nobleman, that's just fine. We'll both just be temporarily displaced misfits down here and figure it out together."

His smile spread, and the blue flecks in his eyes gleamed. The impact was dazzling, and I wanted to find ways to keep that expression on his face.

"Deal. One aspect of being a nobleman in Emrys I have kept is making sure I deliver on my promises. I always keep my word, and you have my word that I will be honest with you going forward. And that if your father is here I will make every effort to get you both home."

Once my breathing was even again, he helped me to my feet. It didn't take us long to make it the rest of the way to his cottage; we'd been closer than I realized. It really was well-hidden between the trees.

Orion held the door open for me as I made my way inside.

"I will have to go to Charon when he calls for me, and you'll have to stay here. There's food on the shelves"—he gestured at the wooden pieces built into the walls—"and perhaps a distraction would help while you wait? What do you enjoy? I don't have many traditional materials for embroidery, but I do have needles and thread and cloth—"

I scoffed.

"Not a talent of mine. If push comes to shove, I could mend a hole in our clothes, but trust me when I say you don't want me to embroider anything you care about."

He laughed, reaching one hand up to tousle his hair.

"No? You did warn me. Honestly, I've grown used to my own hobbies down here. You'll have to tell me what you're interested in doing, and I'll see if I can make it happen."

My legs still felt shaky beneath me. I desperately wanted to run back to the Meadow and search for my father. It made no sense, after years of him being missing, but now that I was here it felt as if I had to hurry or risk Charon finding him first. But Orion was right. If Charon had eliminated the others like me, I needed to be careful.

I sat on the single wooden chair near the fire.

"I enjoy riding on my horse, Pellix. I can play the piano. I like to read."

He grinned.

"I'm fresh out of horses, but I do have several books. You can entertain yourself with those until I get back. Once Charon summons me, I may be gone for a day or two, although of course I would have given you the cot anyway. When I return I'll work on making another one, and another chair."

"Did you make everything in here?"

"Yes, everything, inside and out. I had to if I wanted to survive. I mean, there are times I've questioned whether that was the right decision, but I've stuck with it, so I guess my survival instincts won out."

I didn't get a chance to even begin formulating an acceptable response to such an admission.

Fog descended, filling the small cottage before dissipating.

"That's how I know Charon wants a word," Orion explained.

I eyed the disappearing fog warily, scooting the chair as far away as the space allowed.

Orion gestured to a short, wooden bookshelf that I hadn't given much attention to before. It held an entire row of books, the needle and thread he'd promised, and a few other items. All notable remnants from Emrys.

"How did you get books down here? Or any of this stuff?" I asked.

"That will require a bit of a long explanation, and I shouldn't keep an impatient god waiting. I promise to keep your presence here a secret, and to give you answers. In turn, you have to promise to listen to me. Help yourself to the books, and the bed, and the food. But stay here until I get back. Agreed?"

I didn't like being cooped up, but I far preferred Orion's company to getting myself killed by an angry god.

"Agreed."

"Very well. When I return we'll resume your tour of the Ether, and I'll answer more of your questions then."

He tugged open the door, then walked out, closing it behind him.

I walked to the bookshelf and was starting to read the titles when another thought struck me.

Does he have to walk all the way? Is Charon nearby?

"Orion?" I called out, but there was no answer.

I decided to open the door, just a sliver. I wasn't going to follow him, but I did want to see where he was headed. I looked in every direction, but there was no sign of him. He had disappeared into the woods as easily as his home did.

I'd simply have to stay in the small cottage until he came back.

I made my way over to the table and did end up eating some of the bread and fruit that were available. Then I perused the bookshelf, picking out an adventure story. While I hadn't yet mastered time in this space, I knew I was tired. I lay down on the cot, pulled a blanket up over myself, and began to read.

Within minutes, my eyelids drooped. It appeared that even a night's sleep couldn't stave off the emotional exhaustion of the Ether.

CHAPTER 21

Orion was right when he said he wouldn't return right away. I woke to find him still gone. I ate, then left the cottage only long enough to find there was a small privy built not far off. I wiled away the better portion of that first day rifling through the contents of the cottage and reading.

By the second morning, my skin practically itched, I was so eager to leave, but I'd made my choice. If I trusted Orion about the god, I had to trust him about the rest. That meant there was more in this forest that could kill me, and if I got myself killed I'd never find my father or get home. That, and I'd given him my word.

I started the second day with a new book. This one featured pirates off the western coast of Emrys. The story was full of action, intrigue, and even a romance between the pirate captain and a woman who had been brought onboard at one of the islands between Emrys and the continent of Mejje.

In the book, the whole thing sounded exciting and romantic. It was nothing like the strained relationships we actually had with the other countries. Where our country had its own theories of the origins of the Unseen Hour, everyone else had the same theory.

Since the Unseen Hour had hit Emrys first, it was our fault and our responsibility to fix it. Civility had returned in the ensuing years only because we relied on one another for various goods. Necessity, however, was not trust.

No other country trusted Emrys.

I frowned and returned to my story.

"The amber rays of sunset kissed the top of the waves. Sky and sea, expansive and unknown. Full of possibilities. Just like their love," I read aloud, repeating the passage for a second time.

I'd spent the past year engrossed in the diary, but the writing style of this book kept my attention in a way nothing else had since I'd started my process of finding the Ether.

For all my restlessness, the book was a nice distraction. Once I finished the final chapter, I sighed, leaning back against the dirt wall. For a few moments, I closed my eyes, warmed by the fire, and let the story linger in my veins, as good books tend to do.

"Napping on the job?"

I jumped up to see Orion striding through the doorway. There were circles under his eyes, in spite of his statements about not aging here, and the blue sparks dancing within the grey were dimmed.

What must it be like, assisting Charon? Since Emrys didn't worship him, I had nothing on which to base a guess at his personality. I had recalled his name from texts, but I couldn't claim to be overly familiar with the religions in any of the other countries.

I had already decided that Charon must be the cruelest of the gods, having stolen so many lives and subjected the Shades to the torture of preying on their loved ones.

Orion practically fell into the single wooden chair before the fire.

"You found something to your liking?" He gestured toward the book.

I held it up, showing him my choice.

"I read another book first, and then finished this entire story," I admitted.

"You're a fast reader."

"I couldn't help it. I was engrossed. The way the main pirate character describes the world. The way the two of them looked out for each other, and appreciated each other. The exploration and hunger for new experiences. I've always felt like that's what love should be. A breathtaking adventure."Orion was smiling at me, eyes brightening.

I bit my bottom lip.

"I'm glad you liked it," he said.

"You have good taste in books."

His cheeks went ever so slightly pink, and it drew my attention back to the circles under his eyes.

"How did your meeting with a god go?"

Perhaps the most ludicrous question ever to escape my lips. After learning about the Shade song, I could not have cared less whether Charon was happy, but I found I did already care about Orion's well-being.

It made sense. After all, he was my only real companion here. That probably accounted for the closeness I felt toward him.

Orion ran a hand over his face.

"Charon was pleased. We ended up with the largest number of souls this decade. He smiled when recounting the grand total. As if all these lives we're ending are a good thing."

"Is it the Shades that do the actual killing? You mentioned

the song, but does that just draw people in? Is Charon not the one who deals the final blow?"

"I promised you answers, Starlight, and you'll have them. Just for now, though, could I answer one of your other questions? I also swore I'd give you a proper tour. You should learn your way around the woods. I can tell you what's safe and what to avoid. After we get the basics down, I'll explain where I got the items in the cottage that you asked about."

"And Charon? The Shade song?"

He nodded.

"I'll answer that as well, but being around him is draining. I typically come here and rest for days. Truth be told, I'm quite happy to not be returning to an empty house, but I'd prefer it if we could avoid Charon, just for now."

Once the color faded from them, even his cheeks looked a bit sunken. Just a couple of days with the deity had left him looking ill.

And I *did* need to know about my surroundings. After all, it was likely I would remain in the Ether for a year, and I wanted to be able to look after myself when Orion was stuck performing his duties as Head Shade.

I could wait until he recovered. There were plenty of other things I wanted to learn about aside from Charon.

"Yes, let's go take a walk."

Orion smiled, still looking tired but much more relaxed as the tension fell from his shoulders and he stood up.

"You've already seen the lights and the moon. I think you'll enjoy the rest of the woods. At least I do. Many things are awful about being stuck here, but there's plenty to explore. All sorts of plants you can use for food. Animals. Some I was able to hunt as needed, and some are quite friendly. Others, not so much, but I'll teach you to watch for signs of their territory and avoid those places."

"Animals?" I perked up. I missed Pellix as much as I did my brothers. Odds were, he was fine. Someone would have found him, or he would have returned to the barn for food. He didn't tolerate others riding him easily, but he never missed a meal.

Still, the stallion's welfare weighed on me heavily.

Orion led us back out into the woods. Within minutes, his cleverly camouflaged house had disappeared into the distance behind us, and we were walking on a trail, narrow and faint, that he must have worn over the years. It followed the ribbons of light overhead. They were once again purple and orange instead of blue and green, weaving through the sky.

I'd noted there was no pink, which was just fine with me.

"Is it a way to tell time? Warmer colors are daytime?"

"Very sharp! Took me what I'm guessing was a week here to realize that. When it's just the moon overhead, and blues and greens make an appearance, you know it's truly night. There is no such thing as full daytime here, though, as I'm sure you've already noticed. The nights are long, and as you saw upon your arrival. I follow the colors, but I've lost all sense of a normal routine down here. I do keep a count, though, so I know when the hour is approaching."

"Was it difficult to adjust to that change? And where did you sleep when you first arri—"

Something large and snarling leapt out of the trees toward us. I screamed, stumbling backward and throwing up my hands.

"Get behind me!" Orion yelled, placing himself between me and the creature stalking toward us. Decidedly not one of the friendly animals he'd mentioned, then.

This was a feline of some sort. It looked similar in size to the wolf that had found Pellix and me years ago, though I had no desire to get closer to be certain. Emrys had wild felines in its own wilderness, but they didn't grow past the size of a bear cub. And I'd never been hunted by any, thank both the blasted gods.

I was certain, though, that this creature existed nowhere in Emrys. Its fur was a shimmering green, shining like fish scales.

It would have been the most beautiful creature I'd ever seen if it weren't baring its fangs at us, hissing, and didn't have large claws glinting in the colorful lights.

For the first time in my life I thought I might faint, no corset required.

The cat snarled, swiping at us so I got a good look at its claws, but I forced myself to hold my ground.

"What do we do?" My voice trembled as much as my limbs.

"We distract it and get ourselves away. I hunt in the woods here, but a slycat is tricky to take down. Escape is our best shot."

Something inside me relaxed, just a hair.

Fighting? Fighting was something with which I had very little experience, unless a sharp insult counted. Sneaking and running so I didn't get caught? Those were things at which I excelled. Distraction and a quick getaway: that was the key.

"Are you able to keep it watching you?" I whispered.

Orion tilted his head, glancing at me out of the corner of his eye.

"Are you planning to do something foolish?" he asked.

"I'm planning to help us. Now, can you keep its attention on you?"

"If you move slowly. If I hold my ground and you bolt, it will hunt you down."

The rest of my tension fell away. I didn't have to do this alone. I placed a hand on Orion's shoulder.

"Good! Make it mad."

Orion lunged forward, yelling. The cat jumped back, then snarled again.

While Orion ducked and dodged the cat's paws, I disappeared into the trees around us, searching.

"Come on, come on! Something."

I stumbled around the woods, wishing I knew them as well as the lands surrounding Scopshaven.

"Bloody ghosts!"

I cursed entirely too loudly as my toe found what I was looking for. I'd stubbed my foot on a sizable rock. Wincing at the pain, I crouched and managed to heft it into my arms.

My preference for rides on Pellix rather than embroidery was arguably a deficit in Emrys. Not a usable skill at all when you were trying to advertise yourself as a potential wife. In this case, though? Riding and caring for a horse gave me stronger muscles than most people might have assumed.

I threw the rock as far as I could manage. It arced in the air and crashed into a pile of fallen leaves. The slycat yowled, sprinting to investigate the potential new threat.

"Come on!" I urged Orion, standing and waving him over.

When he reached me, he grabbed my hand and hauled me along as he raced deeper into the woods.

"Let's stop here for some rest," he suggested when we were well away from the slycat.

He'd brought us to a small creek running through the forest.

I sank into a crouch and then fell onto my backside with an ungraceful plop. Tucking my knees up and wrapping my arms around them, I stared at the bubbling creek. The steady sound of the water somewhat soothed my anxiety.

"Are there many of them, those slycat things?"

Orion shook his head.

"Not in this section of the woods. It's part of why I stayed here. When I first arrived, I ran into a mother with her cubs, and then several more sets farther east. I had no desire to live where there was a pack of the things, so I built in an area I saw they stayed away from. The closer you go to the Meadow, the fewer large animals there are. It was a balance, finding a spot away from the Shades but also away from the predatory animals."

I looked at him, tilting my head.

"Why away from the Shades? According to you, they don't do much of anything. Can they be dangerous, too?"

Orion stared at the water, unblinking.

"Not physically, but they're a reminder. A reminder that I'm not dead but not really alive. That I'm under Charon's authority. That I have to lead them up each year to call the souls of their friends and family to this doomed land."

His voice was haunted.

I couldn't even begin to imagine what he had gone through. Losing his life, losing his brothers, and then being forced to repeat the night that ruined everything, over and over. Having to take part in other peoples' suffering.

One trip to Emrys where I was forced to try to hurt my brothers would have been enough to undo my sanity for good. And Orion had gone back to Emrys ninety-eight times after his own hour.

He was still looking at the water, watching it move over the dirt and rocks.

I reached for his arm, and he jumped, looking to where our skin touched. His breath caught.

I gave him a determined stare.

"We'll all get out. The three of us. Together. You must be the strongest person I've ever met to have survived this place alone for so long. But you're not alone anymore."

"I'm beginning to realize that," he murmured in a rough voice that caused a wave of heat to build between my legs.

Orion leaned in, one of his hands reaching up to hold my face, and I nearly forgot how to breathe.

"Starlight?"

"Yes?" I sounded hoarse to my own ears. I felt the thrill of his touch all the way to my toes.

"You're bleeding. You must have scratched yourself on one of the branches. Here. Let me help."

If I was, it wasn't the only reason my cheeks were red. I wrestled with embarrassment. What was I thinking? I had no business being drawn to the Head Shade when he was just trying to help me.

He leaned down, cupping some of the water in his hands and letting some trickle down the side of my face.

"Oh." I was certain I was still blushing furiously. "Thank you. I'll just …" I reached up, wiping at my face with my bunched up sleeve. Just a few drops of red stained the fabric when I pulled away.

I was still in Orion's clothing. Tan trousers and a flowy shirt. No vest or overcoat or intricate buttons. No dress or underclothes.

Just a single layer of fabric.

I swallowed, my throat a little too tight.

Orion wore similar attire to my own, but with darker trousers. The flowing white shirt also looked much different over his chest than mine. Not that I was looking.

"Thank you, for distracting the slycat. And for trusting me," I offered.

"Thank you for luring it away," he responded, breaking into a grin. "Exhilarating, though, wasn't it?"

With a laugh, I had to admit he was right.

"Yes, it was. Much more entertaining than a summer ball!"

"Or a meeting of the lords."

"Or being fitted for dresses."

Some of the torturously sweet tension I felt between us melted away as he continued to speak about our home.

"I concur. Before I came here, the men's fashions in Emrys were intricate. So much pomp and circumstance just to ride into town. I must have wasted so much of my life just getting dressed for the day."

I nodded, thinking his outfits had nothing on the many layers of women's fashion.

"And for what? None of it is comfortable," I said.

"I heartily agree. Another benefit of being down here—you can be comfortable instead of fashionable. Although I'm sure many people would find that horrifying."

I snorted, covering my mouth with my hand. I could think of several members of the nobility who might find a lack of suitable fashions more off-putting than the Shades.

It took me a moment to regain my composure.

"I didn't expect there to be animals. Or woods. Or books. I didn't know what to picture, honestly. I just kept thinking of who I wanted to find and tried to prepare myself for an inhospitable environment awaiting me."

Orion's expression drooped a bit.

"It's inhospitable enough. Unless things have changed in Emrys, you were brought up the same as me—believing in two gods who divvied up souls when they died. An afterlife of shadows, or light. But either way, one of peace and rest. As you can see, the Ether is nothing like that. It's got things that will ensnare you with their beauty, but it's far from an idyllic place to spend a lifetime."

He looked around the forest, and I waited, sensing he had more to say.

"This place may be run by a god, but it's a land just as real as Emrys, or Sez, or any country in Rayus. The only thing it lacks is people, and the influence they bring. There are no roads, or shops, or cities. Just nature and its inhabitants. And of course Charon and the Shades. Not all bad, but I would have traded anything here in a minute to escape my own company. I'm not especially interesting as a conversational partner after a while."

He gave a forced laugh.

"Well"—I beamed at him, my expression equally forced—"now you're stuck with me. You may soon wish you had your silence back."

This time his smile looked genuine, reaching all the way to his eyes.

"Actually, I haven't been in silence. And I think I know what to show you next. My favorite conversational partner, aside from myself, and now you, of course."

He pointed to a branch overhead.

I scrunched my eyes. Then, with a flutter of movement, I saw it.

A small bird with feathers of varying dark blue shades, blending into the darkening sky. The creature hopped through the branches with ease, just a glint of black under its wings.

Orion cupped a hand over his mouth, then gave a series of sharp chirps and whistles. The bird began jumping from branch to branch, flying in short bursts on its way down to us.

"I call them tree hoppers. Very smart little birds. And they like a certain berry that grows in the woods. It's tasty. Perfectly safe for us to eat. I learned a lot from the animals here. It's a shame your first experience was with a predator, but many of them are more helpful than anything else. You can learn from them, and they're good company. I leave food out for the tree hoppers and have even set up some obstacles for them to work through. They're quite clever, and sometimes they bring me things like"—he stopped, giving me a sheepish smile— "They're the closest thing to friends I've had."

If he was concerned about me poking fun, he needn't have worried. After years of friendship with Pellix, it made complete sense to me that the birds could be excellent companions as well.

The tree hopper jumped onto Orion's outheld hand. It tilted its head and clicked its beak.

"Sorry, my friend, no food today. Visit tomorrow, and I'll make amends." The bird took wing and flew away as if it understood. Orion turned to me. "I know they can't really respond, but when you're alone out here …"

"You talk about them like they're your friends and neighbors. I do that with my horse, Pellix, sometimes. He's better company than most of the nobility in Emrys."

Orion laughed.

"If things are similar to when I was there, I'm sure that's true. It's the same for many of the animals here. They're certainly less conceited than many humans I've met. I've always appreciated animals. We had a dog at our estate that I was quite fond of, Terris. He was meant to help with the sheep, but in the evenings he loved to lie at my feet. Long gone now, I'm sure."

My heart lurched. Returning to find Pellix gone would crush me. And the thought of living for decades in a forest with *only* Pellix for company wasn't any better.

He must have been terribly lonely.

Orion was sitting with his legs kicked out to the side, one hand bracing him. Throwing caution to the wind, I reached for his hand, lacing my fingers through his. It wasn't as if it was the first time we'd touched, but this was more intentional.

Orion sucked in a breath, his head whipping toward me.

I gulped.

"When we find my father, that will be even more company for you. Then, at the next Unseen Hour, we can all go back to Emrys. If whatever home you had is gone, my family will help you."

I would do everything I could to make sure Orion had another chance at the life he'd been denied.

Orion smiled.

"Tomorrow, we can begin looking. Charon rules here, but aside from the time just after the Unseen Hour, he takes little interest in the Shades until it draws near again."

When we returned to Orion's home, he fixed us a plate of dried meat and bread.

"You know, you still owe me some answers as to how you have all these things," I reminded him, finishing off the bread.

"If I tell you my secrets, are you going to tell me yours?" He smirked.

"Perhaps," I managed. Maybe he did have a sense of humor, when he wasn't being summoned by a god.

He offered to sleep on the floor again and give me the cot.

"I'll get to work on a second one soon. Then we'll both have somewhere comfortable to sleep," he said when I tried to object.

I crawled under the blankets, warm and comfortable.

Long after his breathing evened out, I was still lying awake.

My thoughts were stuck on everyone I'd left behind. Ambrose and his lectures, Mother and her insistence on pink. Bram and his smile, and Temple with his somewhat haughty charm but quick wit. When I eventually managed to push the thoughts of my family away, they were replaced by Charlotte and Thomas.

My eyes began to water.

"It will be worth it," I whispered to myself.

Soon enough, I'd have my father. Maybe we'd even get lucky and find a way back before the next Unseen Hour.

CHAPTER 23

"Breakfast," Orion announced the following morning, tossing something at my head. I fumbled to catch it. Sometimes, like when I rode Pellix, I could pretend I was graceful. This was not one of those times.

I'd never excelled at any garden games that required hand-eye coordination. The last time I'd attempted shuttlecock the blasted thing had smacked me in the forehead, leaving an ugly red welt. Ambrose and Mother had relented after that, content to let me watch everyone else.

Playing the piano and horseback riding were the only times when I was able to demonstrate any real grace with my movements.

I took a tentative bite out of a round and purple fruit—and then a much larger one, when I realized it was both sweet and tart.

"Delicious," I admitted.

Orion smiled.

With the adrenaline from the first few days wearing off, I was less focused on sheer survival and growing constantly more aware of how comfortable it felt spending my time around Orion.

How natural.

A man whose poetic brother had captured my attention with stories of his adventures; something Orion had already shown me plenty of in person. Maybe the three brothers had been similar.

"Here, try this one."

A second fruit was lobbed at my face. I barely managed to shield myself with a blanket. The fruit smacked the thick threads and rolled down to my lap. I lowered my hands to find a pear— my personal favorite fruit. I bit into it eagerly, the juice sticky on my chin.

"Do the other Shades have to eat?" I questioned between bites. At least I was mannered enough to not ask with my mouth full. Mother would be so proud.

"No, they don't. Another exception reserved for you and me. I have found, though, that I need far less than I ate in Emrys. The garden here has plenty of fruits and vegetables," he informed me.

"Garden?" My ears perked up.

"Yes. I didn't get around to showing you yesterday, since our animal encounter took more time than anticipated. It's just around back."

As soon as we'd finished our breakfast of fruit, he led me around the trees that held up the small home, and I saw the cleared patches of dirt between the trees behind us. Just like his house, it was hard to spot unless you went under the branches looking for it.

"And there's food year round?" I questioned. "Even without sun?"

I'd already decided that the more I knew about this place,

the more likely we would be to succeed. But I also wanted to know because I liked listening to Orion tell me about the Ether.

It was a bit like living in an adventure story, if not for my knowledge that the entire place was little more than an enormous prison.

"The soil here is very fertile. It does rain, but you're right about the lack of sun. Either way, I've never had a problem."

My own gardener would be envious from his toes to his teeth if he knew. Our estate boasted a convenient proximity to town that in no way detracted from the sprawling views, but the openness had made it difficult to protect certain plants from the weather. Scopshaven had a greenhouse, but I knew our gardener, Thestle, would have sacrificed a lot for this kind of natural environment.

"Does Charon eat?"

"Not that I've seen. Why?"

"Then why would he have fruits?"

"The same reason he has animals and plants, I suppose. He has fields of flowers and a forest of trees, as you've already seen. He is not Death, and he enjoys living things. With there being all sorts of creatures in the Ether as well, it stands to reason they'd need something to eat."

"And it's all safe to eat?"

Orion frowned.

"Much of it. What I told you about observing the animals helped me a lot, but I've made a mistake a time or two. It turns out half-Shades can still make themselves quite ill with the wrong supper, but overall I've been lucky."

I was torn between insisting we leave for the Meadow and my innate curiosity. My stomach growled, making the decision for me as I plucked another pear.

"How did you get seeds here to grow things like pears? Did Charon procure them for you?"

The frown that was already becoming all too familiar clouded Orion's face.

"No. I figured it all out myself. Some things I planted already existed in the Ether, but I brought back seeds to grow the others."

Along with his supplies.

He swept his hand out at the gardening tools. Several were clearly handmade, but there were others that must have come from Emrys.

"You've been asking how I supplied myself here. I promised to be honest, but I'll admit to being a bit ashamed as to how I acquired everything."

"Ashamed?"

He nodded.

"I stole it all. During the hour, Shades can't touch and hold things the way people can. That's why barring the doors keeps them out. But I'm not a typical Shade. A few years in, I figured out that I could grasp things. It took practice. As far as I can tell, it's driven by intent and desire. I have to really want something, and focus on it, to be able to grasp it. I never told Charon. I was afraid he'd send me into homes. I try to take only what I need, but I will say my definition of *need* blurred a bit over the years."

"Like with the books."

"Yes. Exactly. Not strictly a need for survival, but believe me, it was necessary for my slipping sanity at the time. A way to feel like I was connecting with another person, even if it was only through their words."

That statement spoke to my heart. He needn't have justified it to me.

"I'm always watchful during the hour. You'd be surprised what people leave outside while running for shelter."

My mouth dropped open.

"Do you think less of me?" he asked.

"Not at all. It was incredibly clever, figuring that out. You did what you had to do. I was just wondering how many items people have chalked up to misplacement or thievery over the years that were actually brought to the Ether."

He ran a hand through his hair, and I stared at the muscles of his forearm when his sleeve slid down his arm.

"I also have taken items from the Shades here, on occasion. That has been rare, and only when I truly did need it. Like the cloak I took to cover you. I just don't want you to think of me as nothing more than a common thief."

"Oh, you're anything but common."

Extraordinary, even. I was in serious peril of finding myself entranced by yet another Holmes brother.

After breakfast, Orion led us back toward the Meadow.

He'd given me the choice of exploring more of the woods or facing the Shades. I felt I'd been delayed from my search long enough.

It was nice, freeing even, to express my opinion with no restraint. I didn't worry about whether I would offend Orion. He'd not once reacted to me as if I were too loud, too opinionated, or too much in any way.

He'd let me use his first name, and his home. Not at all what I would have imagined a man from his time to be like.

I would have wagered anything that Orion wouldn't have assumed I wanted to get married without asking me personally first. Wouldn't have bartered with my brother for my hand when I was perfectly capable of deciding such things myself.

That particular secret was burning a hole in me.

Not that I'd kept it hidden on purpose. Bellamy was far from my top priority. I also hadn't chosen him. My stomach soured, anxious thoughts tugging at my mind when I remembered my unwanted fiancé.

Surely, assuming I was deceased would be enough for him to call off an engagement?

I'd hated leaving my family and friends behind, but with Bellamy? Getting away from him would be an unexpected positive outcome of this entire affair.

"Almost there," Orion said, holding back a tree branch for me.

We exited the forest, and almost immediately I felt the world grow dimmer. Surprising, considering the Meadow that held the Shades was technically lighter, with no foliage overhead to block the sky, and the strange floating orbs that lingered among the Shades. But the floating souls somehow dulled the whole area. Orion was right. The Shades had no real life in them, and this was merely a holding place for thousands and thousands of people in between Unseen Hours.

"What if this is a bad idea after all? Why would my father be among the Shades? Surely he'd be in the forest with you, not here? How would he survive here, where Charon could find him?"

The truth was, I was almost afraid to look. If I found him but was wrong about the state he was in ... I wasn't sure what I would do.

"The woods are large. Perhaps your father has stayed away from me for the same reason you were hesitant to trust me. I'm Head Shade, after all."

"Perhaps."

I still didn't move. I knew I needed to. It was foolish to come all this way and stop now. I'd already looked for him when I first arrived. But now, somehow, the plan felt more real.

A couple of the orbs floated in our direction.

"Do you know what these are?" Orion asked, tone light.

I shook my head. "I tried to figure it out when I got here, but I haven't a clue. I thought they might be lightning bugs in a jar, but I was wrong."

"You were close. Watch this."

Orion placed his palm under one, guiding it gently closer to me. Then he reached his other hand up and stroked a finger over the top of the sphere.

It burst open, the flower-petal soft casing reshaping into two large, luminescent wings.

I gasped.

"It's a moth!"

He smiled, watching my reaction.

"Mostly they float. I think they trap the air inside their wings somehow? Use the heat and light they produce to stay up? But they can fly." He pushed his hand up, and the creature flitted away before wrapping itself back into a sphere.

"Not as clever as the birds, and they mostly stay in the Meadow. They're warm, though."

"And beautiful," I said.

"Yes, breathtaking."

I turned to see him looking at me.

"Ready, Starlight?"

He held out his hand, and I took it, letting him lead me toward the Shades.

CHAPTER 24

"You distracted me so I'd calm down," I observed.

"Did it work?"

"Yes. I appreciate it. It's silly, maybe. I was ready to risk the trip down here, without knowing what was awaiting me. Now that I'm here, though, now that I know there's a chance he could be in the Meadow as a Shade and not how I'd hoped to find him—it's as though if I don't face it maybe it won't be real."

Orion squeezed my hand reassuringly.

"I can relate. When I first got here, when I realized what was happening ... there weren't so many Shades back then, of course. Not in that first hour, when it was only Emrys. I recognized many of the people who had been Taken. Seeing my brothers like that nearly shattered me."

"Oh, Orion. I'm so sorry." I felt ridiculously dense. Bloody ghosts, I'd been going on about my father and hadn't even considered that he'd already found his family in the Ether. That they'd been here with him for years upon years.

If I'd been stuck in the Ether, with no guide and no way of

knowing at first what was happening, and I'd seen Bram floating around, I might just have gone mad.

"You shouldn't have had to go through everything alone," I said.

"It took me a while to adjust to this place. At first, I tried to save them. I tried to find a way out, just like you're trying to do. Then, when I'd come to terms with the fact that I couldn't get them out, I avoided the Meadow for quite a while."

I didn't blame him.

"I grew used to it, eventually. But coming here with someone else, someone alive—it's very grounding. I'm not glad you're *stuck* here, but I am glad you *are* here," he admitted.

In spite of the obstacles I faced returning to my family, and the threat that an angry god might descend, I agreed. I felt more at ease with Orion, wearing trousers and wandering through the woods, than I ever had in a drawing room or at a dance.

I wanted to tell him, but I felt as ill-equipped to express that feeling as he said he was, being human. I was out of my depth.

When I stopped walking, Orion turned to me, put his other hand on my shoulder and looked me in the eyes.

"Are you ready? I know you said you wanted to check the Shades, but I don't want to rush you into anything, either. I want you to find him, but if you don't want to see ... if you'd rather I search the Shades ..."

"I appreciate it, really I do. But I need to see for myself. We should go through the Shades. Although, looking at their numbers, I can see that it might take weeks."

"It's a bit easier when you realize how they're clustered. They float and flit, but I find that they tend to be drawn back to certain groupings, just like they're drawn to who they know in Emrys."

He kept my hand in his as he walked me around the Shades,

and it fought off the worst of the Meadow's chill, warming me all the way through.

"Over there you'll see people from Mejje, in their silks and flowy fabrics from the warmer environments. That cluster adjacent to them is from Sez. The leather and other thick fabrics are designed to protect them from snake bites and sharp teeth. That cluster of individuals wearing warm furs is from Tang, not that they feel the chill here."

"And do you feel it?"

"I think I've grown used to it, after so many years. Honestly, I don't remember ever being bothered by it; just aware of it."

He was clearly thicker-skinned than I was.

We spent the afternoon walking the entire perimeter of the Shades. I could see, when we hit portions of the Shades wearing fashions like what my mother described from her grandparents' generation, that they could be organized by relative timeline as well as region.

There were exceptions, Shades that had wandered farther than others, but they were largely bound by the location and time from which they had been taken.

We did our best to come up with a count based on Orion's memory of each Unseen Hour and some admittedly questionable math on my part from tallying the Shades. Then we divided it by how many individuals we realistically thought we could approach in a day.

I kept a sharp eye out, but I didn't see my father. A combination of relief and worry surged inside me.

We returned to the edge of the woods later in the day, stopping to eat under the sparser tree cover before walking all the way back to the cottage.

Orion passed me a pear.

We chatted a bit more about our lives before the Ether.

"And what about travel? Did you have a chance to do much of that before you ended up here?" I asked.

I knew, based on R.'s journals, that his brother had.

Orion shook his head.

"No. Well, technically yes. I did travel a fair amount, but it wasn't the kind I would have liked. I accompanied my father on some journeys related to businesses our family supports, but I never had the opportunity to explore places in the manner I would have wished. And you?"

He had to know the answer, but he still waited patiently for me to respond.

"No. Ladies rarely get to travel. Although I would like to see everything. The islands of Sez in particular. They're said to have some unique animals and plants. I'm betting I could bring them back with me ... the plants, not the animals. Although ..." I grinned at him, and he chuckled.

"I am hard-pressed to imagine the wild animals of Sez in an Emrys stable, but you distracted the slycat; maybe you'd have luck with Sez's animals as well."

"At least with the Ether, I'm getting to see some interesting wildlife. Honestly, this may be the best, and quite frankly only, adventure I've ever had."

He tilted his head, flashing a grin at me. My heart stuttered.

"Glad I could do something for you, Starlight."

"Thank you, *Ry*." I waited to see what he would make of the new nickname. His face froze for a moment, then he laughed again. This time, his smile reached all the way up to his eyes, and the blue glinted within the grey.

"Ry and Starlight. A duo of would-be explorers who went farther than we ever anticipated," he said.

When he said our names together, something thrilling and dangerous stirred in my chest.

CHAPTER 25

We'd spent two weeks watching and mingling with the Shades. I hadn't seen my father, although I had come across a few vaguely familiar faces from Emrys.

It was disconcerting each time, and I could only imagine what Orion had gone through, watching the number of souls grow over the years. We'd started with more recent clusters of Shades first, so we hadn't gotten anywhere near his siblings. I would follow his lead on how to deal with that situation.

I had tested Orion's theories on interacting with the Shades. If I touched them and got their attention, I could ask them a question. Their responses were muted, and limited, but some of them did engage. Others were frustratingly silent. I'd found that trying to evoke strong emotions brought more reliable responses and heightened interaction.

"I'm sure you'll see your son again someday," I reassured a crying Shade whom I'd upset when I mentioned children being separated from their parents.

It hadn't helped. The woman burst into tears and didn't answer my questions about my father at all. I was thankful the

Shade's tears dried almost as soon as I stopped talking to her, and she went back to floating along with all the others, any signs of despair disappearing as her expression flattened once again.

"Any luck?" Orion asked as he joined me.

I shook my head.

"No. They barely speak to you at all before they get distracted. Some won't even talk to me to begin with." A few Shades stared right through me when I attempted to get their attention. "You?"

"I found someone from Mejje who said they had an Emrys-looking gentleman milling about. It wasn't your father, though. He was far too portly to match your description, and the style of his clothing was nothing like you described. Or his eyes. Those were brown. Then I tried a section with Shades from several years back. I got a couple of reactions from people who knew your father, but no one that had seen him here."

"You're still doing much better than I am. I've upset several of the Shades, which I assure you was unintentional."

I wasn't trying to traumatize anyone.

Orion shrugged, and I watched the slight movement of his strong shoulders. I was back in my brother's riding jacket today. When I wore Orion's clothes, they were loose and baggy, but on him they were fitted and accentuated the muscles he'd gained fending for himself in the Ether.

"I've had a lot more years to practice, that's all," Orion said. "You've already figured out that eliciting those stronger, personal emotions livens them up a bit more. I'd had loads of frustrating one-sided conversations before I stumbled on that knowledge."

"Have you spent a lot of time talking to the Shades?"

He'd said as much, but I hadn't realized the amount of effort he'd put in. Of course he had. He'd had no one else down here.

The Shades were his only option, even if they were duller than an old blade.

"I know a fair amount about some of these Shades. Not that they're aware. They don't really recall much from one short conversation to the next. I tried, though, for the first decade or so, to get them to engage. Since then, I've had some bouts in the ensuing years where I got lonely or frustrated enough with the isolation to try again. It's easier as it gets nearer to the hour, since they're livelier then. But it's not a real friendship."

He'd gone still, glaring at the nearest group of floating Shades. I was learning to watch his expressions, and the way they correlated to his moods. Remembering what he'd gone through in the Ether elicited an immediate frown.

I had all sorts of things I wanted to know, but I had tried to space out my questioning.

I didn't want to cause Orion pain, any more than I wanted to hurt the Shades.

"Why don't we take a break and eat something?" I suggested.

He uncrossed his arms, and I held out my hand. He took it without hesitation. We often walked like this. It kept me warm, and while I couldn't say for certain, he looked more relaxed when we walked together.

The only drawback was that the contact was having increasingly strong results. I'd thought I would grow used to it. Instead, the more we touched, the more my mind wandered to questions like what his hands would feel like on other areas of my body. Whether the rest of his body would feel as warm, pressed against mine.

We stopped under a tree, and Orion rifled through a small bag we'd brought from the cottage. He pulled out a root vegetable that grew here. Deep purple, a bit like a potato, but soft without needing to be cooked. I bit into it eagerly.

Orion watched the Shades while we ate, and I decided to try a different tactic.

"I've seen a couple people I recognize. There was a lady I tried to speak to yesterday. She used to work at a dress shop in the capital. She said hello, and I think I might have seen a brief flash of recognition, but then she got quiet again. It's odd, interacting with people when they're not really, well, people anymore."

Orion let out a short sound that might have been agreement.

"And then I wandered over to those from Sez for a while. Just in case my father decided to hide himself there. After all, if he's not really a Shade, he'd be less likely to stay with groups from Emrys. At least that's my thinking. It might be tougher to stay around people you knew and recognized when they're like this."

"It changes day to day, honestly. At least for me. Sometimes, I wanted to be as far from the reminders as possible. Sometimes, I wanted something familiar, even if I knew it would end in disappointment. And sometimes I did what you tried, for different reasons of course. I'd approach those from other countries. Try to learn in small bits and pieces everything I could about them. Closest thing I can get to real travel in the Ether."

I felt the urge to embrace him. He was as trapped as I'd felt in Emrys.

"You must have learned a great many things. I, for one, have been both shocked and thrilled at the women of Sez. I think we can both agree that trousers are a lot more practical when moving around than layered dresses."

Orion nodded, turning away from the Shades and back to me.

"Too true. And those from Mejje often conceal weapons under those billowing bits of clothing. Between them, and the materials Sez uses for their own outfits, I was able to come up with my own holsters and methods of transporting things. I often carry a dagger around the Ether. Actually, I should make you something so you can have a weapon as well. Not sure why I didn't think of it before."

Likely because he'd been building himself a new bed and chair, as he'd given me his. And he'd had to do it while working around the long hours we'd spent searching for my father.

He smiled, and those blue flecks in his eyes sparked to life.

"Yes, I think some sort of holster would be a fun project. You could wear it on your thigh, since you're not encumbered by layers of skirts, as you pointed out."

"And not missing them in the slightest." I smirked.

His gaze lingered on my leg, and that curious feeling returned. A small part of me wanted to tuck my legs back so he couldn't see, but a much larger part wanted to know what it would feel like to have his fingers trailing their way up my thighs. My heartbeat raced at the thought.

He cleared his throat, looking away.

"Do you know, I would never have expected to see a Hipnosi in anything but layers of pink. You are certainly a surprise, Starlight."

"Did you know any Hipnosis then? Before coming here, I mean?" I asked, intrigued.

"Even a hundred years ago, everyone knew about the Hipnosis. Your family has held wealth and power for centuries, longer than mine, I believe. My family may be dukes, but everyone respected the input of a Hipnosi."

My father wasn't the first to find himself closely helping a monarch. Some long-dead Hipnosi generations ago had been incredibly close to a former king, and the connection had continued for years. My father had even once shared a theory, really more of a family secret, that the Hipnosis had quietly turned down a chance at becoming dukes, or once marrying into the royal family. They wanted to keep the relationship as uncomplicated as possible, not giving the crown any reason to think we were grasping. In exchange, we had wealth and lands that frankly overshadowed any other noble.

"And you interacted with my family?"

"Your great-great-uncle, perhaps, would be the one I knew best. He liked to tinker with things."

"Uncle Albert?" I'd never met him, of course, but we had portraits of the family tree at the Fox Haven estate. My father had told us about our predecessors. Uncle Albert was known as a bit of an inventor, perhaps also a bit of an eccentric, but very intelligent.

"That's the one! He was always entertaining to be around. Always had some new contraption to test out. One time, he brought a whirring, flying thing into the library in the capital. They were furious. He nearly got us thrown out. Would have, if our fathers hadn't stepped in. He was actually part of what inspired me once I was down here. I thought, Albert came up with some ingenious contraptions. Surely I can figure out a way to make the most basic necessities."

I smiled, pleased to hear about the connection.

"Shame we're not looking for Uncle Albert, then. He sounds like he could be quite helpful." I tried to keep my tone carefree but didn't think I quite managed it.

I had known it wouldn't be easy. Still, I'd hoped by now to have some glimpse of my father. Even if he was a Shade, at least I'd have found him. Instead, he was nowhere to be seen, living or otherwise.

I was about to suggest we get back to work when a silent lightning strike hit the ground in front of us. Scrambling backwards, I kept my ears open for the echo of thunder that would typically follow such a strike, but it never came. A figure stood where the lightning had landed, wearing a long and elegant hooded cloak. When the new arrival moved, they floated toward us, and my muscles tensed.

My throat felt too tight to breathe.

"Charon," I managed to whisper, terror shooting through me.

"No"—Orion reached for me—"not Charon." He looked back and forth between me and the advancing figure.

His eyebrows scrunched, head tilting like he was trying to make up his mind about something.

Seeming to decide, he put another hand on my arm and helped me to my feet.

"Come on. It will be all right."

Even so, he stood between me and the advancing figure. I clutched his hand like a lifeline. His warmth spread to me, a familiar comfort even after such a short time. Albeit somewhat lessened by the looming figure that was getting closer and closer.

When the cloaked being drew to a stop in front of us, I craned my neck. The figure was just as tall as I remembered Charon being, even if it wasn't him. As my shock wore off, my natural curiosity flooded back.

I slipped around Orion, now standing directly in front of the individual.

"Hello," I said.

The figure reached up and pulled back the hood of the cloak. I froze.

The woman in front of me was ethereal. Her hair shone with a white light brighter than a star in the night sky. The skin on her exposed neck was the same ivory as bone. Her eyes still weren't visible. Instead, a black silk mask covered them, along with a good portion of her cheekbones, with not even slits to see out of. It was a wonder she could get around at all, I thought. She looked like someone attending a masquerade ball.

Her head craned forward, and I sensed she was looking at me.

"Orion"—the woman's voice was rich and full—"and who is this enticing creature?"

I recovered my manners enough to introduce myself.

"Celia Hipnosi. Charmed to meet you, er—"

I extended a hand, unsure what else to do without knowing who I was addressing. The figure raised a palm, stepping back.

"I'm afraid we'll have to keep this as a 'look but don't touch' situation. At least if you'd like to stay alive," the woman warned.

I gaped, but her voice held no venom.

Orion stepped up beside me, gesturing between me and the woman.

"Celia, allow me to introduce you to Death."

CHAPTER 26

Death.

At least this deity was one I was familiar with. The other countries of Rayus had their own ideas as to how many deities there were and how they divided up tasks. I was kicking myself for not being more of a religious scholar, because then I'd be aware of particulars.

I knew I'd been wrong in regards to the number, but it was somehow reassuring to find out the god I'd been beseeching in my prayers was more than just a figment of my imagination, even if history had neglected to mention she was a *goddess*.

The people of Emrys had thought themselves cursed by Death, or abandoned by Death, but we'd all hoped we could also be saved by Day or Death.

Maybe that was still possible.

"Pleased to make your acquaintance." I dipped into a curtsy, responding on impulse as the reality of what Orion had said hit me and trying to correct my earlier, more casual greeting.

The deity smiled at me with perfectly straight white teeth.

"I hope you don't mind my barging in on what looks like a pleasant afternoon. I had some business with Charon and thought I'd stop by to see Orion. A living Shade is such an intriguing concept, after all."

"I thought Orion said that you and Charon were at odds."

There went my attempt at formality. I threw a hand over my mouth.

Death laughed, the sound musical like chimes in a garden.

"We certainly are that. The others and I are often at one another's throats. It would be more concerning if any of us could die. After all, among six deities there are bound to be occasional squabbles."

"Six!" I exclaimed.

"Yes. Five boisterous men, and me. Hardly fair, is it?" She leaned even closer, and I got the distinct feeling she was winking at me from behind the mask.

I grinned, drawn in immediately.

"It is exhilarating to see another woman in a position of such authority, even if the purview is a bit—"

"Macabre?" Death supplied.

I grimaced.

"Yes. I would say that." I still had no desire to upset a god, but Death was charming. As much as anyone I'd ever come across in Emrys. It was also exciting to have someone else to talk to who would answer back.

Frowning, I turned to Orion.

"I thought you said Charon was using the Shades under the noses of the other deities. If Death is aware of what he's doing ..."

Death laughed again.

"Charon does not know that I know. When I meet with him, I summon him to my own realm. As fun as it is being worshipped across Rayus, we each have our own space to escape to. I invite Charon, and that's when I pop down here, knowing he's stewing over how long I'm keeping him waiting.

It's best to do your snooping when you know you won't be interrupted, wouldn't you say?"

That was something on which I agreed with her. I beamed at the deity.

"Call this a hunch, Celia, but I think you and Orion are going to help create a very interesting event. Very interesting indeed," she said conspiratorially.

I set my shoulders back, barely daring to breathe and determined not to look away. Death was so close that the hairs on my arms stood on end from her static. As if lightning might strike again at any moment.

Strange, I always pictured the embrace of Death as a chilled, empty thing. Not a striking, warm surge of power.

It didn't create the same comfort as Orion, particularly not when Death began to circle me.

"Orion here has been helping to gather some information for me ever since I discovered my brother's little attempted coup. Perhaps you'd like to join him? I could make it worth your while. There must be something you want."

My father. My father and a guarantee that my plan to get home would work. But something even bigger shoved its way in front of those concerns. If I did get him back, I never wanted to risk losing those I loved to the hour again.

My father had tried to get to the Ether because he wanted to protect his entire family. I would do the same. I'd protect everyone, if I could.

"Could you end the Unseen Hour?"

Death smiled.

"I am already attempting that. That's what I've been working toward, and why I've enlisted Orion's help. Now that you're here, I think we might just stand a chance. I will, however, have to put some thought into our methods. If you help, how could I repay you personally?"

A generous god. I doubted even more that she had been the one to curse us, or had any involvement in Charon's actions. Did gods who cursed your country go around handing out benevolent favors?

Small sparks jumped to life on Death's arms before I could respond, and the deity spun around, agitated.

"Charon grows impatient. Think of what I've said. I'll return soon."

Lightning struck the ground, inches from my face, and Death vanished. The only sign she'd been present at all was a small tendril of white smoke rising from where the lightning had hit the Meadow.

I stared at the spot where the deity had stood, cursing the missed opportunity.

Orion laid a hand on my shoulder.

"Don't worry. She'll return. We'll ask about your father then."

I sank into him, and he wrapped his arm around my shoulder.

"Come on. Let's get back to work."

I watched the fading smoke.

"What she said about stopping Charon's coup—does that have anything to do with Charon's own plans for his centennial hour?"

Orion grimaced, his arm tightening around me.

"You can't say, can you?"

He shook his head, the movement jerky.

"Just this. If we can help Death, it would be best for us all, and anyone in Emrys we care about."

As we approached the Meadow, he slowly relaxed again, but I could tell it hurt him. Whatever Charon did, whatever power the god had to force him to stay silent, it was a kind of torture.

I would have helped Death anyway, for myself and my father, but I wanted to help her even more for Orion.

Charon had tormented the Head Shade for a lifetime, and if I could manage it, he would face consequences equal to the crime.

With a god on our side, it might just be possible.

By mid-February, according to my tally of the days, we'd searched a good portion of the Shades. When we stopped to rest, we would talk, or read. Orion had noticed how much I loved the books in his home and had taken to bringing one along in his pack with our food.

The more time we spent together, the more Orion opened up. I'd seen a reduction in his somber expressions, and he'd begun sharing his experience without my prodding or carefully navigating around the conversation.

"I only met Death a couple of decades ago. As you can imagine, I was thrilled to have someone else to talk to. I even asked her to take me with her," he admitted.

Two competing emotions shot through me. Wanting Death, wanting to end the solitary existence he'd had here ... I could understand it, even if I hated it. I only wished he'd had someone here with him sooner. There was a smaller part of me, though, that felt a pang of jealousy. Ridiculous. I had no claim on Orion, and he hadn't even been speaking of the god in a romantic way.

"She said no?"

"She said she wasn't able to. The gods have their own rules, or laws. Whether they are bound by them physically, or they just adhere to them, they've not bothered to tell me. But she was here looking into the hour and wanted my help dismantling that. I was only too happy to offer it. In exchange, she said once it was over the Shades could all be freed."

"And Charon doesn't suspect the two of you?"

"Death thinks he's too prideful, lulled into a false sense of security. At first, the Unseen Hour was as much a secret as Charon hoped. Somehow, with his fog and his freezing of time, I think he kept its existence concealed from her and the other gods. Maybe the other deities just weren't that watchful of what happened in Rayus. She's never told me how she was tipped off, but I've got to imagine that eventually the number of souls *not* entering her realm as expected would have raised an alarm."

"And have you met any of the other gods? Are they helping as well?" I scooted closer, taking a piece of fruit from him.

"No, and Death only speaks of them in vague terms. It's difficult to discern if she has favorites, but she most certainly wants to stop Charon. The whole Unseen Hour, and all the collected Shades, are meant to rival her and her power in some way, but she found out before Charon could act. Charon has his own plans for this hundredth hour, but there's no way Death will stand by, not when she's at risk."

He tensed up for a moment, then took a breath and relaxed. I guessed that last bit was something Charon had tried to keep silent. Maybe if Death had reiterated it, that made it easier for him to share without whatever painful consequences Charon caused?

"Is he trying ... to overthrow Death, or take her place?"

I'd done what I could over the past several weeks to take the things Orion could tell me and collect them. Small clues and puzzle pieces.

He grimaced, giving a curt nod.

I gasped.

"He can't do that!" From my brief encounter with Death,

and what I'd been told about Charon, I could only imagine him exerting his influence outside the bounds of his hour. To have that sort of terror as the norm year-round?

Unfathomable. And we couldn't allow it to happen.

Orion bit into a crisp vegetable as vibrantly orange as a carrot but much sharper in taste.

"And how do you help Death?" I asked, hoping that topic wouldn't cause him any discomfort.

"There's things she's asked about over the years. Tidbits about Charon's residence, the Ether. She can make short forays here, but she can't get into his more intensely warded areas. I, on the other hand, am invited in. And when I'm around her it becomes easier to discuss the things Charon would rather I keep quiet. Sometimes the gods' powers come in handy that way."

Up to this point, I'd only wanted to avoid the gods' wrath. Earn their favor if it helped us.

But I found myself wishing I could help him the same way a god had the ability to do.

CHAPTER 27

"Ry?" I asked a few weeks later, likely into March if our count was right. We were back at his home in the woods for the evening.

We sat outside, staring at the green and blue lights dancing between the trees.

"Hmm," he responded, working with a piece of leather from his stockpile. He was close to finishing the holster for my knife.

We'd fallen into a comfortable camaraderie, one I was worried my desires might ruin. Orion had been nothing but a gentleman, although my own reactions were well into the realm of scandal. Even watching him put the finishing touches on the holster, the sure way his hands moved was torture. My skin pebbled, imagining his hands feeling me, his fingers stroking against my skin.

I cleared my throat, aware he'd been waiting too long on my response.

"How *did* you come to be the head of the Shades? Did Charon assign you that role simply because you're still alive? Was it because you were here with the first group of Shades?"

Orion ducked his head down a bit, fiddling with the knife

that he was using to shape the holster. The muscles in his arms flexed as he worked, his sleeves rolled above his elbows.

"For both those reasons, and I suppose it's because I'm the best at using Shade song. I personally think I excel because I'm *not* a full Shade, and therefore more closely related to those we're drawing into the Ether. That's just a theory, though."

I chewed on the information for a moment, twisting my hair into a bun and then letting it fall over and over.

"Why does it matter, though? Can't Charon claim all the souls himself? What does he even need Shades for? He's a god."

Why pull humans into this ridiculous spat he had with Death? The more I thought about it, the more infuriated it made me. We were pawns, cannon fodder, expendable. It wasn't fair.

Orion gave a tense smile, cutting into the leather with force.

"Even gods have limitations. That's one thing I've picked up in my years here. Just because Charon is powerful, doesn't mean he's *all*-powerful. Shades and Shade song are what allow him to conduct his business within the Unseen Hour. He'd move too slowly otherwise. I suspect he has to expend a lot of his own energy simply to make the Unseen Hour exist. And I've noticed as I become familiar with the magic he wields that he's concealing us somehow during the hour. Not just with the fog, but with the way he impacts time."

"Not just from his victims, then. From Death? Since he's trying to overthrow her?" Understanding the politics of the gods might have been easier if I'd known more about them. I'd searched through Orion's collection of books for answers, and he'd shared the information he'd gotten from the Shades, collected carefully and painstakingly over the years.

Those in Mejje believed in a god that sounded a lot like Charon. They believed in four deities total, but they didn't name them. Speaking the name of a god there was considered blasphemous. The people of Sez had legends that conflicted, with anywhere from four to six. Tang, like Emrys, only believed in two, although they also believed in an older, more powerful third god from the lost country that they said had ceased to exist. Then, there was the lost country itself. I could not find any references to their religion aside from 'gods.' Even more odd, Orion had told me that he'd never seen someone from the lost country in the Ether. Maybe there weren't any people left there.

I realized Orion hadn't answered my question. He was still working on the holster, but I could tell he was tense. Another Charon secret, then.

A couple of tree hoppers landed in front of us. I smiled at them and tossed a few seeds in their direction.

Some grey squirrels joined them, eager for a meal. I'd asked Orion about the squirrels when they'd first appeared; what traits made them different from animals in Emrys.

"Nothing. Apparently everywhere has squirrels," he'd responded. Still, they were cute and harmless.

When the tree hoppers got closer, I pulled out one of my hair pins. This one had a pink jewel set on the end. There was no need for expensive stones here. The rest of the jewelry I'd brought along sat untouched, in a satchel in the cottage.

The birds hopped nearer, tilting their heads as the pin glinted in the blue and green light.

"Here, see what you think. It's more valuable to you than to me."

The larger of the birds snatched it gently from my fingers.

Within minutes, the two of them were using it together to scratch out food from the dirt.

"Ingenious things, aren't they?" I commented.

Orion still didn't respond.

I contented myself with bird watching for several more minutes before he let out a deep sigh.

"I didn't want to do it," Orion said. I rose, moving over to him and sitting on the ground. "I didn't want to sing souls from their bodies, leaving them like empty husks for their families to find. Instead I'm stuck with a job that's even worse."

I didn't want to say anything, afraid of breaking the moment.

"When Death showed up, I was only too happy to help her. We all die eventually, but the Unseen Hour is cruel. The song snares and entices people to their doom. It's a beautiful and vile weapon. And I've been at its forefront each time, leading the Shades as they create trails of frozen bodies. Just as guilty for guiding them as if I'd sung out the souls myself. And I've started to worry. What if we return during this hour, and you …"

"I just won't sing. I'll keep my mouth shut," I insisted.

Orion let out a humorless laugh.

"I think you'll find you're wrong, Starlight. It's like a compulsion, the song. When we hit the surface of the world it bursts forth, whether you want it to or not. Music that needs to escape. All the pain and suffering of being separated from your home over the past year piled up into one hour. It's like the needs and emotions of the Shades are tamped down throughout the year, and the hour is their only release. They can't help the need to free it. When we return here, they're calmer. More subdued, like you've seen them so far."

"And you?"

"Me?"

"How do you feel? Does it help you, being able to sing?"

There was no shame in it, when he couldn't help it. I didn't want him to pile any more suffering on top of what he'd already endured, but he shook his head.

"No. It doesn't help me. I'm aware enough of what we've done to come back choking on my own guilt each time. As soon as the hour, and my subsequent meeting with Charon, is over, I typically shut myself in the cottage for days."

One of the tree hoppers made its way back over, chirruping. I held out a hand and it hopped on my palm, still clasping the hairpin in its beak.

"You're doing all you can to help end the hour. No one could have done more. Don't cast yourself as the villain, Ry. You don't deserve that."

"I'd make a very morose villain. Nothing like what you read about. Large personality and power. Cruelty with flair."

I laughed, the bird cawing along with me. Orion gave me the tiniest hint of a smile in response.

"You'd never do as a villain. More like the determined and adventurous lead, throwing yourself into exploration and new experiences. A bit jaded, perhaps, but more than capable. Like the pirate captain in your books. Now *that* was a good choice. I'm glad you brought it back. I'm sure it's a loss to the library it came from but well worth the thievery."

He busied himself with the holster again, blushing and avoiding my eyes.

"Actually, it was already mine. No one else has read it. I wrote it myself."

My jaw dropped open. It took me a good three attempts before I was able to organize my thoughts enough to respond.

"*You* wrote? But it's so good! Not that I'm surprised, I just didn't realize you liked to write." *Maybe a family trait, given his brother's diary?* "Is there more?"

"I started a few things, but I abandoned them all over time. I wasn't as excited for it once I got down here. I could never quite get the stories right. I could never come up with a happy ending. It always eluded me."

I gulped, inching even closer.

"It doesn't have to."

"Maybe not," he agreed, setting the holster aside and grabbing one of my hands.

The longer I was in the Ether, the closer I wanted to get to him. I'd always enjoyed my own company. Even with Bram, or Charlotte, eventually the feeling of someone other than myself in my vicinity became too much. Like an itch that had been ignored too long and demanded to be addressed. I had to find my own space.

Not with Orion. He'd been summoned by Charon once more since my arrival, and I'd spent the entire two nights he was gone wishing he'd come back.

If it hadn't been for my search, Charon, and my concern for those I loved and had left in Emrys, I'd have to admit I liked it in the Ether. Orion was a large part of why. Always ready with new information about our surroundings, but still striving to learn more. Curious, intelligent. And apparently just as poetic as R. and his diary.

I knew our situation wasn't sustainable. When we returned home, I'd have to contend with my family, and possibly Bellamy, and who knew what story Orion would have to tell people. Unless everyone became aware of what we'd done, unless we had proof, we'd never be believed.

He might still be lost to his estate.

Orion dropped my hand, and the familiar chill of the Ether returned. I swallowed disappointment as he retrieved the holster.

"Finished," he announced, placing it in my hands. He flipped the knife so the handle was toward me, and then handed that over as well.

I slid it into the holster, then started trying to get the contraption placed over my thigh. The leather was soft and pliable and had plenty of give. No doubt it would be easy to move in, but I couldn't quite figure out how I was meant to keep it in place.

"I might require some assistance," I admitted.

"Of course. Here, let me." Orion reached for my leg and tied the holster in place with strips of very thin pieces of leather looped onto the larger harness. His fingers brushed my leg through the fabric of my borrowed trousers, and his cheeks went as red as I imagined mine were beginning to.

"Starlight," he started as he continued to work with the holster, "there's something else about the Shade song. It's the *only* way to save people, in a sense. Do you remember what I told you your first week here, about the others like us who I saw? The ones that Charon destroyed?"

I nodded slowly.

"They weren't the only ones he's done that to. He prowls the streets alongside us during the Unseen Hour. He enjoys the hour, even if he can't be everywhere at once. I've seen him in action. There have been a few times where a Shade was struggling to sing out a soul, or resisting. Charon eliminated the Shade—and the resisting soul."

I gasped.

"Eliminated? How—"

"No resting in the Ether. No going to Death. They cease to exist in any form."

"That's horrid! Why kill his Shades, if he needs them?"

"He said once that a soul not easily separated from a body wasn't useful to his purposes. If we don't sing them out, he destroys them. It's part of why I don't work harder to resist the song, and leading the Shades with it. I know the consequences if I do."

Everything I learned about Charon made him sound worse and worse.

What if that's what had happened to my father, and Orion hadn't been there to witness it?

Even if I managed to find my father, even if we escaped and Orion came with us, this was the risk we opened the world up to every year. And how could I help? If I did make it back, who would believe me? It was one thing to know the Unseen Hour killed people, quite another to show up announcing that a god no one in Emrys believed in was attempting to overthrow Death. To convince them that he had spirited peoples' souls away to an adjacent realm where he was rallying them for some strange and hostile takeover. I barely believed it myself, and I was living it.

No, the only way to stop it was to defeat the Unseen Hour.

All I needed was for Death to return.

"Finished," Orion announced, but he kept his hand on my leg.

Warmth shot through me, and an aching need.

When Orion moved his hand I nearly reached for it.

"I know it won't be much help against a god, but it could help with a slycat. I'll teach you to use the dagger. I'll feel much better if you have it, and I want you to feel comfortable defending yourself as well."

"I'd be glad for the help, but I can't promise I wouldn't try it on Charon if I ever do meet him. Especially after what he's done to everyone I care about. To you."

"Are you saying you're growing fond of me, Starlight?"

I wanted to get closer. To feel him. We'd been in the Ether together for weeks. No one from Emrys was there to pry. No one to gossip or judge.

Just the two of us.

"And if I am?"

I stared at him, part longing and part determination. We

had no idea what might happen to us before the hour. I wasn't wasting the time we had remaining.

Orion's eyes went wide; then, in a flash, his arm was around my waist, pulling me close.

"If that's the case, I might have to admit I'm falling for you," he told me.

He pulled me closer, until my face was an inch from his.

Falling for you.

True, he hadn't confirmed it, but it was more than a strong hint. I'd told myself for years that if I got a chance at adventure, I would take it.

I reached up, letting my fingers trail across the stubble on his chin.

"If that is the case, do you intend to do anything about it?"

"Starlight. May I—"

I crushed my lips against his before he could finish the question.

CHAPTER 28

Orion's fingers tangled in my hair. His lips were full and soft against mine.

Instead of sating the desire in me, the kiss just fanned it into a flame. As the weeks had gone on, I'd found myself thinking more and more frequently of what it might be like to have Orion's hands on me.

I reached out, wrapping one hand behind the back of his neck, pulling him closer. It still wasn't enough.

Orion moved his attentions, kissing just below my jaw, then all the way down my neck. I gasped when he reached a particularly sensitive spot.

He pulled back, looking down at my hand. Then, he leaned and kissed each finger.

"I've been wanting to do that for weeks now," he admitted.

"You're not the only one."

His kiss had awoken the increasingly familiar combination of heat and need between my thighs. It was the sort of longing a *real* lady would have ignored, if she'd had such a sensation to begin with.

I had no desire to do that.

The longer I spent with Ry, the more time I wanted to spend with him. We hadn't had any discussions about what life would be like in Emrys if, and after, we'd accomplished what we'd set out to do.

Part of me had wondered if he was afraid to get his hopes up.

We'd certainly made no promises to one another, and I knew that the situation would be complicated for many reasons. His long absence, my own reappearance, Bellamy—although I had to believe he'd moved on after months of my absence—plus the potential that we'd have a very upset deity after us for ruining his hour.

"You're frowning," Orion observed. "Now, I'll admit to being out of practice, but surely I can't be that bad of a kisser?"

"I've never been kissed," I said.

"Really?"

I shrugged.

"Keeping up with some sort of tryst, or becoming infatuated with someone I wasn't engaged to ... it would only have put me at risk of gossip."

"I got the idea that didn't bother you."

"It doesn't, but I never met someone worth the trouble."

He smirked.

"What about now?"

I put a finger to my chin, pretending to think.

"I suppose I'd to be open to it, if I found the right man."

He threw a hand over his heart.

"You haven't found him? I'm wounded. Tell me then, Starlight, what do you require from a suitor?"

"I want someone I can trust to carry my heart. Someone who has the same thirst to learn, and see, and explore. Someone who sees me. Not a Hipnosi, not a woman who needs to mind her place, but me."

And I'm pretty sure you're exactly that man.

Orion put a hand on each side of my face.

"I see you, Starlight. Since the moment you got here, it's been difficult to look at anything else. Your determination, your resilience, and your light."

"Ry. I never thought I'd find someone like you. Not here, of all places."

Then again, I'd been upset over the lack of options in Rayus.

A sudden chill tore through me, and I clung to Orion. Fog circled us.

"Bloody ghosts!" Orion cursed. "I have to go."

I was ready to march up to Charon myself and tell him off for ruining the moment.

"I know. I'll be here," I said instead.

I followed him out to the garden, grabbing a few of the purple potatoes while he walked away. He was lost in the trees in a matter of seconds.

Orion returned late the following night with news.

"He's growing paranoid. He's still tight-lipped on details, but he mentioned the other meddling deities. Either Death has been pushier than anticipated, or more of them are involved. Either way, he's said he plans to 'see for himself' what state his Shades are in. He'll be in the Meadow for the next few days."

In light of that rather large obstacle, we took the opportunity to spend more time in the forest. We hadn't gone far from the cottage since our slycat encounter, but it was always possible that's where my father was, anyway.

I'd felt better about his odds among the Shades or hiding in the Meadow than deep in the woods, with predators. Though perhaps the chances were about even.

I shuddered, picturing Father facing an angry slycat and its claws. He was smart, though. An experienced hunter. Surely he would know how to elude predators? After all, if he was in the forest, he'd also remained a secret to both Orion and Charon.

The following afternoon, we wandered through the trees. Just as we'd mapped out the Shades, Orion had sectioned off areas around his home to begin our search of the woods.

The swirling lights were purple and orange in the trees. The day had been pleasant. My hand was firmly in Orion's, feeling as if it had belonged there all along.

"I used to love being outdoors at home. Riding Pellix, or sneaking off to bother the gardener."

"At the rate you've gone through them all in the evenings, I'd have thought you spent most of your time reading books," Orion observed.

He wasn't wrong. I'd read everything on his shelf at least once, and some as many as three times.

I hopped over a log in our path. Taking a deep breath, I decided this was a good moment to bring up a particular book I still hadn't mentioned. R.'s words had comforted me and drawn me to the Ether. But it was Orion's words, and more importantly actions, that had caused me to fall for him once I was here. I wanted to be free of this particular secret, which was starting to seem more silly and less serious the longer I held onto it.

"I do enjoy books, but I like being outdoors even more. The year before I ended up here, there was one particular text that I took with me. In the garden, in the sitting room. It was a constant companion. A diary of one of the doomed Holmes brothers."

He stopped, eyes going wide.

I barreled on.

"I discovered it quite by accident, and I wasn't the first Hipnosi to do so. My father had written into the margins, between the lines, in every available space. He was working for the royal family, on a mission to try to figure out the king's disappearance. He thought the answer lay in the Holmes writings. That's where he got his idea for Thipp's root as a means to come down here, and where I did as well."

I kept walking, avoiding his eyes and waiting to see how he would respond.

"Once you told me about your father, I understood why you wanted to get here so badly. I've just never asked for more details about your methods. I didn't want to imagine you suffering. And now you say you figured the entire thing out based on a few scraps of writing? If all you had to go on was the word of a few papers, that must have been difficult for you. I'm graced with company as intelligent as she is intriguing."

I gaped at him.

"You're not going to ask about the Holmes aspect of the whole thing?"

"We'll get to that in a moment. After all, we have plenty of time to talk. I assume you're not going anywhere?" He smiled, eyes glinting.

He helped me over another, larger log, and I sucked in a breath as he released me, still feeling the places his hands had been.

"Not for several months yet. And if I did, we'd be going together."

There was no point denying it, because I had already made up my mind that I wanted to stay with Orion. I hadn't worked out how that would play out in Emrys, when we were subject to certain restrictions again, but I was hopeful the two of us could figure out something.

If he wanted to, of course.

And the sooner we accomplished what I'd initially come down here for, the more time we would have to discuss that.

Orion held back a branch so I could walk along the path easier.

"How *did* you figure out a way to get down here in the first place, and come up with the antidote idea?"

"It wasn't easy. There were times where part of me was tempted to give up."

"Not that you'd ever give in to such temptations," he said, an amused half-smile on his face.

I gave him my own wry grin in return.

"Of course not. Stubborn to a fault, that's me."

"I would have said *determined*."

I threw back my head and laughed.

"I like your version, I must admit. Truthfully, if I'd been caught, it would have been devastating. For my reputation— which I could have survived without. But I wouldn't have wanted to shame my family. The Hipnosi daughter, running around town in her brother's trousers and breaking into the library, what would people have made of such a thing?"

Orion scowled.

"Hearing you say it aloud highlights how ludicrous it is. While I wish you'd had the opportunity to put your investigative talents toward something less morose than finding your way to the Ether, it undoubtedly required skill. I ended up here by accident. You found a way here purposefully. I gave up on any hope of sending myself back, or ending the Unseen Hour, until Death showed up with a plan, but you came prepared to work for both goals. Even though we've been unsuccessful at locating your father, your resolve hasn't wavered."

He helped me through a tangle of thick branches. Tree hoppers filled the area around us with song, and I could hear the chittering of the grey squirrels as they clambered up the trunks of trees.

I sighed.

"You're not completely right about me. My resolve *has* wavered. I miss my father, and he is the main reason I wanted to come. The longer I'm here, though, and after talking to you and Death, the more aware I am that the stakes are much larger than even my love for my family. Seeing the Shades day after day makes that fact impossible to ignore. Everyone in that Meadow was someone's ... someone. My main objective is the same, but with Death's help I want to ensure no families suffer like ours again. That's part of why I wanted to talk to you about your brother's journal. Your family has suffered, too."

"I won't argue with you on that front. I'm torn on how I feel about the journal. Not that I mind you reading it," he rushed to assure me, "but I don't want to feel responsible for your being stuck here."

"Technically, your brother is responsible." Although I could understand he still felt, as an older sibling, that he was at fault.

"Actually, Starlight, that diary was mine."

CHAPTER 29

All the words I'd fallen in love with, and the man I'd fallen for. It had been Ry the entire time.

"Yours?" I took a step back. "But it said R. Holmes. Reginald? Remington?"

"Rion," he supplied. "I wrote it."

"But you told me you hadn't traveled much! The brother who wrote that traveled quite a bit!"

"I said I hadn't been able to travel in the manner I wished. That's true. All those trips were strictly business, first with my father, and then in his place after he passed and I became Duke Holmes. No opportunity to really explore."

He stared at me as I chewed my lip.

"Was there something else, Starlight?"

"To be honest, I'm a bit relieved. When I read the diary, I ... well, I ... I developed feelings for the author. It would have been incredibly awkward to tell you that I'd been pining after your brother for the better part of a year."

He smirked, pulling me into an embrace.

"Are you telling me you were enraptured with me before we even met? I'm even more romantic than I thought. I really should provide tips to the other gentlemen. Apparently, they don't stand a chance against my charms."

I laughed, pushing against him without really trying to get away.

"I never said *enraptured*! I merely meant that—"

Orion opened his mouth, but he was cut off by the cracking of wood in front of us. I noticed that the tree hoppers had gone silent, and I couldn't see a single squirrel.

A thundering roar erupted from the trees.

Orion shoved me behind him.

For a moment, I thought we were in for another slycat encounter. I began to reach for the knife at my side; then three creatures shoved their way through the tangled branches and into the clearing where we stood.

Each was notably larger than the slycat. Bears, of a sort. They were furred, with large heads and enormous clawed paws, but the shape was wrong. They had long snouts, more like a wolf than a bear, and a long tail with a series of small points at the edges.

"Orion, what are they?" He took a few steps back, with me still pulled against him.

The three creatures had paused, watching us.

Orion's voice was barely a whisper, and he spoke through the side of his mouth, not opening it fully.

"Great bears. Celia, you need to run."

"What about you?" I hissed as the great bear to our right let out another roar. The other two shook their heads, appearing to recover from the shock of finding two half-Shades in their woods.

"I'll try to distract them. Don't come back for me, no matter what you hear."

"I could help," I insisted, bending down again for the knife.

Orion grabbed my arm, holding it firm.

"No."

Ry had been a stream of information on the plants and animals in the Ether. What they ate, how they behaved, if they were dangerous. If he wasn't sharing a plan on how to beat these creatures, it meant he didn't know of a way.

"I'm not abandoning you!"

The largest of the three creatures lunged at us. Orion threw us on the ground, rolling us awkwardly away from the great bear.

Unfortunately, the one on the right was prepared, and as we stood it snapped at the Head Shade. Orion dodged its jaws, shoving me out of the way, but the side of the creature's massive head slammed into Orion's ribs.

He grunted, stumbling backward and clutching his side. With what appeared to be difficulty bending over, Orion reached toward his boot and pulled out a dagger.

"I'll hold them off. Head back to the cottage. Please, Celia."

I'd spent more time than I wanted to admit admiring Orion's physique, his muscled arms and strong shoulders. But facing the three great bears, it was clear that he was utterly outmatched.

We weren't going to fight our way out of this.

Not with a couple of small knives, in any case.

We needed another solution. My mind raced like Pellix through the fields as I struggled to find any way to help us.

If only we had the stallion with us. Pellix could run faster than any animal I'd seen.

"Pellix. That's it! Pellix!" The idea was so far-fetched that I knew it might get us both killed. Still, I couldn't let Orion die while I ran away.

"Celia!" Orion yelled as the smallest bear moved in my direction. He swiped at it, and it redirected its attention toward him. "Run!"

"Hold on, Ry," I whispered, ducking into the branches. They scratched at my clothes and skin while I tried to stay out of sight. When I passed around the lightest-furred great bear, it raised its snout, sniffing the air.

Don't see me. Don't smell me, I beseeched silently.

It turned its head and ran toward Orion.

Not what I meant.

I found a tree with decent handholds, and an open area underneath it, and got to work. Climbing was much easier in trousers than it would have been in a dress and corset, and my muscles had been built from my hikes with Orion, time in the garden, and even carrying our food back and forth from the Meadow.

I didn't need to reach the top of the tree. I just needed to be taller than the bears.

Then came the part that really required bravery.

Below me, barely visible through the leaves, Orion screamed. He stumbled back into view, his right trouser leg in tatters and a sickening crimson coating the material.

"Over here! This way!" I yelled at the creatures, keeping one arm tight around a branch and waving the other furiously.

Two started toward me, but the largest kept its attention on Orion as he backed away. Ry's right leg gave out, and he fell against a tree. The great bear swiped, and Orion threw himself, dragging his weight by his arms, to get out of the way. He slid behind another tree, creating just a few seconds of confusion as the largest great bear looked for its prey.

"Come and get me!" I shouted again. I broke off a small branch of the limb I clung to, beating it against the tree to keep the eyes of the two other great bears on me.

The smallest one slammed its front paws against the tree trunk, standing on its hind legs and snarling so I was staring down into a mouth of saliva-dripping fangs.

The other, with its russet fur, was circling the tree.

Thank both gods that I'd spent all those hours riding Pellix around the ruins.

I'd never attempted it from a tree, and my feet weren't as steady as they had been on a thick bit of stone, but it was this or a dead Head Shade. One of the bears lumbered just underneath my branch.

"Now!" I yelled as I jumped from the tree, plummeting toward the snarling beast. I landed on its back with a *thwump*, and scrambled to get ahold of its fur. It was much larger than Pellix, and without being able to get my legs around its sides, I began to slide.

"No, no, no!"

"Celia!" Orion screamed, and his voice was followed by the sound of cracking and splintering wood as the biggest great bear took another swipe at him, splintering tree bark.

I dug my heels in, trying to fix my awkward angle.

The great bear roared, rearing back.

I screamed, clinging to it.

The smallest bear had noticed me by that point. It swiped out a paw, and it was only because of the beast's movements beneath me that I was twisted out of its path. Instead, the great bear underneath me was hit by its pack mate's claws. It plunged back onto all four legs with a bellow.

Both creatures forgot me for a moment, snarling in each other's faces instead.

Seeming to sense something amiss, the largest great bear roared at the other two, turning its head and making its way over.

I scooted up the creature's back until I was seated in the nook between its shoulder blades. Before the larger bear could reach us I leaned down and punched the head of the creature beneath me with my fist.

"Hello in there!" I yelled.

The beast roared, tossing its head and nearly clocking me in the nose. I grasped the fur of the creature's shoulders as it reared back again and then stomped into the ground.

All three great bears started shouldering one another, pushing and snarling. I was certain I was about to roll off and fall beneath a flurry of waving claws when I heard Orion in the distance.

"This way!" The call was followed by the sound of someone crashing through the undergrowth of the forest.

All three bears turned and barreled through the woods after him.

I knew Orion had no chance of outrunning the beasts but didn't see him ahead.

The treeline thinned, and my grip on the great bear grew tighter. In front of the lumbering creature was what appeared to be a sheer drop-off into a deep canyon. I could hear water rushing somewhere below.

We were headed directly for the edge, with no signs of stopping.

CHAPTER 30

"Both gods save us!" I gasped.

Admittedly, I hadn't had much of a plan after leaping onto the bear, but I'd envisioned a less deadly exit than a sheer drop.

My hope had been to distract and lure the bears away from Orion, find an opportunity to grab a low-hanging branch, and disappear into the trees while the creatures lumbered on.

Clearly, I'd miscalculated.

I craned my neck around while bouncing on the creature's back. The other two bears were right behind us, but mine was the quickest, and the distance between them was growing. The creature slowed slightly as we neared the cliff, turning his head right to snarl. I looked that way just in time to see a rock hit the bear's side.

"Right here! You want me!" Orion yelled as he stepped out from behind a large boulder, waving his arm, his right leg dragging behind him as he came forward.

His eyes found mine. I knew my own were wide and terrified.

"Jump when I tell you!" he called.

"What?"

The great bear stopped and threw back its head with a roar. I struggled to grasp the fur in my sweating palms.

Orion was yelling back at the beast, imitating its roar.

I heard a whistle—something flying through the air—and felt the bear jerk back when the object made contact with its front.

"Now! Jump!"

Trembling, I squeezed my eyes shut, released the bear's fur and flung myself off the creature's back. I hit the dirt with force but managed to tuck and roll as small pebbles embedded themselves into my legs, bruising my knees and shins despite my sturdy trousers. I scrambled away from the still-roaring bear, toward Orion's outstretched arms.

"This way!" he urged as he grabbed my hand and yanked me back toward the rocks.

The bear I had been riding was thrashing and twisting, Orion's dagger protruding from its large neck. It was either luck or direct intervention of the gods when it stumbled into the path of the other two creatures, who had spotted us and were now racing toward us.

There was a tangle of fur and claws, and as the injured beast extricated itself, it took a few lumbering steps back on its hind legs.

Then it stumbled over the cliff edge.

My eyes wanted to follow the falling bear, but Orion took advantage of the distraction and tugged again at my arm. "We're going upwind, where they can't find us as easily."

With his injury, he was moving slowly. I wanted to suggest stopping so I could take a look at it; there was entirely too much blood soaking his leg. Then another ear-splitting roar sounded, reminding me that if we didn't get away from the remaining bears, there would be no point in worrying about an injured limb.

We plunged farther into the trees.

"Are you all right?" Orion asked, his chest heaving for breath, once we had gained enough distance and the roars had faded behind us.

We stopped under a large tree, sheltered by branches that arced down like willow boughs and provided some cover.

"Am *I* all right? What about you?"

He waved me off.

"Minor inconvenience. I've been in worse scrapes than this before. You're sure that you're not hurt?"

He took my face in his hands, then my arms, examining me for any wounds. Longing shot through me as he pulled up my sleeves, his hands moving over my skin.

"Orion."

He pulled back, eyes widening as though he'd just realized that he'd had his hands all over me.

"Sorry, I just wanted to make sure that—"

"I don't mind." I stepped forward, reaching for his hand. He wrapped his arms around me, but sagged against me, and I readjusted my stance to hold his weight.

I looked back up at his face and saw a sheen of sweat. Panic woke in my heart.

"Ry! You look feverish. We need to get you home. Now."

When we stopped to catch our breath again, we were close to the cottage. It was deep into night by this point, the greens and blues of the Ether's forest serving as only a mild comfort. I was exhausted, but Orion looked far worse. His skin had a pale, sickly pallor. Strands of hair were slicked against his face with sweat.

"What do we do about your leg?" I asked, cursing myself for how useless I felt.

"We'll have to clean it, and brace it."

I helped him stay upright until we reached the cottage.

"No, just set me outside," he insisted when I reached for the door. "I'll get blood everywhere. There's another dagger inside, on a shelf behind the table. Get that, and we can cut some material to wrap around the wound."

"I still have the one in my holster."

He shook his head, then winced.

"We've been sitting in the dirt, wandering through the woods. It'll be dirty. We need a clean blade."

Bandaging gruesome wounds was not something with which I had experience, but I swallowed down the queasiness rumbling in my stomach and pushed the door open. If he said he needed a specific blade, I'd get it.

Both gods be praised, or however many gods be praised, the knife was exactly where he had indicated. I snatched it, careful to keep my touch only to the handle, and went back outside.

"Rinse your hands. Then you'll have to cut around the damaged skin and get rid of any material stuck to the wound," he instructed.

He had, in addition to his many other useful contraptions, a piece of wood that he'd attached to a branch above the garden, which directed rainwater into a bucket below. I dunked my hands into the bucket of fresh rainwater—we'd had a shower the previous day—then went back to Orion.

My hands trembled, and I crouched over his leg so he wouldn't see me shaking. I would have to slice most of that pant leg off, a good way up his thigh. My cheeks heated, and I chastised myself. This was no time for modesty.

I pulled a piece of tattered fabric away from the wound, and Orion hissed. Some of the blood had dried, and bits of shredded fabric were stuck in the wound, as he'd predicted.

"You're awfully prepared for this scenario. Just how often have you upset one of these great bears?" I teased, trying to take his mind off the pain.

"I've encountered them a handful of times before, but I've managed to avoid a direct conflict with them. Although—" he hissed as I cut away another bit of fabric.

"Go on," I urged.

"—there was a time I accidentally stumbled on a slycat with a cub. That was an exciting day. Had to stitch up my own arm."

I'd seen the scar when he'd had his sleeves rolled up, working in the garden.

He gasped as I sliced away another chunk of fabric.

"This will leave another scar, I'd wager. Probably not the way most people picture a duke."

He hissed again at the next bit of fabric being pulled from his skin.

"Almost done," I assured him, not reminding him that I'd then have to wash the area. "And I think you're far more handsome than any duke who's done nothing but sit on his estate."

There was no biting comeback, no flirtatious commentary in response. That worried me more than anything.

"You know, I have a scar as well," I admitted.

"Really. Tell me." His voice was hoarse.

I told him about my fall from Pellix and our encounter with the wolf as I did the best I could to clean the area thoroughly without causing him further agony.

"Brave woman. Brave stallion. I think I'll like Pellix," he said.

Then his eyes fluttered closed.

I clutched his face, leaving streaks of dirt and blood on his cheeks.

"You have to stay awake! Tell me how to brace your leg!"

Something told me that if I let him slip into unconsciousness, he'd be in even worse danger.

I kissed him, desperately, trying any contact to rouse him that wasn't painful.

"Maybe ... should get injured ... more often."

I was crying by that point but kept my composure as well as I could.

He walked me through the steps to brace his leg, his voice growing fainter and fainter.

I used wood and rope from the garden supplies, along with some torn strips of clean fabric, following all his instructions to create a splint.

"There, done!" I looked up at him as I finished tying the last bit of fabric, gasping when I saw his eyes closed and his mouth hanging open.

"Orion! Ry! No!" I kissed his cheek, but he didn't even move. I took him by the shoulders, shaking him. I didn't want to hurt him, but I needed him to stay conscious. "You're all right!"

If I said it enough, it might be true. I pulled him toward me, hugging him tight against my chest.

"Please wake up!"

"You know, this might be counterintuitive if you want me to have room to breathe, not that I'm complaining."

I practically threw him off me, sobbing and laughing at once.

"You wretched man! You terrified me."

I didn't have any time to puzzle over whether he'd meant the comment to be as flirtatious as it had sounded. I just had to keep him conscious.

He'd made a soup a couple of days before, and I heated some over the fire. I brought it out along with some of the purple almost-potatoes, hand-feeding him. I sagged with relief as some of his color began to return.

Once I'd lectured him into sipping some water as well, he looked to be in no immediate danger of passing out again.

"Thank you, Starlight."

When he stood, he swayed, but with me supporting him under his arm we made it inside. I helped him onto the second cot he'd set up after my arrival but kept him sitting up, his back against a wall.

I put the back of my hand to his forehead. Not feverish, thank all the blasted gods.

He let out a sigh.

"Much better."

"You're not going to expire on me, then?"

"No. I'm afraid you're stuck with me."

"Maybe I like being stuck with you. If that bear ... if something had happened ..."

Blasted ghosts!

I was starting to cry. All the adrenaline had finally leached from my system, leaving room for me to focus on how close we'd come to death. How close I'd been to losing Orion.

As tears started to roll down my cheeks, Orion reached out and tugged on my hands. I sank down next to him, kneeling at the edge of the cot. I would have loved to lean against him, or tuck myself into his arms, but I didn't want to jostle him.

He reached up, cupping my cheek. His palm came away wet.

"I wouldn't leave you alone down here. That's a promise. Is that what you were worried about?" he whispered.

I was too tired to play games with my words.

"I wasn't worried for myself. I was worried about you. I would have been devastated. You've been down here all this time, and you're so close to getting home. If it had been my fault ... if you'd died down here because you were trying to save me, I never could have forgiven myself. You deserve to go home too, Ry. You deserve a life."

"Mmm-hmm," he mused, "and what about you? You jumped onto the back of a great bear—a creature I've never managed to hunt here—and nearly got yourself trampled. You would have come all this way for selfless reasons, compassionate reasons, and would have died because you were more concerned for me than yourself. I did tell you to run away, you know."

His voice was soft and soothing. I scowled at him but didn't pull away from his touch. His thumb traced my jawline.

I shivered.

"Yes. I know. But I couldn't leave you."

"You, Celia Hipnosi, are remarkable. No man could tell you what to do. No man should try. If we do make it back, after we break the Unseen Hour, I'll help you with whatever other goals you seek to achieve. I have no doubt you can shatter any barrier you set your mind to."

"What do you mean?"

"I know how you've said you hate 'flouncing around,' as you put it, in restrictive pink dresses. While I'd give quite a bit of money to see you in a pink, puffy dress, you have a right to wear what you like, and go where you like, and I'll do all I can to see that hope achieved. A hundred years ago, I attended all the same endless social events of the season that you've endured. I met every eligible woman in Emrys, and I can assure you that I've never met someone like you."

"Someone who caused this much trouble?"

Orion shook his head.

"No. Someone I cared for this much. Someone who woke something deep in me that I thought had been long extinguished. I will defend you from anyone who tries to cage you, just like I did with the great bears. Not because you can't do it on your own, but because you shouldn't have to. I won't allow anyone to take your spark, or snuff it out. No one gets to hurt you."

The blue flecks in his eyes were blazing.

My heart stuttered.

Could we really find a way to change things, even back in Emrys?

And do it together?

The idea was intoxicating.

"Starlight, I'm going to kiss you, if you'll allow it."

"Do you really think you're recovered enough for that?"

"I'd say it might just be the best possible remedy."

I leaned in and pressed my lips to his.

CHAPTER 31

This time, his lips were demanding as they pressed against mine. This was nothing like our first, tentative kiss. It was wild, and I craved more of Ry.

When his teeth nipped at my bottom lip I gasped, and when his tongue slid across mine I couldn't repress a low moan from climbing up the back of my throat.

While I'd never thought the trysts that created such a scandal in Emrys should have been the ruination of someone's reputation, I had never participated in one. I'd never cared enough about anyone to get this close.

With Orion, however, the closer he got, the closer I wanted him to be.

I placed my hands on his chest, running them up his tunic, and then grabbed it and pulled him even closer. A small voice in the back of my head reminded me that he was injured, and I needed to be careful.

It was silenced when he deepened our kiss and I moaned against him.

When he released my lips, I was disappointed for only a moment, and then he slid my hair over my shoulder and began kissing my neck. When he gave another soft bite at the spot where my shoulder and neck met, I felt my knees tremble.

I'd heard the phrase 'weak at the knees,' but I'd always thought it was a dramatic and unnecessary exaggeration. I hadn't realized it could be entirely accurate.

Just like some of the romances I'd read.

In his book with the pirates, Orion had written a couple that I'd initially envied, but I didn't want any fantasies. I wanted Ry.

He was the adventure I'd longed for.

His mouth found mine again, and one of his arms wrapped around my waist. I reached up with one hand, running it through his hair.

The next time he broke off the kiss, I sat back, creating space before he could find my neck again.

"I ..." I paused, at a loss for words and feeling embarrassment I'd never felt before. "I would like to continue, but I have no experience with what comes next."

Orion held out his arms, and I moved back into them, careful not to touch his injured leg.

"I won't lie to you, Starlight. I'd love to explore every inch of you."

"You have mentioned your love of travel," I teased.

"And by your side is the place I've most longed to be. That being said, we'll move at whatever pace makes you comfortable."

"As eager as I am to keep going, perhaps I should be insisting you rest instead, given your grievous injury."

I kept my tone light, but I could see his leg shaking.

"I wouldn't call it grievous. Besides, this is a welcome distraction. But, I will defer to your judgment." He winked.

With a combination of concern, regret, and a desire to throw both to the side and throw my lips against his again, I extricated myself.

I got him a glass of water and then helped him lie down on the cot.

Once he was settled, I dragged my own cot across the floor so it was next to his. By the time I had it situated, he was already asleep.

The following morning, Orion was in no state for a visit to the Meadow or anywhere else. I didn't like the idea of leaving him, and he didn't like the idea of me wandering the forests or the Meadow alone.

We would need to stay near the cottage until he was more mobile.

As anxious as I was to keep moving, there was something serene about staying in the small space with Orion.

"I think I may take up journaling again," Orion said as I closed one of the books from his shelf.

When I looked up, he was grinning.

"Trying to win me over with your words?"

"Would it work?"

"It already has."

Orion adjusted his position, grimacing as his leg moved. I got up to help, but he waved me off.

"I'll be okay. I just need to be distracted. Tell me, how *did* you find my journal?"

"When I was first mourning my father, I used to go to the library. Unlike my home, there was no chance of my family stumbling upon me there. I didn't want my own grief to make things worse for them. My mother, especially, had a tough time at the beginning. The library has patrons, of course, but I stuck to the Estates section. Hardly anyone goes there. My first foray was into a random stack, but after that I continued to return to the section housing 'H' papers, because it began to feel safe. It wasn't near enough the beginning of the alphabet, or the end, to abut other sections of the library. That meant it was even more deserted than the other shelves."

Once I started, the truth came out in a rush. How, in the fall before the ninety-eighth hour, I'd sunk to the floor crying. How I tried to pull myself up and sent books tumbling. How I discovered the diary, and then my own father's writing in the margins.

"He was working for the queen? To find Emrys's king?"

"Yes. I've kept an eye out for him as well but haven't seen him down here. He was lost at sea, so it's possible that he wasn't a victim of the hour. Maybe he was a victim of the storms that plagued the Talwin Sea that year. The ship sank. Bits of wreckage were found later, but no survivors."

Orion frowned, and rubbed the splint on his leg.

"I wouldn't recognize the current king of Emrys, but I haven't seen anyone with a crown. Nothing like that. Maybe he drowned?"

"It's definitely possible. But from what I could tell, my father was less motivated by the thought of finding the king and more excited about making it to the Ether. Not that he knew that was his destination. He just wanted to uncover the secrets of the hour. The queen wanted to send an army down here."

Orion laughed.

"Ah yes, overthrow a deity with brute force. Charon would at least have been surprised, but I doubt it would have been successful."

"My father wasn't certain, either, but he was driven to protect his family. If he could have the queen's backing to look into the hour, all the better. He scoured all sorts of books and bits of history. I'm guessing that's how he found your journal. He might have been one of the few individuals actually interested in the Estates section. He wrote his notes, and I found them. That's when I decided I really could do something about my situation. Of course, I didn't put the pieces together to realize that *you'd* made it here alive. But I knew Father was trying to work out the Thipp's dosing and had his own ideas."

Orion's hands clenched his blankets.

"I tracked the doses my brothers and I were being given before our demise. It was sheer luck that I survived and my brothers did not. Good luck, or bad luck, is hard to say. I would have said the latter, up until recently. Now that you're here, though ... if I had to wait all this time for someone like you, then it was well worth it."

I blushed.

"Your journal mentioned that you'd all been ill and taking Thipp's to help you with insomnia. Did all three of you realize something was amiss?"

"We all knew something was wrong, but I was the one to suggest it was intentional poisoning. The first to become convinced that someone was sabotaging the three of us, although I never managed to figure out who, or why. But it made no sense. No one else on the estate was ill. Just us three."

"Maybe someone wanted the estate? Wanted your money?"

"Always possible, but doubtful. The cousin who would have inherited was cordial with us and in no need of funds himself. And he was abroad during that time. He enjoyed Tang immensely, for all its winter weather. I doubt he'd have wanted to return, although he could have at any time."

The more I thought about it, the odder it seemed.

Three prominent noblemen were targeted just before the hour began.

But they couldn't be connected. No one knew the hour was

coming. No one except Charon, and he'd already proven that his methods were less subtle than slow poisoning.

"Why were you out that New Year's Eve?"

Orion sighed.

"It was my idea to go out that night, following the trail of the person who delivered the Thipp's root. We were told by our butler that someone from town brought it directly from the apothecary. We trusted our staff implicitly and, as we lived on the same grounds, we had no reason to suspect any of them. We thought that maybe the person bringing it was swapping it for something dangerous, or being paid to do so. Now, of course, I realize the Thipp's itself was dangerous enough. But that theory still stands."

"So you waited for a delivery, and you followed him?"

"Yes. We were so ill by then, though. My youngest brother, Remi, stumbled and fell before we'd even made it off the estate. I asked Reg to take him home, and I kept going. I should have stayed and helped them. If I had, we might all three have made it back into the house. Then none of this would have happened. Instead, I insisted on going on alone. I'm the reason my brothers are dead."

His expression was anguished, his eyes watering.

I moved over to him and sat down carefully, on the side of his uninjured leg. I put a hand on the side of his head, and he leaned against my shoulder.

"Oh, Ry. That's not true. You were trying to save them."

"I was the eldest, and the only parental figure my brothers had left. I should have suspected something sooner. Noises and clamorings on the estate and throughout the manor that no one could find the source of? The sudden onset of symptoms that plagued all three of us? Someone goaded us into seeking out a cure."

I wanted to promise that we would find the person responsible, but whoever it was would be long dead themselves.

It would almost be better if they'd ended up in Death's realm, instead of the Ether. I couldn't imagine Ry having to see his brothers' killer for nearly a century, even if he wasn't sure who it was.

I ran my fingers through his hair, my hand pausing.

"Have you talked to them? Your brothers?"

He'd mentioned seeing them and trying to get them out, but he'd never told me whether they'd been at all responsive.

"I tried. But they're typical Shades. Wandering in the Meadow. When I first saw them here, I was overjoyed. I didn't realize what had happened to us, you see. Then, I saw what they'd become. I didn't have a name for this place, or the hour, or anything. For weeks I lived outside, on the edge of the Meadow, barely surviving. I approached them every day, pleading with them to engage with me. After a while, it became clear they wouldn't. They couldn't. That's when I began avoiding them. It became easier as more souls joined the Ether. I didn't see them as often. I've spoken to almost every soul here, but I can't bring myself to return to them. I wish they knew how badly I wanted to save them. I have no words adequate to apologize for what was done to them."

His voice was rough, and my heart ached for him.

"Ry, this was not your fault."

He wiped at his face.

"I've had time to grow used to it. That's part of why I made my deal with Death. When we stop this hour and she frees the souls, my brothers will finally be where they belong. That's how I make things right."

"What about Charon?"

He *harumphed*, adjusting his leg again.

"What about him? I don't care a single jot for what happens

to that cursed god once his hour is gone. So long as we're away from here and Death feels like she can face him without his Shades. I'm fine if he rots in the Ether."

"But, when you arrived ... he always greets the new souls. While you were here with your brothers ..."

"Yes. He saw me first thing. A bumbling, grieving half-Shade. He was so triumphant, walking around that initial crowd of souls. Then, he came to me. Looking for my brothers, panicked, half-convinced that I was still in Emrys and the poison running through my veins had caused me to hallucinate. I was not at all how he'd pictured that celebratory first hour, and he was less than pleased."

"What did he do?" I was afraid to find out, and he was well within his rights not to tell me.

"Lashed out. Those wings he has are for more than just flying. He swatted me with one and I careened into one of the Meadow's trees. I was more banged up then than I am now, if you can believe it. Had to borrow what I could from some of the Shades' pockets to fix myself up. I was ashamed of it, too—a grave robber as well as a careless brother."

"You only did what you had to do!"

"Still, I try to avoid taking from the Shades, when I can. On occasions where it can't be avoided, I always ask. Not that they'll always respond. The cloak I took for you was likely the closest I've come to true thievery in a while. To be fair, you did look much better in it than the man who originally wore it."

He gave a weak smile, attempting to add some humor to the moment.

I gave my best attempt at a smile back, but inside I was seething at Charon. And whoever had harmed the Holmes brothers.

Only one of them was still within reach, and I intended to make him pay for every single soul.

CHAPTER 32

April in Emrys was typically our last month in Fox Haven before the season. It meant flowers, afternoons with short windows of rain, and rides on Pellix in the sunshine that followed.

In the Ether, it arrived around the time Orion's leg had healed enough to return to our search.

We were back in the Meadow again, checking several clusters of older Shades. Orion walked with a wooden cane that he'd fashioned himself. I worried that his leg wasn't healing quite as it should, but given the amount of blood that had poured out of the wound, I was thankful it hadn't been worse. Ry's movements were stiff, and part of me suspected he'd insisted on checking the Meadow again because he wasn't quite ready for the rougher terrain in the woods.

We'd give the Meadow another week and then resume our search among the trees, assuming he felt up for it.

For the time being, I carried blankets with us so we could sleep at the edge of the forest and Orion wouldn't have to walk back and forth to the Meadow each day. We'd continued sleeping next to each other, although still on separate cots, and twice now we'd woken up with our hands clasped together.

There had also been several additional, passionate moments of kissing, but it had yet to progress further.

"Thank you," I offered to the Shade I'd just finished speaking to. He'd only said a few words, but it felt right to show appreciation.

Another day full of strange faces and conversations that hardly ever made it past a turn or two.

"Bollocksing, bloody, blasted ghosts!" I kicked at the grass.

I'd been in the Ether all the way into spring, and I was ready to see some progress. I took a deep breath and walked toward Orion, calming myself down with each step. He was feverishly writing, with his leg propped up.

"Storytelling?"

I knew he'd started a new book, although he'd refused to let me set eyes on it quite yet.

"Not today," he responded without looking up. "Drawing up plans. I'm mapping out the rest of the Ether and how we can cover the different sections. I know you don't really anticipate finding him in the Meadow at this point. You're just humoring me and my leg. This way, at least I can feel like I'm doing some- thing useful."

I looked down at the map. The canyon from our great bear chase was marked on it, along with the Meadow, and the place where I'd entered the Ether. He had several additional land- marks described in the forest, including a known slycat den.

West of the Meadow he'd crossed out a large portion of the map and written *Charon's*. It was too large to all be his home, but Orion had given the deity a wide berth.

"You're sure we can't go there?" I asked him as he added some details to the area bordering Charon's section.

"I would highly advise against it. The rest of the Ether could take us months. But"—I held my breath—"if we get close to the hour and see no sign of your father anywhere else, we'll have to figure something out. Although I warn you, Charon wouldn't be happy about finding us near his home. We'll have to be very careful, and very stealthy."

"Sneaking and stealth is something I can definitely do. I know he's a real danger, but the way you describe him he also sounds annoying. Worse than any member of the nobility I've ever met."

Orion looked up at me, the grey in his eyes stronger today than the blue.

"Too true. By the way you talk about it, I'm guessing there are still some very pompous individuals running around during the season."

"And the rest of the year. Ry, what were you like before you got down here? I know you liked to travel, and you were a protective brother. But what about as a duke? Were you a stuffy sort of lord?" I asked.

"Stuffy?"

"Yes, you know, were you someone concerned with your appearance? Someone who would have blanched or held his handkerchief over his mouth at the sight of something ghastly, like a woman whose dress showed her ankles. That sort of thing?"

Instead of laughing at me, Orion tilted his head, musing over his answer.

"I would have noticed something like that, if I'm being honest. I wouldn't have minded, and I'd have thought those making a fuss were being a bit ridiculous, but I would have noticed."

"Because you're so attuned to details?"

"Honestly, I was a bit removed when I was Duke Holmes. I cared a lot less about the season, and the gossip, than I did about my own properties and the people close to me. I was consumed with making sure our estate was a success and that everyone who relied on me was taken care of. It's a lot of responsibility, having so many people look to you, and I didn't want to let anyone down. My father passed away when he was still fairly young. I was the youngest duke the house of Holmes had ever seen. I tried to rise to the title."

"You looked after everyone else, just as you did your brothers."

"I tried. It's part of why I was so certain our staff had nothing to do with what was going on, at least not purposefully. I knew everyone who worked for us and with us very well."

"My father always said that to be a good leader, one must serve others," I said.

"I think I shall like him quite a bit. We'll have a lot to talk about, assuming he doesn't challenge me to a duel for the way the two of us have been living down here."

Orion raised one brow, smirking at me.

I just laughed, and when Orion winked at me I dissolved into a full-on fit of giggles.

I'd already explained my father to Orion, telling him almost as much about the head of Scops as myself. Orion was well aware that Father would be only too thankful to anyone who helped rescue him and keep his daughter safe, regardless of the means.

"Even my brothers will be won over by you," I promised him.

Ambrose might not be, but the longer I stayed here, the less I cared. Didn't I also deserve to be happy? Was I really willing to fall back in line once I returned to Emrys, simply because it was expected?

Orion moved even closer.

"I doubt that. Not when I've spent a good portion of your time here with my lips on your neck."

I gasped as he leaned in, his breath teasing that sensitive spot at the curve of my neck.

"Ry," I breathed.

His arms went around me, and I leaned into him.

"Starlight," he whispered, his breath sending pleasant shivers down my spine. "When we do get back, will you travel with me? Seeing Shades from all over Rayus isn't enough. I want to take you to Mejje, Tang, Sez, anywhere you'd like to go."

"Like the pirate in your books?"

"If that's what you want." He trailed kisses down to my collarbone, then gazed at me with a look that was almost reverent. "Everything down here was dull and lifeless until you arrived. You breathed life into me again. I want you to have the things you dream about as well; the things we both dreamed about before we came here."

It wasn't exactly a proposal, not in the marriage sense, but it was a commitment. He wanted to stay with me.

"We'd make a ghastly scene," I warned him.

He just laughed.

"Oh, I haven't been gone so long that I've forgotten that. Let them all talk. We've seen and experienced things that most people in Emrys wouldn't believe, even knowing about the hour."

It was harder and harder to imagine that I would let a bunch of prideful nobles' opinions cow me, after this place.

"There's no one I'd rather see the world with," I told him truthfully.

He smiled, leaning back in to kiss me again.

His tongue was sliding across mine when I saw a bright flash, even from behind my closed eyelids.

Lightning struck the ground in front of us, and we leapt apart.

CHAPTER 33

We'd been waiting for Death to reappear for weeks, but I had to force a glare off my face. Deities had no respect for privacy.

The lightning sizzled, and the hairs on my arms stood on end. I had the strangest urge to reach out and grab the light, even though I was quite certain it could spear me through as easily as regular lightning.

It certainly gave off enough heat.

Death stepped forward, and the stunning deity threw back her hood, silken hair falling over her shoulders. Once again, she wore a mask over the top portion of her face. This one was silver, made of metal.

"I did say I would return soon." Death flashed her dazzling smile at us both.

I might have argued that weeks and weeks hardly counted as *soon*, but who was I to debate a god? In Emrys, letters could take over a week to reach someone in the wrong weather. I wasn't about to question the timeline of a goddess.

She gasped as she turned toward Orion.

"You've hurt yourself. Not Charon's work, I hope?"

Orion shook his head.

"Bad interaction with some of the local wildlife. It's healing nicely, though, and we're ready for whatever you have planned next."

For a moment, I wondered whether Death might be able to heal it the rest of the way. Exactly what powers did she possess? And was she limited by the Ether?

The deity turned her dazzling smile on me.

"Have you been thinking of what you want from me, young human?" She leaned in close, and I could feel the crackling and dancing static across my own skin.

I took a deep breath and forced steadiness into my voice.

"Could you heal Orion?"

"Celia!" Orion's voice rose.

Death tilted her head to one side, then the other.

"Unexpected. I am very rarely surprised. I thought your request would have something to do with what brought you down here."

I gasped, although I shouldn't have been surprised that she knew. She was a goddess, after all.

She laughed.

"I do make it my business to know things about the other gods and their realms. It's why I'm not taken unawares, as they risk being. We're allies, yes? I can't fix his leg for you, but I can give you a bit of advice connected to what I came to discuss, and that will help Orion."

I breathed out a sigh of relief.

"Thank you."

I sagged, and Orion put an arm around my shoulder, letting me lean against him. My one request, and I'd used it, but I couldn't feel bad about it.

"Now then, what else?" Death prompted.

I snapped my head back toward her.

"But I just ... you still want to offer me something else?"

Death clucked her tongue.

"Do not bore me, small humans. Please. The other gods are tedious enough, and none of us like to be repetitive. I need you both, and I need you in shape enough for a trek. Besides, I'm merely giving you a hint when it comes to Orion's leg. I shall ask once more: what is it you'd like in exchange for helping me end the hour?"

The answer spilled out in a rush; I was worried she might just retract the offer if I delayed.

"I want help locating my father. We've been looking for him down here since my arrival. I believe he is a half-Shade, like Orion and myself."

Death threw back her head and laughed.

"How quaint. Neither of you is a *real* Shade, I can assure you of that."

I looked between Orion and the floating souls in the field. I couldn't argue when it came to appearances, but there were other things that were undeniable.

"But Orion can sing just like the others, and Charon has him leading them, and I—"

"I only mean that you do not face the limitations of a real Shade. You, unlike these Shades, can escape. Just as I promised before. If"—she raised a finger—"you do what I ask."

I nodded.

"Of course. If you'll help find my father, and we can destroy the Unseen Hour and go home, we're more than happy to help."

Even if we weren't, I couldn't imagine how we were meant to refuse a god. But as long as Death was being generous, I felt no need to point that out.

Death nodded, her silvery mask shimmering with the movement.

"Good, good. Then I will locate your father. You believe him to be here?"

I sighed.

"I thought he was here, but we haven't been able to find him. We've covered the Meadow and the area closest to where Orion lives, but we still need to check the remainder of the Ether's woods."

Death tapped a slender finger against her pale chin.

"And Charon's lands?"

Orion frowned.

"Yes, and those. *If* we can't find him elsewhere. That will be our final stop and last resort."

"Very well. I will look at Emrys, and the other countries. If he is alive, I will locate him. I can also check my own realm. If he is dead …"

I gulped.

"I still want to know. I don't believe him to be, but if he is, will you know what happened?"

"I will be able to give you insight into his death, yes, if he is in fact deceased."

Orion kept his arms around me, giving me the strength to swallow down the urge to cry.

"You'll search for him yourself? Can you do that and still monitor Charon?" I asked.

"That will be of no issue. I'll monitor the investigation, but I'll send my Reapers to find your father."

"Reapers? What are those? How do they work?"

Death smiled again.

"I like you, little human. You don't shy away from bold questions. I send my translucent horde to collect souls when they depart this life, but unlike the Shades, they do not alter the timing of when someone dies. They merely ferry the souls home when it is their time."

"To your realm? Or to Day's?"

Death waved a finger at me.

"Now you're trying to snoop. Bold is good, but there are some mysteries not everyone is meant to know. My Reapers are gentle shepherds. Charon has his Shades, and I have my Reapers, but they are very different."

Churches in Emrys held portraits of Day and Death. Day was often depicted in warm, light colors: yellows, pinks or orange. Death was shrouded in blacks and blues. Day was shown sometimes as a tanned, muscular figure with dark hair and eyes. Death was shrouded, a pale face visible within the hood, the body that of a broad-chested man. Eyes that were grey, but dull, unlike Orion's. And skin just as pale as actual Death's, but without any of the vibrance. There was no mention of lightning.

Day sometimes carried a sheaf of wheat and a scythe. Death was depicted with a sword or a vial with unknown contents.

"She's told me a bit about them, but I didn't think to mention it since it wasn't relevant to our search. Emrys got many things wrong," Orion informed me. "Reapers are the ones who carry a scythe. They use it to separate souls from their mortal bodies, but it doesn't hurt. Unlike the Shades, they don't use an ability, but a weapon. Without their scythe, they wouldn't be able to help Death."

"No abilities? What about moving through the world unseen and transporting souls to Death's realm?" I questioned.

"Those aren't the abilities I mean. I'm talking about actually separating the soul from the body. *That* is something that only Death can do without a weapon. Her Reapers aren't nearly so skilled. Shades don't have to carry anything physical to do our jobs. Our song is always with us."

Orion may have loathed what happened during the Unseen Hour, but he sounded certain when it came to the power the

Shades possessed. Since my first day in the Ether, I hadn't heard him sing. Hadn't heard his voice take on that enticing quality, although I still found him just as tempting.

"Do Shades not carry anything at all, then?"

He pointed at his neck.

"Only our voices."

I hadn't yet attempted the Shade song. I hadn't wanted to. In Emrys, I'd performed for my family and close friends. I'd been told my voice was lovely, but it didn't seem the sort of hobby that one used to strike fear into the hearts of mortal men. Besides, I'd always been better at the piano.

Death gestured toward Orion.

"You should show her. I'll actually need her to sing for my plan to be successful."

I put a hand to my throat. Why should either of us need to sing, if breaking the Unseen Hour was the entire point?

Before I could protest, Orion nodded.

"It may be better for you to see it now and understand how it works. Then it won't take you by surprise during the hour."

Whether I wanted to hear the song or not, I did trust Orion.

"All right," I agreed.

Orion let go of me, backing up several paces. He cleared his throat, then opened his mouth, and as he did I lost all sight of blue in his eyes. They were as deeply grey as the fog that covered Emrys during the hour. A sound reverberated from somewhere deep within him, echoing with such force that he might as well have been yelling up from a well, or a long tunnel.

It was a single note at first, long and clear. Then, it changed into a beautiful melody. Haunting and mesmerizing. No words, but they were unnecessary.

I had always had a fondness for the theatre. I cherished the times my brothers had accompanied me to the opera, or to see an orchestra. I particularly liked stringed instruments. There was something about them that carried me through an emotional journey along with the performers. When they plucked and played the strings of the instrument it felt like they were pulling on my heart, tugging me toward feelings I'd not yet explored.

Some moments I'd spent with Orion were the closest I'd come to the same sensation. As if something was physically pulling my heart closer to him.

That was the sensation the Shade song caused. I was drawn to it, focused solely on the music. I envisioned rides on Pellix, soaring through the fields. The smell of the gardens in spring. The feel of pages turning beneath my fingers as I sat uninterrupted in the library. The sound of the piano keys under my fingers.

Orion's voice cut off without warning, leaving me off-balance. I stumbled forward, shaking my head to clear it. I threw a hand out as I began to fall, and it landed on Orion's chest. As I pushed against him to right myself, his hand came up, grabbing mine and holding it in place.

"You're warm," we said in unison.

I pulled my hand back.

No need to stumble about like a lovesick fool in front of an actual goddess.

Not that I thought Death shared the same morality as the people in Emrys. She'd made no commentary on the situation between the two of us. She focused only on the Unseen Hour and Charon, and I liked her all the more for it. But I wanted her to see us as capable, not distracted.

My feelings for Orion had been growing, and I enjoyed his company, but the song brought out something else entirely. It had pulled me toward Orion without thought or reason. I would have walked off a cliff if he'd been on the other side.

"The Shade song is dangerous," I said.

With Death looking on, I tried to ignore the fact that I'd been close enough to catch the scent of crisp winter air and snow that clung to Orion in spite of his warmth.

"You smell like the cold. Normally you smell like fresh earth and rain," I commented.

Death let out a trilling laugh.

"You two have become quite familiar, I see. It's because he used the song. He probably smells however he did on the night he ended up here. You see what I mean now? The Shade song makes people lose their reason. It's why people go quietly to their doom instead of running, screaming through the streets and away from the Shades. You'd hear the victims otherwise."

I winced.

"But why would we need to use it? I thought we wanted to end this entire abomination."

"You will still need the song to accomplish that. Before I get to that part, though, let us start at the beginning."

Orion reached for my hand.

"I'm sorry, Starlight. I didn't want you to feel it or hear it for the first time during the hour. With thousands of Shades singing, it might have been overwhelming."

I shook my head at him.

"Don't worry. It was … beautiful, but disconcerting. I'm glad you showed me, though. You're right. I'd rather know what I'm in for. Should I … do I need to attempt it now?"

Death was the one to step between us this time.

"No. Not now. The song will come naturally, and you won't need it until the hour. Instead, I have a task for the two of you. It involves taking an item from Charon, and it's the beginning of my plans to unravel his precious hour."

<h1 style="text-align:center">CHAPTER 34</h1>

"We'll help you defeat him," I swore, holding a hand out to Death without thinking. I hastily put it down when the deity didn't respond, recalling her warning about her deadly touch. "I promise."

Death held her hands up, interlocking her fingers as they crackled with electric current.

"Excellent. I'll tell you what we need. What I'm sharing with you is a well-protected secret. All the deities have our own methods of intervening in Rayus. Charon's Shades and my Reapers are some examples. I was the original, but greatness breeds imitation. I have an item that connects me to my Reapers. It essentially binds some of my power to them, so that they can act on my behalf. Charon has something similar. Two things, actually. He's nothing if not cautious."

"What are they, these items that help connect your kind to ours?" Orion asked, stepping toward the deity.

Death tapped a crackling finger on her chin.

"I have a much larger scythe, similar to the smaller ones my Reapers carry. Charon will have followed a similar pattern. Items connected to the ability his Shades are granted. Retrieve those, and then I'll tell you how we can use them. By the time this next Unseen Hour is over, the Shades will cease to exist."

Death grinned, and Orion nodded along, but I gnawed my lower lip.

"Then what will happen to them?"

Death turned back in my direction, her mask creating a blank look.

"Freed Shades would return to the realm in which they belong. Mine. Their souls will be at peace. Able to enjoy their eternities instead of existing as barely existent shadows."

"And us? We'll be able to return to our lives? I do still have the antidote for the Thipp's, which is how we all ended up here in the first place."

"That won't help you, but I can. Get me what we need, and I will handle the rest. I do not have the purview to return life, but you aren't *really* dead, so it's only a small obstacle. I'll take care of that part of the plan, and you all retrieve what we need."

Purpose sparked to life in my chest. This is what I had been waiting for. If I couldn't find my father on my own, then I needed something else to focus on while Death searched for his soul. The goddess would succeed where I had failed; I was sure of it.

The deity held both her hands out, palms up. I watched, entranced, as she laid out her plan.

"This victory relies on a two-fold strategy. First, you must retrieve the items that Charon has kept secreted away in the Ether. Reunite them, and we are halfway there. Second"—she lifted her left palm—"we use both to stop the hour. But for now, we will focus on step one."

I fidgeted, thinking as I did so how Mother would have chastised the restless movements. I couldn't help it. Stillness had never appealed to me.

"What do we need to find?" Orion asked.

I pictured the mighty sword Death was sometimes depicted with in Emrys. Perhaps they merely had the wielder wrong, and gods did carry weapons. After all, the Reapers had the scythes that their art associated with Day. From what I could tell, those in Emrys and the other countries had been right on at least portions of our lore.

"The first item you will be looking for is ... a baton."

I stopped fidgeting, eyes scrunching.

"A baton?"

Death nodded, silvery mask glittering under the blue and green lights that cast the faintest glow at this edge of the forest.

"A conductor's baton. My brother must tie his ability to his Shades. So we all must, with those who serve us. To share his song with the Shades, he needs a means to control the ability. That is the baton. He sees himself as the grand conductor of this scheme."

She snorted out a laugh, a shocking sound coming from an immortal being.

It made sense, with music being Charon's most dangerous weapon.

"You mentioned a second item. What is it? Will they both be kept together?" I asked.

"They will not. I'd wager he's kept them separated as an extra means of security. It's what I would do."

"And do you have another item, in addition to your scythe?"

She grinned, perfect teeth more menacing then dazzling that time.

"That is another secret I think I'll keep to myself for the time being."

Orion frowned.

"Would Charon not keep the baton or this second item with him? He is meticulous. Surely he would—"

"He is also paranoid and growing more and more suspicious

of me and the rest of the deities by the day. My brother is closing in on the date of his attempted coup, and he has no desire for me to locate the item on his person. I am somewhat familiar with this realm. I know of a few locations close to his heart. All of us were close, before we weren't," Death admitted.

"You called him *brother*. Are the gods siblings, then?"

Death shook her head, her hair glinting in the changing light.

"No. None of us, in fact. Although we were just as close, once. We're more like 'brothers-in-arms' than real family. We squabble like family, but we're not related in any way. In fact" —she waved an arm—"never mind. But no, we are in no way truly related."

"Why did you grow apart?" I asked, still curious at the bit she'd chosen to leave out.

Whatever had come between them, I wanted to avoid getting more involved with the issues of deities than we already were. Fetch the items, end the hour. That was all I wanted. They could settle the rest themselves.

"It was rather more intense than merely growing apart. Don't worry, the squabbles of the gods should not interfere with your lives. I'm stepping in now because that's exactly what Charon's actions are doing. This will not end well for him."

"And the baton?" Orion asked, taking a step closer to me.

"There are two places he might keep it. One is in a cave at the bottom of a canyon, deep in his forest. It has crystals inside that glitter and glow just as bright as the lights in his night sky here. He used to go there to be alone, away from his creatures and even us. It is a sanctuary to him. That's where you'll find help for your leg. The waters within the cave can also be a place of healing."

I had difficulty picturing gods with their own sanctuaries. Who would they worship?

And why would Charon need something that could heal? Unless the gods were more vulnerable than we'd believed.

"They can be wounded, then, the other gods?"

"They can be vanquished," Death answered, hedging. "Gods can stand against gods. Can you find the canyon?"

Orion dipped his chin.

"We know where it is. I got my leg injury near that location."

"Good. I don't envy you the climb down, but I'd suggest starting there. Then, even if it's not where he's keeping the baton, you'll be working with both legs."

I tensed. From what I remembered of the canyon, it was a steep drop. Any pathways down the sides would probably be narrow and treacherous. I wasn't looking forward to the trip.

We'd have to be careful, and playing it safe would mean moving slowly as well.

At least we'd be taking care of two tasks at once. We'd been planning to go back to the forest soon anyway to expand our search for Father. We could look for him and the baton at the same time.

"And the other possible location for this baton?" Orion asked.

"The Ether is vast, but it has distinctive areas. The entrance back to Emrys is the farthest northern point, and the Shades are in the central region of his domain. My brother resides in the west, and the forest where you reside, along with the canyon, are in the east. I believe you know most of this. If the baton is not in the canyon, you would need to go south. You will come to an area of vast emptiness—flatlands with grey sands stretching for miles."

"Like Mejje," I interjected, recalling its deserts from books I'd read.

Death shook her head.

"Not quite like Mejje. These sands are cold, and the air dark and damp. Eventually you will reach a rocky beach. My brother does love his water, and I'm not sure he even realizes how he stays close to it. There, you will find several large stone formations. The baton may be hidden in one of those."

"Is there a significance to this spot?" Orion asked.

"If you find it, perhaps you'll figure that out. Which location he has chosen for the item will also give me some insight into his actions."

"And once we've found the baton?" I asked her.

"You can retrieve the second item. I don't know exactly *what* it is, but I do know where Charon will be keeping it. Well, I know the general location. It resides in Charon's home. It will have something to do with music, I've no doubt."

Orion rounded on the goddess.

"Charon's *home*? We'd have to be mad to go in there. I only go when I'm summoned. He's got it protected and only allows me access. *I'll* retrieve whatever is in there, alone."

Death threw out her hand, and small arcs of lightning struck the ground.

"No. This will take both of you. I will take care of distracting Charon while you search, making sure he's kept busy for a while. In fact, I have him waiting in my realm as we speak, so I'll need to leave soon. Once I can ensure he'll be out of the Ether for a while, I'll send a lightning strike. That's your signal to start searching."

"But what if—"

Death put up a palm, stopping Orion before he really began.

"I almost forgot. It matters how you transport the items. Orion, you should hold the baton. You've got years of experience as Head Shade, and I think you'll tolerate the power in it easier. That means that only Celia should hold the other item. Both contain large amounts of magic, and I'm not sure either of you would be able to handle both items, since they're meant for gods. I recommend you not risk it, unless you'd like to see my realm first-hand."

Orion ran a hand through his hair, the brown and coppery strands pulled back from his face.

"Respectfully, goddess, how am I supposed to get Celia into Charon's home, when it's built to keep Shades and other creatures of the Ether out?"

Death patted the air above his head as though he were a favored pet but avoided actually touching him with her crackling hand.

"I can help with that. Let it never be said that I'm not the most generous of all the deities. Now then, I'll need you to hold hands."

We did so, and she waved her own hands over ours, sparks of lightning emitting from them.

"There!" she declared after a few moments. "When you first enter the boundary of Charon's property, you'll be able to pass through. Once you're in, you're each free to wander about as you wish. Celia just has to make it past the barrier of the grounds. When you find the object, leave as quickly as you can. Remember, watch for my lightning, then go. I'll meet you here again when I'm able. Best of luck."

Death turned to walk away, then spun back around.

"Oh. One more thing. I should warn you that you may not be the only ones looking. Keep both eyes open."

"May Day and Death protect us," I whispered out of habit.

Death tilted her head.

"Day does not deign to involve himself in human matters. Day ensures you all are born, and then leaves you largely to your own devices. Truly, I do believe he gets too much credit. Now then, get to work, and I will see you soon.”

Lightning struck the ground, and she was gone.

“Shall we get started?” Orion asked, already picking up the items we’d brought with us to the Meadow.

“Yes.”

We had a deadline, and I intended to meet it.

CHAPTER 35

By the time we reached Orion's cottage, we were well into the Ether's night. I looked overhead, watching the vibrant blues and greens dancing in the sky.

"This is one thing I might just miss," I told Orion before we made our way inside.

"I'd most miss the tree hoppers," he responded.

They were clever birds. And I had noticed that several in particular returned over and over to his cottage.

"How long do you think, until she gives us the signal?" I asked.

"With Death, who knows? You've seen her idea of a short time. I vote we stick close to the cottage and prep some bags. We'll need food, water, and a few blankets. There's no telling how long we'll be sleeping outdoors once we leave. I'll grab an extra knife." He was already moving around the small space, gathering items. "And we'll also want to take some waterskins along."

"Will you bring your new book?"

I was still dying to see it, but he'd kept it closely guarded.

Orion pulled it from the satchel we'd taken to the Meadow and set it on his bookshelf.

"Better not risk it. We don't know what we're going to run into in the woods. If Charon does somehow find us, well, I'd rather be concerned with items to help our survival. Not personal things that could give away secrets."

"What do you mean, secrets? It's not another journal, is it?" He'd told me it was a novel, like the one with his pirates.

Ry shook his head.

"No, but all the same. Charon reads into things."

Ry busied himself with preparation, and I went out to the garden and collected some food for our supplies. When I returned he'd already packed the remainder of things we would need.

Orion was on one of the cots, leaned up against the wall with his leg kicked out. He held up a blanket for me.

"I'll roll these into our packs when we get the signal. Something you said before, about what you would miss, got me thinking."

I made my way over to him. He tucked the blanket around my shoulders and pulled me close so that my head was on his chest.

"Do you think," Orion started, "that Charon is going to realize what we've done? We still have months left here."

I wanted to reassure him, but I'd had the same thought. He ran one hand up and down my arm. The comforting touch lulled me into relaxation and lit me on fire at the same time. His hands were callused from years of work in the Ether, and I appreciated them all the more for that. Orion was capable, and he didn't back down from any challenge.

"I think Death has the most insight into this situation. If she's asking us to get them now, then she must be at least somewhat confident that he either won't go looking or that she can distract him from it. Think about it: if he really is worried about her meddling, or another god's, he might not want to draw attention to the locations."

"So he might be less inclined to visit them and check," Orion guessed.

"Exactly."

"But as it gets closer to the hour, particularly with this being his end goal, I can't imagine he wouldn't do everything he could to ensure his success. That has to include monitoring his Shades and the way to control them."

"We'll have to ask Death about it, once we have the items and see her again."

The deity had indicated she'd show us what to do with the two things, and that she planned to return at least once more before the hour. When she did, we could come up with a ruse for Charon.

"If your theory is right, and I suspect it is, that means that searching the canyon and the beach is likely a very safe move. We'll be more hidden from Charon there than his Meadow," I said.

Orion relaxed a bit, although I could still feel his muscles where I leaned into him, strong and solid.

"Feeling tired, Starlight?" Orion asked when I almost nodded off, waking as my head fell into his lap.

"I didn't hurt your leg, did I?" I jumped up, but he pulled me back against him.

"Not in the slightest. You're welcome to stay right here." He ran his hands through my hair.

"You know," I mused, "the only thing that might improve this would be a story. I don't suppose you're at point of sharing that newest story yet, since you won't bring it along?"

He laughed, and I could feel his chest moving behind me.

"It's not finished. How about, instead, I tell you about the time I went on my last treasure hunt? My brothers convinced me there were enchanted beans in our kitchens."

I snorted.

"You must have been very young."

"Eleven, but I went along with it mostly because it amused them."

He told me about the scavenger hunt his brothers had created to lead him to the supposedly magical objects, how he'd found it and pretended to cast spells, how the two of them had clapped and cheered.

Just the way he spoke about them told me how much he loved them and still missed them.

A week later, I woke in Orion's arms, side by side on his cot and wrapped beneath a blanket. We'd kept close to the cottage.

I tried not to move, afraid of ending the moment. His embrace was reassuring and warm, and even knowing what we had to do, I longed to stay there.

Lightning struck the ground inside the cottage, not burning anything but leaving familiar white smoke.

"If I pretend to be asleep, will you stay with me, or will you worry my leg's finally finished me off?" Orion whispered against my hair.

I laughed, twisting in his arms to face him.

"It is nice being here like this, but we should go. We made Death a promise."

I tried to rise, but Orion kept his arms tight around me.

"I warn you, Starlight, I think you've utterly ruined me for spending the night alone ever again."

"Then I'll simply have to stay until you grow tired of me," I teased.

He released me with a smile, and my heart lurched, watching the blue flecks in his eyes.

Everything he'd said, and everything he'd done, told me Orion was dependable. Even so, I couldn't help feeling a small flash of doubt. He hadn't had his own life in Emrys for a hundred years. If he got his estate back, depending on whether the rest of Emrys found out the truth about his situation, he'd be incredibly busy as the duke again. If he didn't, then he'd be rebuilding an entire life.

There was always the possibility that he found something, found someplace, or even found someone that drew his attention. After all, in the Ether I was his only option.

"Something on your mind?" he asked as we got up.

He handed me my satchel and slung his own pack over his shoulders. I saw that he'd stuffed our blankets inside.

"Just thinking about going back to Emrys."

"Then let's get moving. This will take us one step closer."

There was no point in bringing up a worry so far in the future. We had so much else to sort through first.

The canyon was mere hours from Orion's cottage, but getting to the bottom was another matter entirely. Purple and orange lights danced above us as we stared over the edge.

"I can see some areas where we could climb down, but I'd guess it would take a full day or more for the climb, and who knows how long for the actual search. Getting up again is also another matter, although I'm hoping we'll find whatever Death said would help with my leg. That would speed things up considerably."

I knew he would reject it, but I wasn't going to let him risk himself without at least offering.

"I could go down, and you could wait up here. Especially since Death said she'll be trying to keep Charon distracted, so we're not likely to see him, and I'll be safe."

Orion shook his head.

"No. I would never stop you from going, but I'm going with you. Charon may not be our biggest worry at the moment, but all the other things in the Ether could be."

"I know your leg still hurts after too long on your feet. We'll take more frequent breaks on the way down."

He frowned down at his leg, looking offended at the appendage.

"I can make it down. But if something does go wrong before I'm fully healed, you need to run. Don't let me slow you down."

"Come on, we should get going," I responded, walking to the rim of the canyon.

"That's not agreement."

"No, it's not," I tossed over my shoulder. I wasn't going to lie to him, and I wasn't going to leave him behind.

We had to walk quite a bit of the way around the canyon rim before we found a good spot to begin our descent. Along the way, Orion had pointed out signs indicating the great bears had been through the area.

"Looks like they've been through here as well." I gestured, pleased to put some of the things he'd taught me to use. "See? Broken branches, rooted-out vegetation at the base of the trees."

"It might be great bears. Although the brush boars also like to do that," Orion warned.

"And those are? Hopefully something friendly and cuddly? But by the sound of your voice, I somehow doubt it."

Orion let out a laugh that fell flat.

"Brush boars are large swine-like creatures with skin that's pale pink under a coating of wiry, silver hair. It glints like metal, and it can pierce like metal, too. It's more spike than hair, really. I've hunted them before, but I pick off one at a time. You have to be careful if there's a sounder."

"Sounder?"

"A whole group of them. They often travel in groups."

Both gods save us. If we had any luck at all, they'd have passed through ahead of us and wouldn't notice our descent.

What I wouldn't have given for tree hoppers. That was an animal I could support. Friendly, clever, and had never once tried to kill us. Or even the squirrels. Not particularly useful, but also not aggressive.

"Brush boars also have enormous tusks that extend from both their upper and lower jaws," Orion added as we started making our way down the interior wall of the canyon.

"Then why risk hunting them?"

"They're just as tasty as Emrys' bacon." He winked, and my stomach fluttered.

I could think of several things I'd prefer to be doing rather than climbing down a canyon wall while avoiding predators, but given our situation I didn't feel safe enough to engage in any of them.

We had already made one hairpin turn, but we were mere feet below the rim of the canyon when a tree hopper swooped down from above.

"Hello there, my friend," I crooned to the bird. It clacked its beak. "Don't worry. I didn't forget you."

I took a handful of dried fruit, seeds and nuts Orion had packed and scattered it on the ground. Soon four more tree hoppers had joined the first. They cawed and snapped at the little banquet.

"You're spoiling them," Orion warned with a smile.

"I wish I could take them with us to Emrys," I admitted. "You don't suppose Death would add on a few birds to the deal?"

"We could always ask."

I couldn't imagine the deity agreeing to such a request, but I liked his idea better than giving up on the comforting creatures.

The birds swooped and hopped behind us for a while, clacking and cawing. At one point my foot slipped on a loose bit of rock, and I clung to the canyon wall. One of the tree hoppers dove, pulling at my hair.

"A valiant attempt at rescue," I told it with a smile, trying to hide from Orion how much the slip had shaken me.

"Do you need to rest?" Orion was already digging through his pack for food.

"No. I'm all right. At least I'm dressed for a walk." I gestured to my attire—yet another set of his borrowed clothes—with a grin.

"Do you plan to go back to dresses?" Orion asked when we made our next turn on the route.

I scoffed.

"Not if I can help it. I'll just be known as a wild woman."

He chortled.

"And I will defend you from any naysayers. You and your army of birds." He pointed, and I saw the treehoppers were still swooping above us.

When we reached an outcropping that was flat and wide, we sat for a rest.

Orion grimaced and rubbed his knee. The birds landed with us, and one poked at his injured leg.

"I'll be all right," he assured the bird, tossing them all another piece of fruit. "We've got a plan."

I pulled a waterskin from my own satchel. Thank both gods, and I suppose whichever others weren't awful, that Orion had bothered learning enough when hunting to figure out how to make the things. I'd have been desperately lost on my own. I tilted the skin, taking a long drink and then passing it to Orion.

In exchange he handed me a strip of dried meat and some berries.

I chewed furiously, trying to take my mind off our precarious height, intermittently tossing a stray berry to the birds, who swooped and dove to catch them in the air.

The largest landed and began preening his feathers.

"Bravo!" I applauded him.

"I like seeing you happy. Death will find your father, I have every confidence. And if he's in danger in Emrys, or anywhere else, we'll go after him as soon as we've returned home."

I reached over and placed a hand on his arm, reveling, as always, in the warmth.

"My valiant knight," I teased.

After our short break we hiked for a few more hours, then stopped on another ledge to sleep.

We began moving again when the orange and purple lights danced above our heads once more. The birds had slept in a leafy branch that grew from the cliff wall.

"Do you think they're just following us for the food?" I asked, somewhat disconcerted. The tree hoppers were more intelligent than any birds I'd ever seen. Perhaps even more intelligent than Pellix, not that I would tell the stallion so. I imagined they had ulterior motives. They visited often, but they'd never stuck close for so long before.

"It's possible they want to know what we're after. They're

very observant, and they've probably noticed that I've never come down here before."

After another lengthy session of hiking, we reached the base of the canyon. It was covered in a gritty sand, with a stream running through its center. We were near the apex of the canyon on its northern edge. I could see the arc of the canyon wall where the cavern must be.

All the water came from the direction of the cavern entrance. As we approached, the water grew calmer. Farther downstream from the cavern's entrance, it became deeper and more erratic, growing from a small creek to a raging river. In the distance I could hear rushing rapids.

No matter; we'd stick to the shores and the cavern and hike back up the canyon walls.

At the cavern's entrance, the water was as smooth as glass. It was crystal clear and no deeper than our knees.

"How could it be so calm here, and grow so rapidly as it leaves the cavern?"

Orion glared at the water. "Charon. His realm. His rules. It will not move like any normal river, and we'll want to be on our guard. Stick close to me while we're inside."

I kept my hand in his as we waded into the water and entered the cavern.

CHAPTER 36

I froze once we were inside. It was a sanctuary, just as Death had described. The whole thing was like the interior of a cathedral. Instead of stained glass, there were shimmering crystals scattered down the curved walls, from the towering roof of the cavern to where the walls met the sands. All covered in glistening purples, blues, and creams.

"It's beautiful," I gasped.

The water was spilling out of a raised pool rimmed in steel-gray stone.

We approached the pool, climbing several slabs of stone as though they were a set of altar steps.

"Do you see the baton?" Orion asked.

"No."

Tree hoppers swooped outside the cavern's entrance, perhaps keeping watch, or just not interested in flying inside and feeling cooped up. I looked at the crystals, the sand, and around the stone and crystals for any sign of the baton.

"Ry. Maybe ... do you think ... the water?"

The water within the stone pool was glowing. If there was

some sort of magic relic within the cavern, I was willing to bet it was in those depths.

"Could be, but it could also be warded by Charon in some way. I'll check it."

"I can help."

"I know you can, but I've been around Charon for a hundred years. If there is some sort of defense in place, maybe it's like his home? Where I'll be able to break the barrier easier than you? I'll try, and if anything starts to go wrong, you can absolutely come to my rescue."

I still didn't like it, but I let go of his hand as he stepped over the stone rim of the pool and made his way into the water.

"Well?" I asked as he waded around the pool, water up to his waist.

"I feel fine. I'm going to search the bottom."

Orion took a deep breath and sank beneath the water. He resurfaced after several moments, took another breath, then dove again. He repeated the action several times.

"No baton. But I feel wonderful. My leg isn't aching at all."

"The cure Death mentioned! It's got to be this pool."

I was elated. Orion had a grin on his face as he clambered out of the pool. Knowing he wasn't going to be in pain anymore was a relief, but there was no baton.

That meant one thing.

"We'll have to go south to the beach."

He nodded.

"Yes. And if we're going to need to trek back up the side of the canyon and hike through the woods, I vote we rest here first."

"You're not worried about being found here?"

"Not if Death told us to come. She said she'd distract Charon for now, and we made it here fairly quickly. This might just be the safest place for us. We're protected from the elements better here than on the canyon wall."

"That's true."

"And I'm fully healed," Orion added.

He gave me a lingering look, slowly glancing at me from my head to my toes. The cavern suddenly felt much warmer.

"You are. And did you have anything in mind?"

"Several things." He smirked. "Should I tell you all my most scandalous desires, Starlight?"

I'd sworn I wasn't going to shy away from what this year might hold, not when it could all be taken away at any moment.

"You could, or you could show me."

He was on me in a moment, pressing me gently up against the cool stone between the crystals, capturing my lips in his.

"Ry!" I couldn't help letting his name slip out in a moan when he nipped at my neck.

"I could get us a blanket?" he offered, his breath sending delicious shivers down my spine.

"Yes. Let's do that."

I was tired of feeling any separation between us, and with Orion healed and Charon distracted, this was the perfect moment to rectify that.

I was so eager that I tripped forward in the sand as I moved for our satchels. Orion attempted to catch me, and we went tumbling. I landed on his chest.

"Ry! Are you okay?"

Blasted ghosts.

If I'd hurt him after he'd just fixed his leg, that might put a damper on things. Even if we did have a magically healing pool with us.

"Excellent," he wheezed. "This was all part of my devious plan."

He smirked, reaching up and pressing his lips against mine. I leaned into the kiss.

Ry wrapped an arm around me and rolled us so my back was in the sand. I laughed, at least until I looked into his eyes. The blue sparked, and Orion looked ravenous.

"Starlight," he groaned, tugging the neckline of my shirt aside and leaning down to trail kisses along my collarbone.

"Why *Starlight*?" I asked, then gasped as his body pressed against mine. I could feel his hardened length pressing against my core. Heat shot through me, and an urgent need.

"Orion."

He stopped, looking at me and running a hand through my hair.

"I called you Starlight because I've been trapped for a hundred years in a realm with no stars. The Ether may have beautiful lights, but as for stars, it doesn't have even a single one. I've always loved the stars—watching them and planning my adventures. Thinking of how you can see the same constellations from every country in Rayus. You can't see any here, and I've felt adrift for so long. Alone, and in the dark. Then you arrived, and you lit up this entire realm. Your presence is brighter than any star in the sky, and I knew I was lost to you the moment you entered the Ether. But also that my soul had been found again. It's not the sort of thing you admit right away; I didn't want to scare you. But I've been yours since you arrived."

My eyes threatened to fill with tears, so I did the only logical thing. I wrapped a leg around him, pulling him even closer. His eyes widened, then his mouth met my own again. We were a desperate clash of limbs.

"Orion, I'm ready."

"Really?"

I gasped as he nipped at my neck.

"Yes, all gods yes."

I pulled at his back, desperate to have him closer. He'd mentioned grabbing a blanket, but I didn't want to let him go. Not ever again.

Loud caws sounded, and the tree hoppers swooped into the cavern, flapping furiously.

"Bloody ghosts!" Orion cursed. "What could be—"

Something loud and deep echoed outside the cave.

"Ry! Did you hear that?"

Surely Charon couldn't be here. Not unless Death had failed to live up to her side of the bargain, and if that was the case we were in even worse trouble than we'd imagined.

From outside the cave came a growl, sending an echo through our crystal sanctuary.

Orion's eyes went wide, and he reached for me.

"A great bear. The tree hoppers were warning us."

"You don't think it's the one that went over the ledge?"

"No, it wouldn't have survived the fall. I'm surprised more of them could even get down here. The pathways are so narrow."

Unlike Orion and me, though, the bears had all the time in the world to meander through the forests. It was very possible wider or less visible pathways existed somewhere along the canyon.

A squeal and snort followed the next roar.

"What was that?" I asked, knowing in my gut that it was indeed the worst-case scenario.

"Brush boars."

A yowl joined the other calls, and my heart sank further when I recognized the slycat call.

"Ry, what do we do?"

One of the bears lumbered past the entrance of the cavern. It didn't charge us, but it lifted its head and sniffed, then roared and wandered back outside toward the other predators.

"They're like guardians of this realm for Charon. Even if he has no idea what we're up to, they must have realized that someone who's not Charon entered the area," Orion guessed.

"Then why not come in and kill us?"

"Maybe they'll keep us trapped here until the god does eventually realize someone's here? Or maybe they will grow bored, and we'll end up dinner after all."

I paled.

"That's not at all reassuring."

Orion scowled.

"No. It's not. I'm going to say this, and you're not going to like it. I recommend we do what I suggested during our first encounter with the great bears. I'll distract them, and you run."

"There's no way I'd leave you, and there's too many animals anyway. We'd never make it. I have a better idea."

It was a foolish plan. Haphazard and dangerous, but at the moment I thought it significantly less of a risk than the gnashing teeth. I explained to Orion what I wanted to do: we would make a run for it, straight out on the sands and then into the rapids. Once the water got deep enough, we could use the current to deter the animals and make our escape.

I twisted my hands.

"It's completely mad. Don't worry, you can say it. I happen to agree with you. But it's also our only way out. These creatures are all stronger and more sure-footed than us on land. They'll tear us to pieces. The rapids are dangerous, but they're our only chance. Besides, you said yourself the waters flow south. We'd be closer to the beach Death asked us to look for," I reminded him.

"Yes, but we could also drown. Even if we survive, I doubt we'd get out of this unscathed."

He was right, of course. And we still had to make it past the predators far enough down the bank that the waters were strong enough to prevent them following us.

"Orion, the water. We empty our waterskins and take more from the pool here. Hopefully it could help any injuries we might incur."

He frowned at the glowing water.

"I still don't like it, but I can't see that we have another choice. The predators are certain death. Waiting for Charon is certain death. The waters give us a chance."

"Then let's hurry, before they decide to come in after all."

We made quick work of emptying our water supply and filling the skins with Charon's glowing water. Once we had everything packed tightly in our satchels, we walked hand in hand to the entrance of the cavern.

The animals went quiet, perhaps sensing we were on the precipice of something.

Orion looked at me, the grey in his eyes eclipsing any blue.

"Ready?"

I gave a firm but shallow nod, worried that if I opened my mouth a sound of terror might escape.

"Now!" Orion yelled, charging forward. The two of us ran for everything we were worth.

All gods help us. We just have to make it to the rapids.

We ran along the very edge of the shallow water where it met the sands, sprinting south and following the rushing sound of churning waters in that direction.

A heavy body splashed into the shallow waters behind us. I turned and saw a great bear, charging at us. To each side of it ran multiple slycats.

"We'll never make it."

Orion charged on as if he hadn't heard me.

The tree hoppers swooped down, pecking at a few of the

slycats and clawing at them. The cats yowled, breaking off and batting at the loyal birds.

Please let them be all right, I begged as I kept running. I just had to trust that they were in better shape than us, since we most certainly couldn't fly.

I heard a snarl, closer than before. Two slycats leapt for us. The first was blocked by a charging brush boar, and the two creatures tangled and tumbled in the sands. The second slycat was headed directly for me.

"Hold on!" Orion screamed, flinging me toward the deepening waters. My feet slipped underneath me, and I fell back. I sputtered and flailed, trying to keep my head above water as I was pulled farther from the shore and into the increasingly violent rapids.

My plan no longer seemed like a safer option. I might well get us both killed.

"Orion! Ori—" I yelled, coughing and sputtering whenever my head surfaced. The waters were too deep, and too strong. I'd lost sight of him. I was moving faster than I'd anticipated, and it was all I could do not to drown.

I twisted and was pulled under again.

The next time I surfaced, I spotted his head over the waters. His mouth was open like he was shouting, but I couldn't hear him over the rapids.

I tried to swim for him, but the water forced us apart.

Yowls and roars faded into the distance as we were washed away.

CHAPTER 37

My eyes burned from all the water that had assaulted me. I hacked and coughed, feeling like I'd ingested more of the river than was possible.

The waters had slowed again—not as gentle as those in the cavern, but tamed to a soft flow instead of raging rapids. The high canyon walls had fallen away, and we were in a hilly area with trees along the banks.

I tried to swim for shore, desperate to grab onto a long branch or a downed log. My muscles were screaming, exhausted and numb. I could only imagine how they would feel when, or if, full sensation ever returned to them. I had to be seriously bruised from bashing against rocks in the midst of the rapids.

By some miracle of the gods, my satchel was still twisted around me, but who knew what state the contents were in, or whether they'd been pulled out of it by the current.

"Orion!" I attempted to yell, but my voice came out a hoarse rasp. I waved my arm, but my hand drooped feebly.

Tears threatened to spill from my aching eyes as the water continued to pull me along.

The rapids had been my idea. If anything had happened to him, it would be my fault. I might have made it down to the Ether by following a plan, but nothing since then had gone as expected.

Meeting Orion had erased any disappointment in that. He was worth the year in the Ether, worth the risk of Charon, and worth facing any predators the forest could throw at us. But if he was gone, and if it was because of me, I'd never forgive myself.

My chest felt as if it might rip open. I envisioned Death arriving again, only to tell me that Orion's soul was now in her domain.

I couldn't bear it, I thought. I'd ask to go with him. I'd request that Death return my father home to Emrys, and then take me, along with Orion.

Losing my family had been hard, but even the thought of losing Orion was simply unacceptable. A reality that could not be.

"Starlight!"

I whipped my head around, regretting the action instantly. Everything that wasn't numb ached, including my temples.

"Celia!" The voice was hoarse, just like mine. I saw movement along the bank—a waving arm.

Orion. His clothes were torn and tattered, and his hair disheveled from the water. He ran alongside, screaming for me.

I tried to swim to him but was barely able to move, stuck in the center of the current. My vision went hazy. When I saw Orion again, he was waist-deep in the water and extending a solid branch.

"Grab it!"

He sloshed farther into the river, but I could see him sway. He wouldn't keep his footing if he went any deeper, I thought.

Summoning my last reserves of energy, I kicked with my

battered legs, pulling at the water with my arms. The progress I made was scant, but it was enough. The fingers on my right hand brushed the edge of the branch, and my left closed around it, clutching the lifeline.

Slowly and steadily, Orion pulled me out. When the water was shallow enough for me to stand, I tried and nearly collapsed. Orion rushed to me, scooping me up in his arms and carrying me on his own unsteady feet the rest of the way to the grassy bank.

After setting me down, he collapsed on the ground. I crawled until I was next to him. We were both soaked and, as I had predicted, covered in bruises. My shirt clung to me, and I felt an extra chill where there was a hole ripped in the fabric.

"What now?" My voice hadn't recovered in the slightest.

"We head to the beach."

I groaned in response.

"As soon as we've had some rest," Orion added.

He held an arm out. I laid my head on his chest, and his arm wrapped around me as I curled against his side. Even the small gesture made a world of difference.

My shivering gradually stopped. I knew I needed to get up. We needed to figure out what our supply situation was and make our way to the second location, where the baton most likely was. At the very least, we ought to find somewhere more sheltered to rest, but I couldn't bring myself to move.

I stared overhead, watching the twisting lights of the Ether.

We stayed like that until my stomach growled.

"I still have a bit of food," Orion offered. "I put my pack down to run after you. Give me a moment."

He walked back upstream, and I sat looking down at myself. Orion's holster was still in place, the thin straps of leather soaked and frayed, but the knife safely at my side.

Once I untangled the straps on my own pack I found that

several items within had been sucked out by the water, but there were still a few soggy things left.

A couple of waterlogged purple potatoes, a few pieces of jerky that were soaked and loose in the satchel, and the best prize of all.

"The waterskin! Orion, we can use this!" I held it up and waved it. He was walking back with his own pack.

"I lost mine, but I still have a few fruits, some jerky, and one soaked blanket that nearly drowned me when it fell out of the pack and got wrapped around my legs. And my own knife."

We moved a bit further into the trees. The blanket wouldn't be any use to us wet, so Orion hung it overhead to dry out instead. He gathered some kindling and built up a fire. I gratefully warmed my hands next to the flames.

Neither of us had used the glowing water.

"You should take it. It's only practical. I'm not trying to insult myself, but you're the stronger of the two of us. You're more familiar with the Ether," I said.

"That's why you should take it! I can make it out of any scrapes I get into here, but you need all your strength in case we find ourselves in more trouble. And there's no way I'd let you hurt while I healed myself."

He had been fully immersed when he was healed in the cavern. We had no way of knowing how much water was necessary, which made it difficult to ration. We didn't want to waste it entirely by each using only a small amount and being no better off than before.

My stomach growled again.

"Why don't we figure this out on full stomachs?" Orion suggested.

I wouldn't have imagined soggy jerky and a damp root vegetable could taste so delicious, but they were more than welcome. I wolfed both down, smacking my lips.

"When we do return home, I think I'll eat all my meals this way. No cutlery, and with my hands. What do you think the queen would say?" I asked.

"If she's a smart woman, she'll join you. Fewer dishes. Much simpler." Orion laughed.

After we ate we made our way back to the bank, crouching down to rinse our hands off in the water. I cupped my hands and drank, even though I wanted to run from the water screaming. If I never saw a river again, I thought, it would be too soon.

"I think we should follow the river," Orion said.

"I have had enough water for a lifetime."

"I hear you, but think about it. We were at the northern end of the canyon, and the water ran directly south. Now, I'll grant you that water could have done some serious twisting and turning, but I think we're still generally headed south. The baton wasn't in the cavern, so the beach is our next stop, and we might as well stay close to a water source."

"I agree. I hate it, but I agree. It's the most sensible thing."

Not that I would have accused myself of being overly sensible, but I did want to survive, and more than that, I wanted Orion to survive.

"We're low on supplies and we have no idea how long it'll take us to reach the beach, but I have a lot of scavenging experience. It took me a lot of trial and error, getting sick by eating plants I shouldn't have ingested, but I have a pretty good idea of what's edible."

"As much as I would kill for some of the puff pastries at my favorite Fox Haven bakery, I'm more than happy to eat some roots right out of the ground, if that's what it takes. Edible is just about my only requirement."

He ran his hand through his hair, some of the lighter brown strands falling right back over his face.

"I wish I could offer you better. You deserve more than what the Ether has available."

I went over to him, grabbing his hands and placing them around my waist.

"The Ether has you. That's the best thing it could possibly have given me."

"Would you let me give you one thing, aside from barely edible plants? Take the water?"

I sighed, dropping my hands.

"How about this? I try a small trickle on one of my larger bruises. Maybe my ribs." They'd been terribly painful, and I knew I must have bruised a few. "We watch that spot for results, and based on how well it does or doesn't work, we can ration out the rest."

"Deal." Orion grinned.

He grabbed the waterskin from among our sparse possessions and brought it back over.

"You'll have to pull your shirt up," he told me.

What remained of my shirt, anyway. No spare clothes had survived our tumble in the rapids, so we'd have to make do. I lay on my side and pulled the tattered garment up past my lower ribs.

Orion sucked in a breath, reaching out to run his fingers lightly over the mottled bruising.

"I didn't realize it was this bad. We could use the entire thing."

"No. Just a small amount. And we need to save some, anyway. Who knows what we'll find at the beach?"

Orion scowled at me, but I knew it wasn't me he was angry at. It was the fact that I'd been injured in the first place. He opened the waterskin and poured a small trickle of the still-glowing liquid onto my injured side. Instead of dripping off, it pooled over the bruise.

I let out a low moan as the water warmed, soaking into my skin and chasing away the constricting pain.

"It's working," Orion whispered.

The reddish-purple of the injury faded until it was almost entirely gone. I let out a sigh of relief, finally able to breathe without pain.

"There. Now we know we can use it in small doses. You should have some as well."

"Yes. Fine." Orion responded, but his gaze was still glued to my side. The blue flecks surged like flames, bright against the grey.

"Ry?"

"I was just ... thinking about the cavern. Before we got interrupted, that is."

I smiled.

"I haven't forgotten. And I stand by what I said, but maybe it's best to wait until after we have the baton?"

He scowled.

"You're angry at me," I guessed.

He shook his head.

"No. I agree with you. But this is one more reason for me to hate Charon. For nearly a century I've had to bury most of my feelings to survive this place. Having you here has brought them back to the surface, but I'm thankful for that. I'd become as listless as the Shades, but now I actually feel real hope. Admittedly anger as well, but all the fury is for Charon. Assuming Death's plan does work, I'd like to have a hand in doling out whatever consequences she's got in mind."

"You don't think losing his hour will be enough?"

"I know it can't be, if we don't want to be looking over our shoulder forever, but it's a start."

CHAPTER 38

We ended up using perhaps a third of the waterskin for our more serious injuries, or at least the ones that would have the largest impact on mobility.

After taking shifts to sleep, we started our trek for the beach. The rest of my bruises did nothing but blossom throughout the day, tender to the touch and as colorful as any dress I'd ever owned. Still, things could have been far worse.

I'd wanted an adventure my entire life. I wasn't going to complain, now that I was on one with Orion and both of us had made it through the rapids.

However many blasted gods there actually were be praised, we didn't run into any large animals. We wouldn't have stood a chance, and I didn't want to try escaping into the water again. I would have liked to see the tree hoppers and assure myself they were okay, but they were nowhere to be seen either.

The farther south we got, the sparser the trees became, until we didn't see even the familiar gray squirrels. We kept close to the shoreline, following the river as it wound its way south, convinced it would eventually lead us to the sea Death had mentioned.

When we woke on the third morning, and after a breakfast of actual roots Orion had foraged, I did a bit of mental calculating.

"I'd say we're officially into May."

Orion nodded.

"I was thinking the same thing."

"If I were back in Fox Haven, we'd be headed to the capital and preparing for the first events of the season."

"You don't miss it, do you?"

I scrunched up my nose.

"Not most of it. But I do miss my friends. I wonder if Bram or Temple will propose to anyone this season. I wonder if Thomas will even be in town, or if he'll be traveling. I wonder if Charlotte's married yet or not."

More than anything, I wanted to make sure they were all well and to apologize for any hurt I'd caused them.

"I'll make sure you get back to them, Starlight. They'll forgive you. We'll stop the hour, and they'll realize that everything you did was for a reason."

Even if the rest of Emrys never found out what had happened to the hour, I'd have to explain things to my family. There was always a chance they might think I'd lost my mind at first, but I'd have Orion to back me up. And if they truly couldn't accept what I had to say, I'd leave.

I loved my friends and family, but I'd rather take my chances traveling Rayus with Orion than allow myself to be locked in a room as the crazed sister who spoke of gods no one believed in.

"What do you most want to do when you return?" I asked Orion.

A lot depended on how much people knew and were able to believe.

"Be with you. Without hiding you from Charon, and without the hour hanging over our heads."

Since I'd arrived, Orion had considered my safety.

"I hope you know," I started, "that you are the most important person to me. Wanting to make sure everything else is—"

"I know. I've never felt threatened that you still have family and friends to return to. I hope it works out for you. I'll do everything I can to make sure they believe and support you. I have no one else, Celia, but that doesn't mean I expect you to abandon everyone you ever cared about just for me."

But I would.

"Things do need to change, though. Emrys needs to change."

I shouldn't have to worry about choosing between Orion and my family's reputation.

He smirked.

"Then we change it. Bring a little bit of the freedom from the Ether to Emrys."

I couldn't help laughing. He made it sound simple, when I knew it would be anything but. Although ...

"I suppose for two people who have ended the Unseen Hour, anything is possible."

"That's the spirit, Starlight. Now then, why don't we figure out something to eat? If we had tools, I could catch a fish," Orion lamented when we saw some swim by.

"You could always wade in and try to scoop one up with your hands." It was a half-hearted attempt to tease him, but my aching joints stole all the humor from my voice. The pain hadn't even fazed me during our activities before our rest, but I'd been too distracted to notice.

The blue and green lights of the Ether's sky, faint as they were in this vast landscape, were high in the sky when Orion threw his arm out, signaling a stop.

Adrenaline rushed through me and all my muscles contracted.

"What is it? A brush boar? A bear?"

"No." Orion shook his head. "It's a sound. Waves."

He was right. Rhythmic and insistent, the sound wasn't the same as the river.

"There!" Orion pointed in front of us. Under the light of the pale blue moon, I could see distant waves.

We'd reached the beach.

There were shadowed shapes looming, sticking out from the sands and towering above our heads. When we got close enough, I saw that they were rock formations. These were not sunny and forgiving shores; they were rocky and dangerous.

"Death said we'd be looking for rocks," I said.

"Yes. Should we try to find the baton now?" Orion's voice was hesitant, but I nodded.

We gave it a half-hearted search, realizing quickly that the limited light would make it nearly impossible when what we were after was such a small item. Something easily confused with a small stick.

The waves were such a deep blue they were almost black. We needed the brighter orange and purple lights to have much hope of spotting anything between the dark stones and grey sands.

"Ry, what if you sing? Do you think that could help? Death did say the baton was tied to the Shade song. Maybe you'd ... feel something?" I turned away, blushing. I knew only the barest bit about Shade song, and that it was a sore subject.

A gentle hand turned my cheek so I was staring into Orion's eyes. Even in the darkness I could see the blue flecks glinting.

"You are brilliant! Maybe stand far off, though? I don't want to risk you coming to harm."

I shivered, picturing myself walking directly into the sea.

I moved well away from the area, back past where the rocks began. Even then, I could hear some of the clearest notes as Orion sang.

I did my best to resist, but when the music stopped I found myself halfway across the beach.

"I think I've found it!"

I ran, stumbling through the sands to where Orion stood.

"This one. This has to be it." He pointed to one of the rock piles.

The stones were larger than any of the others, and arranged in a pattern. The biggest, a tall rectangle rounded at the corners, was placed at the back, with other rectangles curving around it to form an arc that served as the backdrop to what appeared to be a stone altar.

The cavern had crystals surrounding the healing pool. This place had a stone box.

"There's writing on here. I'm certain of it. Feel," Orion insisted.

I knelt down, running my hands over the stone lid. He was right. Etchings of some kind. I'd have given all of the money at Scops, taken it from under Ambrose's nose, to be able to read it. For just one lantern, or one of the floating orbs that lit the Ether's meadow.

"I'm almost certain the baton is inside. I can feel it. We'll just have to wait for it to get brighter so we can read it."

"Think it could require a key?"

"No. There's nothing I felt on it that would be a keyhole. Only the writing."

I wasn't convinced, but it made as much sense as any other theory. And I trusted Orion. If it was important to him, we would try it.

I looked around the beach. It appeared empty, but I couldn't shake a wary feeling.

"This time, let's not linger by the altar, just in case," I insisted.

We trekked back to where I'd stood while Orion sang and then rested, waiting for the sky to lighten and give us our answer.

CHAPTER 39

The beach was awe-inspiring under the purple and orange lights of day. The sands stretched on for what seemed an infinite length in both directions before they disappeared into fog. The water extended the same way in front of us, waves as far as the eye could see. The shore, and the shallower waters, were dotted with the black rock formations we'd seen the night before.

Orion passed me a handful of jerky. We'd been saving it for the beach. I gnawed on my piece.

"I've been thinking. You should try to read the box and open it. I'll stand watch near the stones so nothing can sneak up on us from behind them. We don't want another incident like at the canyon, and Death said you should carry the baton," I reasoned.

"And what if wild animals *do* rise from the seas? You're not fighting them alone."

I threw my head back, trying to get my unruly, sea-air soaked hair out of my eyes.

"No. I'll give a signal for us to make ourselves scarce if I see anything suspicious. But you're the one with the Shade song. You should be the one to open the box."

"All right. I'll work quickly, and then we'll leave as soon as we have what we came for."

"Deal." There would be no arguments from me on that front. The beach spot, like the cavern, did have an eerie sort of beauty to it, but I wasn't planning to stay and see if Charon had more guards.

The light confirmed what we'd been able to make out in the dark. The formation we had focused on was notably larger than any other. The stones were placed in an arc shaped like a crescent moon, and I paced its perimeter, making sure no one could sneak up on us from those directions.

"I can read it!" Orion called.

I paused, taking in a shaky breath and letting it out slowly. *Thank all the gods.*

"Listen to this. *I shall see you again in whatever fate awaits the gods,*" Orion read aloud.

I shivered, from the breeze and words in equal measure.

"It's like what you'd see on a headstone," I whispered.

"Who would Charon have to mourn?" A few moments passed in silence, and I prayed he'd be able to work quickly.

"The box is still shut tight! Reading it did nothing, and I can't pry it loose," Orion called.

"Blasted ghosts!" I cursed, kicking the sand a few times. "All this way for a locked box and no key. Unless … Ry! Check the sides. Maybe there's a latch or a catch somewhere?" My father's desk had held a hidden compartment. Gods and men were different beings, but maybe the same when it came to protecting their secrets.

"There's something here! More writing, very small, on one edge." Orion's voice got quieter and he murmured something, probably reading the inscription.

I heard a resounding pop, like the cork in a bottle coming loose.

"I've got it! There was a small compartment that slid out from the bottom." Orion's voice grew louder, and he rounded the back curve of the stones. "We've got it!"

He scooped me up, spinning me in a circle. My heart soared along with the rest of me.

When he released me, I saw his left hand held a wooden baton. I threw my arms around his neck, pulling him back to me. My fingers ran through his unruly hair. When my lips met his, he tasted like the sea air.

"I'll need to be finding secret, Unseen Hour–ending items more often, if that's the result," Orion teased.

"Now that we've got it, we can go home."

"We still need whatever's on Charon's property before we can return to Emrys," Orion reminded me.

I blushed.

"Actually, when I said *home* I was referring to the cottage. I know it's technically yours, but—"

"Starlight, you could have anything of mine, and I would give it gladly."

"Then let's go home. We can recoup and resupply before we find the second item. Decide what to do with the baton. And finish what we started at the canyon?"

Orion's pupils widened, his look turning hungry.

"If that's what you want," he choked out.

When I made a decision, I committed. Back in Emrys, no one had kept me from rides with Pellix, or from leaving the estate at night, or stealing books from the library.

And nothing would keep me from Orion. I wanted all of him, and I wanted him to have all of me.

Just as soon as we were back to the safety of the forest.

"Let's go, before a great bear or something ruins the moment," I urged, grabbing his hand.

The ground shook, and Orion reached out, steadying me.

"Cursed gods! Really?" I looked around for the source of the noise.

"What is that?" Orion pointed further down the beach.

My gaze locked on a glinting mass that had just appeared near the waves. I couldn't help feeling like I'd called bad luck down on us with my words.

Orion's grip tightened on my arm, and he hauled us behind one of the rock formations.

"Nothing good." He looked around.

If we moved, we'd be exposed.

To hide, or to run?

"Hiding didn't work at the canyon. We should move," I whispered.

"Quickly," Orion responded, nodding his head toward a stone formation northwest of us, farther from the waters.

He squeezed my hand, and we ran for it. I threw a glance over my shoulder. The figure was closer, looking wholly out of place on the grey shores, silhouetted against the orange and purple sky. A man. Tall and barrel-chested.

"Not your father, I take it?" Orion asked as I picked up my pace.

"Definitely not! I'm fairly certain whoever's out there isn't even human. Another god?"

"He's definitely not Charon!"

"Foolish beings! Do you really think you can run?" A deep voice boomed across the beach.

Orion threw us behind the next rock formation. I poked my head out, trying to figure out where the god was. Closer still, and with a malicious gleam in his eyes.

He was muscled and covered in armor. It looked almost like

leather, but it was green. Green with copper studs and spikes along the chest and arms. He had long red hair tied at the neck, and a beard of the same shade.

"No sense hiding!" the god shouted.

"He's right. If he can move like Charon or Death, he could just appear wherever he wants. He's toying with us," I said.

"But we have to try."

We didn't have a choice.

"On three, we go for the next formation. A few more and we can be off the beach and into the trees. Maybe we can lose him there. It's our best shot. Three, two, one, go!"

We sprinted for the next formation. I could see the god out of the corner of my eye as we moved from that one to the next. We had one more to go before we were off the actual beach.

The god lifted his hand, spinning a weapon he held. It was a hammer, several times larger than the ones I had seen black-smiths in Emrys using.

He stalked closer, his steps carrying him an impossible distance, but he still didn't transport himself directly into our path.

His brows were lowered in a glare.

His size, and ferocity, added to my certainty that we faced yet another deity. This one looked much less friendly than Death.

"Why do you invade Charon's lands?" the god demanded. Strong winds buffeted us as the words hit my ears.

If any of them had been a god of war, I imagined it would be the deity on the beach. He swung the hammer in a circle above his head, seemingly creating the wind himself. The copper on his armor gleamed.

Orion positioned himself in front of me.

The god lowered his hammer, pointing it at us.

"You have no right to be here. This realm is for Shades, not women of Emrys."

He recognized me for what I was—alive—just as Orion had said Charon would. And he'd spoken to me personally. I gulped.

"You won't touch her." Orion glared at the god, looking every bit as angry as when he mentioned Charon.

"And you, *Head Shade*," the deity's voice dripped with disdain, "will feel the wrath of Odos's hammer."

The answer to my question of which god we faced no longer felt relevant. Knowing his name wouldn't help us beat him.

I leapt out from behind Orion, shaking my fist.

"You cannot have him!" I screamed.

Odos threw back his head and laughed.

"Look at the two of you. Such fiery tempers. Fierce. Certain of yourselves, even when you're outmatched. Not that I'm surprised. After all, you made it down here, and you—"

"Celia, run!" Orion shoved me, and the two of us tried to sprint farther from the beach.

I had no interest in finishing our conversation with Odos, and we couldn't let him get the baton, either. It was our only bargaining chip with Death.

The sand rolled, and I went flying. Odos lifted his hammer, striking the beach a second time. The ground beneath me shook, and I was slammed onto my back. I sat up and struggled to breathe. My lungs refused to take in the air my body was begging for.

I looked for Orion, only to see him on his feet. His expression was positively feral as he faced the god. He charged at Odos, screaming.

The god raised his hammer, and I reached uselessly for them.

"Orion, no!"

Lightning slammed into the sands between the two of them. My heart leapt.

Death didn't appear, but Odos had stopped and was looking up at the skies.

A familiar voice boomed overhead.

"Leave or fight me, brother."

I recalled what Death had said about their not truly being related, but she'd been right about one thing: they definitely fought like siblings.

Odos glared at the skies overhead, and then at Orion.

Ry had been thrown back from the lightning, and was pushing himself up from the sands.

"You have no authority here!" Odos yelled at Death's disembodied voice.

She laughed, the sound echoing around us.

"No more than you. This is foolishness. Leave, before he senses us. You could ruin everything."

"But he—"

More lightning peppered the earth, striking the sands. Where it hit, brittle curved structures that looked like warped glass rose from the beach. Odos struck each of them down with his hammer, a defiant scowl on his face.

I took my chance, rushing over to Orion and helping him to his feet. The two of us stumbled away from the arguing gods, making for the sparse treeline.

"Don't stop!" Orion shouted at me when the ground beneath us rolled again. I almost tripped, but he held me up.

"Leave them be, Odos!" Death's voice boomed again, followed by more lightning. I risked one glance over my shoulder.

The god continued to glare, but his wind stopped chasing us.

"This isn't the end of it," he warned, voice echoing as his form faded on the beach and we distanced ourselves from the sands.

CHAPTER 40

We didn't stop until the trees grew thick around us.

I fell on my back, winded.

"Are you all right?" we asked each other at the same time.

"I'll live." Orion laughed, then sucked in a sharp breath. "Although my ribs may be useless for a while. I appreciate Death's help, but I landed all wrong. I do have one bit of good news, though."

"And what is that?"

He reached into his pack and pulled out the glistening wooden baton. Its color matched the trees near Orion's hut, and the handle was smooth but gleamed with the same color as the cave crystals.

"We did it!" I yelled, leaping to my feet and regretting it instantly as pain shot through my newly bruised legs. I sat down, staring at the baton in Orion's hand. "*You* did it," I said again, softer.

He sighed.

"One step closer to defeating Charon, and his hour."

We used a small trickle of water on Orion's side but

preserved the rest. After all, we still had Charon's residence to get through.

Orion sighed as the water went to work.

The first full day of walking back was largely uneventful, aside from the scenery. At one point the familiar trees fell away, and we found ourselves surrounded by a growing number of large hedges. After a while, we couldn't see anything over the plants.

"It's like we're in a maze," Orion observed.

"We could try and circle back, find where it starts and go around the perimeter?"

Orion was frowning at the tall shrubbery around us. It was quiet within its bounds.

"I don't love the idea of spending more time in an unfamiliar portion of the woods with potential predators and possibly Odos on our trail, but I think I like this place even less."

We turned around but had barely begun to retrace our steps when it became evident that wouldn't be an option.

"They've grown around us. There's no way out. Bloody ghosts!" Orion cursed, staring at the solid wall of greenery where a path had one been.

We were quite literally hedged in.

Orion pulled the knife from his boot, slashing at the leaves and branches. Bits of hedge fell at our feet, but as quickly as it hit the ground, it grew again, thicker, giving us less space.

Orion stopped. He put the knife back and scowled at the hedges.

"Sometimes I forget just how much power gods have," I whispered, watching to see if the hedges would continue to close in.

They didn't.

Orion sighed.

"We've got a long journey ahead of us. The good thing is

that it looks like if we don't harm the plants, they won't harm us."

"And I'm guessing you've never seen anything like this before?"

"No. Even with all my time in the Ether, I haven't seen everything. I've focused on survival. Once I had an area that contained what I needed, I left it at that. I marked boundaries based on where I encountered trouble, and stayed away. All those years I wanted to be free to explore, and once I got down here I lost my desire. Things are different now, of course. I should have looked at every square inch of the Ether several times over."

But he'd been alone, and he'd lost everyone and everything. It was no wonder he had wanted to protect what he had left. His life, his cottage, his safe area in the forest with the tree hoppers and squirrels. Even his trips to the less-than-responsive Shades.

"Don't worry. We'll figure it out together. Why don't we keep moving forward?"

Orion held my hand as we turned back in the direction we'd been going before the hedges closed in.

We had no stars to navigate by, but we could watch the directions the lights ran in overhead. They'd gone back to deep purple and blue, but from what we could tell we'd continued in roughly the same direction walking overnight.

I yawned, putting the back of my hand over my face.

"They are pretty, although they're a bit repetitive," I observed as we continued down a long opening between the hedges. The leaves were large and had several points apiece. They were lush and green, held together by twisting limbs.

"Look!" Orion pointed, and I saw that ahead of us there was a break in the monotony. A tree.

We ran for it.

I was worried the hedges might block us off from our exit, but they never moved. We made it out of the plants, and just like that, we were back in a forest of familiar trees.

"I've never been so happy to see a tree in all my life." I threw my arms around the nearest one, laughing when my embrace sent a gray squirrel skittering up the trunk.

"Sorry small friend! Just happy to be free of the maze."

Once we were far enough that we could no longer see the hedges behind us, we felt safe to stop and rest.

"We can take it in shifts. I'll watch first," Orion said after I'd gotten settled on our one blanket.

I didn't have the energy to argue with him, but I made him swear to wake me up when he needed rest as well.

I was exhausted enough that sleep came easily, and I was so deep into it that I wasn't sure where I even was when I first felt something grabbing at my arm.

After a couple of confused moments I jerked upright, convinced Orion was hauling me up.

Were we being attacked? I felt something else on my leg.

"Ry? What is it? Is something wrong?"

He was walking a perimeter around where we'd stopped, looking out into the trees. He turned back to me.

"Everything's fine. You can go back to sl—"

His eyes went wide, and something snaked around my face, covering my mouth. I screamed, but my voice was muffled. Looking down, I saw vines trailing across the ground and twisting themselves around my legs and wrists.

"Starlight!" Orion charged over, pulling out his knife and hacking at the vines around my face.

As he did, I was slammed into the ground when the vines around my legs tightened and began to pull.

"Ry!"

Panicked, I twisted and flopped, trying to reach my own knife, but I couldn't. I gasped in pain as I was dragged over rocks and rough patches. In the distance ahead, I saw the hedges again. The area where we'd exited was no longer a welcome sign of freedom. It looked like a yawning mouth, ready to swallow me up.

"I'm coming!" Orion yelled, running after me as the plants hauled me over the ground at surprising speed.

He threw the knife, and it wedged itself in a thick vine that was wrapped around one of my arms. That bit of vine went slack, and I was able to slide my left arm loose. Small thorns went flying from the vine in Orion's direction.

I struggled more when I realized the plant was fighting back. It was alive enough not merely to grab me but also to respond to Orion's attacks.

"Your knife!" Ry yelled, who now had several thorns stuck into his arms and pant leg. I was able to reach it with my left hand; I pulled it out and began hacking at the vines around my leg.

One released, and my left leg slid loose. Orion continued to chase me as I got to work freeing my other arm.

Just as I did so, I was slammed into the ground and felt my chin get knocked into the dirt. It was almost as if the plant knew what I'd done and was offended. I tried to twist around and reach the remaining vine on my leg, but it held firm and was now whipping me side to side.

Unable to focus on the vines themselves, I changed strategies and dug my knife into the dirt.

Orion ran past me. I twisted my neck in time to see him retrieve his own knife and begin hacking at the remaining vine holding me. More vines slid past him, twisting around both my legs. One snapped him in the face, and I saw a line of red appear on his cheek.

"Ry!" I yelled, then screamed as the knife holding me fast started to slip out of the dirt.

It wobbled, and my grip loosened. I tried to grasp it and slam it back in the ground, but the moment I adjusted my grip I was pulled backward, losing my hold entirely.

"Ry!" I screamed again as I flew past him, being dragged backward by the singular vine still intact.

I was pulled into the hedges, and the last thing I saw before they closed in was Orion's wide eyes as he ran for me.

CHAPTER 41

Vines twisted over me, thorns digging into my arms, my leg, my side.

"Orion!" I kept screaming, trying to break free.

I heard him yelling for all he was worth on the other side of the hedge; then, for a moment he got quiet.

"I've got an idea!" he called before going silent again.

I stilled, trying not to do anything that would bring forth a response from the plants and further injure my limbs.

He'll come back, he'll come back, I repeated to myself.

Vines slid over my neck, and even with all the adrenaline coursing through me, my vision began to go black.

I could still hear Orion yelling, but I didn't think he'd make it through in time.

"Let her go! Let. Her. Go!" he yelled.

There was a flash of light, and the vines began to retreat. Fire. Eating the leaves and stems and thorns.

A hand closed around mine, and Orion hauled me to my feet.

"We have to run, Starlight, can you run?"

I tried to nod as the vines around my neck slid away, but it was too much of an effort. I could barely breathe. Smoke, and whatever the vines had done to hurt my throat, made it impossible.

"It's all right. I've got you."

Orion scooped me into his arms and ran, directly through a wall of flames and disintegrating hedges.

"The. Fire." I managed in a hoarse rasp as we got farther away.

"If it saved you, I would burn the entire Ether down without regret," he responded.

As he spoke, it began to rain.

Orion stopped at one point to bend down and scoop up my lost knife but then continued on carrying me.

He'd had no sleep, but he didn't set me down for what felt like hours. When he did, he examined the areas where the vines had dug in. His touch was gentle, but the slightest pressure was agonizing on my throat where the vine had twisted around it.

"Can you speak?" he asked.

I opened my mouth, but nothing came out. Swelling must have started since we'd run from the hedges. It was ludicrous, since I'd been breathing the entire time, but I grasped at my throat, feeling like I was short of air.

"It's all right, Starlight. We'll fix this."

Orion lowered my hands and got the healing water for me. After it took effect I was able to manage walking at his side, but I was so shaken that it was a while before I felt safe to speak again.

"This was Charon. Even if he doesn't know about you specifically, he's the one who created these hellish traps. I'll kill him for this, I swear it."

My muscles tensed at Orion's declaration. How could he possibly take down a god, unless it was with Death's help? Another part of me, though, understood. Orion was right about his emotions becoming more prevalent, and he had a right to them.

He said nothing further, and we moved in companionable silence until we got back to a part of the forest Orion recognized.

I was certain we'd see Death on the journey back, but she never made an appearance.

"She warned Odos about alerting Charon to their presence. I'd guess that she's being very careful about her trips down here." Orion said.

I was inclined to agree. And I hoped that the fact she wasn't back was a good sign. At any rate, we hadn't seen Odos, Charon, or any other gods since the beach. I chose to believe that meant Death's plans, or her interference, were working.

It took several more days to get back to the cottage without the water to carry us. The last couple of days we began seeing the tree hoppers again.

"Thank you, friends. I'll have something special for you when we make it back," I promised them.

"In the hundred years I've been here, I never thought I'd be so thrilled to see this place," Orion said when we made it to the cottage. It was still cleverly concealed between the trees, but I'd memorized the area of the forest around his home and recognized it more easily now.

When we made our way inside Orion stared at the two cots. He ran one hand over the back of his neck.

"I was thinking, we should push them together. I want you to fall asleep in my arms. I'll be able to protect you better if you stay close."

For a brief moment I considered flirting and asking if that was the only reason, but then I felt the phantom pressure of vines squeezing my limbs. Smoke that didn't exist filled my lungs.

"I think that would be best."

I woke to the feel of Orion's arms warming me, tucked close against his chest.

"You've ruined me for sleeping any other way ever again," he whispered before kissing my shoulder.

He'd been right. It was much better sleeping together. I curled into him, longing to stay like that. After a few moments though, I threw back the blankets.

We just had one more item to find, and then Death would be able to help us end things once and for all.

Ry and I made our way outside to resupply our packs.

"We'll just keep going as though nothing happened with Odos," he said as he stuffed some purple almost-potatoes into his satchel.

I nodded along, shoving a bite of pear into my mouth and chewing furiously.

"Yes, as much as I don't like it. We have to keep going. We've gotten this far, and searching for the items has been a distraction from my father."

From my failure.

"I'm sure Death is being diligent in her search."

And Odos had pulled her away from her efforts.

I squeezed a fruit I was packing too tightly, and it burst.

Without a word, Orion took it from my hands and wiped my fingers clean with a bit of cloth.

"We'll find out where he is. As long as we're alive, it's not too late."

I laughed.

"What?" he asked.

"I was picturing Death's face if we had been killed in the canyon, or the beach, and appeared in her realm instead. I don't think she would have been happy."

Orion grinned.

"I expect not. And I'm sure she'll be able to help your father, Starlight. She has all her Reapers. If she can't figure it out on her own, she'll find a way."

I was drawn to the deity. I wanted to be like her, although I would certainly never be a goddess, and I did want to retain a little more warmth than even the most benevolent god we'd met.

We ate ravenously as we finished our preparations.

I heard a familiar cawing sound, followed by a handful of tree hoppers fluttering down.

"Wait right here!" I ran back into the cottage.

When I returned, I had a handful of silver buttons, pulled from Temple's riding jacket.

They were lovely, but the birds would get far more enjoyment out of them. They had a love of shiny things.

One tree hopper jumped over, tilting its head to the side to give one of the buttons a closer look. He clacked his beak happily, picked it up and flew to a low branch to examine it further. The other birds followed suit, and soon we were surrounded by glints of silver reflecting the purple and orange lights in the sky.

"Without you all, we would have been lost," I told the birds, wishing I knew a better way to express my gratitude.

"Do you still think we should ask Death about bringing them back?" Orion asked.

"Absolutely."

He grabbed my hand, pulling me toward him and kissing me. I sighed into the softness of his lips, the reassuring solidness of his chest. The beating of his heart that reminded me we'd made it this far.

"Before we leave, there was something I needed to discuss with you."

"Yes?" I stayed pressed against him, warm and safe.

"As much as we laughed at it earlier, the idea of losing you terrifies me. Not just because I've been alone so long. What I mean is, I'm not just desperate for any company. I'm grateful for *you*, Starlight. As fierce and fearless as you are though, anything could happen. I'm not fool enough to think I can prevent everything, but I would like to address one issue that could keep us apart in Emrys."

"And what is that?"

"Will you marry me?"

CHAPTER 42

I drew back, the words echoing in my head.

"Marry? You and me? The two of us?"

"That is generally how marriages work. At least that's how they worked a hundred years ago."

I'd been in the Ether with him for months. Engagements in Emrys could happen within a week during the season. Not that I intended to measure my own life by their standards anymore, but I shouldn't have been surprised.

Still, it felt sudden.

"Are you certain? I'm not doubting you," I assured him, "but we're in the middle of something that could impact all of Rayus, not just Emrys. We're tangled in a web of strife created by the gods. Do you not want to wait until things calm down? To make absolutely certain this is what you want once things settle?"

He liked me in the Ether, but things might be very different after the hour.

Orion knelt in front of me.

"No. I don't want to wait and I don't want to reconsider. I've waited over a lifetime for something that I thought might never come. I lost everything that mattered to me. I thought helping

Death was all I was good for anymore, but that's not true. *You* matter to me. I will do whatever I can to help you, to protect you, and to make you happy. And at the risk of being far too traditional, I'd like to do it as your husband, not just a man you met in the woods."

Tears pricked the corners of my eyes.

"You could never be just another man to me. You are the voice that spoke to me in my dreams, before I'd even met you. You're the one who's kept me going down here, and who has never once tried to change me. Of course I'll marry you."

He threw his arms back around me.

"This is truly the happiest moment I've had in the Ether. I know you wouldn't want me asking your family's permission, but I also know how deeply you care for them. I'll find a way to win them over."

I scoffed, picturing Ambrose with his nose in the air.

"I don't care what they say. I won't be separated from you."

He'd waited all this time to return, and he was more concerned with how those closest to *me* would react. The only family he had left was a distant cousin who had taken over the estate, and even if by some miracle of the gods we could prove that Orion was in fact the rightful heir, where would that leave him? He'd be alone without family in a large house, on a large estate, and at odds with the cousin whom he'd just ousted from the position.

"What about you?" I asked him. "What of your family seat? Are you going to try and take back your estate?"

If he wanted it, I'd support him as well. I'd do anything I could to make it happen. I'd dig through every Holmes record in the library. I'd help forge documents if that's what it took.

"Truthfully, I'd just as soon not. My goal hasn't been to be the duke for years. If I never see my title again and need to pick up a trade, that would be fine. After my time in the Ether, I'd be happy to be a gardener on an estate, except..."

He stayed silent for so long that I worried he wasn't going to answer at all.

"Except?" I prompted gently.

He looked away.

"What would I have to offer you, then? How could I ever ask for your hand with nothing to my name?"

My breath caught in my throat.

"There is no one else I want by my side. I would live with you anywhere," I answered honestly.

I would not let the people around us be the thing that kept us apart. I would make my own decisions. I couldn't control the consequences, but I was free to decide who I wanted to spend my life with.

"Oh dear!"

I threw a hand over my mouth.

"Should I be concerned?" Orion gave half a smile as he said it, his voice light.

There was one person in particular who might argue I wasn't free to offer my hand to anyone. What was Ry going to think? Bellamy had started as a small annoyance, and now he might be the undoing of the best thing to ever happen to me.

"It shouldn't be. There's ... something I haven't told you. Something that I should have, but at first it simply wasn't the priority on my mind. Then, I didn't think it mattered, because the issue had surely resolved itself. But you do deserve to know. And it's not that I've been trying to hide it. I haven't even thought about it in weeks."

I wrung my hands.

"Whatever you have to say, even if it's a 'no,' I will listen openly. You know I'll help you no matter what, whether you accept me or not."

"I've already accepted. This has nothing to do with a lack of interest. It's a problem with me, not with you. Once you hear it, you might want to take back your proposal."

"I'm going to have to disagree with you there."

The words were right on my tongue, but it took great effort to push them out.

"It's … an engagement. Another engagement. I am engaged. I mean, I was engaged. Before this. I'm sure he thinks I'm dead now. But before the last Unseen Hour, there was a proposal and—"

I was doing an awful job of explaining myself, and I knew it.

Ry's mouth twisted down, his eyes focused on the dirt.

"I see. You have a fiancé. There's already someone waiting for you."

"It's not what you might be thinking," I rushed to assure him. "I am engaged, but I never even really said yes."

Orion looked back up at me, the blue in his eyes flashing dangerously.

"You didn't say yes? This was a forced situation? Who arranged this?"

His anger was justified, as far as I was concerned. He may have spent a hundred years in the Ether unbothered by etiquette or society, but he was well aware how it worked. How it had worked in his life as well as mine. This wasn't unheard of.

Women agreed, but not often because of love.

"It wasn't technically forced. My mother had started pressuring me to find a husband. Truthfully, she should have done it years ago, based on my age. She'd only held off so long because she was grieving the death of my father."

"So she's responsible?"

I shook my head. I was explaining everything horribly.

"No. My brother Ambrose is the one who agreed to it when

asked for permission. There is a man. A Marquess. Bellamy. Bellamy Bonds."

"Marquess Bonds. I've not heard of the family." His voice was still tense, but I grabbed ahold of the distraction.

"You wouldn't have. His family moved to Emrys a couple of generations ago. In fact, I think they likely rose to prominence within a few years of your disappearance. Bellamy's grandfather was from Tang and was a noble emissary. He married a noblewoman here and was a favorite of the king at that time, I'm told. They were granted a position and lands. Newer money in Emrys, but money for generations in Tang."

Orion steepled his hands, placing his fingers under his chin.

"Was that the reason for your brother's acceptance? Financial? I know you're not a product to be purchased, but if money is what they require, then I will find a way. I know what I said about losing my estate, but I'll fight for it if that's the only way to gain your family's favor."

I shot him a glare.

"You're right about one thing. I am not a product to be purchased. My family doesn't need money. We already possess an utterly unsensible amount. As for my family's favor ... I'd marry you without it."

I wanted them to appreciate Orion as much as I did, but if they didn't, I'd settle with him somewhere new. We had survived the Ether; we could survive a journey to Sez, or Mejje, or even the lost country, if we had to live in the wilderness to truly be free.

I would miss Charlotte and Thomas, and my family, but I wasn't going to let anyone's opinions or rules keep me from Ry.

I glowered.

"This is all about tradition and expectations. I'm too old to be unmarried, still in the house with my brother and his new wife. Bellamy means nothing to me. He's just insufferable and persistent, and has dreadful timing. He wanted to get married before Wintertide, but I convinced him to move the ceremony. I knew I'd be gone before the actual wedding took place."

Orion's glare faded.

"Was he aware you didn't really want this marriage? Did he pressure you in any way?"

"No. He's just another self-important bore. I don't think he had any inkling that I wouldn't be interested. He's awful, but mostly because it's so dull being in his company, and he's not a fantastic dancer, either."

Orion laughed as he finally displayed a smile.

"Well if that's all, then."

"He wanted to propose during the last season, and my friend Thomas helped me by pretending to consider my hand. Thomas and I have only ever been friends," I rushed to assure Ry, "but he was more than willing to assist me when Bellamy expressed interest. I'd hoped that would hold him off until I could enact my plan to come after my father, but at some point he realized Thomas wasn't serious about my hand."

"I will owe Thomas thanks."

I sagged in relief. For once, someone wasn't questioning my motives when I very clearly defined what Thomas was to me.

"He and Charlotte are lovely, and he really did try. Bellamy approached my brother in the fall. I would have said no outright, but it would have caused such a commotion, and I didn't think it was necessary. I thought if I could get down here, and then return with my father—"

"They'd all be too focused on his return to worry about forcing you into a marriage. Whether or not you tell your family the true story of the Ether, your father would know the truth. He could side with you and rescind his acceptance. Your family is established, and wealthy, and no protest Bellamy could make would hold water."

I nodded.

"Precisely. As far as I am concerned, I am a free woman. I don't feel any loyalty to Bellamy whatsoever, but I did feel you deserved to know. Are you angry?"

"Not at you, although I'm more than willing to release some anger if anyone questions your decision. Now that everything is out in the open, let me ask again. Celia Hipnosi, will you give me permission to marry you? And to adventure together, no matter where life takes us?"

"Yes!" I threw myself into his arms again, grinning. "Now, do you think we have a little more time before we have to leave?"

"For?"

I trailed a hand down his neck, then pulled him in for a kiss by his shirt collar.

He grinned when he pulled back.

"Starlight, I can always make time for that."

CHAPTER 43

Orion and I returned to the cottage, which felt much smaller than it had previously.

Or perhaps it was that Orion took up more space as he turned to shut the door behind me.

"Did you mean what you said in the cavern? About being ready."

"Yes," I answered without hesitation.

There was a lot of uncertainty in our future, and our situation in the Ether, but that was one thing I wasn't going to change my mind about.

I wanted Orion.

"I don't want you to think that because you said yes to me, that you're obligated to me in any way."

Many men in Emrys would have felt differently. Orion was exceptional, and I wanted to make sure he knew it.

"If anything, I think you'll find my desire for you will only grow."

"Is that so?"

He prowled forward, just as predatory in his movements as some of the Ether's animals. Soon, my back was pressed up against the cottage wall. His arms rested to the sides of my head, and he leaned closer. I was boxed in, but instead of feeling caged, all I wanted to do was get closer.

"Ry."

One of his hands dropped to the back of my neck, and he eliminated the remaining distance between us. The kiss was bruising and insistent. His hand trailed down my side.

"I need to see you, Starlight," Orion insisted. "No layers of fabric between us, and no secrets either."

He'd seen me before, but this was different. He'd helped me treat wounds, or felt me underneath layers of clothing. Now we were in front of the fire, and I could see and feel everything. Nothing to focus on but each other.

I ducked out from underneath Orion's arm, giving myself more space.

I tugged at my borrowed shirt. When he twisted around and saw what I was doing, the flecks in his eyes practically glowed.

"May I help?"

I nodded, barely daring to move my chin.

As his hands pulled the shirt he began kissing my neck, sending a pleasant shiver trailing down my spine.

"Ry, I want to feel you."

I'd barely gotten the words out of mouth when Orion groaned into my neck, pressing the length of his body against me. He ground his hips, and I let out a mewling sound that wasn't in any way controlled, and certainly not dignified.

Heat pooled between my legs, and an aching need had me reaching to pull him in closer. He trailed bites and kisses down my neck. He only paused long enough to finish pulling the shirt over my head.

I'd just as soon have him rip it off, but our clothes were limited.

I reached for his shirt in turn, and he obligingly pulled it over his head with one arm. The need for him, the desire to be closer, was driving me. It drowned out any lingering voice in my head that might have insisted on propriety.

I stepped out of my borrowed trousers, only pausing for a moment. I didn't think he'd noticed it in the woods, but I had that large scar from my incident with Pellix and the wolf. I knew Orion wouldn't judge me for it, but would he be disappointed?

I was fully exposed to him at that point but refused to let embarrassment stop me. Orion grabbed at my waist, tugging me back against him.

"Magnificent," he whispered as his hands crept higher.

He palmed one of my breasts, then ran his thumb along the nipple. Another shiver trailed down my spine, and that same helpless sound escaped my throat.

I tried to clamp it down.

"Oh no, Starlight. I want to hear every sound you make." He repeated the motion, and I whimpered. When he leaned in toward my neck I could feel his grin against my skin.

"Much better."

His hand delved lower, until his fingers brushed against my clit. I'd had no experience with the trysts in Emrys, but I was very familiar with my own anatomy. There had been many nights in my own bed at Scops when I'd touched myself, but it didn't compare in the slightest to the feel of Orion.

He swirled his fingers over my clit, and I began to moan. He captured my mouth in his.

I was on the verge of losing myself to the moment entirely.

"Ry!" I squirmed beneath his hands.

I wrapped my arms around his back, my fingers digging into his shoulders as I clutched him against me.

"I want all of you, please," I begged.

He broke off our kiss, tugging off his trousers hurriedly. I'd seen him working outdoors without his shirt on before. But I'd never seen him fully unclothed like this.

He was breathtaking. Muscled arms and chest from his work in the Ether, and no small number of scars. He'd told me that he made mistakes when he was first figuring out how to survive here, and I saw them like a timeline along his skin. I reached out and traced a finger over a long, thin scar on his forearm.

"So many," I murmured.

He laughed.

"I'm not the most handsome man at the ball, but as long as you don't mind—"

I shook my head.

"I wouldn't want anyone else. I'd let you escort me to a thousand balls. Even without a shirt."

He beamed.

"You'd get us thrown out, Starlight. What would people say?"

My reputation was already destroyed a thousand times over by now, but as long as I had Orion, it didn't matter in the slightest.

"We'd both be effectively ruined," he insisted.

I reached up, my fingers weaving into his hair as I pulled him down.

"Then ruin me."

One of Orion's hands trailed down my side, clutching at my hips. His touch made me want to jump out of my skin; every nerve responded to him.

My entire body lit up as his fingers trailed along the most sensitive part of me, not lingering, teasing with light touches.

"Ry!" I gasped, pressing myself closer.

His fingers pressed against my clit again, circling in a way that made me want to come apart.

"Again," he whispered.

"Ry, that feels—"

I clutched at his back, trailing my fingers down his shoulders and writhing against his hand. Everything felt tense, like my entire body was contracted and focused on that one point where his hand moved.

"I can't! I can't!" I squirmed, needing to move, needing more of him, needing something.

"I've got you, Starlight, I'm right here," Orion soothed, then he kissed that sensitive spot on my neck as he pressed harder and the whole world came apart.

I screamed his name, pleasure rolling through me. All the tightness released at once, flooding my body. My knees threatened to give out, and I felt my limbs trembling. Waves of sensation echoed through me, and it took several moments before I could form a coherent thought.

"That was—" I couldn't even describe it.

Orion held me, lowering us both down on the two cots we'd shoved together. He lay down beside me, pulling my head against his chest so we were positioned just like we'd slept together before.

"That felt incredible," I said.

The words hardly did the moment justice. All those nights imagining my mysterious author, and I was in his arms.

I reached down, brushing my fingers against his cock. He sucked in a breath.

"Starlight, when you touch me like that—"

I wrapped my hand around him, trailing it up and down.

"Touch you like what?" I whispered.

"Bloody ghosts!" he choked out, throwing his head back. He only let me continue for a few moments before he reached for my hand.

"Keep doing that, and this is going to move much quicker than I'd hoped for," he warned.

I'd no sooner released him than he grabbed me and flipped us so my back was pinned to the cot. My mouth dropped open, fully prepared for a witty remark when he leaned down, his mouth closing over my right breast.

As he sucked and licked I moaned, no longer capable of any rational speech. Then he moved lower, kissing my stomach and my hips.

When his tongue flicked against my clit, all the same needy tension returned, magnified tenfold. I bucked under his mouth.

"I've been dreaming of this," Orion growled into my skin.

Everything was sensitive; every nerve on alert. Each movement he made with his tongue sent my need mounting higher and higher, until once again it felt like I wouldn't be able to take it anymore. My body craved release.

His mouth pressed against me, his tongue growing more insistent and one hand clutching at my hip. With his other he pressed a finger against my core, then slid it inside me.

When he added a second, his tongue still teasing me, I screamed his name.

"I could never tire of hearing my name from your lips," he murmured before continuing.

I knew my nails had to be clawing new marks into his back as I pulled at him, but I was utterly helpless to stop myself.

He pumped his fingers into me, and his tongue flicked against me, shattering me again. I'd never felt anything like this. It was pure rapture.

I was breathing hard, trembling as I came down from my release.

Orion crawled up my body, kissing from my hips back to my neck. I felt his cock against my center, hard and insistent.

"Still ready?" he asked.

I managed a nod, not trusting my own voice.

I gasped as Orion entered me, pressure and a sharp pain shooting through me.

"I'll go slow," he assured me, his movements steady and slowing, just as he'd promised.

He continued to trail kisses down my neck. After a few moments the pressure eased, and the pain decreased. It was still there, but mounting alongside it was that increasingly familiar sense of growing tension and desire.

Just like the first time he'd kissed me, I needed him closer, deeper.

My hair fell back against the blankets. If I was ruined, I was ruined. And it wasn't because of the shame for anything we did.

It was because Ry had captured me, heart and soul, and I was ruined for anyone else.

Orion's rhythmic movements sped up. He braced himself with one hand to the side of my head, staring down at me.

"All gods, you are stunning. I never thought that I could have this. Someone here, someone who understood me."

I wrapped my arms around him, my fingers trailing through his hair.

"Until Emrys and all the gods' realms fall, I will be yours, Ry."

He groaned, and I gasped in response, the two of us moving together.

Ry drove into me, his thrusts speeding up as he pushed deeper. I kissed his neck, trying to match his rhythm.

He reached between us, his fingers finding my clit again as he continued to thrust into me. It didn't take long for me to reach a peak, and then that same shattering release.

I came apart beneath him, and his entire body tensed.

"Starlight!" he yelled my name like a desperate plea. I could feel his release, and I wanted nothing more than to keep him that close forever.

For several moments afterward we lay completely still, utterly spent. Then he moved, rolling so he could hold me.

"How are you feeling?"

"Overwhelmed," I admitted. "I fantasized about you even before I knew who you were. I fell for words on a page, and never thought I'd meet the author."

"And now?"

"I feel closer to you than I even imagined I could. It's nice, but also terrifying."

"Because it's one more thing you might lose?"

"Exactly." I knew he could relate to that sentiment.

Night had fallen outside. I could see blue and green creeping in from under the door.

"It's similar for me. I've had no one this entire time, and now that I have you, I won't let even Charon stand in the way. I would do anything for you, Starlight," he whispered into my hair.

"Would you let us delay until tomorrow?" I couldn't imagine letting him go at the moment, even to go after Charon's second item.

"We can leave first thing in the morning," he said.

After Orion had fallen asleep, I was still awake, thinking over our next destination. The Unseen Hour had taken Ry from Emrys once, and if we were found out, Charon might remove him for good. I knew I was also in very real danger, but I'd chosen to take a risk when I entered the Ether. I had gained Orion, and an ally in Death. We'd been given the chance to end the Unseen Hour once and for all.

He'd had to wait for this moment for a century. I couldn't let him be the one to suffer if things went wrong.

The thought that we might fail welled up in me. I bit down on my lip, determined to force down the urge to cry.

"What are you thinking?"

Ry was curled against my back, one hand combing through my hair. The light touch sent a pleasant sensation tingling down my spine, and it almost made me forget what I'd been so focused on moments before.

I'd promised him honesty. No layers between us.

"I was thinking that I could lose you."

He laughed.

I rolled to face him, my nose scrunching as I scowled.

"Do you mind explaining how that's humorous?"

He just grinned.

"I was thinking I might need to improve my technique, if you're envisioning ways to get rid of me afterward."

I placed one hand against his bare chest.

"You know that's not it. I was thinking that I couldn't stand to lose you. That everything we're doing, even if it saved Emrys, wouldn't be worth it if it costs you."

His smile grew softer, the teasing tone in his voice taking on a soft edge.

"That will not happen. I'll do everything in my power to make sure of it. And I couldn't stand to lose you, either."

One hand was still wrapped in my hair, and his eyes darkened, his gaze hardening.

"No one will take you from me, Celia. As long as you want me here, I'll be by your side. Nothing will prevent that, not even a god."

He leaned in, kissing me, and I responded hungrily.

It was only later, as I was drifting off to sleep, that the doubt crept back in.

CHAPTER 44

We'd headed west before the lights had even changed fully to purple and orange. We hadn't even made it halfway to the Meadow when fog swirled. It circled Orion like a tornado.

"Celia, I'm sorry, but—"

The cold of the Ether was nothing to the chill that struck deep in my bones.

"Does he know?"

What were the odds that the god of the Ether would summon Orion just after we'd returned from stealing a prized magical object from him?

Low, I was willing to bet.

"Can you refuse? Could we run?"

Even if we made it north of the Meadow and to the Ether's entrance, it wouldn't open until the hour. Maybe we could call Death? I had no idea how, but my mind raced trying to come up with a solution.

"I can't refuse him. I haven't shown you this, but I suppose you're about to see. I get the fog as a warning; then he pulls me to him."

I was trying to wave the fog away.

"What do you mean, he pulls you?"

Orion grabbed my hands. "Look, this could be a good thing—"

"A good thing! You could be killed!"

"He's not killed me yet. I'll be able to find out what he knows this way, and I'll do everything I can to share that with you. Go back to the cottage and wait there."

"I will not! I'll keep going. At least to the edge of the Meadow."

That was where Death tended to meet us. If I could get the other deity to intervene, that seemed the most likely spot.

I threw my arms around Orion, but he pried me off.

"I'm sorry, Starlight. I don't know what would happen if you do that. Look, you're about to see something disconcerting. But I'm all right. You need to remember that. Don't panic. I'll be o—"

In front of my eyes, Orion faded into the fog, and then that dissipated as well.

I stared for a few moments, wide-eyed, at the empty space in the woods in front of me.

Then, I screamed.

For several chaotic moments I was certain I'd just seen the man I loved die. He'd already told me that Charon had disintegrated some of the Shades when they didn't do what he wanted, and the other people who had made it to the Ether alive.

But, he'd said *ash*. There was nothing left of Orion. And he'd gone with the fog.

I took several shaky breaths in and out, still too fast and shallow to actually be much help.

He'd told me he was all right. He'd acted like he knew something was coming for him.

Come to think of it, I'd never seen him go to Charon. Not really. He'd left when he saw the fog, and then I'd assumed he'd walked the full way. But that made no sense. Given that Charon's residence was west, well past the Meadow, Orion couldn't have traversed the distance and back to his cottage in the time he'd managed in the past.

Somehow, Charon had transported him via the fog.

I put a hand to my head, feeling like I might fall over.

It was almost too much to wrap the mortal mind around, but it had to be right. The alternative was unacceptable.

"I'll follow him. I'll keep heading to the Meadow."

And if I didn't meet with Death on the way, I'd keep going. I would walk all the way to Charon's if I had to. Without Orion touching me, I wouldn't be able to get on the grounds. At least according to what Death had said when she'd connected the two of us.

It didn't matter. If I needed to, I would stay outside whatever border his estate had and throw stones, yell, and shake the gates until he saw me.

I didn't want to die, but I would risk anything for Ry.

I ran, my satchel bouncing on my back. The path between the trees had become familiar, and I leapt over twisted roots and ducked low branches without a second thought. I'd never been so coordinated, but memory served me well.

I only slowed when the trees grew sparse and I could see the Meadow. A few of the glowing orb moths floated by in front of me.

We were getting closer to the hundredth hour, and Orion was right about the Shades. They moved quicker and farther afield. Their faces, from what I could see, were still impassive. But some zig-zagged in erratic patterns as they floated above the flowers. Certainly more animated than in January.

My mind made up, I approached the Meadow on my own.

There wasn't any sign of Orion or Charon. No chill, and no fog. If the god of the Ether was distracted with his Head Shade, then he wasn't watching me.

I took a deep breath.

"I could use some help! We got what you wanted, but he's got Ry!"

A few of the Shades looked over at me, in itself a sign that they were more attentive, but Death didn't respond.

She'd never given us a way to summon her. She just appeared when she wanted to. I'd accepted it because she was on our side, and we needed the help, but at that moment I resented it.

Why did our nature as humans give the gods a right to toy with us? From what I could see, they weren't superior in any way that mattered. They were more powerful, but not more moral. Not more compassionate. Not kinder in any way.

Even Death was willing to put us at risk.

I knew I wasn't being fully fair. She was risking the only two half-Shades she had available, to end the hour and save countless lives, but I was desperate for Orion and in no emotional state to be charitable.

"Come down here! Please!" I had no idea if she could hear me. "He's got Ry, and Ry has what you wanted us to get!"

The baton was in Orion's satchel, and if Charon figured that out, we truly were in trouble.

In return for my screams, I got nothing but a few Shades floating in my direction, weaving around me but giving me a wide berth. I didn't see my father, but then again I no longer expected to. I'd have to rely on Death for that, because I'd run out of other places to look. One more thing that depended on a deity when I wanted to do it myself.

I needed to be stronger.

I'd keep going to Charon's, but I knew my chances of

success were slim. I screamed one last time, dropping to my knees.

Static danced across my skin; the hair on my arms rose and the air crackled. I hiccupped, looking at the sky, but still no Death.

Confused, I stood, wiping down the feeling on my arms. The static that told me if I touched the wrong thing I'd be shocked. But if Death wasn't in the Ether, then how ...

Lightning slammed into the ground, forcing me to stumble back.

"You're making quite the racket, little human," the goddess observed, this time wearing a mask the color of champagne.

"Death! I need your help. Charon summoned Orion, and he's got the baton, and—"

I ran for her, hands out. She backed away with a frown, putting an arm out to stop me. I was less than an inch from touching her when I remembered. The hairs on my arm rose again, and I could tell I was being shocked, but I was too concerned about Orion to care.

And I hadn't touched her, so it wasn't too bad.

"Slow down. Now, what has Charon done this time? Did you get the baton?"

I nodded.

"Yes. We got it. The two of us were headed here, and then Charon's, for the second item. Orion is carrying the baton in his satchel, but he got summoned by Charon. He disappeared into fog. He said he'd be all right, but if Charon realizes what's happened ... is that why he called for him? Could he know?"

Death tilted her head, maddeningly silent for several moments.

"No. No, I don't think so. I saw him recently and he was agitated at me, but he didn't give any indications of fear. If anything, he's growing more aggressive, confident. I'd say he's still convinced he's going to be victorious."

"Then Orion is safe?" All my muscles were tense, ready to leap into action and run after him if the answer was no.

"I should think so, unless you run in and cause a scene. *That* would take the odds of survival for both of you down considerably."

I sagged, partially in relief and a bit in defeat.

"Then how do I help him? Even if it's likely he's all right, we can't be sure. If I don't go after him and something happens. If he's hurt—"

"Then it will be up to you to help finish this hour. Small human, I have no desire for the half-Shade to be hurt. I've enjoyed our talks these past decades. But if you enter Charon's personal grounds now, you're doing nothing but increasing Orion's risk. Although, if he is with Charon that means the god of the Ether is distracted. Which presents us with an opportunity."

"An opportunity?"

I tensed again. More items to find?

"I think you should learn a bit more about the other gods. Odos's interference showed me that my fellow deities are growing as restless as I am. You should know who and what you're up against."

I couldn't have agreed more, although I wished she'd thought to share sooner.

I kept looking past her.

"And it may distract you from your paramour for the moment. Hear me out, and we'll wait for him to return."

"What do we do once he's back? If he's just been to Charon's, if the god is feeling paranoid, then can we still go after the second item?"

"You leave Charon to me. I've seen him recently, so it may

look suspicious if I call him again, but I can certainly goad one of the other deities into causing some trouble. Once Orion has returned, I will leave and make sure that Charon stays occupied while you find the other item we need."

I let out a deep breath. I still didn't like Orion's absence, but this might have turned out to be a good thing. If Death knew our exact timing, she would be better able to keep the god of the Ether away from us. It would be the best and possibly only opportunity to get the second item without worry that he would descend on us the minute we crossed his gates.

"All right," I agreed.

Death smiled, perfect teeth shining as she clapped her hands together.

"Good. Then it's time you learned about the other gods."

CHAPTER 45

Death's whole form sparked with small arcs of lightning.

"I've already told you a bit about how we intervene in Rayus. My Reapers assist your souls out of the world when they are meant to die, and I collect the dead. That is my purpose. Life for humans is so short, and then my realm stretches for eternity. I am responsible for souls longer than any of the other deities, which you would think would mean something. But the others ..." She shrugged.

"And the other gods?"

"You've met Odos now. When we began, he undertook the responsibility of *misfortune*. He throws obstacles into paths. He hardens hearts and deafens ears to keep them from listening to logic. A troublemaker, all around. But he's also a supporter of strength, so he's handy in a war if you gain his favor."

I knew it.

Emrys didn't recognize him, and a god of misfortune and war is something we'd never considered, but he'd immediately struck me as ready for battle.

"I've already told you of Day. Overseas birth, and that's

about it. I think you humans associate birth with growth, and tie it to harvests, and that's how he got credit for that bit of Charon's role. To be fair, I'd be annoyed as well."

"And that's all Day does?"

She shrugged, the movement stiff. It was as if Day annoyed her in particular. I supposed they were cast as opposing forces, life and Death.

"Then, there's Grim. He oversees illnesses, injuries and the like. He can be a healer, or usher people all the more quickly to my realm. He's also got an odd obsession with pretty things, so he's the deity of art, if that means much to you." Her tone suggested that she didn't think much of the power of a painting.

I silently tallied the number of gods, my mind reeling.

"And the god of the Ether?" I pressed, more interested in the enemy we faced than the others.

Death scowled, small arcs of lightning dancing across her skin.

"He was meant to nurture the world around you humans, the only one of us who did not directly interact. To support the plants and animals that surround you instead. He's always envied my role."

I couldn't wrap my head around that. I loved the gardens back home, and Pellix, and the tree hoppers. It made sense, then, that the Ether allowed things to grow. That there was a wide variety of animals and intelligent creatures, not to mention both edible and deadly plants.

It was his purpose.

"And he'd rather kill people than nurture those things?"

"He's always been jealous of me. Always wanted what he sees as a showier and grander option. I have souls the longest, and he never gets them at all. As you've seen, he also has an interest in music."

Her voice got softer, more gentle, on the last bit. She might not have thought much of art, but she clearly enjoyed music, even if she hated Charon.

I scowled. Charon's purpose was beautiful. And honestly the one I would have wanted most if I'd been a deity myself. He hadn't appreciated his role, and the selfish ambitions of a god I hadn't even known existed had cost me, Emrys, and all of Rayus for too long.

"Why did we only hear about you and Day in Emrys?"

Death shrugged.

"People figured out for themselves who held the real power, and worshiped accordingly. As you can imagine, Charon gets little credit. He used to have churches, but they've fallen away. Humans, if you'll excuse my observation, tend to be inherently selfish. Why would they heap worship on a god that didn't directly benefit them? Charon should have accepted his lot. The rest of us know our place."

I was annoyed that I felt the smallest spark of sympathy for Charon. Offering something unique and beautiful, only to be unappreciated and forgotten. Not wanted unless he could be used, unless his abilities affected lives directly.

But he'd taken things too far. He'd done too many vile things for me to be tempted to forgive him.

"You mentioned six gods. The god in the lost country? Who are they? What was their role?"

"That god, we do not speak of anymore. A betrayer to the rest of us, and what should have been a cautionary tale for Charon," she warned.

She took a deep breath, tilting her chin up.

"Your paramour will be joining us soon. Which means I will be leaving, since Charon's attention may wander."

"Wait! My father, did you find him?"

"Odos pulled me from that search, but my Reapers are still

working."

"And the hundredth hour. What is Charon's plan, if he succeeds?"

Death smiled, but the expression held no warmth.

"Destruction. He would decimate everyone you hold dear. He thinks he finally has enough souls, and he plans to challenge me for my seat. He wants my job, and he wants the souls for eternity. I don't intend on giving them up."

"But how would—"

"We're out of time. Make haste for Charon's, and I will ensure that he stays focused elsewhere. Hurry, small human. The clock is ticking."

Lightning struck the ground, and Death was gone.

Destruction.

That's what she'd said. And the hour already ruled through death and fear. Charon would be able to take any soul he wanted, at any time. If he was so inclined, he could take all of them.

A chill that had nothing to do with the Ether ran down my spine.

A figure was approaching, walking through the Shades with purpose.

I retreated back to the edge of the trees, watching to see if he was winged.

As he got closer, I saw his brown hair and strong shoulders. I leapt up and ran to him. It took him a moment to notice me. Orion was scowling at the ground, shoulders hunched and jaw clenched.

When he glanced up, his eyes widened, like he hadn't expected to find me at the edge of the Meadow.

"Ry!" I threw my arms around him, and he hesitated for a moment before embracing me. "Are you all right? What happened?"

"Charon is ... frustrated. Suspicious." He said the words through gritted teeth, as if they cost him.

"He asked you not to discuss it?"

Pointless, since as far as Charon was concerned, he had no one to discuss it with but silent Shades. Just another sign of his twisted need for control.

I wanted to meet the god, if only once, so I could show him what I thought of him.

"Charon's proud. I'm less a person to him and more a journal. Ironic, considering I completed one prior to arriving here. He and I have that in common, I suppose."

"He is nothing like you!" I insisted vehemently.

"In some ways. I would never force all my secrets onto another person, but he needs to vent his thoughts, and I'm the individual available. I think he's under the impression that if he orders me silent I can't endanger him, or help the other gods. He's ..."

Orion grimaced, clutching his jaw like he was trying to pry it open.

My fists closed around Orion's sleeves. Charon would pay. For Orion, his brothers, my family, and so many others.

Orion let out a breath, running his hands through his hair.

"He knows the other gods have been here?"

Ry gave a quick, tense nod.

"And he knows you've been helping them?"

His head jerked to the side.

"*Suspects* you? Suspects they might approach you? He's worried about your interference, at the very least?"

Another terse nod.

"He's angry."

Orion reached down to lift his shirt. I gasped, stepping back to find several red bruises on his side. I walked a circle and saw more on his back.

"He hurts you. Has he been hurting you this whole time? Ever since you arrived?" For a hundred years.

He dropped his shirt.

"Charon looks for ways to express his anger, and that's often by punching or throwing things. Breaking things. Including his Head Shade."

I clenched my fists, trembling.

"He's going to die for this," I hissed through clenched teeth.

"I know we need to find the other item, but he's going to be on high alert right now. Should we wait until he drops his guard?" Orion asked.

I filled him in on Death's visit and her promise to keep him preoccupied, potentially by working with at least one of the other deities.

"Then we go now."

"But you're hurt! At least use some more of the water."

Orion shook his head.

"No. It's good to know that Charon will be gone, but I'm still worried about his grounds. I know what Death promised, but I want to make sure you're safely inside before we waste any more."

I opened my mouth to protest.

"No. Listen, please. If we make it inside and nothing happens to you, I'll take some then. Deal?"

I knew arguing with him when he thought my safety might be on the line would be a wasted endeavor.

"How long will it take us on foot?" I asked instead.

"I'm honestly not sure. I've never walked the entire distance," he admitted. "The fog takes me from where I am to his gates and then returns me, typically to the Meadow."

"Then we'd better get started."

We made our way past the increasingly restless Shades.

If we succeeded, soon they would all be free.

CHAPTER 46

Charon's abode, it turned out, was quite a bit farther from the Meadow than we had anticipated. It took two weeks of walking before the scenery started to change to something Orion recognized as Charon's.

"I'm glad that this time I overpacked the supplies," Orion grumbled on the tenth day. We'd also continued to make use of anything familiar and edible that we found along the route.

It was tiring, but I hoped that our trek had given Death plenty of time to implement whatever plan she had to keep Charon away from his home.

Orion and I moved as swiftly as we were able. At night we rested, but also used it as a chance to repeat our actions from the cottage. I already felt connected to Orion because of who he was, and I was surprised at the additional layer of intimacy I felt from sex.

I'd wanted it, but my observations of scandals in Emrys indicated it led only to trouble. I should have known they were as wrong about that as they were about many other things.

The ground slowly gave way from all the grass and flowers

that filled the Meadow to large stones and boulders and a mossier ground covering.

"We're getting close. I recognize this scenery," Orion said when we made it to an area covered entirely in black stone.

When we came to a towering wrought-iron fence, my mouth dropped open.

"I don't know what I expected, but this—" I swept an arm out, gesturing at the scene beyond the fence.

Charon's home was built onto the black rock, directly on the edge of a drop similar to the canyon we'd traversed before. I could hear the rush of water tumbling over the side. The house had whole walls made of glass, with metal holding it in place. There was a large porch that wrapped around the outside of the property, and two dark doors at the entrance.

I'd never seen anything like it.

Homes in Emrys were typically brick or stone. Nothing like this.

"How should we go about this?" I asked Orion, who was staring up at the gates.

"When I'm summoned, the fog leaves me here. I'm just able to push open the gates. Simple. Hold my hand, and I'll see if it will give way."

When he grabbed onto my hand, his was too warm, uncomfortably so. I normally relished the sensation, with the Ether's chill. I wondered if he had a fever. Charon had harmed him, and he'd refused the entire journey to use any of the healing water until I made it onto the property.

His bruises were mostly faded, but it still worried me.

As long as we both made it through the gate all right, I'd insist that he use some after we got whatever was in Charon's home.

"Well, here we go," Orion said, pressing the hand not holding mine against the gates. "I'll enter first."

The left gate swung open without so much as a creak. Orion stepped across and onto the grounds, and with my hand firmly in his I followed just behind him.

I held my breath, tensing and awaiting pain, but nothing happened. Orion's grip tightened around my hand, and he kept moving forward. We stepped slowly across the rock, making our way to the door of Charon's home.

"If we can get in here and nothing happens, then I'll let go," he said.

Death had promised I could get on the grounds after she'd joined Orion and me, and that had been true. She'd promised to distract the deity, and he hadn't shown up when we retrieved the baton. There was no sign of him on his grounds.

The smallest tendril of hope grew in my chest.

I could feel the mist created by the waterfall as we stood in front of the door, but the house itself looked dry.

"Death did say he liked water, and she wasn't wrong," I observed.

Orion's shoulders stiffened as he pushed against the doors of Charon's home. There was no knocker. Just flat, smooth black.

I could only imagine Orion's mixed feelings. Charon had kept him alive but essentially a prisoner. This home was where he'd had some of the only real conversations during that time, but the god had harmed him.

"Will you be okay, going in here?" I asked.

Orion turned, and the door cracked open behind him.

"If we succeed here, we have everything we need to bring down a god. Trust me, Starlight, this is the first time I'm happy to be here."

Just as we had with the gates, I let Orion step through first and then followed.

"Nothing," I said after several moments standing in the entry of the house.

Orion blew out a long breath.

"Death was right. Blasted ghosts, but I was nervous."

He let go of my hand, and we both stared at where we'd been touching for several moments, but I stayed whole and unharmed.

"You'll use the water, then? You were burning up outside. I'm worried that he hurt you badly enough to bring on some sort of illness," I told Orion.

"Once we get what we need here. Yes. I'll use some," he agreed.

The floor in Charon's home was made up of the same stone that littered the ground on his lawn, but it was smoothed and gleaming. The floor-to-ceiling windows allowed the colorful lights of the Ether in, but the fog and sea spray kept it dim regardless.

The interior was just as different from Emrys homes as the outside. I was used to grand rooms, but nothing with this sleek and tailored feel. The interior was all blacks and greys. The room where we'd entered was a massive diamond. At the points on each side, there were halls leading away, but at the back there was a clear view of the falls, rushing past the window.

"There's another story above us, where you can see the top of the falls. He has a balcony out there. It's one of the few locations I've actually seen," Orion said.

Around the edges of the room were a few short standing columns, each holding a small sculpture or vase on top. Everything was grey, white, or beige. No bright colors to speak of, which I found odd, considering the Ether's forest was so vibrant.

The only exception was a ribbon of blue running through

the black stone under our feet. It mimicked lights in the night sky in the Ether.

"When we're not outside, this room is where Charon meets with me." Orion gestured to the entryway around us.

I saw no comfortable seating, or even seating at all. Orion would have had to stand and wait for Charon each time.

How could he treat the man I loved like that?

But Charon didn't view us as people, with love and relationships. He viewed us as souls that could be used in his petty squabbles. We didn't understand the intricate nature of the gods' realms, their relationships, or their powers. But how could we?

He'd soon find out, though, that love could fuel vengeance as readily as anger. And I had plenty of both.

"Where should we start looking?" I asked Orion.

He rubbed a hand under his chin.

"If I were Charon, I'd keep the key to the Shades somewhere personal." Orion followed a vein of blue in the floor and chose one of the darkened hallways off the main room.

The first hall led to a room that had to be an office, containing a large desk made of a blackened wood with sweeping curves at the corners. The walls were made of the same bark as the Ether's trees, and I was surprised to see books on Charon's shelves.

We pulled several down, but none that I could read referenced music in any way. There were some in the languages of the other countries. While Emrys primarily used a universal language heard across Rayus, I knew Mejje and Sez had their own local languages as well.

"I'm very rusty, since my education was well over a century ago, but I did learn the basics in both. I don't see anything here related to music," Orion said as he placed a few books back on the shelf.

The desk did not open easily for us. The drawers were locked tight.

"If it's in there, then we'll have to pry it loose," I said, tugging on one of the closed doors for a third time and making no progress.

If we did that, though, surely Charon would figure out someone had been in his home.

Orion shook his head.

"I think we'll be drawn to it, just like the people of Emrys feel and are drawn to the Shade song. We felt the baton. I'm not picking up anything in here, are you?"

I shook my head.

The only thing that changed in the hallways was the color running through the stone floor. It might be purple, orange, blue, or green. Only one at a time, and always a color that mimicked the sky.

Eventually we made our way up a sweeping staircase on the side of the home to the upper story. What a god like Charon used these rooms for was beyond me. There were a few set up as bedrooms, but I couldn't imagine the god playing host to guests.

"I never rest here. I have to stay in the entrance for as long as Charon cares to keep me here," Orion said as we closed the door on yet another room that didn't hold what we were looking for.

And I knew there were times he was gone for days. He had to be exhausted as well as the victim of Charon's frustrations.

My fury grew with each room we explored.

The whole house was maddening. I tugged at my hair as we shut the door on a room that had been empty except for dozens of the glowing orb moths that lit the Meadow.

"What does he think he's playing at? Do you think he knew

we were coming, or that Death would send someone? What if he's just having fun at our expense?"

Orion shook his head, his jaw tense.

"I doubt it. Charon, from what I've seen, has no sense of humor. I don't think he gives much consideration to most of this space at all. Maybe it was different back when the deities were more cordial. Perhaps that's the purpose of the extra space."

Anything was possible. The bedrooms were the only section of the home that didn't follow Charon's color scheme. One even contained pink flowers in a vibrant blue vase. The sight had almost brought me to tears—it was the first pink I'd seen since I left home. I didn't think I could ever bring myself to miss pink dresses, but I did miss the family home the color represented.

We were nearing the end of one side of the oval on the upper level when I threw out an arm to stop Orion.

"What is it?" He tensed, head swiveling to check the hall.

"I feel something. A tug, drawing me, like when you sing. It makes me want to move closer."

I paused, trying to center myself. There was that desire to go in the direction of the feeling, but something new as well. Something pulled at my throat, urging me to sing. Surely it had to be connected to the Shade song.

I followed the feeling, Orion at my side.

We entered a room that had the same floor-to-ceiling windows overlooking the cliffs that others had. There was the roar of the waterfall outside, and mist and droplets sprayed against the windows.

That wasn't what held my attention, though. Inside this room was a gorgeous grand piano. Sleek and black, with the lid open and ready to play. The bench looked plush and comfortable.

We'd found our answer.

CHAPTER 47

I crossed the room in several strides to the piano bench. I sat down, running my fingers over the keys without pressing down.

Aside from Pellix and my family, I had also missed playing music. It was the only acceptable talent at which I excelled and also didn't loathe. I'd spent hours practicing, reasoning that if I couldn't be outside or curled up with a good book, it was the next best place to be.

Music, like books, carried me away to places beyond Emrys.

"And now I'm somewhere else, and maybe it can take me home," I whispered to myself.

"What do you think?" Orion asked, still walking the room's perimeter and looking around.

"I can feel it. We're in the right spot. You can tell, right?"

His head tilted, brows furrowing over his eyes.

"I definitely feel something, but I can't quite put my finger on it."

"You don't think it's the piano, do you?" I fretted. If it was, we'd never be able to carry it.

"I doubt it. At least, Death didn't indicate it could be something that large. Although ... what if it's *inside* the piano? The baton was inside a stone box; perhaps the piano is the container."

He checked around the instrument while I looked underneath the bench, then each of the pedals. There were no strange notches or markings.

Orion came back around behind me.

"Maybe we need some sort of code before the item will reveal itself?"

"Maybe ... could it be the music? We had to read the box, and we have to play the music?" I guessed.

"The Shades have song, and he left sheet music."

"It's worth a try," I agreed.

"Can you play?"

I nodded, a strand of hair falling across my cheek before he reached down and tucked it away again.

"Passably well. Actually, more than passable." No need for feigned modesty in the Ether. "I'm really quite good. As part of his negotiations with Ambrose, Bellamy assured him that a piano and music room would be made available to me."

Orion's look darkened, his brows drawing down.

"Yes, your fiancé."

"He's not my fiancé anymore."

Even if Bellamy tried to reignite our engagement upon my return, it was too late. I had survived the Unseen Hour, I was allying with Death, and I was sneaking through the home of a god. I would not be cowed by my brother's negotiations or Bellamy's desires. *I* didn't agree to the engagement, and therefore I considered it null and void.

When I returned, my life would be my own. That wasn't up for negotiation, no matter the consequences.

"I suppose I should thank my mother for all those lessons," I grumbled as I flexed my fingers.

For the first time, I paid attention to the actual notes written on the sheet music in front of me and was surprised to find they were familiar. It was a classical song. The original had been composed centuries ago, but the song had become popular again after being featured in a theatrical production within the past few years.

The piece would be difficult. I had played it before and knew that it had been written for someone with larger hands. The spread between the notes was tricky for me, but I was determined not to miss a single one. If this really was the key, who knew what the consequences would be for messing up the song?

After another deep breath in, and slowly out, I began.

The moment I hit the first note of the sheet music, I knew I was right. My fingers flew over the keys, as drawn to the music as I was to Orion's singing.

When I'd previously played the piece, I had created cheats and trills to bypass having to play some notes so far apart that I could not reach them easily. This time, I stretched the span of my hands wide, just managing to hit all the right notes.

As I played, something warm lit up within me. Not whatever magic the gods exuded. This was just joy.

The song reached a crescendo, and I followed the dizzying set of notes up and back down the keyboard with enthusiasm. As I neared the end of the piece, only then did the notes slow.

The melody grew clearer, simpler, and ended with a sweet refrain.

It was a piece written about the intense passion of a love affair, and then the moment of a proposal. At least that's what we'd been told when seeing the production at the theatre. That was just the first movement, though.

There was a second section, and a third. Only the first

movement had been revitalized, and the sheet music in front of me ended on the first movement as well.

When I hit the last note, I held it, letting the sound linger. Without thinking, I'd closed my eyes on the last bit, when the melody was easiest. I'd let the music and memory carry me.

I opened my eyes as I released the note and looked to see Orion's gaze locked on me. The blue in his eyes blazed with heat. I ran my tongue along my lip, trying to find my voice again.

"Well, what do you think?"

He leaned down, one arm circling behind me and pulling me across the bench until my face was mere inches from his own.

When he spoke, his voice was rough, and breathless.

"That was beautiful, Starlight. Just like you."

My breath caught.

"Orion."

The last note from the song continued to echo.

"Wait! The key!" I twisted back around and looked for the last note I'd played, an A. I'd looked at all the keys before, but this time, when I touched the A, I was able to move it. The key slid off, and rolled tightly within was another piece of paper, tied in pink ribbon.

"Orion, do you think?"

"Death said you should carry this one. Can you unroll it and check?"

Carefully, I slid the ribbon off the paper and placed the A key back on the keyboard. I unrolled the paper. There were more musical notes on it, stretched horizontally across what turned out to be a narrow, but long, strip of parchment. Just a single note at a time, in one continuous melody.

"I think ... I think it could be sung," I said, letting my right hand reach out to the keyboard.

I played the first few notes, and then Orion joined in with his voice. There were no words, just smooth, clear tones.

Shade song had pulled me in before, but this intoxicated me. The warmth inside me became a raging fire, and it took all I had to keep playing the melody instead of reaching for Orion to pull him toward me.

Something told me it was important to finish the piece. Just to be sure. To *feel* that we had the right item.

This time, when I let go of the last note, the music went silent almost immediately.

I turned to look at Orion. He was practically panting, and one of his hands was braced on the edge of the piano.

His pupils were wide.

I licked my lips again, hungry for the Head Shade.

He leaned down, his hand moving to the bench to steady himself as he sat beside me. His other arm wrapped around me, pulling me as close as I could get without climbing onto his lap.

"Celia, Starlight, I—" His voice was tense, desperate. I felt it as well.

His lips found mine, insistent and needy. One of his hands tangled in my hair as I moaned into his mouth, flicking my tongue against his, then pulling back to suck on his bottom lip.

He groaned.

"Ry, should we? Charon?"

"Is gone. Death made sure of that. And if he's searching for treachery, his eyes are on the other gods. This is the last place he'd look."

"But Charon—"

"I don't want his name on your lips again, Starlight. Just mine."

His hand moved from my hair to my waist, then slipped beneath my borrowed clothes. His fingers swept over the part of me that most longed for his touch. Need tore through me as he continued, building that sweet but unbearable tension inside me.

He leaned back in to kiss me again. His tongue swept across mine, and I was lost.

I could only hope he was right. We'd been promised that this place would be empty, and up to now the location had meant only suffering for Orion. Maybe a better memory would help.

One of my hands twisted in his hair, tugging him even closer, needing more. With Orion, I would never get enough.

When his hand moved away from my clit I groaned in protest, but then he grabbed me around the waist and hauled me into his lap without breaking our kiss.

One of his hands slipped underneath my shirt, trailing up my ribs and then lightly squeezing one breast. Each touch sent bolts of lightning stronger than Death's through me. When he ran his thumb over one nipple I sucked in a breath at the sensation that rocketed through me.

I moved my legs so I straddled him, rocking my hips against him, driven entirely by the desire to feel every inch of him. When he matched his movements to mine, I felt his cock, hard and rubbing against me. I made a sound in the back of my throat that was involuntary and desperate. I reached between us, tugging at the waistline of his trousers.

Orion grinned at me.

"What are you thinking?"

I knew what he was asking.

"That I need you. Please, Ry."

He carefully slid out from under me, removing his own trousers, and then mine. They were thrown in a heap on the god's stone floors. Orion lifted me onto the keys, discordant music filling the room.

"Orion," I whispered, gazing into his eyes.

He thrust into me, hard and fast. I gasped, doing my best to match his rhythm. Something told me the piano should have been uncomfortable, but I was driven by desire for Ry, and if it was, I didn't notice.

The notes changed with every movement, and I clung to Orion, my own voice adding to the strange melody.

With one hand, Orion braced himself on the instrument, and with the other he reached between us. His fingers swirled over my clit as he continued thrusting, and I nearly came apart right then. He flicked and swirled over the spot until my need mounted and I was practically whimpering, my hands digging into his sides.

"Ry, please!"

He added pressure with his fingers, and drove even deeper into me.

Release crashed through me, and I screamed his name again as it broke into waves of pleasure. I still hadn't come down when Orion screamed my name, all his muscles tensing, shuddering as he found his own release.

He lowered us both back onto the bench, looking around the room.

"We'll have to make sure it doesn't look like anyone was in here."

He'd tossed our satchels alongside our clothes, and from them he retrieved some torn strips of cloth he'd thought to pack in case one of us was wounded. We got dressed, and then wiped down the piano. I rolled the music back up, wrapped the pink ribbon around it, and tucked it into a pocket.

We started to make our way back to the entrance.

A shot of white lightning illuminated Charon's home.

Orion looked at me, eyes as wide as my own.

"But she promised," I started.

He grabbed my hand.

"It could be we took longer than she expected, or something went wrong. Either way, we're out of time. We need to go. Now."

We were still in the hall, but once we made it to the entrance we'd be exposed by the wall of windows that lined the front and back of Charon's home. We'd be sitting ducks.

"We need to hide," I insisted, pulling Orion back in the hall.

"He can't find you here. We have to get out. Wait!" Orion led us to one of the rooms on the upper floor that we'd searched. It was near the center of the house and had large doors on the back of the room, looking out at the falls.

"We use the balcony, and go around the side of the house," Orion said.

We made our way outside and even found a staircase that led down from the upper to the lower balcony, but it was quickly apparent that the plan would lead nowhere.

Once downstairs, we'd be exposed to more windows. If Charon was down there, he'd see us for sure.

There was only one other means of escape.

I gulped.

"Orion, you're not going to like it, but we do have one way out. If we jump ... "

He followed my gaze over the railing, to the falls.

"We barely survived the rapids! We'd have to be out of our minds!"

"I don't like it any better than you! Charon is here, and the front of the house is floor-to-ceiling glass. Even if we made it down and around to the front, he'd be sure to spot us before we made the gates. We have to chance it, unless you think Charon would forgive us for this." I pulled the rolled-up music from my pocket.

That was our only other problem. We had to protect what we'd found, or the entire endeavor was for naught.

"Here, use this." Orion pulled out a waterskin, one holding regular water, not the supply from the cavern. He turned the waterskin and poured the contents over the balcony, shaking out the final drops. Then he handed it to me.

"Damp is better than destroyed," he reasoned.

I tucked the music into the waterskin, shoving the stopper on tight. The waterskin had its own strap, and I wrapped it several times around my forearm, tying it there and then tucking that arm against me.

The other, I held out to Orion.

"We go together!"

He nodded.

"Together."

He helped me over the railing, and I teetered on the thin ledge on the opposite side.

Orion was barely over it himself, hand clasping mine again, when he shouted.

"Now!"

The two of us leapt.

The roar of the water was deafening, and I prayed to all the gods, except Charon, that we wouldn't strike a rock on the way down.

CHAPTER 48

ind whistled in my ears. The spray from the falls battered my face.

I only had time for a split-second of relief when we hit the water below, followed by terror as the force of the current pulled us under. We'd survived the rapids, and I wasn't going to lose Orion so easily after everything we'd been through together.

The water twisted and spun me, but I clutched at Orion's hand like a lifeline. With my other arm I held the waterskin close.

When my head broke the surface, I was still attached to Ry.

I hacked up water and began kicking for all I was worth.

"All right, Starlight?"

I nodded my head, getting my sopping hair in my eyes. I didn't dare let go of the music or him to fix it.

"Just splendid," I managed.

"This way."

We moved toward calmer water. Directly under the falls, it had been churning, but it quickly quieted the farther away from them we got, thank the gods. My joints were still ringing like

Fox Haven's clock tower with its echoing chime on the Unseen Hour, but I forced my legs to kick.

We let the current carry us downstream a bit, but the water remained fairly calm. When we were out of eyesight of Charon's home and could reach the bank, we swam for it. Orion hauled us both out of the water. We sat for several minutes, panting. I wrung out my hair and checked inside the waterskin. All gods be praised, the music was all right, all the notes still readable.

Orion sat with his knees bent up, his arms slung over them.

"Another fun adventure, wouldn't you say?"

I laughed, but my throat was so raw that it soon turned into a hacking cough.

"I don't know if those are the exact words I would have used. Although it hasn't dampened my desire for travel in the slightest."

He looked me up and down.

"Oh, you're most definitely damp."

"That may be the worst joke I've ever heard."

I laughed anyway, then stood and spun, showering him with water droplets.

The thrill of escaping Charon, getting the second item, surviving the falls, and the lingering adrenaline from all three was thrumming through my veins.

I was sure my body would pay for it later when exhaustion kicked in, but for the moment, I had plenty of energy to move.

"Northeast, right?" I asked.

Orion stood as well, checking his satchel, which he'd managed to keep a hold on somehow.

"That's right. And I suggest we cut a wide path around the Meadow."

It would take longer, but if Charon was worried about his hour, it was possible he'd spend more time checking on his

Shades. I hadn't come this far only to be discovered on the brink of victory.

As predicted, my excitement waned once we'd been hiking for a while and my aching limbs made themselves known. Both of us decided not to use the remaining water from the cavern.

"Besides," I tried to joke, although I knew my tone was frustrated, "I'm still dripping, so the last thing I need is more water. I have no desire to be this wet anywhere but the bath."

A warm bath sounded like perfection in that moment, not that I truly needed one.

"And would there be room for two in that bath?" Orion nudged me.

The whole thing would have been unspeakably romantic, except for the fact that we were both still sopping and I was beginning to grow chilled.

I leaned into him as we walked, sighing as he lent me his warmth.

"It will be well into August by the time we reach the cottage, won't it?" I asked, trying to make sure I had my count of the days right.

"I believe so. As the hour gets closer, I check the Shades. We might want to give it a bit of time, make sure Charon doesn't notice anything amiss or wander through the Meadow, but then I'll go check on them. I can tell by their behavior when the hour is getting close."

There were a couple of Shades in particular that I hoped to meet, but I wanted to ask Orion's thoughts on it before introducing myself to his brothers.

"We have both items. The next thing we need is to make sure we know where your father is," Orion said.

And we were running out of time. I trusted Death, but I didn't want to leave any stone of the Ether unturned. I knew in my heart that if he really was in the same realm as me, I would probably have found him long ago. But I wasn't one for giving up, either. Until I heard otherwise, I would look for him. I'd kept my eyes open the entire way to Charon's, and I was doing the same on the return journey.

"We've got both items with us. Could we take a bit longer getting back to the cottage and check this area thoroughly on our way?"

"Absolutely, if that's what you want. Although it will mean more foraging. Or hunting. You still have your knife?"

I checked my leg, finding the holster still in place. I was useless when it came to actually hunting anything, but Orion could make use of it, and I'd do my best if we ran into another predator.

The area we walked through as we weaved south of the Meadow combined portions of Charon's home and the forest. There were trees, but the ground was rockier and harder to navigate.

"That's part of why I didn't choose to settle here," Orion told me several days in. "There are enough dangers in the Ether. I didn't want to add the possibility of breaking my leg by falling over a rock to the list."

But if my father was still hiding, maybe he'd had a different strategy.

Orion kept the baton safely in his pack, but I couldn't resist checking on the music frequently.

"I don't think it's going to disappear. It may *belong* to a god, but it's not a god," Ry reminded me for perhaps the thousandth time.

"Do you want to take a look at it?"

He shook his head.

"Death wanted you to keep it. And we know it's powerful. That melody ... it was irresistible."

My mind went back to our actions in Charon's piano room. Utterly shameless, and I didn't regret one second.

"Do you think the music influenced our actions, somehow? Similar to how the Shade song affects people during the hour?"

"Shade song brings people to their death. This sheet music doesn't do that. But I can't deny that I felt something. Would you sing again? Your voice is beautiful."

"Not as much as yours," I countered.

"That's only because I have Shade-enhancement. Yours was entrancing when you were humming to the first song you played, not just the one Charon wrote."

"I was humming?" I hadn't even noticed. "My piano skills are better than my voice."

I was speaking from accuracy and not some ridiculous sense of self-deprecation.

"One song? Would it help if I told you that I'll have the new book ready for you before the hour?"

How could I refuse that promise?

Instead of Charon's Shade song, or the first piece I'd played in the god's home, I decided on a another classical piece from Emrys. I'd always enjoyed it. It was from a theater production where a man fell in love with a beautiful woman he saw in his garden. He thought she was a ghost, because he only saw her walking through the plants and singing at night.

In the play, it turned out she was the princess of a lost kingdom. At the end, the two marry and he joins her in her land. That last bit had always appealed to me, but it was the song she sang walking through his gardens that I chose. It was one of loss, but also longing.

My own voice wasn't as high as the original, but I changed the song's key and managed to make my way through. At the end, there was a high note the piece called for, but I chose to go an octave lower.

When I'd finished I looked over to see Orion's reaction, but he was no longer next to me. I spun, searching for him and finding him frozen a few feet behind me.

"Stunning," he gasped. "I've never heard anything as breathtaking."

I laughed.

"Now I know you are flattering me. My voice is good, but it certainly wouldn't stop a man in his tracks, or bring him to his knees."

Orion dropped, shuffling over on his knees, the look of awe replaced by a wicked grin.

"Oh, wouldn't it?"

I laughed, swatting at him.

"You are impossible!"

"No, I am enraptured." He reached out, grabbing my hand and planting a kiss on it. Then he stood and began trailing kisses up my arm. "And as for enjoying our last few months here, I think I know just what to do when we return home."

My father was nowhere to be found on our way back to the cottage. I swung back and forth between anticipation of our possible victory and regret that I still hadn't found him. Along with worry at what that could mean.

What if Charon had him? Not free, like Orion, but kept somewhere in that house? What if we'd missed him?

The thoughts chased themselves round and round in my head, but I wasn't going to let them keep me from the rest of our mission.

We'd kept close to the cottage for days, but then Orion had gone to check the Shades.

"They're too restless. Either they can sense the importance of this particular hour, or somehow our count is wrong," Orion said when he'd returned.

Either way, the remaining weeks until the hour were dwindling. We still needed Death's final details, but there was plenty we were doing on our own. We didn't know what we would need to do on the hour, but we spent hours each day reviewing the landscape of Emrys, in case that's where Death needed us to be.

Orion taught me what he could about the other countries, because it was also possible that whatever strategy Death was relying on involved us entering Rayus in another place.

I'd worked with my remaining jewelry, knowing the tree hoppers' love of shiny things, and taught them to follow me as I held the glinting jewels. We couldn't exactly stuff them in a satchel, so we'd try to get them to follow us out of the Ether. But ultimately it would be their choice whether to leave or not—assuming they even could.

Orion had also been working with me more on using the dagger I still kept strapped to my leg. It was no use against Charon, or a Shade, but we wanted to be prepared for anything.

"Again, but this time, when you lunge watch the weight on this leg." He demonstrated a better stance. "That way, you won't lose your balance as easily."

"All this for a foe we may not even face," I griped, although my voice didn't have much sting in it. I was tired from training, but I appreciated what Orion was doing.

He wanted to protect me, but he understood how much I wanted to be able to look after myself as well.

I took a few steps in the clearing where we practiced, where several tree hoppers were cawing from the trees. After a sip from one of the waterskins, I took the stance again and went through Orion's paces.

I lunged toward a stuffed dummy he'd set up. Grass and discarded bits from the garden were stuffed into some material and then hoisted up by a stick. I stabbed it in its center, then stepped back and readied to try again.

Lightning struck the training dummy, setting it ablaze.

Death stood in front of us, wisps of white smoke wafting from where she'd appeared.

"I've set Charon on Odos's trail for the time being, but I

expect that won't keep him distracted for long. I've meddled too much, and he's more and more hesitant to leave his realm. Although he's also more and more smug. He really thinks he's going to win—all the better for us. He'll be taken by surprise. You did get the second item, yes?" Death asked, leaning forward and holding a hand out.

Today's mask was black again, a dark void hiding her expressions.

Orion nodded.

"Yes. Sheet music, hidden within Charon's home, just as you had guessed."

"Excellent! I knew the two of you could do it."

I sheathed my knife, then went and got the music, holding it toward her.

"Here, if you unfurl it, there are notes written along the paper."

I moved to place the music in her palm, but she pulled back.

"I won't hold it. It should stay in your hands. Charon won't notice they've been moved while they remain in his realm and still technically under his control. During the hour, he'll be busy with the Shades, and his plans, which should give you time. I won't touch it, but I can tell you how we'll use both items."

What Death laid out was simple in theory but would be complicated in execution.

The way she described it, the gods of our world had once been much less powerful.

"Not exactly mortal, like you, but much closer than we are now. Emrys, and the surrounding lands, used to hold long-lived beings and abilities that you people now cannot fathom. At one point, we realized that power, or magic if you'd prefer the term, was fading from Rayus. Experts from many fields experimented with all sorts of ways to keep ourselves healthy and powerful, but with lackluster results. I was part of a group of several intelligent individuals brought together, each with their own talents, determined to search for a solution. We were trying to prevent death itself. It didn't work, as you can see. No one can prevent this."

She gestured to herself, the portion of her expression I could see so wry that I couldn't help letting a small laugh escape, but my mind stuck on the rest of her statement. Things in Emrys, and the rest of Rayus, had been far different than I would have thought. And if our ancestors from generations ago had been more powerful, was there a way to work back to that?

"Initially, we'd worked with basic plants and herbs, like what your apothecaries would sell. That didn't fix the problem, though. We searched further and delved deeper, looking for a better option. We found the answer in what you humans now call the 'lost country.' No herb, or potion, but a substance. Running through the earth. It took us time to extract it and experiment. You could crush it and ingest it, and the results were"—she took a deep breath—"exhilarating, but short-lived."

What she spoke of sounded less like science and medicine and more like superstition. Darker than the Unseen Hour.

"One of the others eventually figured it out. We could fuse the substance to ourselves, permanently. But how best to use it? We didn't have enough for all of Rayus. Instead, we chose to split it between the six of us, making us into gods. One from each country, with the exception of Emrys. It has always had the highest population, and we concluded that two spots were warranted. At least, we did after some debate."

I could only imagine, if their bickering now was any indication, how unfriendly that debate must have been.

I tried to think of how to word my question in a way that wouldn't sound impertinent but couldn't come up with one.

"Why you six? What about the rest of the world?"

"Because we were the ones who had discovered, researched, toiled, and spent countless hours conversing about this potential gift. And ultimately, it was for the good of everyone. With these powers, we would be more equipped to help the people around us."

She spoke passionately, but I couldn't help noticing that things hadn't turned out that way. At least not in my time. The hour was proof enough of that.

"And you, a woman, became the most powerful one?" I asked, once again unable to come up with a style of questioning that was guaranteed not to offend.

Death smiled, looking wholly unbothered.

"Women have always been powerful. I will admit that Emrys has become more than a bit disappointing. We were wilder in my time, freer. That is something I would like to see again."

Then why not help? But maybe she couldn't. She'd already said it was beyond her purview to bring life back, and perhaps it was just as impossible for her to interfere in Emrys, with the trajectory of our lives.

"We gained our powers and used them to improve things for those around us. To bring the chaos of their existence under better control," she continued. "The churches in Emrys, and around the world, were initially set up as tributes to us. Over time your understanding of things, and even the rumors of which god and how many, have been blurred. Each nation favored its own deity at first; then, as people evolved, some nations adapted differently from others. The key here is the churches. That's why I mention this at all, because it pertains to our plan. Many of you have grown apathetic, but the buildings still hold power. The original ones, anyway. Do you know where the original churches were in Emrys?"

"Fox Haven," Orion answered without pause. "Centuries

ago, it was a favored location, for its farmlands and ready access to water. Eventually, things moved to Karith, where people could construct a larger city without sacrificing the farmlands."

Death nodded, her smile still in place.

"Precisely. The church in Fox Haven may have Day's face plastered on it alongside mine, but initially it belonged to me. Just as we gods tie a bit of our power to the items that control the souls who help us, we did the same with those original churches."

Fox Haven's church was beautiful. Breathtaking stonework, stunning stained-glass windows.

"Did you know that Charon also had a church in Emrys once?" Death asked, turning to me.

"I'd never even heard of him until my arrival here. And I've never seen another church," I said.

"Oh, I'm not so sure about that. The foundation still exists, but no one cares for it anymore. Mine still shines like the sun, but Charon's has been abandoned for years. All that remains is crumbling stone and a cemetery of long-forgotten graves."

I gasped.

"The ruins?"

"The very same."

All this time, I'd been riding Pellix to Charon's church. I'd found escape in the shadow of the god who had cursed my world. I'd chosen his seat of power as the location where I was Taken.

I'd been taking comfort from a place devoted to my enemy.

CHAPTER 50

Something like betrayal hit me as Death went on.

"For our plan, you will each need to be in a separate location. It requires living souls, wielding the power of gods. Now that you're both here, we have the means. Celia, you will carry the sheet music to my church. You need to take it to the altar within the church and destroy it. First, sing the melody written on it. Then, rip it in half, burn it, do whatever it takes. But it must be damaged beyond repair."

It almost hurt to think of getting rid of it. Charon's music was deadly, but beautiful. For my family and Orion, though, I would do anything.

"I can do it," I promised.

"Good. Orion—"

"Why are the churches so close together? Emrys is large, as you said. Why not put the churches in two locations?"

Death turned to me, lightning dancing on her skin.

"The relationship of the gods is complicated. Charon and I were not always as we are now. Now then, Orion. The baton is the other piece. Take it to Charon's ruins and the graveyard that surrounds his former church."

I wanted to know more; I was no better than the worst gossip in Emrys. But whatever had happened between the gods didn't matter nearly as much as how we could save Rayus.

"You need to use your song and pull the Shades to you. As long as you are holding the baton, they will answer your call from all over Rayus," Death was telling Orion.

"I'll do it," he promised.

"When you first exit the Ether, head straight there. Sing, and do not stop. Conduct them toward you. While you're doing that, Celia will be at my church destroying the music. Keep singing the Shades to you and don't stop. Once she succeeds in her part, the Shades will be released, free to go to their real afterlife. Their spirits will be transported to my realm, where they belong. That's when—"

"And what about us? What will happen to us?" I asked.

Freeing everyone else was something I desired greatly, but I needed to know Orion would be saved as well.

For a split-second, a muscle in Death's jaw twitched, and I was reminded that I was speaking to a deity and not a friend or even my brothers, where an interruption or informal word could be quickly forgiven.

Death smoothed her expression into a smile.

"You will both be alive. Although"—her smile faded—"Charon will be well aware of what we have done. He will notice when the hour is broken, and I am certain his wrath will be immense. After all, this was to be his grand victory. This was the hour when he intended to use the Shades to overpower all of Rayus."

Cold swept through me, all the way to my core. If we failed, it would not just mean another year of victims from the hour. It would mean the loss of everything in Emrys and Rayus that we held dear.

Death held a hand out but didn't actually grab mine.

"I will handle that part. I'll settle things between us, but you should still be on your guard."

While I appreciated the warning, I had no idea what good it would do us. What could we do against an angry god? We just had to hope Death could keep him at bay and protect us from his wrath.

"I will see you both after it has been done. Now, then, I have something I need to—"

"How long until the hour?" It was Orion who interrupted this time. "The Shades are more restless than they typically are this time of year."

"This time of year? What do you mean?" Death frowned.

"I've watched them for a hundred years. Normally they wouldn't grow this restless until a few weeks out from the hour, but it's only August, isn't it?"

Death froze, the lightning dying on her skin.

"That wretched fiend! He must be changing the timing of this realm. He can, you know. I'd wager he's made the days and nights longer with his dancing lights"—she gestured at the sky that was currently filled with dazzling purple and oranges—"to make the days and nights longer than usual. He doesn't know I've involved you, I'm sure of that. If he did, you wouldn't be standing here. But he must be concerned."

"So the date?" I asked.

"It's December. The people in Emrys are preparing to celebrate Wintertide soon. It's why I came down, so we could have everything prepared in time."

"December!" Orion shouted.

"December?" My own voice was quieter as I grappled with the reality.

An entire year. We'd been counting based on the system that had worked for Orion for years, but Charon had changed the rules.

We were almost out of time.

"Charon is returning. When you get to Emrys, you know what to do. Take the music to the church once Orion has the Shades. They'll disappear, and you'll be truly alive," Death said.

For a brief moment, I thought I saw Orion frown, but it was gone as quickly as it appeared. I reached a hand out and placed it on his arm.

"We're both anxious, but we're so close. Mere weeks until the Unseen Hour, and all of this will be behind us. We'll protect each other."

Orion held my hand.

"Yes. And I'll know when the hour is here, no matter what he's done. He'll summon me. Then you can go to the church, and Death will help protect you from Charon."

The deity smirked.

"I've been in touch with the others. We'll be having a *discussion* with Charon. He'll have more important things to worry about than two lost Shades, once this is over."

The way she said the words made me quite certain that I didn't want to be on the receiving end of such a discussion. Charon, however, deserved whatever consequences were coming for him.

Her face softened when she turned back toward me.

"I have only one thing left to do before I take my leave, and I hope you will understand why I've saved it for the last. I needed you both able to give your full attention to our plan, because many lives depend on it. Celia, I need to share something with you, if you would follow me."

My heart was heavy in my chest, each beat like a weight against my ribcage. I clutched Orion's arm, and it calmed slightly.

"Whatever you have found, we should both hear it," I told her.

Death paused, then brought her arm down.

"Very well. I searched throughout my realm, and I must extend you my deepest condolences. Your father is not in the Ether. He has been with me. It may be of some comfort to know th—"

I collapsed, tugging Orion down with me, still clinging to his arm. A sob tore free from my throat.

"His soul has been looked after. I promise you, Celia, he's in no pain," Death assured me.

But what about my pain? What about my family's?

I clutched at my chest, unable to stop crying. Tears streamed down my face. "He was supposed to be here. He has to be here! Or in Rayus somewhere! There was no ... no body. He wouldn't have just left us!" My voice grew harsher on each word.

Orion knelt behind me, wrapping his arms around me. I leaned into him, my tears staining his sleeves.

Death knelt down, too, running a hand a few inches over my hair. I felt the crackle and static as my hair lifted, but it was strangely comforting.

I wished I had my own lightning. A way to vent my emotions that was visible, and powerful.

"There, there," Death soothed. "I know humans have difficulties with parting. But I am just another continuation of life. You will see him again, and now you know where he'll be waiting. And you have my assurance that he is well."

Death had revealed very little of her realm, or what people's spirits really went through after death. I was aware by now that Emrys's preachings of a land of darkness and a land of light were probably wrong.

The words did help, though, if only a little. Death had done so much for us and now was offering us a way home. She would look after Father. At least he hadn't been in the Ether, alone and lost, unable to reach anyone he loved.

I forced myself to take deeper breaths.

After a few minutes I hiccupped, still crying but no longer with heaving sobs that shook my chest.

"Thank you," I choked out, "for finding him."

"There is one other detail," Death said as Orion helped me to my feet. "I hesitate to mention it, but I swore to bring you all the information I found. I am a goddess of my word."

I sniffled, nodding along. "Whatever it is, I want to know."

"Your father is safe now, and in my care. In regard to his manner of death, however … "

I tensed, clutching Orion's arms lest I collapse again. I didn't want to know. I wasn't ready. I opened my mouth to stop Death from speaking.

"He was murdered. His death was intentional, and his killer lives."

Death reached for me as if she might steady me. Small shocks crackled across my skin, and some of my grief morphed into purpose and rage.

"Tell me who did it!"

I would ensure that they didn't live past another Unseen Hour. The anger that spiked through me was almost physical, so hot and sizzling that for a moment I felt like I could call down Death's lightning if I wanted.

Death tilted her head to the side, and for once I was frustrated by the mask and not intrigued. It was so much harder to read the deity's emotions without seeing her full expression.

"We must bring them to justice! This cannot stand," I insisted.

"You will seek revenge? Tell me, small human. What will you do when you find them? Alert the constabulary? Call for a trial?"

"Rip them apart with my bare hands!" I swore.

Death laughed, and I lunged. Orion held me back.

"This is the furthest thing from humorous! How dare you!"

Death raised a finger, all signs of laughter gone.

"Careful, little human. We are familiar, but there are some things I will not tolerate. I did not mean to insult your grief. I merely meant to point out the glaring error in your plan."

"And that would be?" I demanded.

"Take it from me, as someone who knows. To cause Death, you must be willing to kill. You're angry now, but ask yourself, are you a killer?"

I sagged in Orion's arms.

No, I wasn't.

I'd never killed, but I'd learned a lot during the year I'd spent in the Ether. What the gods were willing to do, and what I was willing to do.

"I'll do whatever it takes. But I need to know who they are."

"I'm not denying you, but I need you both focused solely on your work with the Shades, not a vendetta. Free the Shades first. When you have succeeded in ending the Unseen Hour, and I have Charon handled, I will give you a name. I promise you that."

It would have to be good enough. There was only so much bartering one could do with a god, and I needed that name.

"Until the hour," Death said, before disappearing in a flash of lightning.

"Come on, Starlight, let's head home." Orion wrapped an arm around me, looking as defeated as I felt.

We were on the verge of a great victory, but it didn't feel that way.

All the reading, and deciphering, and sneaking, and planning, and searching.

My father hadn't been in the Ether at all.

CHAPTER 51

The remaining weeks passed by quickly, and with each day, Orion's mood grew worse. He was as kind and compassionate with me as always, but then he'd get quiet and moody, and retreat into the woods.

Charon hadn't summoned him at all, and with the Unseen Hour so close, he expected it any day.

When the moment finally arrived, I almost expected it to reduce some of his tension. That was the only roadblock left—whether Charon said anything that indicated he knew what we were up to. After a kiss goodbye, Orion readied to meet the god, his expression gloomy.

"One more hurdle. Survive this last bit, and then we can go home," I reminded him.

He lifted my hands in his and kissed my fingers.

"I won't let him ruin this for you, or for us," he assured me.

Without his restless energy in the cottage, I fell into the same tense mood myself. It was as if the situation demanded anxiety, and at least one of us had to fulfill the requirement. I was too jumpy to read. I needed action.

With Orion keeping Charon busy, there was one other thing

I'd been considering for some time, and the Meadow would never be safer.

We'd spent nearly a year searching for my father with no success, but somehow I knew it wouldn't be as difficult to find the people I wanted to see. When I reached the Meadow, I headed directly for the area in the sea of Shades where I knew the oldest souls tended to congregate.

The two people I sought took me a laughably short time to locate. One with lighter hair than his brother, and one with darker. One with grey eyes, and one with blue.

"Remington? Reginald?" I asked as I approached them.

Both were dressed in the more intricate male fashions of Orion's time. One in a deep blue tailored coat, the other in silver.

The two Shades turned and watched me but didn't respond. Still, it was almost the hour. All the Shades were more active. This was my best chance.

"You're Orion's brothers, aren't you?"

The one with grey eyes blinked heavily.

"Yes. That's us. I'm Regi," said the one with blue eyes.

"And I'm Remi. Our brother Rion. Do you know him?" asked the other.

I felt tears forming in my eyes. I had no idea how much they would be able to understand or remember, but for Orion I wanted to try.

"I'm in love with your brother," I started.

I told Remi and Regi everything. How they'd ended up in the Meadow, where Orion was. I didn't go into detail on what their brother had been through; that was his story to tell. But I gave them the broad strokes. That he'd been alone for nearly a century, that there was an angry god ruling the place, and that Orion and I would be going to Emrys with the god on the hour.

I told them how much their brother missed them, and how I felt about him. That I wanted to help them as well. I even told them about my father.

"I was too late for him, but we can still help both of you. That's what I want. To help you, and Ry," I finished.

Miraculously, they kept their attention on me through the entire story.

"He's doing all this to free us?"

"Yes. To free all the souls. But if we succeed, he'll never see you again. I wanted you to know everything he's doing for you. How much he loves you."

Regi's blue eyes blazed in a way that reminded me of his older brother.

"We never did find out who meant to harm us. But Rion was willing to die trying, to keep us safe. It sounds like he's still doing it."

"And we can help. You're going back as well? Let us shield you. We'll stand at your side when we leave for the hour. We'll keep you hidden while you cross over," Remi promised.

It may have been an empty promise. They were this responsive only because the hour was so close. When I returned, I thought, they might have no idea who I was. But I was touched either way.

Three brothers bound by love for a century. Each still willing to do whatever it took to help the other. As much as I cared for my family, I hadn't trusted any of them enough to share this much.

But Orion's brothers immediately accepted what I said and expressed a desire to help. They were every bit the wonderful men Ry had said they were.

"I'll return on the hour, then, and look for you. I wish there was something else I could do. I just didn't want you to … I didn't want you to leave this realm without knowing just how much Ry cares for you."

"And we care for him as well. Always. Can you give him this?" Remi reached into his pocket and pulled something out.

"And from me," Regi seconded.

They each handed over a small, dry bean.

"The kitchen? When you set up that scavenger hunt for him?" I asked.

Remi laughed.

"He told you about that? He was always such a good sport."

"The best older brother," Regi agreed. "We always had the most fun in each other's company. When our father died, a lot of responsibility was put on his shoulders. We just want him to know we saw how hard he worked. That we appreciate what he did."

"That he didn't fail. He has looked after us all this time, and we love him," Remi added.

Tears fell down my face as I accepted the small tokens and put them in my pocket.

"I'll make sure he gets them," I said.

"Watch out for him, please. He deserves someone to look after him as much as he looks after others," Regi urged.

"And welcome to the family," Remi added.

They both leaned forward, hugging me. Their touch was frigid, but I welcomed it.

Family.

I'd come to the Ether to save one family member and was too late, but I could still free others.

I returned to the edge of the woods, losing sight of the brothers in the sea of Shades.

Orion didn't return until the orange and purple lights were long faded and blue and green were ruling the night. I'd made it back to the cottage quite some time ago.

"Are you hurt?" I asked when he walked through the door and went to sit in front of the fire without a word. "Does he know? What did he say?"

"According to him, he's been traveling," Orion gritted out, as though each word cost him.

"Dealing with the other gods?" I pressed.

Orion's jaw clenched, but he managed a nod. I wondered if only Charon had this power to protect his secrets, or if Death could have ordered us to behave similarly.

"He doesn't know about the music?"

"No. I'll be joining him on New Year's Eve to gather the Shades. When I go to the Meadow, I'll hide the baton. You stay here and follow later with the music. Stay in the back of the crowd, so he doesn't notice you."

His brothers had already offered to hide me, so that worked perfectly.

"Ry, while you were gone I went to the Meadow."

I'd half-expected him to worry, even though I was in no danger as long as Charon was away.

"I thought you might go," he said instead.

"Why?"

"To look for him one last time. Just to make sure Death wasn't wrong."

"Actually, I went for you."

"Me?"

The entire story spilled out.

"I hope I didn't overstep. I know you haven't been to see them in quite some time, and I didn't want to meddle."

He got up and moved quickly toward me. He pulled me into a hug.

"It's perfect, Starlight. It's exactly like they told you. You're my family, and their family. And I'm glad you got to meet them. I said my goodbyes long ago. To find out that at least they got to hear that I never stopped loving them, or fighting for them ... it means more than I can express."

"They wanted you to have these." I pulled the beans from my pocket and handed them to Ry.

He took them, laughing, and beginning to cry at the same time. He placed them in his own pocket.

"The three of us would have done anything for each other. Go with them tomorrow. If they can help it, they won't forget. They'll keep you safe. And so will I. No matter what it takes, or what happens, Starlight. I will make sure you get home."

He'd said as much before, but he sounded more fervent this time.

"I know, Ry. I trust you, and I'll have your back."

"I have something for you as well. The book. It's not what I'd call finished, but I still feel like you should have it."

He went to the shelf to pull out his latest story. I flipped it open and thumbed through the pages carefully, drinking in his familiar handwriting. I read a few passages, not in order, but on whatever pages fell open.

"Wait. This is ... this is *us*. You wrote us."

There was a section about the cavern, and the woods. On seeing me for the first time. Our entire story for the past year, from Ry's perspective.

In one moment the spark I'd been missing for a hundred years returned, lighting up my entire world.

A love story, and an adventure, from his perspective. The same poetic writing I'd fallen in love with, but it was directed at me.

I clutched the book to my chest, overwhelmed.

"I never expected something like this."

Orion ran his hand through his hair.

"I'm glad you like it. I'd hoped to work on it more in Emrys, but this seemed like the best time."

I shook my head.

"Not the book, although I will cherish it. I never expected a love like this."

I threw myself into his arms again, and he kissed the top of my head.

The Ether hadn't provided what I expected at all.

And I had no intention of letting Orion go.

<h1 style="text-align:center">CHAPTER 52</h1>

Our last full day in the Ether sped by faster than I'd imagined possible. I'd thought time would drag on while we waited, but the purple and orange lights overhead were already giving way to blue and green. The following evening, we'd be in the Meadow.

Orion would be leading the Shades along with Charon, and I would be hidden in the back of the crowd, hopefully with tree hoppers in tow.

I wanted to go after my father's killer as soon as possible. They'd already escaped justice for years, and I didn't intend to let that continue.

But Orion had waited all this time to go home, for decades not really believing he ever could. If he needed time to adjust to being back, I would give it to him.

Orion ran a hand over the back of his neck, stretching. We were plucking a few last fruits that I'd try to carry back in my satchel. Maybe we could grow some of the Ether's food in Emrys, or wherever we ended up.

Ry grimaced, and I went to him.

"Did you hurt yourself? You've been working too hard."

He'd claimed Charon hadn't harmed him on his visit. I'd seen no bruises, but he'd looked pained on more than one occasion.

Orion wrapped his arms around me, pulling me into a hug. When he released me, he stepped back. His eyes met mine for barely a moment; then the blue and grey flicked downward, as though he couldn't bear to hold my stare.

"Starlight, there's something I have to tell you. I'm not supposed to share this, but I must." He was breathing faster, a sheen of sweat on his brow. "It's about the hour. The Shades. When we free the Shades, and ... and—"

"And free ourselves. Yes?"

He was trembling. Whatever he had to say, Charon wanted it kept secret, badly. He clutched at his chest with one hand, and I rushed forward, but he shook his head.

"I have to say this. I can't ... You can go home. But I can't."

He huffed, falling to his knees.

"Ry!"

"I have to, get it all, or I won't. I can't start again. Charon knows. Not about us. He knows I want to leave. Told me, I can't. I'm connected."

My stomach sank.

"We can't leave? Why? Why not?"

I looked around frantically, half-expecting Charon to show up in the cottage and kill us both. I put one hand on the dagger at my side. For Ry, I would try to fight a god.

Orion shook his head.

"*You* can go. I can't. I belong here. I can't leave."

He started to take deep breaths, and though he still had a sheen of sweat on his skin, his muscles relaxed a bit.

Ignoring his protests, I bent down to help him up. His skin was fevered and blazing. Almost uncomfortable to the touch.

"You can't? Did he threaten you? I don't care if he is a god!

I'll go back to his home right now and—" Orion's hand gripped my wrist.

"No. Starlight. We have to do what we promised we would. End the hour. Save the souls. Then you'll be safe. And I will survive, just like I always have."

I blinked, unable to absorb his words.

"I can't believe what I'm hearing. I don't think you believe it, either. Did he threaten *me*? Is that it? He's found out about me and he's trying to keep you in line?"

I had no proof, but I knew the god was ruthless. I wouldn't put anything past him.

"It wasn't about you. It was about me. He asked how I felt about being Head Shade, and living in the Ether. He could tell I longed to go back to Emrys, and he told me it wouldn't be possible. Charon is many things, but he's not a liar. Everything he's ever threatened has happened."

I froze, then turned my head to look at him. His shoulders sagged, and his gorgeous blue-flecked eyes were fixed on the ground.

"Not when it comes to his hour. He thinks he will win, but he won't. *We* will. And then you can go home. We can go home. Together. We have the music, the baton, Death's instructions, and each other."

He shook his head.

"He told me that I'm stuck here. That even though I'm not dead, I can't hope to escape back to Emrys. I was angry, and I argued with him. I'm honestly surprised he didn't resort to violence, but I think he got more enjoyment from crushing my hopes. Told me that even if I tried to hide in Emrys and avoid returning, it wouldn't work because I have no anchor. I mentioned the other souls that he'd destroyed and he said that if they'd escaped they would have stood a chance, because they still had people to go back to. It's too late for me. There's no one else alive waiting for me. I have no anchor back in Emrys."

I grabbed his shoulders and planted myself in front of him.

"Ry, you can still go back. You will have an anchor. When we break the hour *I* will be alive, and I know you. I love you. I would miss you. I'll come for you, as soon as the music is destroyed. I'll meet you at Charon's church and make sure that you stay."

My heart was cracked, and I waited to see if he would shatter it or not.

He heaved out another deep sigh.

"All right. All right, Starlight. We'll try."

I wanted assurance, but I would take what I could get. He'd been beaten down by Charon so many times before. I would believe enough for both of us that this time, Orion could win.

I would be strong for him. If necessary, I'd be the one to face a god.

"This is it," I said, crawling into our shared blankets later that night.

"It is," Orion agreed.

The following morning was when he would meet Charon. He would lead the Shades with the god. I would sneak to the back of the mass of Shades as they exited the Ether, as far from Charon as I could get. Once we made it to Emrys and Charon went off on his own, Orion would go to the church ruins and the cemetery. I'd go to Death's church.

We had one shot.

Orion paused before climbing under the blanket with me.

Once we returned, our sleeping arrangements would no

doubt differ. I had to believe we would be successful in keeping Orion in Emrys. That meant our relationship would cause gossip the likes of which Fox Haven had never seen. A long-dead duke and the missing daughter of the Hipnosis? Instant news. A Hipnosi daughter returning after a year-long disappearance with a mysterious man at her side? Just as good for gossip fodder. Even if we had to leave Emrys to be together, if someone saw me we'd be the main topic of conversation for years.

It wouldn't bother me either way, but I hoped my family wouldn't suffer. I was going to be infamous no matter what, reappearing after a year. Our story would depend on how much of what happened was witnessed by the people of Emrys. Would they see our action with their own eyes, or would we just be the town fools, laughed at for our fantastic tales?

Would I even have Orion, or would I be back around everyone I loved and feel entirely alone?

And what of him? My own feelings were the least of my concern. What would happen to Ry if he were trapped in the Ether by himself again, with only the creatures for company?

"Starlight? What's the matter?" I jumped as I realized Orion was kneeling in front of me. He reached a hand up and wiped away a tear.

"We will succeed. You will see your home again. You have my word."

That just made it worse, and more tears made their way down my face.

"That's not it," I managed, struggling to keep some hold on my emotions.

"Then what?"

I took a few shaky breaths, trying and failing three times to get the words out before I managed it.

"*You* are my home. I don't want to lose this."

I sat up, reaching for Orion. He wrapped his arms around me.

"You will always have me. You own my heart. No matter what forces try to come between us, I belong to you."

I sprang forward, kissing his cheeks, the stubble across his chin, his full lips. His tongue swiped against my bottom lip, and I opened my mouth to him.

He pressed me back down against the blankets, holding his body above mine as he continued the kiss.

Orion peppered a trail of soft bites down the curve of my neck. The contact sent a thrill along my spine, and I sighed, leaning into him. Like so many times before, our clothes quickly ended up in a pile on the floor, nothing more than an inconvenience. I never wanted to see another dress again. I'd never have removed a corset or layers so quickly.

Orion's mouth continued downward. His tongue grazed my hipbone, and I jerked.

"Beautiful," he murmured. "Adventurous, compassionate, strong. I never thought I'd find someone like you."

Then, he pressed his tongue against my core, and brought up one hand to rub against my clit. He continued his torturous teasing, and I moaned, throwing one arm over my mouth to muffle the needy sound.

Orion reached a hand up, tugging my arm down.

"I want all of you, Starlight. Every shiver, every moan, every shudder. I want every sound and moment of your pleasure, uninhibited."

With his hand he gently held my arm down.

Familiar pressure built in me. Orion's tongue flicked out, and I shattered, screaming his name.

"Ry!" I broke his hold, both my hands reaching and pulling on his back, tugging him toward me. His mouth captured mine again.

"I need," I said breathlessly when we broke apart.

"Tell me," he urged.

I smirked, grabbing his cock instead. He gasped. I guided him toward me, and when he thrust into me I screamed again, throwing my head back against the blankets.

Orion lifted me, and I wrapped my legs around him. He held me against the wall, thrusting into me, one hand anchored above our heads to steady himself.

When he tensed with his release, I came apart all over again.

"Starlight," he panted against my chest as I shook. After a few moments, he carefully helped me climb down him so I stood on the floor.

He'd gone without stars for a century, and I would make sure he saw them again.

CHAPTER 53

The next morning I barely managed to contain my tears as Orion got ready to leave. He had the baton hidden at his thigh, sewn into a bit of fabric.

"And don't forget, you'll have to bring—"

"The music. Don't worry, I'll have it with me," I assured him.

"And we meet at the church ruins."

"Yes. As soon as you can get away from Charon. Sing the souls toward you, and when I arrive in Emrys I'll run to Death's church."

And once the music was destroyed, I'd return to Orion. He would be waiting. He had to be.

When he reached the door, he turned back and rushed to me, hauling my body against him. He kissed me like he wanted to devour me, and I threw myself into the embrace.

He left for the Meadow, and I tried to distract myself.

Waiting to follow him was pure torture. I busied myself with a final round of showing the tree hoppers the jewelry, then rewarding them with food when they came to my side. When enough time had passed that Orion was well ahead of me, I set out.

I fixed a pair of glimmering pink earrings into my ears and a matching bracelet around my wrist.

The tree hoppers flitted through the trees, keeping pace.

The walk to the Meadow felt shorter than ever before. I was so ready to go home, but this was it. No matter what happened, everything would change for us. Even if Orion returned to the Ether, and I had to come back for him, our situation would be drastically different. I would make my way back to Charon's stronghold if that was what was required.

Either entering an empty realm or facing a defeated god well aware of what we had done.

When I reached the edge of the forest, I could see the Shades moving. They were becoming more alert as they went. More agitated. There were a few yells, and I could hear crying. All the emotion they'd tamped down for the year was welling to the surface. All the longing, compelling them to sing.

Please let them remember.

At first, I didn't see them, and I worried that as Shades they hadn't been able to stay alert enough; that they'd forgotten me.

Then, two men floated toward me. Their shoulders were pulled back, and they moved with purpose. I could imagine them striding if they'd been able to touch the ground again. Even with their features faded and washed out, I was still struck by the resemblance. Regi's hair might have been black, and his eyes wholly blue, but the sharp lines of his jaw and the stubble on his face was all Orion. Watching Remi was like looking at a younger Orion.

My stomach twisted as I joined them. Regi stayed slightly in front of me and Remi at my side, ready to shield me from prying eyes if Charon decided to have a last look at his unwilling troops.

I reached out, taking Remi's hand. He gasped, looking down at where we touched. His limbs felt light, like they might float away, but he still looked strong.

"Thank you," I managed, tears building. "I wish you could stay with us."

It was a miracle I couldn't manage for Orion, but I could give his brothers peace.

We followed the crowd past the Meadow. I was relieved that the tree hoppers stayed near me, flying low enough that they could also be easily lost in the crowd.

We made it to the sparse area where I'd first entered the Ether. Light, pure and blinding, forced me to close my eyes as we kept walking.

When the light faded, I blinked my eyes open as my vision adjusted.

Somewhere near us, the clock sounded.

It was midnight, and I was home.

Remi and Regi were still with me, but the Shades drifting away from us were fewer in number. How Charon ensured each soul came out at the country of its death I couldn't begin to fathom, but the souls weren't my main concern when it came to my plan.

I looked around but didn't spot Orion or Charon. Ry had told me that the god went from country to country during the hour. He could be anywhere in Rayus. As long as he was far away from Orion, our plan would work.

We'd arrived just inside the Fox Haven gates.

"This way!" I waved the brothers onward, toward Death's church, but they didn't respond.

Orion's brother let go of my hand, and the two of them began to drift away.

"Remi! Regi! What are you—"

They weren't listening. They were singing. The streets were filled with fog, and the lanterns were dark.

There was a clacking sound, and I looked up to see five tree hoppers circling overhead. Somehow, they'd made it out. I flashed my wrist, a pink bracelet glinting through the fog. The birds cawed in response.

I swallowed down the lump in my throat. I could do this. I could stop this whole thing—hopefully before the brothers or other Shades hurt anyone else. It was possible Orion had already started singing at the ruins. At any moment, the Shades might all follow his voice.

I raced over the cobblestones in the center of town, forcing myself not to stop at any of the familiar landmarks. As I neared the clock tower, the urge to turn west toward my family's estate was stark, but I ignored that as well.

Just one more night. You'll have plenty of time with them soon enough, I reminded myself.

As I raced past the clock tower, I saw more Shades. They were grouped together around the apothecary. Singing, with their hands joined.

Orion had said Shades tended to target their old friends and neighbors. I supposed they could be patients, but he'd never indicated Shades could behave this cohesively.

I paused when I heard the door creak open.

Dr. Stephans emerged.

"No! Don't come out here!" I ran for him, but he froze, dropping to the ground before I could reach him. Within seconds, a new Shade wearing Dr. Stephans' face joined the crowd.

I put a hand over my mouth, covering a scream and backing away in horror.

Dr. Stephans and the other Shades moved as a unit to the next building.

This was how Charon planned to win. He had enough Shades, and perhaps enough Shades with their emotions built up over so many years, that walls and doors weren't enough anymore.

If I didn't succeed, the entire town would be dead by the end of the hour.

I'd tried to prepare myself to fight against the urge to sing. I'd brought extra cloth to stuff in my mouth, but I didn't have the slightest inclination to join the Shades.

Maybe the music I held in my hand kept me immune.

I sprinted the rest of the way to the church, past other groups of Shades.

The massive structure loomed over me. I put a hand out to the twisted metal of the church door-knocker, but I couldn't grasp it. I wasn't really a Shade, but I'd been in the Ether for a year. Orion had said it had taken him years to work out how to grab things in this realm, and he'd never breached someone's sanctuary when they hid during the hour.

I'd beat the other Shades to this particular location, but I knew it was only a matter of time.

On instinct, I wanted to start beseeching the gods for help, but one was already doing as much as she could. One would kill me if he found out what I was up to, and the others hadn't bothered to answer me anyway.

I was on my own. This plan had to work. With new determination settling in, I reached for the knocker with one hand, and the handle to the right side door in the other. I took several steadying breaths, and squeezed.

I couldn't help the surprised squeak followed by the sigh of relief as my hand closed around the cold metal. I could feel it.

I tugged hard, but the door didn't budge.

"Blasted ghosts!" *Think, Celia.* Of course they had barred the door for the Unseen Hour.

The church was a safe haven. Desperate people without a home of their own, or who had ended up out alone too near the hour, had probably sought refuge within it.

Refusing to give up, I turned and began circling the church. I went around the side of the building, pressing my head up against each darkened stained-glass window. The scenes depicted were beautiful in the sunlight, but in the dark of night appeared haunting. The face of Day looked down on me, eyes dark and disapproving without the sun to make them shine. In his hands, he held the wheat and scythe.

"That's not yours," I murmured, staring at the scythe.

I had to be careful. If I entered and left an opening behind me, the other Shades might lure people out before I could destroy the sheet music. I'd be a killer as much as if I'd sung them to the Ether myself.

There were very few individuals I would happily see dead, and I doubted any of them were hiding in the church.

I looked again at the stained glass, then at the ground around me.

I was sending up a silent plea for forgiveness as I bent down and grabbed a rock. I was about to bash in a window when I saw movement.

Someone was walking toward the doors.

CHAPTER 54

I ran, yelling. The tree hoppers had followed me to the church, and they squawked, echoing me.

"Please! Please let me in!" No one responded. There was no way for me to know whether they couldn't hear me unless I was singing, or if they were ignoring me. It wouldn't be the first time someone had begged for help during the Unseen Hour only to be left out in the cold, dead the next morning. It sounded harsh, but villagers feared opening their homes and risking their own lives.

I remembered being a small child and hearing a frantic stable hand who had been chasing a loose horse pounding on the doors. The screaming and bustle of the responding staff had drawn me to my door, still awake during the unholy hour even at the age of seven.

I'd crept stealthily from my room, since at that age a nanny was supposed to keep an eye on me and ensure I stayed inside. When mine went to see about the noise, I curiously followed.

I listened at the edge of a hall as the staff debated what to do. In the end, my parents opened a side door themselves, after sending the staff to a closed room. The stable hand tumbled in and my mother slammed the door shut immediately after. He was white as a sheet and mumbling to himself about haunting sounds.

It wasn't until now that I realized he'd heard the Shade song. My family's peers had called them mad for risking such a thing.

I could only imagine how these people inside were feeling, with my desperate attempts to get in creating a moral dilemma. The memory, however, had given me an idea.

There was one trick left, and maybe I could do it without completely destroying the window. I studied the panes carefully, and instead of launching the rock through the center I used it like a hammer, cracking the glass in one triangular area. A green piece of glass gave way, breaking inward and giving me a fist-sized opening directly into the church. Ignoring the hesitation that tugged at me, I shoved my face up to the opening and started to sing the song written on the sheet music.

I hadn't felt the urge to sing when I'd arrived in Emrys, and I could only attribute that to the overriding desire to succeed and end the hour. But in that instant, I needed the music.

Even when I was the cause, I couldn't get over the haunting but beautiful nature of Shade song. A melody that somehow spoke to the soul. After only a few moments an individual holding a candle walked into sight. It was the vicar. He had on a soft robe rather than his vestments. I cringed when he made eye contact with me, and I could see the terror on his face.

Carefully and slowly, I made my way down the line of windows, breaking the smallest triangle or square in the stained glass I could find in each one as I led the vicar closer to the front door. There were no windows on the doors, but there were two that were regular glass to each side. They were too high up to climb through or reach, and I was forced to throw a rock through one. This still left only a small hole, and I hoped it would be enough to keep those inside safe from the other Shades for just a short while.

I tilted my head up, singing toward the ruined glass.

Just as I began to lose hope, the front door of the church creaked open and then swung wide. Before any Shade had time to notice and could grab the emerging vicar and snatch his soul, I leapt forward, shoving him back inside and slamming the door shut behind us.

I stopped singing, and the vicar stopped moving, but his gaze remained unfocused as he stared intently at a wall.

I rushed past him—and quite a few other individuals in the pews. One or two were lying straight across them, attempting sleep. Most were kneeling and praying. A couple cried out as I swept past, but no one called my name. No one pointed.

Just as it had taken effort for me to grasp the rock or door, I thought the rest of my body might not be fully solid or visible yet either.

That could only help.

I ran to the altar at the front of the sanctuary. On one side was a basin of holy water, a reference to Day and the fuel of life. On the other side was one of the fires that the church always kept lit. A testament to the funerals held for our deceased, and their journey to Death.

I tried to rip the music in half. It refused to let me do so.

Singing, Celia. Singing!

My voice was shaky, not at all the way I'd sung when Orion had kissed me on the piano bench, but I got through the piece. The people in the pews still didn't react by pointing, but they began to move toward me, following the song. When I came to the last note, there was a crowd around me.

I tried destroying the music again.

"Please. Please," I begged, holding it over the fire. It didn't blacken right away, but after a few moments I saw the edges begin to smoke. I wanted to snatch my hand back as the temperature soared but forced myself not to. The piece of parchment felt thinner. Reaching up with my other hand, I ripped it down the center. Then I turned it and ripped the pieces again. I tore them up until they were mere fragments of their former selves, then cast them all in the fire. I watched until each piece was nothing more than blackened ash beneath the dancing flames.

Lightning slammed into the altar, and I was blown backward. My back hit the floor, knocking the wind out of me. As I pushed myself into a standing position I realized one of my hands was blistered.

But it had worked! The music was gone.

I had to get to Orion.

I stumbled down the steps in front of the holy water and fire, then ran through the center aisle between the pews. The inhabitants of the church might not have seen me sneak in, but they definitely saw the lightning and the lingering smoke. They were screaming and running. Some cowered underneath the pews. One pointed at me as I ran past.

"Isn't that a Hipnosi?"

"It's the missing daughter, I'm sure of it!" cried out a second individual.

"I thought she was dead," I heard someone argue back.

I flinched. I had to see my family, and explain, but first I had to ensure everything had worked as planned and Orion was safe.

They can see me. I'm back, and they can see me.

I put a trembling hand on a pew as I passed, and it immediately felt solid beneath my blistered hand. Even the pain, I welcomed.

I knew the layout of the sanctuary by heart. My family often attended here when we were in Fox Haven.

There was a large mirror in a hall off the side of the sanctuary. I passed it on my way to the doors. My reflection stared back at me—hair a bit wild and eyes wide and scared, but I was undoubtedly solid.

I ran my hands over my shirt and pants.

"We did it!"

I kept going all the way to the entrance doors of the church. Several people were crowded around the vicar. His eyes were clear again.

I tugged on one of the large doors.

When the others realized what I was trying to do, the shouting started again.

"Stop her!"

"She'll kill us all!"

"She's gone mad!"

The door creaked, opening just a crack before strong arms hauled me backward. It was the vicar, his hands squeezing my arms. A woman from town that I recognized as a baker grabbed me around my middle, helping the vicar.

"We have to open the doors! I must get to him!"

Several of the other townspeople argued amongst themselves.

"We can't just treat a Hipnosi like this."

"If her family finds out—"

"No one will find out if we're all killed!"

I turned my head wildly as a few more people grew brave enough to approach.

I whispered a silent apology, then I stamped a foot down on the baker's shoe. The woman howled, and I elbowed her in the gut. The vicar and I went tumbling as she released us. A few more townspeople moved to grab me, but the tree hoppers had followed me into the church, and now they swooped down on my would-be assailants with beaks and claws.

"Cursed ghosts!" one woman screamed.

"She's possessed!" added another.

"She's bewitched the birds!"

The vicar's hold loosened as he tried to gain his footing. I twisted, breaking his hold.

Before the others could reach me, I tugged the door open and ran into the night, with the birds overhead.

<h1 style="text-align:center">CHAPTER 55</h1>

Screaming voices, and then the sound of the door slamming shut, told me I was safe. No one had come after me once I was outside the church.

It appeared no one wanted to risk their lives, not even for the rewards rescuing a Hipnosi might bring. Particularly if that Hipnosi had gone stark, raving mad, in the eyes of the locals. I didn't blame them in the slightest. I knew how I must have looked. After this night, there would be all sorts of rumors about the Hipnosi daughter who'd returned during the most cursed time of the year, besmirching a church and fighting the good-hearted townspeople with her possessed birds.

I laughed, looking up at the still-dark sky. Orion and I needn't have worried about what my reception would be. My reputation was already in tatters, and I'd only been back a few minutes.

I didn't care in the slightest.

I ran through the streets, screaming for him.

"Orion! Orion!"

I didn't see him, of course. I still had some distance to go to reach the cemetery, but I also didn't see any Shades. I didn't feel any, either. The fog that filled the streets during the Unseen Hour was dissipating—another sign that we had been successful.

Ahead of me, the gates to the town were open wide. I had no idea whether the watch had fled or the Shades had sung them out before I'd succeeded.

I reached the town wall, running so fast I practically sprinted past the stables where the city watch kept their mounts.

A familiar whinny brought me to a stop.

"Pellix," I breathed. It was impossible, but there was the grullo stallion, in the end stall.

Pellix snorted, stomping a foot like he always did when he was trying to get my attention and go out for a ride.

Had the watch found him and kept him after I'd disappeared? Did my family not know where he was? Or had they given Pellix to the watch, in hopes his speed would aid in looking for me? Or, even worse, could they not bear the sight of him after I disappeared?

Whatever the reason was, luck was on my side.

"Pellix, I have missed you," I whispered as I approached the stallion. He pushed his head forward, and I stroked his face.

"I'm so sorry. I promise you a real apology later, but I need you now. Are you ready for a ride?"

Pellix whinnied, stomping his hoof decisively.

I unlatched the gate holding him in. Pellix went still as I stood at his side, and with a grunt I heaved myself up. My chest rested against his back. Another grunt, and another strained heave, and I swung my leg up and over.

"I promise you I will give you endless treats and adventures after this. Orion and I won't leave you."

I had no reins to rely on, and instead I fisted my hands in Pellix's mane, trying not to pull. I leaned forward.

"We have to make it to the ruins. He has to be there."

I gave a gentle nudge with my heels, and that was all the stallion needed. Pellix was off like a shot, running across the cobblestones and through the gates. I looked overhead and saw the tree hoppers soaring above us and keeping pace.

"Orion!" I screamed as Pellix sped over the hills, toward the ruined church and its cemetery.

Without reins, I didn't have the same control, but I gently tugged Pellix's mane to the right, and he cantered to the structure when we got close.

When I saw a figure standing in the cemetery, I slowed Pellix to a walk, leapt off him and landed in the dirt. I stumbled to one knee, and a hand wrapped around my arm and pulled me up.

"Ry! Ry, I'm so glad you're—"

I pulled back when watery green eyes met mine instead of stormy blue and grey.

"Bellamy!" I said, too shocked to think of what else to do but greet him.

Bellamy gave me a simpering smile, and a small bow.

"Celia, darling. I was so relieved to hear you were safe. I've spent this past year worrying myself sick, and your family has as well. They'll be so happy that you're back."

Pellix whinnied, and I tried to move over to him. Bellamy tugged on my arm, and Pellix stamped the ground. I heard *caws* overhead.

"What are you doing here? Why would you be at the ruins, on this night of all nights?" I demanded, keeping myself close to the stallion. Bellamy gave Pellix a scrutinizing look.

"The risk was worth it. Your stallion was found near here after the last hour, and I saw bootprints at the ruins. When the past year of searching turned up nothing, I thought I'd try the location you disappeared, on the anniversary of when you went missing."

The answer technically made sense, but suspicion ate at me.

No one went outside during the hour on purpose.

Well, except for me and my father. But we'd both done it for love. Me, because I loved him, and him, because he loved his family.

Bellamy might have proposed, but I was under no illusion that whatever he felt toward me was love. He didn't even really know me.

"I appreciate the gesture, Lord Bonds, but as you can see I'm just fine. And I need to find someone else who is supposed to be at these ruins. A man, tall, with brown hair. He has grey eyes. Have you seen him?"

The Marquess snorted, giving me a disapproving look.

"Meeting a man in the middle of the night, unchaperoned? Really, Celia, what *have* you been doing this past year? It's a wonder you've managed to avoid a public scandal so long, if this is how you've been behaving. What will your brothers think?"

I still couldn't see Orion, and I had not come this far to be judged by the Marquess, of all people.

"Listen here, Bellamy! I really don't have time for this nonsen—"

"Celia." Bellamy glared, but then plastered a smile back on his face. "You're merely traumatized. Who knows what you've endured while you've been away. I'm sure you're anxious to get to your family, darling, and into more suitable clothes. My carriage is right over here. If you'll just come this way."

He grabbed onto my arm again, trying to lead me away from the church. I yanked it back, scowling. Pellix nipped at Bellamy, who barely pulled his own arm away in time.

"Really, Celia, this is ridiculous! There's no point in fighting me! I have your family's backing, and I am your fiancé! You *will* obey me."

"No! I need to find Orion! Toss off!" I threw my arms out and shoved him.

Bellamy stumbled back, mouth hanging open.

"Ry! Ry! Where are you?" I was growing frantic. What if he *had* gone back to the Ether? I needed Death. I needed a way back to him.

I entered the ruins themselves, continuing to shout. Bellamy was on my heels, and Pellix whinnied from outside the structure. I heard flapping, uncertain whether the birds had remained with the horse or followed me into the dark church.

"Celia, do you hear yourself? Wandering around in men's clothes, yelling for some man! You sound hysterical. We need to get you home before anyone else witnesses this ... scene."

"I'm not making a scene! Bellamy, this is important! I—"

"Not another word!" he yelled, then cleared his throat. "Dear. Come now, let's get you home." He wrapped an arm around my torso and hauled me across the stones. I saw a carriage waiting across the cemetery. I struggled against him.

"Bellamy, you're not listening!"

"Cursed gods! You're being so difficult! One would think you had run off with some man on purpose!"

I dropped to my knees, and he stumbled, releasing me as I became dead weight. Flustered, he barely managed to right himself.

"I *did* choose another man on purpose! I will *never* marry you, Bellamy Bonds! The fact that you decided we were engaged without ever asking me convinced me of that before I even met Orion! But now *he* is my home, and you will not keep me from him. I've been living with him for a year, and you can't undo that. Your wishes and my brother's orders will make no difference in the matter."

I stood and stamped my foot. His face turned red, and he was waving his arms.

"You insolent, crazed harlot! You belong to me! And that is what will not change. The fact that you've given yourself over to some other man just shows me that you're not worthy of the respect of a wedding ceremony before I take what I'm owed."

Bellamy lunged at me, pinning my arms and shoving me against a crumbling stone wall.

"Let's see if this changes your mind," he told me before shoving his lips on mine.

He pushed his body against me, and I was horrified to feel that he was hard, aroused by the assault.

My arms were trapped, but I could still fight. I brought my knee up to his crotch, and he wheezed, dropping my arms and clutching his trousers.

"You wretched cu—"

I slapped the Marquess clean across his face and reached for the knife at my side. I leaned over him, yanking him up by his hair and placing the blade at his throat.

"If you don't leave these ruins right now, I will leave you bleeding on the church floor," I threatened.

I threw him aside, running farther into the ruins.

"Orion!"

"Celia!" Bellamy called, voice hoarse.

Then, I heard the clacking of beaks and Bellamy yelling at the birds.

They could handle the Marquess for the moment.

After I clambered over a pile of rotting beams, I stepped onto a square area that looked as though it had been recently swept. It shook beneath me. I screamed, stumbling back.

It was a cellar entrance, built directly into the floor of the church. A muffled voice came from behind it.

"Starlight!"

"Ry!" Relief flooded through me.

He wasn't in the Ether. I still had him.

I knelt down and spotted the lock that had evidently been slid into place. "I'll get you out. Wait a moment!"

It was half-rotted and didn't want to budge, but I managed. I tugged the bolt back, and it slid with a squeal. Several times, I checked behind me, dagger sitting at my side and ready, but Bellamy didn't reappear. Maybe, between my self-defense and the tree hoppers, he'd given up.

I tugged open the door at the same time Orion pushed. He clambered out from the cellar.

"Starlight!" He embraced me. "Thank all the gods. I knew you'd succeeded. I was waiting here, but then—"

A shot sounded outside, followed by a loud whinny.

"Pellix!"

I charged through the wreckage, Orion on my heels, swearing to bury my ex-fiancé under the church if a single hair on Pellix's mane was harmed.

"Bellamy Bonds, you rat!" I screeched as I flew out of the ruin, running toward his carriage.

I heard a snort and saw Pellix trotting beyond the graves. There was no visible blood. All five tree hoppers circled above him.

"Oh, thank all the gods!"

Bellamy stood beside his carriage, gun still in hand. I snarled at him like the wild woman he thought I'd become.

"How *dare* you shoot at my horse, or my birds! And if I hear you're the one responsible for imprisoning my fiancé—"

"Fiancé?" That snapped him out of it.

"Yes. I am re-engaged."

He sneered.

"I was right. You *are* a whore."

Orion lunged past me faster than a shot. His fist connected

with Bellamy's jaw. The Marquess fell in an awkward heap, and the gun went flying.

Bellamy rubbed his cheek, his eyes watering. He glowered at Orion.

"You have no right! She belongs to me."

Orion stepped over the Marquess, and I thought he might hit him again. Instead, he leaned forward, his expression as cold as the Ether.

"She belongs to herself you utter waste. Insult her again, and I'll make use of the graves in this cemetery."

My heart skipped. It was possible I ought to examine why Orion's threats against the Marquess made me even more attracted to him, but I didn't get the opportunity.

Bellamy shrieked, diving behind one of his carriage wheels. Orion was impressive, but I was surprised the Marquess had been cowed so easily.

It was only then that I noticed the fog spilling over the church grounds. Orion ran to me, shielding me from what was coming.

A figure I'd only seen from a distance was landing amid the graves. Feathered wings beat the sky, and this time, he didn't get rid of them when he hit the ground.

Charon pulled back his hood, his steely grey eyes landing on the two of us.

He pointed an accusatory finger, and his voice echoed across the grounds.

"You did this."

And I had no doubt we were going to pay.

CHAPTER 56

The same fog that blanketed the ground during every Unseen Hour rolled over the grass.

"You might as well face me, little Shades. I know what you've done." Charon's cold voice cut like a steel blade. "I doubt, however, that *you* know what you've done. You have ruined my plans and didn't even realize what they were for."

I leaned into Orion but refused to cower.

Grabbing his hand, I stepped forward to meet my fate. My heart lifted when he walked with me, instead of pulling me back.

Bellamy whimpered behind us, hiding near his carriage.

"We know what you were doing. You were trying to overthrow Death and take her place. You were angry about your role as a god; that it was less than hers. And you were going to destroy Rayus in retribution; create your own realm full of death. This is a petty squabble that the entire world has been paying for, and now you've lost your army. If we'd left it to you, then all of Emrys would have succumbed."

Charon grinned, a mirthless, dangerous expression.

"Is that what you think? Then you know nothing. Someone just as powerful as me has been whispering in your ear, feeding you lies." He raised his voice. "You might as well make your presence known. I'm sure you have something to say!" he yelled at the sky.

Lightning slammed into the ground, burning away some of the fog and replacing it with clean, white smoke.

Death landed between Charon and us. She stood facing the god of the Ether, with her back to Orion and me. When she pulled back her hood, her hair spilled out. Lightning danced over her hair and across her hands.

"You truly thought to deceive me, Charon? Did you really believe I would not find out about your theft of souls? And yet you stand here accusing me. You are nothing if not confident."

I leaned to peer around Death's cloak, watching the god of the Ether.

Charon, for his part, looked unrepentant. He stood tall in the face of his accuser.

"I've been claiming souls for a hundred years now, and you've taken no notice. You never really saw me. You're only here now because my traitorous Shade tipped you off."

She laughed.

"Is that what you think? Is that really what things have become between us? You're wrong. I recruited your Shade years ago. You've grown too arrogant. You've tried to upend the order of things. You went against your fellow gods, and you know the consequences."

Charon raised a finger and jabbed it toward Death.

"*You* are at fault for this. I trusted you. I cared for you, and you betrayed the rest of us. You're the reason we lost Epi–"

I was thrown into Death's cloak, thankfully missing her lightning-laced skin, by a gust of wind. Odos slammed onto the church grounds to our left, his hammer shattering a gravestone.

Bellamy came sprinting from behind the carriage, only to cower behind the newest arrival.

I'd balked when he called me mad, but now I had to question if this had all fractured *his* mind. Did he have no idea the danger he was in?

"I gave you one task, and you couldn't even do that!" Odos yelled at the cowering noble. "A worthless descendant, that's what you are. And now Charon's stands free."

My head spun. None of this was making sense.

"Day! Grim! You're part of this! No sense staying out of things now!"

There was a beam of warm, amber light, and then a deity stepped out from its depths. Where Death's skin was so pale it resembled a bone, this deity's skin was a warm, light brown. He had brown eyes, full cheeks, and a thick beard.

"Day, you finally grace us with your presence." Death greeted him while Charon scowled at the three deities.

Orion's grip on me tightened, and I glanced to our right to see something oily bubbling up from one of the graves. I screeched, jumping back as another deity stepped from the ooze, his clothes somehow entirely clean. When he first emerged, his face looked gaunt and sunken, his skin covered in sores and blemishes. By the time he stood on the grass, he'd changed. He had striking pale blue eyes, black hair, and a smile that would have weakened the knees of most women in Emrys.

"Grim," Death acknowledged.

The god of illness and decay. I recoiled from the handsome hand of disease.

Charon kept his glare in place as he looked around at his fellow deities.

"She's fooled you all, then? You're not even going to try to stop her?"

"Don't make a scene, Charon," Death chided, almost

reminding me of Bellamy when he'd latched onto me earlier. Except this time, a villain was on the receiving end of the tirade. "They've seen the evidence. You could have killed everyone. You're a threat to the rest of us. You know what happens next."

Charon raised his arms, fog lifting and obscuring my view. I heard his wings beating, and the temperature dropped sharply. For a moment, I thought he would fight.

Then, the fog disappeared. His wings stilled, and Charon held his arms out.

"I'll go peacefully, but this isn't the end of it, Death. Mark my words, you will get your due someday."

"I highly doubt that," she responded, voice light. She snapped her graceful fingers, and Day and Grim each grabbed one of Charon's arms.

Charon ignored the other gods, turning toward us instead.

"She wants to be the last one standing. Goddess of everything. And trust me, if you think I'm bad, it's nothing compared to what she has planned. She's as dangerous to you as the rest of us."

Death snapped her fingers again, and Day and Grim disappeared, Charon in tow.

"I had your word, Death, don't forget," Odos growled. Bellamy continued to clutch at the large, muscular god, looking even smaller by his side. But I saw that Bellamy had always been a small man.

Orion spun to face me as Death spoke to the remaining god.

"Starlight, I think, with him gone ... Yes. I can. I can say it. You need to know something. What I couldn't tell you before, in the Ether. Another reason I thought I couldn't stay here. Charon isn't just the god of the Ether. I mean, he is, but he's also my ancestor. He said I was tied to the place. To the Ether, *because* of him. That I couldn't leave, and even if Death bested him, I'd have to stay. The Ether needs a god. All the deities have some-one, Celia. A descendant, one per generation. It's another fail-safe. Another way to spread out their power. Just like the churches, and the items like the scythes and the music."

"You. Charon. You're his ... then there's five more descen-dants? Who?"

"Oh, little Shade, now you've gone and spoiled the secret," Death trilled.

She turned to face us, and I gasped, taking several large steps back from her.

"It's not possible." A trick. Dark magic, just like the Unseen Hour. That was the only explanation. Death was mocking me.

In front of me was the same deity I'd seen before, but without the mask hiding her eyes and half of her face. Death had paler skin and hair, but those were the only things sepa-rating her features from my own. Without the mask covering her, I saw that our cheekbones were the same. As was our eye shape. But that wasn't the convincing piece. Death's eyes were not black pools of despair, as I might have assumed. They were vibrant, shimmering, and undeniably pink.

Death looked like an avenging angel, a harsh woman bent on war, and capable of winning it. She looked like she had real power.

"You ... "

Death nodded.

"Yes, you're beginning to understand now. I told you we didn't always have the power we now possess. There was a time, after acquiring our abilities, that we tried to live among other people. A disastrous experiment. People do not like being reminded of power they don't have, and circumstances like Death which they cannot hope to change. But we also learned through their attacks that we might be vulnerable. One day, surely, they would find a way to get rid of us. And with that, bring destruction to themselves."

"What did you do?"

"We left descendants. Each of us, a line, to keep our ties to this world before creating and retreating to our own realms. Individuals we could call on, or utilize if the situation arose. I had always thought it would be us, the gods and our descendants, against an uprising of citizens who wanted the power we possess. Instead, we've ended up fighting one another."

My mind was spinning like the gears in a clock, ticking away and driving me mad as the pieces clicked into place.

"That's why you wanted to help Orion. You realized Charon hadn't told him initially, and you thought you could gain another victory by having him on your side. Then, when I showed up, you were happy because ... "

"Because I had Charon's descendant and my own, stuck in the Ether and only too eager to help me, yes. I needed you. You see, we have certain rules with each other, certain boundaries we don't cross, as Charon was trying to do. And we have certain protections afforded to our descendants. You're vulnerable, but not nearly as much as a typical human. And you have enough of our power that you can do things, like handle our artifacts."

"The baton? The music?"

Death nodded, looking pleased.

"Precisely. Orion can hold the baton, and conduct the Shades. Not because he was in the Ether, but because he has Charon's blood. And you, Celia, are capable of even greater things, because you are *my* descendant. Orion was right: one descendant per generation. I know you've worried about your lack of power compared to your brothers. They have more social influence than you. Well, how does it feel to know that you could have the power of a goddess?"

"I wanted to be allowed to wear trousers, ride my horse, and choose my own husband. Not fight with gods!" I yelled, far too overwhelmed to censor myself. "Bloody ghosts!"

Descended from gods of death. Both of us. And deities on separate sides of a potential war. Charon had told Death that this wasn't over. The gears in my head ground to a stop, and whatever powered my heart protested, pain shooting through me that was so real I clutched my chest.

"What happens now?"

Death tilted her head, and it was eerie seeing eyes so like my own observing me in such a way.

"Now? Charon will be imprisoned. Just like Epiphany, the only other deity to ever attempt a stunt like this. We'll stick him in what you all call the 'lost country' for a few centuries, until we forget him or he learns some manners. And until then, the Ether needs a god. There are no more Shades, of course, but someone has to do Charon's job. Balance of nature and all that."

"No. He's not going back!" I threw my arms out, shielding Orion as if I could fight her off. "And we can't help you, anyway! We aren't deities."

Death scowled.

"Haven't you been listening? You haven't *mastered* our abilities, but you have so much potential. You could learn. Just because you haven't yet done something doesn't mean you can't. I'm sure you've figured that out."

Did that mean? Orion's connection to the Ether. His ability to get into Charon's home with me. The way he influenced the Shades.

"Did we need your help to get into Charon's home?" I asked her.

She laughed.

"Now you're getting it! No. You never did. Orion could have

taken you at any time. The Ether is his as well. He just has to learn to influence it, and he has plenty of time. I'm more than happy to support the new god of the Ether, under my guidance, of course."

"No! He doesn't want to go!"

Orion was frozen at my side, silent as the graves around us. He probably had a hundred years of memories playing through his mind, all in a potentially new light.

"Stop being unreasonable! We had a deal. I got you back, and you're both alive. And I'll tell you how to track down the person responsible for your father, as promised. But Orion will go."

She reached for him, and I snapped.

"You can't have him. He is *mine!*"

Lightning shot between us, and I screamed, fully expecting to burn. I slammed my eyes shut, and when I opened them, I saw Death was wide-eyed, her jaw hanging open.

"How did you manage that?"

I looked down, realizing the smoke was rising from my hand. I'd done it.

She beamed.

"Even more powerful than I'd hoped! Perhaps being in Charon's realm has been helpful to you. Oh, yes, this is wonderful. After this whole debacle, I'd already decided that keeping my descendant closer would be the best thing. Orion will return to the Ether, and you will come with me, to my realm."

"She will not!" Orion yelled, breaking his silence.

The temperature dropped again, and I looked around for Charon, but there was only Death, smirking.

"And you as well, little Shade. My, my. It is a momentous day. Charon was always adept at adjusting the temperature. You've been doing it for months, without noticing, although normally you are making it warmer for my precious descendant."

I stared at Orion. He was able to ward off the Ether's cold because of his blood? That's how he'd kept me warm?

"I will be going, goddess. My sniveling descendant will be coming with me." Odos grabbed Bellamy by his collar, dragging him away.

Bellamy Bonds? Odos was a god worshiped in Tang, and Bellamy's family was from there, but I couldn't imagine the whimpering, slimy man as Odos's descendant.

And he'd imprisoned Orion. On Odos's orders. Another god with plans we hadn't been aware of and motivations I trusted as little as I had the others.

The two of them vanished in the wind.

"Now then, it's time to get going," Death urged. "I think you'll enjoy my realm. And once we're there, we can figure out the best way to unseat the rest of these gods. Charon was right in that at least. They're all useless. None of them are doing their duty as intended. Together we'll replace them and start again."

"You really do want to be the last one standing."

She nodded.

"I certainly do. No better individual for the job."

There was no way to best her. We'd only defeated the hour because she was on our side. All I could hope to do was delay her.

"You once said that a hundred years was nothing to a god. Did you mean that?"

"Of course. Human lifespans are sad, paltry things. I do plan to pay a bit more attention in future. Charon only kept his little hour secret for so long because I don't deign to check in on Rayus so often. Something I'll remedy, I assure you."

"We don't need a hundred years. We only need one. I want to track down the person who killed my father, and I want to say a proper goodbye to the rest of my family. My brother Thomas is probably traveling again, so it may take a while to reach him. Orion has to settle things with his estate. He's been missing for a hundred years. It'll take time. When those things are done, then we'll leave."

Death laughed.

"Bargaining with Death? You have no leverage. What would I get out of this?"

"A willing pupil instead of one who is trying to fight you. Assurances that the Ether will not try to defy you or your realm again."

She tapped her chin.

"You amuse me, little human. Or should I say, small descendant. And you would be willing to let Orion go? He is returned to the Ether, and you go with me?"

"Yes. *If* you give us this year."

"A wise choice. Power is superior to love in every way. You have a year. Not a day longer. And here is the information I promised regarding your father." She handed me a folded slip of paper that appeared in her hand. "We will meet in this spot, and you will come willingly, or face the consequences."

Her expression turned vicious just before lightning struck her, and we were left alone in the graveyard.

I clutched the paper and collapsed. Orion caught me.

"Remember what I said, Starlight. Nothing will keep me from you. Not even Death. I will find a way," he assured me.

He brushed a stray hair away from my forehead.

"We stopped the Unseen Hour. We have saved Rayus. We'll avenge your father, and we will solve this problem, together."

Charon was defeated, but had promised vengeance. Death had given us a reprieve, but it had come with a threat. Odos and Bellamy might well cause trouble of their own. I didn't even know enough about Day and Grim to guess their motives. There was only one individual who knew what it was like to face down the other deities.

"Whoever harmed my father will pay, yes, but I already have plans for how we're going to stop Death."

"Oh?"

"Yes. We're going to the lost country, and we're going to free a trapped god."

ACKNOWLEDGMENTS

No book is a truly solo effort, and this has been no exception. So many wonderful people have helped to make this fantasy romance a reality.

Doreen, Mary, and Eve-from the first look to the last comma, the three of you provided such valuable editorial feedback. I can confidently say that this story would be lacking some of my favorite elements if not for your keen observations.

Krista Walsh-phenomenal author and unparalleled critique partner. You read the first version, the final version, and so many versions of the blurb that I'm sure your head was spinning. I cannot thank you enough for your unwavering support on this project.

David Gardias-thank you so much for the inspiring cover art. I fell head over heels the moment I saw it, and I cannot wait to share the next book's art with everyone.

To my family and friends-with each book I write I am so thankful for your support. I am incredibly fortunate to be surrounded by people I can call to bounce ideas off of, vent, share, or just take a much-needed break and then go back to my work with fresh eyes.

To every reader-I will never stop being absolutely overwhelmed with gratitude for my readers. You have made this indie author's dreams come true more than once, and I am happy to place this story in your hands. I hope you enjoy it.

ALSO BY SILAS REAMES

The Shifter Vengeance Series

-A Completed Urban Fantasy Series-

Never Before

Never

Never Again

Never Ever

Never More

Never Say Never

Never Mind

Never Ends

The Societies Trilogy

-A Completed Science Fantasy Trilogy-

(Under Pen Name Sydney Reames)

Assimilation

Serpentina: A Societies Novella

Alliance

Ascension

www.ingramcontent.com/pod-product-compliance
Lightning Source LLC
Chambersburg PA
CBHW030728310726
48969CB00005B/1138